**Praise for Leslie Meier and
her Lucy Stone Mysteries**

TURKEY
"Timely . . . Mei
cozy a serious
—F

BRITISH MANOR MURDER
"Counts, countesses, and corpses highlight Lucy
Stone's trip across the pond . . . A peek into British
country life provides a nice break."
—*Kirkus Reviews*

CANDY CORN MURDER
"Meier continues to exploit the charm factor in her
small-town setting, while keeping the murder plots as
realistic as possible in such a cozy world."
—*Booklist*

FRENCH PASTRY MURDER
"A delight from start to finish."
—*Suspense Magazine*

CHRISTMAS CAROL MURDER
"Longtime Lucy Stone series readers will be happy
to catch up on life in Tinker's Cover in this
cozy Christmas mystery."
—*Library Journal*

EASTER BUNNY MURDER
"A fun and engaging read. It is quick and light and has
enough interesting twists and turns to keep you turning
the pages. If you like this type of mystery and this is
your first meeting with Lucy Stone, it will probably
not be your last."
—*The Barnstable Patriot*

Books by Leslie Meier

MISTLETOE MURDER
TIPPY TOE MURDER
TRICK OR TREAT MURDER
BACK TO SCHOOL MURDER
VALENTINE MURDER
CHRISTMAS COOKIE MURDER
TURKEY DAY MURDER
WEDDING DAY MURDER
BIRTHDAY PARTY MURDER
FATHER'S DAY MURDER
STAR SPANGLED MURDER
NEW YEAR'S EVE MURDER
BAKE SALE MURDER
CANDY CANE MURDER
ST. PATRICK'S DAY MURDER
MOTHER'S DAY MURDER
WICKED WITCH MURDER
GINGERBREAD COOKIE MURDER
ENGLISH TEA MURDER
CHOCOLATE COVERED MURDER
EASTER BUNNY MURDER
CHRISTMAS CAROL MURDER
FRENCH PASTRY MURDER
CANDY CORN MURDER
BRITISH MANOR MURDER
EGGNOG MURDER
TURKEY TROT MURDER
SILVER ANNIVERSARY MURDER
YULE LOG MURDER
HAUNTED HOUSE MURDER
INVITATION ONLY MURDER

Published by Kensington Publishing Corporation

HALLOWEEN MURDER

LESLIE MEIER

KENSINGTON BOOKS
www.kensingtonbooks.com

KENSINGTON BOOKS are published by

Kensington Publishing Corp.
119 West 40th Street
New York, NY 10018

Compilation copyright © 2018 by Kensington Publishing Corp.
Trick or Treat Murder © 1996 by Leslie Meier
Wicked Witch Murder © 2010 by Leslie Meier

All rights reserved. No part of this book may be reproduced in any form or by any means without the prior written consent of the Publisher, excepting brief quotes used in reviews.

If you purchased this book without a cover, you should be aware that this book is stolen property. It was reported as "unsold and destroyed" to the Publisher and neither the Author nor the Publisher has received any payment for this "stripped book."

All Kensington titles, imprints, and distributed lines are available at special quantity discounts for bulk purchases for sales promotion, premiums, fund-raising, educational, or institutional use. Special book excerpts or customized printings can also be created to fit specific needs. For details, write or phone the office of the Kensington Sales Manager: Attn. Special Sales Department. Kensington Publishing Corp., 119 West 40th Street, New York, NY 10018. Phone: 1-800-221-2647.

Kensington and the K logo Reg. U.S. Pat. & TM Off.

ISBN-13: 978-1-4967-2158-7
ISBN-10: 1-4967-2158-6
First Kensington Trade Edition: September 2018
First Kensington Mass Market Edition: September 2019

ISBN-13: 978-1-4967-1835-8 (ebook)
ISBN-10: 1-4967-1835-6 (ebook)

10 9 8 7 6 5 4 3 2 1

Printed in the United States of America

Contents

TRICK OR TREAT
MURDER

PROLOGUE

"**I** could just kill him."

Monica Mayes pressed the gas pedal of her little BMW to the floor and zoomed around a pokey Dodge Caravan, cutting it a bit too close as she pulled back into her lane. The driver of the Caravan braked, and the van swerved, but Monica didn't notice.

"How could he do this to me?" she asked herself, pulling out the cigarette lighter. With a trembling hand she held it to the end of a Virginia Slim and took a long, slow draw. No longer used to the smoke since she hadn't had a cigarette in years, she coughed.

"He's not worth it," she decided, tossing the cigarette out the window. She was damned if she was going to sacrifice her health for him. He'd gotten enough from her already. Thirty-two years of marriage, three grown children.

Tears welled in her eyes. She couldn't believe how much it hurt, actual physical pain. Her chest ached with every breath; she could hardly swallow. He'd never laid a finger on her, but she felt bruised and beaten anyway.

She hadn't seen that final blow coming. If she had she

might have taken care to avoid it. But she'd never suspected a thing.

She'd left the house at a quarter to one for her weekly shift at the Hospital Auxiliary thrift shop. Realizing she'd forgotten a couple of Roland's old suits that she'd planned to donate, she returned home. She'd hurried upstairs, thrown open the bedroom door, and was halfway across the room before she even saw them.

Roland and Krissy, her aerobics instructor. Her aerobics instructor, for God's sake! And in her own bed—their marriage bed.

"How could he do that?" she asked herself. He was such a bastard. Why hadn't she realized it sooner? She'd just gotten used to it. She gave and he took. That's the way it was. Her job was to please him. She cooked for him. She cleaned for him. She washed and ironed for him. She entertained for him, and decorated the house for him. She dressed for him, and dieted, and even took aerobics for him.

She'd been a fool. She'd thought their marriage was as important to him as it was to her. Him. The doctor. The head honcho. The chief of staff.

Angry now, she impatiently brushed the tears from her cheeks. She'd show him, she decided. She'd hit him where it hurt. He wasn't going to get off scot-free. He'd have to pay. She began making a mental list as she flew along the turnpike, empty on this weekday night now that the tourist season was over.

First of all, she wanted the house in Tinker's Cove, and all the furniture. She'd need her car, of course, and money. A nice little nest egg, plus a big fat alimony check every month. It was her due. She'd earned it. She wasn't going to settle for less.

Was that her exit already? Braking hard she careened off the highway, almost losing control of the car on the tight curve of the exit ramp. Shaken, she pulled to a stop at the intersection and paused, taking a few deep breaths. Then she proceeded, carefully turning onto Route One and was soon driving down Main Street, surprised to find it empty. Of course, she reminded herself. Until now, she had only been here in the summer, when the town was full of tourists and summer residents. Now it was fall. Darkness came much earlier, and the only signs of life were the lighted windows of the houses.

She stopped at the blinker and turned left, then left again onto Hopkins Homestead Road. The road was named for her house. Hopkins Homestead, the oldest house in Tinker's Cove.

She took one last turn onto the familiar dirt driveway and parked the car neatly in the vine-covered carport behind the wood shed.

Her key turned easily in the lock and the heavy pine door swung open. She eagerly inhaled the spicy, old wood smell of the house.

Ignoring her reflection in the spotted glass of the hall mirror, she stepped into the tiny parlor and switched on a lamp.

It was just as she remembered. Bare, wide plank floors, a camelback sofa, a scarred old sea chest serving as a coffee table. There were no curtains on the windows; Monica loved the way the garden became an Impressionist landscape when viewed through the wavy old glass. Anyone passing the house could have looked in and seen her, but no one did.

She went into the next room, the dining room. A collection of Currier and Ives lithographs hung on the wall, and a pine drop leaf table stood in the center of the room, surrounded by six yellow painted chairs. The chairs were the first purchase she'd made for the old house, hesitantly raising her hand at a country auction. "Sold," announced the auctioneer, bringing down his gavel. The bidding was over almost before it had begun. Soon she'd become a regular, rescuing fine antiques from the greedy dealers who stripped off the original finishes and slapped on high prices, taking advantage of ignorant buyers.

Passing through the kitchen, she stepped up into the homing room. Here, close to the warm kitchen hearth, was where the first inhabitants of the house had given birth, nursed the sick, and died. This was where she had put her most prized possession, the curly maple sleigh bed.

Monica pulled back the blue and white handwoven coverlet and found crisp, white sheets. So, she had left the bed made after all. She paid a quick visit to the bathroom, grateful she'd decided to put off closing the house and draining the pipes. Why had she done that? Had she known on some subconscious level that she would need the house? Shivering, she checked the thermostat and raised it to sixty-eight.

Then she pulled off her shoes, slipped off her slacks, and climbed into the bed, pulling the covers around her shoulders. Involuntarily, she let out a long, shuddering sigh.

She was so tired. Here was where she would rest, lick her wounds, and gather her strength. The house was old; it had endured centuries of nor'east storms, winter blizzards, summer heat waves, and decades of neglect. She had restored it and brought it back to life. Now, it was the old homestead's turn to shelter and protect her. She felt safe here. She reached up and turned off the light. She slept.

CHAPTER ONE

"This place is a firetrap. It ought to be torn down."

Sue Finch bit neatly into a crisp apple, closed her eyes, and raised her face to the warm October sun while she chewed. She was sitting on the ramshackle porch of the Ezekiel Hallett house, once the grandest mansion in Tinker's Cove. Now, it was little more than a decaying pile of tinder.

"How can you say that?" asked her companion, Lucy Stone. She thought of the fantastic tower rising above their heads, the mansard roof, and the fanciful urns that perched on every corner. "It's a fabulous example of Victorian seaside architecture. It ought to be restored."

Lucy spoke softly. She didn't want to disturb six-week-old baby Zoe, who was asleep in the red corduroy baby carrier she wore strapped to her chest.

"As what? It's much too big for a family."

"It could be a restaurant, or an inn. Just look at this view."

From where they sat on the porch the two women could see the little town of Tinker's Cove spread out before them. Low, rocky hills sheltered the harbor where a few Cape Island boats bobbed at anchor off the fish pier. The water was a deep blue today, and the tree covered hills wore their fall colors of red and gold.

"Think of the heating bills," said Sue, pulling her sweater off over her head and shaking out her hair.

"That's new, isn't it?" asked Lucy. "Where'd you get it?"

"At the Carriage Trade," said Sue, naming an expensive specialty shop. "Twenty bucks. Last spring."

"Some people have all the luck," grumbled Lucy. "When I go there all I find is real expensive stuff that I don't have any place to wear. Even if I did find something on sale, I wouldn't know what size to buy. I can't seem to get rid of these extra baby pounds."

"There's a new aerobics studio opening across from the Laundromat. If we weren't so lazy we'd sign up for something. What's the latest? The step, the slide?" said Sue, yawning.

There was a pause in the conversation. The bright sunshine and fresh air, combined with a hearty lunch, was making the women drowsy.

"Are you making Halloween costumes for the kids?" asked Sue.

"No way. Toby's going to wear his werewolf mask and hairy hand gloves from last year. The girls are going as ballerinas—in the tutus they wore in the show last spring."

"They'll freeze," warned Sue.

"I'm having them wear pink tights and turtlenecks underneath. They won't be out too long."

"Is there a party at the church, or the youth center? Something to keep them out of trouble?"

"Not that I know of," said Lucy. "I wish there was. I don't even like them trick-or-treating. You always hear about some maniac who poisoned the candy or put razor blades in the apples. Toby won't go with me and the girls—he wants to go out with his friends. I hope they don't come here. A place like this is a real magnet for kids. Especially on Halloween.

Think what could happen if they played with matches, or experimented with cigarettes. It wouldn't take much to burn this place down."

"Like the Hopkins Homestead," said Sue.

"Bill was awfully upset when he heard the news on the radio this morning. That house was his first big project."

Lucy's husband, Bill Stone, was a restoration carpenter.

"That's too bad." Sue was sympathetic. "They said it burned to the ground."

"It did. I drove by on my way to your house. Nothing's left but the chimney. I'm worried Bill's going to take it hard. He really put his heart and soul into that place."

"Is there insurance? Do you think they'll rebuild?" Sue was practical.

"I don't know. Bill tried to call the owners, but there wasn't any answer. He wanted to tell Monica himself, before she heard it on the news or something."

"Her husband's a doctor, right?"

"Yeah. They live near Boston. The house was really her project. Bill said she was the perfect client. Lots of money, and good taste, too."

"A rare combination," said Sue.

Lucy smiled. Zoe was shifting around in the baby carrier and it felt a bit like being pregnant again. She got up on her feet and walked back and forth on the porch, hoping to lull the baby back to sleep.

"Doesn't it seem like we're having an awful lot of fires lately?" she asked, leaning against a post.

"Well, yeah, now that you mention it. There was the old movie theater just after the Fourth of July. It was damaged, but they were able to save it. Winchester College is going to renovate it, turn it into a performing arts center."

"Then there was that barn out on Bumps River Road," said Lucy, sitting down Indian fashion and undoing the carrier straps so Zoe could nurse. "When was that?"

"Mid-August. I remember because I was getting Sidra ready to go back to school." Sue's oldest daughter was a sophomore at Bowdoin.

"Who did that belong to?"

"Nobody. It was listed 'owner unknown' in the tax files."

"And now the Hopkins Homestead."

"Don't forget that fire at the old powder house. They caught it before it did much damage."

"Right." Lucy nodded. The powder house, a tiny relic of the Revolutionary War, stood in Brooks Park. "It's kind of suspicious, isn't it? All these fires?"

"Not really. They were all old buildings, but old buildings are more likely to burn. The wood gets dry." Sue picked off a bit of shingle and it crumbled to dust in her hand. "I'll bet this place is next. Want to take a look inside before it's gone?"

"Can we? Isn't it locked up?"

"I know how to get in." Sue grinned mischievously.

"Okay," said Lucy. "Zoe doesn't seem very hungry." Standing up she rearranged her clothes and refastened the baby carrier. "I'm game if you are."

Hopping off the porch, Sue led the way around to the back of the mansion. Pushing aside some overgrown bushes she revealed a flight of stone steps.

"This is the kitchen entrance. We wouldn't want tradesmen muddying up the front hall."

"Of course not," agreed Lucy, watching closely as Sue pulled off a loose board and opened the door. "You're pretty good at this. How long have you been breaking and entering?"

"Practically my whole life. When I was in high school we used to sneak in here to smoke cigarettes and drink beer."

"I'm shocked," said Lucy, following her friend into the darkness. Zoe's eyes, peeking out over the corduroy carrier, were very large and round.

"This is the kitchen," said Sue, in her best real estate lady voice. "Very roomy."

"It's enormous," said Lucy, glancing around at the cavernous, dungeonlike room.

"All the latest in modern appliances," said Sue, waving her arm. "The stove." She pointed to a rusting hulk in one corner. "The dishwasher." Sue indicated a soapstone sink complete with hand pump. "The refrigerator!" Throwing open a pantry door, she sent a startled mouse scurrying for shelter.

"Yuck. Can we go upstairs?"

"This way, madam."

Sue led the way up a flight of surprisingly sturdy wooden steps and opened the door to the dining room. Lucy blinked at the brightness; dusty sunlight streamed through the filthy windows. Long brown ribbons of wallpaper were peeling from the walls, and the carcasses of dead flies crunched under their feet.

"The dining room needs a bit of freshening up," conceded Sue. "The living room is this way, through the hall."

Stepping into the hallway, Lucy paused and let her gaze follow the long curving staircase upward. Long ago the house must have been lovely, and beautiful young ladies in long gowns would have descended these stairs to greet the handsome beaux who waited for them below.

"I see this old place is casting a spell on you," said Sue. "Would you like to see the ballroom?"

"Ballroom?"

"I kid you not." Sue tugged at a pair of warped French doors and finally succeeded in opening them. She bowed with a little flourish as Lucy entered the room.

It was a long, rectangular room with three sets of French doors along one side. There was a magnificent, ornate marble fireplace at one end and a balcony for musicians at the other. Facing the French doors there was a wall of matching mirrors, now spotty and dusty. The panels between the doors were decorated with carved wood shaped into lavish bouquets of flowers. Gilt sconces, long since robbed of their crystals, lined the walls.

"Sue, how can you say you want to see all this demolished?" asked Lucy. "It's fabulous."

"It could be, if somebody had hundreds of thousands of dollars to spend fixing it up. But that's not going to happen. It's been empty for a zillion years, falling apart bit by bit. A rock through a window here, a piece of paneling ripped out there, it's like the death of a thousand cuts. I'm all for a swift mercy killing."

"You really care about this old place."

"They just don't build 'em like this anymore. Hey, I want to show you something."

Returning to the hallway, Sue opened another oak-paneled door and revealed a tiny cabinlike room, barely ten feet square.

"This is the house Ezekiel Hallett was born in. When he got rich he built the mansion right around his boyhood home. They say he used to come here to get away from his social-climbing wife and daughters."

Lucy examined the rough-sawn plank walls, the packed dirt floor, and the crude hearth.

"This was the entire house?"

"Yup. He was one of seven or eight kids. There's a sleeping loft overhead."

"From this to that," said Lucy, trying to imagine raising a family in such cramped quarters. "It's incredible."

"He did it the hard way—selling guano."

"What is guano, anyway?" asked Lucy, heading for the door. She found the tiny, windowless room claustrophobic. "I'm gonna go out on the porch. I need some air."

"Okay," said Sue. "I'll lock the door behind you and backtrack through the house."

"I forgot. We didn't come in through the front door, did we?"

Lucy stepped outside and busied herself gathering the picnic things. She was struggling to her feet when Sue reappeared.

"You know, Lucy, it might be kind of fun to try out that gym," she suggested.

"I think I'm past help. Besides, I don't have any energy to spare."

"They say working out gives you energy, though I don't quite see how," admitted Sue. "I'll give them a call. See if they've got a good deal."

"Don't forget to ask if they have child care," said Lucy, opening the car door and beginning the process of transferring Zoe from the baby carrier to the car seat.

"I'll call," said Sue, hopping into her little sports car and starting the engine.

Lucy watched as she zoomed down the dirt driveway, disappearing in a swirl of dust. Finally clicking the last strap in place, she looked down at the baby. "Do you think I'm too fat?" she asked.

Zoe folded her hands across her chest, and closed her eyes. She was as inscrutable as a little Buddha.

"Okay, be like that," said Lucy, settling herself behind the steering wheel and turning the key in the ignition.

CHAPTER TWO

Ted Stillings, editor-in-chief, reporter, photographer, and publisher of *The Pennysaver,* parked his aging subcompact in front of the Hopkins Homestead and climbed out.

"Whew," he said, shaking his head. He'd covered a lot of fires in his career, but never one this bad. There was literally nothing left of the house. The massive chimney, now black with soot and surrounded by a mound of charred rubble, was all that remained.

A yellow plastic ribbon encircled the site, and a few curious onlookers stood politely behind it. Inside the cordon, Fire Chief Stan Pulaski stood chatting with Police Chief Oswald Crowley. Ted lifted the yellow ribbon, ducked under it, and approached them.

"Hey, you! Stay behind that line," ordered Crowley. He knew perfectly well who Ted was, but enjoyed being as obnoxious as possible.

"Cut it out, Crowley," yelled Ted. "I need some information."

"You think writing that paper of yours gives you special privileges or something?" Crowley narrowed his eyes, and picked at his yellow teeth with his fingernail.

"People want to know what happened and I want to tell them," said Ted, turning to face Pulaski. "So, Chief, what's the story?"

"I haven't finished the report yet," he answered affably. "Soon as I do you can pick up a copy at the station."

"Thanks." Ted surveyed the scene. "Mind if I take a few pictures?"

"I guess that'll be all right. Stay clear of the debris, okay?"

"Sure."

Ted walked off a short way and pulled his camera out of the worn bag that hung from his shoulder. He busied himself screwing on a lens and adjusting the exposure while keeping one ear cocked. He wasn't above a little discreet eavesdropping.

"Damn reporters," he heard Crowley mutter.

"Better get used to it," advised Pulaski. "This is gonna be a big story, soon as somebody figures out we've had four fires in four months."

Ted looked through the viewfinder and stepped a little closer to the two chiefs.

"He's late." Crowley consulted his watch. "Girl in his office said he'd be here at nine."

"Here he is," announced Pulaski, nodding as an official blue van pulled into the driveway. Neat white letters on the side and back read FIRE MARSHAL.

Ted whistled softly to himself, pulled out his notebook, and joined the two chiefs in greeting the newcomer.

"Mike Rogers, assistant fire marshal," he said with a grin, extending his hand. Rogers was a friendly fellow.

"Ted Stillings, Pennysaver Press," said Ted, shouldering his way between Crowley and Pulaski and grasping his hand. "Have you got Sparky with you?" Ted knew all about Sparky, the accelerant-sniffing dog, from the frequent press releases issued by the state fire marshal's office.

"Sure do. He's right here."

Rogers opened the back door of the van and released the

dog, a youthful black Labrador, from his portable wire kennel. Sparky gave an enormous yawn, stretched, shook himself, and waited patiently while his leash was fastened. Then, walking smartly beside his handler, he went to work.

"This dog's been trained to identify more than a hundred different accelerants?" asked Ted, pointedly ignoring Crowley's disapproving glare.

"That's right. He went to a special school in Michigan. I went, too. We work as a team."

"Is that right?" asked Ted, scribbling away in his notebook. "Where does Sparky live?"

"He lives with me. He's part of the family. When I go to work, he goes, too."

"Is he a good pet?"

"He's great. My kids love him," said Rogers, pausing at the edge of the debris and scratching the dog's neck. "Okay, the way we do this is we sweep the site in a systematic way, working from the outside in. Don't follow me, Ted. There may be hot spots and I don't want to disturb any evidence."

"So what made you call in the fire marshal, Chief?" Ted threw out the question in a deliberately offhand manner as he peered through the viewfinder. "Is there something suspicious about this fire?"

Crowley and Pulaski exchanged glances.

"It was a very fast, very hot fire. The house was completely engaged in a matter of minutes. That doesn't happen unless there are multiple points of origin." Pulaski took off his peaked cap and wiped his forehead with a large white handkerchief.

"You mean arson?"

"Maybe."

"Crowley, have you got any suspects?" There was a slight challenge in Ted's tone.

"No comment." Crowley's attention was on the dog, who had assumed a classic pointing position. "There?" he called.

"Yup," said Rogers, squatting down and opening a toolbox. As they watched he took a sample of the burned material and carefully placed it in a jar.

Sparky indicated the presence of accelerant in three more locations along what had been the outside wall of the house. Once he began investigating the inside, however, he didn't seem to find anything. The man and the dog worked slowly, stepping gingerly among the blackened boards and other charred remains. Ted had plenty of time to get some dramatic photos of Sparky in action.

Rogers spoke softly to the dog, encouraging him and keeping his mind on his task. They had reached the far side of the house, behind the chimney, when the dog began whining and scratching frantically at the rubble.

"What's he found?" shouted Pulaski, hurrying over. "More accelerant?"

"No." Rogers shook his head. "I'm afraid you've got some human remains here."

"A body?" Crowley was doubtful. "This is just a summer place. Nobody's here after Labor Day."

"He only does this when he finds a body," said Rogers. He glanced at the dog who was standing rigid and shivering

"There is no body here," insisted Crowley. "I don't see a body. There's nothing but ashes."

"It was a hot fire," Rogers reminded him. "There's probably teeth, bone fragments, maybe even jewelry. I'll have to call in specialists from the medical examiner's office. Meanwhile, let's get this area secured and covered with a tarp."

"Winchell," Crowley yelled to a young officer who was stand ing nearby. "Find Carter. Get on this right away."

"Okay, Chief," he said, setting off across the yard at a trot.

"I think we're about done here," said Rogers, gently tugging at Sparky's leash and leading the trembling dog back to the van. "Good boy." He stroked the animal behind his ears. Sparky gave him a look of doggy adoration and licked his hand.

"What happens now?" Ted asked the chief. But before Crowley could tell Ted to mind his own business he was interrupted by Winchell.

"Chief, Carter's found a car behind that shed. A BMW."

"Damn," said the chief. The last thing he wanted was a homicide.

"You, Stillings." He stabbed a fat finger at Ted's chest. "I want you out of here." He cocked his thumb. "Now."

"Okay, okay," said Ted, holding his hands up. "I know when I'm not wanted."

He started off toward his car, and Pulaski joined him, walking companionably alongside. Unlike the police chief, Pulaski understood the value of a good working relationship with the local media.

"Check at the station, Ted. We'll be scheduling a press conference this afternoon, tomorrow morning at the latest."

"Thanks."

"No problem." He paused. "I have something to say." Ted got out his pad, and when he was ready, Pulaski continued. "I hate arson. Every time my men go out to fight a fire, they put themselves at risk. Every time. And now we've got a death. Somebody died in this fire.

"This is my pledge to the people of Tinker's Cove: I'm going to catch this bastard. But I need help. Anybody sees any suspicious activity, especially around a vacant building, call us. Call right away. Arson's hard to prove, unless the perpetrator is caught in the act. Got that?"

"Got it."

Humming softly to himself, Ted got behind the wheel of his car. He was already rearranging the front page in his mind. Scratch the photo of the jack-o'-lantern, put the "Healthy Holiday Treats" interview with the school dietitian on page five, move "Officer Culpepper's Rules for a Safe Halloween" to page six. Arson, homicide, this was going to be one hell of a Halloween issue.

CHAPTER THREE

There was an annoying buzz in the room. If she didn't stop it, it would wake up the baby.

Lucy sat up in bed. She opened her eyes. Zoe was sleeping peacefully in her white wicker bassinet. She couldn't find the hum.

"Lucy, turn off the alarm."

"Unh." She reached out and pressed the button. She flopped back on her pillow and felt herself slipping back in the warm cocoon of sleep. So easy to drift off, except for the tug of her conscience. She had to get the kids ready for school, and Bill off to work. She threw off the covers and sat up, groping for slippers and robe. Standing, she staggered slightly and caught her balance on the door frame.

She crossed the hall to her eleven-year-old son's room. Picking her way carefully across the dirty clothes and sports equipment that littered the floor, she gave his shoulder a shake. "Toby, it's time to get up."

Next she stuck her head in Sara and Elizabeth's room. "Good morning, girls," she called. Elizabeth was nine, going on twenty-nine, and Sara was five.

She went down the steep back stairs to the kitchen, made

the coffee, and continued on into the downstairs bathroom. She splashed cold water on her face and looked in the mirror. Short black hair stuck out all over her head and there were bags under her eyes. She looked terrible. What did she expect? She'd been up most of the night with the baby. She brushed her teeth.

Back in the kitchen, she poured herself a cup of coffee and sat down at the table, resting her head on her hands.

"Mom, I need you to sign this." Toby's voice pulled her back to consciousness.

"What is it?"

"A pledge that you won't abuse your body by taking any illegal drugs."

"No problem," she mumbled, scribbling her name. "Got any speed, man?"

"What?"

"Nothing." She took a long swallow of coffee.

When she next opened her eyes, she saw Bill standing at the counter, dressed for work in a plaid flannel shirt and jeans, buttering a pile of toast.

"Sara, that pink scrunchy is mine," said Elizabeth.

"No, it isn't." Sara's voice started to climb the scale. "It's mine!"

"Let her wear it," said Lucy.

"That's so unfair. You're always siding with her." Elizabeth stamped across the kitchen and plunked herself down on a chair.

"What's the matter with your eye?" asked Bill, setting a glass of orange juice in front of her.

Lucy squinted suspiciously at Elizabeth. She reached out and ran a finger across her eyelid.

"Eye shadow! Wash it off."

Elizabeth glared at her, then stomped off to the bathroom.

"More coffee?" Bill had the pot ready.

"Please. Intravenously."

"Mom, can you come to school tomorrow?" asked Sara. "Officer Barney is visiting our class." Sara was in kindergarten, and she loved it. After watching Toby and Elizabeth go off to school every day, she was finally in school, too.

"Sure," said Lucy. She looked up as Elizabeth returned. "That looks much better."

"All the other girls wear makeup."

"Right." Lucy heard the roar of the school bus engine, as it began the climb up Red Top Road. "You better get going. The bus will be here any minute."

The kids pushed and shoved, grabbing their backpacks and lunches, then clattered out, slamming the door behind them. Lucy picked herself up and started up the stairs, heading back to bed.

"What the hell?" Bill was peering out the kitchen window, thoughtfully stroking his beard.

Lucy joined him. "Oh, my God," she groaned, spotting a huge old Chrysler Imperial turning into the driveway, narrowly missing a whiskey barrel planted with bronze chrysanthemums. "It's Miss Tilley. What could she want so early in the morning?"

"The old witch probably hasn't been to bed yet," said Bill. "Probably been riding her broomstick all night."

Stifling a yawn, Lucy opened the door. "Miss Tilley, what a nice surprise!"

Like most everyone in Tinker's Cove, Lucy didn't dare address the old woman by her first name. Only a select group of her dearest friends referred to Julia Ward Howe Tilley, the former librarian of the Broadbrooks Free Library, as Julia.

Casting a disapproving glance at Lucy, who found herself involuntarily buttoning up her ratty old velour robe, the old woman wasted no time getting to the point. "Bill, it was really you I came to see," she said, baring her complete set of rather dingy original teeth in a ferocious smile.

"Me?"

"Sit down. I have something I want to discuss. You too, Lucy."

Meekly, they obeyed, waiting while the old woman settled herself.

"As you know," she began, folding her knobby, arthritic hands together on the edge of the table, "I am a member of the Tinker's Cove Historic District Commission. The chairman, in fact. Unfortunately, we have a vacancy now that Porter Lambkin has resigned. He has cancer and says his treatment will prevent him from attending meetings." From Miss Tilley's expression, it was clear she disapproved. In her eyes, sickness was usually nothing more than a convenient excuse for neglecting one's duty.

"I wouldn't have expected it of him," she fumed. "He's left us in a terrible predicament."

"What do you mean?" asked Lucy.

"Remember when the commission was created? It was supposed to protect the town from tasteless, rampant development. People saw what happened in Freeport, and wanted to make sure that could never happen here. They voted to designate almost all of the town as a historic district, and set up the commission to review all proposals for change within the district. No one who owns property within the district can make any changes without getting a certificate of appropriateness from the commission."

Lucy and Bill knew all about the commission, usually referred to in *The Pennysaver* as the TCHDC. More and more, however, people were calling it the "hysterical commission." While most everyone agreed it was important to preserve the character of the town, they resented having to get official approval whenever they wanted to change the color of the front door.

"I've been on the commission from the beginning, and so has Porter and Hancock Smith. You know Hancock—the president of the Historical Society. And then there was Kitty Slack and Gerald Asquith from the college. Gerald decided not to run for reelection, and, well, you know all about Kitty."

Lucy did. Only a few months had passed since Kitty, a wealthy widow, had jilted her faithful suitor Gerald Asquith and left town unexpectedly, accompanied by a silver fox of a time-share salesman.

"Only three people were on the ballot for two seats, and one of them was Kitty. It was too late to get her name off the ballot so Jock Mulligan and Doug Durning really ran unopposed. We used to have a nice unanimous board, but those two apparently have a different agenda. They will approve anything. It didn't matter while we had Porter, but now that he's gone the commission has been stalemated. Our votes are always tied. We can't even agree on a fifth member to fill in until elections next year. Then I thought of you, Bill."

He shifted uncomfortably in his seat. "Me?"

"You." Sitting with her back to the window, Miss Tilley's white hair glowed angelically. Her blue eyes twinkled. She smiled sweetly. Anyone who didn't know her would think she was a perfectly nice old lady.

"It's positively Machiavellian, if I say so myself," she cackled. "They can't say no to you. You're a restoration carpenter. You have impeccable credentials."

"I'd like to help," said Bill, "but I don't think I have the time."

"Really?" She raised an eyebrow. "And what do you do most evenings?"

Bill squirmed uneasily.

"I bet you watch TV. Mental masturbation, that's what I call it."

Lucy pressed her lips together, to keep from giggling, and looked at Bill.

"There's nothing the matter with TV," he grumbled. "How often does this thing meet?"

"Once a month."

"I guess I can manage that," he agreed. "But I'm warning you, I'll have to vote the way I see fit."

"Of course, you must vote your conscience," she said, laying heavy emphasis on the last word. "Then we'll see you tomorrow night. Seven o'clock at the town hall."

"Tomorrow? That means I'll miss *Seinfeld!*"

Miss Tilley silenced him with a stare. Only one avenue was left. Bill grabbed his lunch box, gave Lucy a peck on the cheek, and hurried out.

"I'm glad you asked him," said Lucy. "He has a lot to offer. It's about time he got involved. He needs something to take his mind off the Hopkins Homestead fire."

"My thoughts exactly," said Miss Tilley, casting an appraising glance at Lucy. "My dear, I hope you'll take a little bit of advice from an old friend. Even a spinster like myself knows you'll never keep a man interested if you let yourself go the way you have."

Lucy ran a hand through her hair, suddenly self-conscious.

Miss Tilley rose. "You're really quite attractive when you make an effort, my dear. Now, I must be off."

Lucy watched from the door as she trotted across the yard and climbed into her huge old Chrysler, a 1974 Imperial. That was some car, thought Lucy, guessing it was nearly ten feet long. A dinosaur of an automobile decked with tons of chrome. She winced as it lurched into gear, and Miss Tilley slowly wrestled it through a three-point turn. Built on the theory that size equals comfort, the designers had given little thought to maneuverability. In this car you didn't avoid obstacles, you ran right over them.

Miss Tilley finally had the car pointed in the right direction, and gave Lucy a little wave before flooring the gas pedal. Lucy wondered if she could actually see over the steering wheel as she careened down the driveway. She never even noticed when she knocked over the mailbox.

Lucy shook her head, and was thinking of slipping back between the sheets for a quick nap when the phone rang.

"Are you okay?" inquired Sue.

"Sure. Why?"

"You sound so groggy. Do you have a cold?"

"No. Zoe didn't sleep much last night."

"Six-week growth spurt?"

"Probably."

"Listen, Lucy. I had a great idea. I want to have a big Halloween party for the whole town in the Hallett House. Whaddya think?"

"Sounds like fun. Will the fire chief let you do it?"

"I just got off the phone with him. He said he'll issue a temporary occupancy permit if we clean the place up and it passes his inspection."

Hearing a cry from upstairs, Lucy was distracted.

"What? I think I hear Zoe."

"Listen, Lucy, will you help with the party?"

Zoe's cries were coming more frequently, threatening to become a full-blown wail. "Sure. What can I do?"

"Cupcakes?"

Zoe was now screaming, and Lucy could feel her breasts tingle as her milk let down. All she could think of was the baby. "Sure. No problem. How many?"

"Twelve dozen?"

"Okay. I gotta go. Bye." Lucy slammed the earpiece onto the hook, hiked up her long flannel nightie and robe, and started up the stairs taking them two at a time. "Hang on, baby! Mommy's coming!"

CHAPTER FOUR

"What's all the fuss about?" crooned Lucy, bending over the bassinet. Zoe's face was red with rage; she was in no mood for small talk. "I bet you want your breakfast," said Lucy. She scooped up the baby and perched on the side of the bed, offering her breast.

Zoe took it greedily, and began sucking energetically. Feeling herself beginning to relax, Lucy considered falling back on to the pillows, but Zoe was having none of that. She suddenly pulled her head away, leaving Lucy to clamp a diaper over her spraying milk ducts. Lucy tickled the baby's cheek with her milky nipple, but Zoe wasn't interested. She had a soaking wet diaper, and knew perfectly well that it was time for a change and a bath. Lucy knew it, too, but had hoped to postpone it for a bit.

"You're so . . . conservative," she said, placing the baby on her shoulder. "If it's eight-thirty, it must be bathtime."

In the kitchen, Lucy propped Zoe in her plastic baby seat and set it on the counter. She flipped on the radio and began loading the breakfast dishes into the dishwasher. She gave the counter a quick wipe, lined the big porcelain sink with a hand towel, and began filling it with warm water.

Cocking an ear to the radio for the morning news, she gave Zoe a big smile, tickled her tummy, and eased her out of her rather damp terry suit. Removing the wet diaper, she slipped the naked baby into the water.

Cradling her head in the crook of her arm, Lucy listened to the Oil Peddler promise 24-hour delivery as she gently splashed water on Zoe's round tummy.

"Regular exercise can make you look and feel better," advised a feminine voice.

"That's right," said Lucy, nodding and smiling at the baby. At six weeks, she was looking less like a newborn and more like a real baby. Her little limbs were no longer folded tight against her torso. "You love to exercise, don't you? You love to wave those arms and kick those legs."

"My name is Krissy Wright," continued the voice, "and I'm inviting you to stop by my new exercise studio, the Body Shop, for a free introductory class."

"Shall we do that? Would you like to work out? Oh!" said Lucy in surprise, as Zoe splashed her in the face. Zoe gave a little chuckle, and smiled.

"Is that a smile?" cooed Lucy, returning the gesture.

Zoe's eyes were fixed intently on her mother's face, and she smiled again.

"Definitely a smile," crowed Lucy. "Aren't you a smart little girl!"

Zoe agreed, and flapped her arm rhythmically in the water, startling herself with the resulting splash. Before she could cry, Lucy distracted her by singing along with the radio. "Hey, where ya goin? I'm goin' to the Lobster Bar, 'cause that's where the best . . . lobsters are!"

Lucy hummed along with the radio as she quickly soaped Zoe's silky, tiny body, and rinsed her off, then wrapped her in a fluffy towel. With the baby propped against her shoulder, she waltzed around the kitchen gathering the diapering supplies.

Spreading the towel beneath her, she laid Zoe down on

the kitchen table. Whenever Lucy saw her like that, naked and helpless, she felt a little stab of fear. So many things could happen to a baby. Just last night she had watched a TV news segment about a dangerous cradle. Nine unwary mothers had tucked their babies in for the night only to find them dead in the morning.

Then there was her own private nightmare, in which she drove off on an errand and forgot the baby. She'd dreamt it often since coming home from the hospital, and always woke up in a panic. Then, she wouldn't be able to get back to sleep until she checked the bassinet and made sure Zoe was safe. After four babies one wouldn't expect these irrational fears to keep popping up, but they did.

"You babies sure know how to drive mommies crazy, yes you do," crooned Lucy, pulling a clean diaper out of the basket of unsorted laundry in the corner. "I'm crazy over you," she sang along with a popular tune, snapping the diaper cover firmly in place. She was just tucking Zoe's arms and legs into a stretchy little suit, when the music ended and the announcer read the news tease.

"Police say a suspicious Tinker's Cove fire claimed the life of at least one victim. More in a moment."

"Oh, no," she muttered, as she settled herself in the rocking chair. As Zoe nuzzled her chest, now eager for a late breakfast, Lucy wondered who the victim could have been.

It couldn't have been any of the Mayes, she assured herself. The family only used the house in the summer. Perhaps it was a vagrant or homeless person who had broken into the empty house looking for a night's shelter.

"Please, please don't let it be one of the kids," she sent up a little prayer. There wasn't much to do in Tinker's Cove, and Toby's friends sometimes did things they shouldn't. Exciting and forbidden things, like entering someone's deserted summer cottage.

Lucy began to nurse, gently stroking her baby's downy

head. She bent down and sniffed Zoe's clean baby scent. It was the best smell in the world. Just then the announcer's voice interrupted her reverie.

"The fire that destroyed the Hopkins Homestead early Tuesday morning also claimed the life of its owner, Monica Mayes. Remains found at the site by state fire investigators have been positively identified by the medical examiner."

Lucy sat motionless as Zoe continued her rhythmic sucking. It took a minute for the information to sink in. Gradually, grief engulfed her and tears ran down her face.

"No, not Monica," she whispered.

"This means we are no longer investigating a case of arson," Lucy recognized Police Chief Oswald Crowley's voice, in a recorded sound bite. "This is now a homicide investigation."

Homicide? Who would want to kill Monica? She remembered Monica laughing, recounting how an inept young traffic cop had tied up traffic for miles on Route 1, by stopping the line of cars for every pedestrian who wanted to cross the street. They'd been standing outside, and Monica's coppery hair had blazed in the sun.

Lucy thought of the flames, flickering brightly as they consumed the Homestead.

She remembered Monica flipping through wallpaper books, determined to find exactly the right paper for the bathroom, and her excitement when Bill showed her the 1703 penny that had been placed under the threshold to guarantee prosperity.

Lucy thought of her husband, busy at another old house. He had been so fond of Monica, just as she had. He shouldn't hear this on the radio. She ought to tell him.

Zoe was asleep in her arms. Lucy knew she would sleep soundly for a couple of hours. She carried her upstairs and tucked her in the bassinet, then quickly showered and dressed herself.

An hour later, steering her little silver Subaru wagon along the back roads with Zoe securely fastened in the safety seat, Lucy thought of Monica.

She had been one of Bill's first clients, and initially had seemed to be just another pampered, rich doctor's wife who wanted a summer place that would impress her city friends. When they first discussed the restoration of the Homestead, Bill had come prepared with estimates for alarm systems, air-conditioning, even a Jacuzzi tub.

"I don't know," Monica had said doubtfully, shaking her head. "This is a very old house. Somehow these things don't seem to belong. I know we can't be one hundred percent authentic, after all, this isn't 1703 and I don't want to use an outhouse! But I'd like this to be a place where we live simply, and get back to the basics, know what I mean?"

Bill had nodded.

"What about your husband?" Lucy had asked. "Men don't like to give up their gadgets."

"He says he wants to make a woodpile." Monica shrugged. "I'm not sure he knows how. He's a gynecologist." She changed the subject. "This means so much to me. I've always wanted to have an old house."

At first, Lucy had been a little jealous of Monica. She had money and social status, and although older than Lucy, was still extremely attractive. Her skin was nourished and revitalized, her hair was highlighted and carefully coiffed, and she was a living testament to the benefits of regular exercise.

At the time, Lucy was struggling through the first months of her pregnancy with Toby, and she felt bloated and nauseous. Lucy was pretty sure that if Monica had given Bill the least encouragement, he would have hopped into bed with her.

But she never had. She'd become a friend to both of them. She'd become Bill's eager student, listening carefully as he explained the old construction methods. She insisted that he do what he thought best for the house and refused to cut corners to save money. As a result, the house had been one of Bill's most satisfying projects, and he was justifiably proud of the work he did there.

She took Lucy along to country auctions, and together they learned how to tell the treasures from the trash. When Lucy fell in love with a golden oak high chair, but was quickly outbid by a dealer, Monica noted the buyer's identity. She bought the chair from him, and surprised Lucy with it as a baby gift.

That was the sort of person she was. She quickly became involved in people's lives, and showered them with affection. Always quick to smile and laugh, revealing those pearly white teeth.

Did they use her teeth to identify her? Lucy wondered, with a stab of pain. Had Monica been quietly overcome by smoke in her sleep, or had she woken in a panic realizing the house was on fire? Had she found the doorway blocked by flames, and struggled to open a window? What were her last moments like? Had she been afraid? Had she suffered?

Lucy couldn't bear to think about it. She wanted to remember Monica as she'd been. A beautiful woman who loved life.

How was she going to tell Bill? How could she soften the impact? Bill wasn't the sort of man who expressed his deepest emotions openly, but Lucy knew he'd taken the fire very hard. He hadn't said much, but she knew he was simmering with anger. As she pulled the Subaru up next to Bill's truck and braked, Lucy felt heavy with the weight of the terrible news she had to deliver.

CHAPTER FIVE

Moving automatically, Lucy opened the car door and got out. She pulled open the rear door and reached in to loosen the straps that held the baby seat. Bracing herself, she awkwardly lifted the cumbersome plastic shell that held the baby. Then she climbed the makeshift steps and entered the spacious hall of the Hathorn-Pye house. The house had recently been purchased by the Maine Museum of Fine Arts, and Bill had been hired to restore it.

"Bill?" she called.

"I'm in here," he answered. Lucy followed his voice and found him bent over a window frame in one of the front rooms.

"This is a nice surprise," he said, looking up.

"Zoe was restless," improvised Lucy, trying to ease her way into breaking the news, "so I took her for a drive." She set down the heavy baby seat, and tucked a shawl around the sleeping baby.

"I thought you'd be back in bed."

"I wish I was," she confessed, crossing the room to stand beside him. "Sue called and the phone woke the baby. Wotcha doin'?"

"Taking a paint sample, so I can figure out the original color."

"This is a lovely house," observed Lucy, looking around. "I love the proportions."

"It's a classic Georgian," said Bill. "The museum was smart to buy it. They got it for a song. It's a fine house, Captain Hathorn spared no expense when he built it. It was his statement to the world that he had arrived." Bill began carefully dismantling the window frame.

"I love the big front hall, and those stairs."

"That hallway told visitors the captain had money to waste on space that wasn't needed for cooking or sleeping."

"I wonder what the captain's wife was like," mused Lucy.

"Which one?" asked Bill, carefully prying off a piece of window casing. "The first three all died in childbirth, not one lived past twenty-five. The fourth was a rich old widow who already had six children."

"My goodness," said Lucy, recalled to her grim task. "Bill, I've got some bad news. Terrible news."

He straightened up and turned to face her.

"Monica was there," said Lucy, her voice breaking. "She died in the fire."

He shook his head, refusing to believe her. "It must have been somebody else. A vagrant or something. Monica was never there except in the summer."

"She was there. They've identified her." Tears were now running down her face.

"Where did you hear this?" Bill's voice was sharp.

"On the radio."

His face went white and slack; he looked as if he'd been kicked in the stomach. Then his jaw tightened and he turned away, facing the wall. Raising his fist, he slammed it against the tough old horsehair plaster, raising a cloud of dust.

Lucy reached up and touched his shoulder. He spun around and drew her against him, burying his face in her hair. They clung together for a long time. Finally, he pulled himself away and began to pace.

"Dammit," he said, suddenly stricken with guilt. "It was my fault. There was no smoke alarm in that house. They changed the code a year or two later. If I'd thought to put one in she might have lived. At least she would have had a chance to get out."

"It's not your fault. You did everything you were supposed to. She was just in the wrong place at the wrong time."

"Damn. I hate fires."

"I know," said Lucy, thinking once again of the flames, remorselessly consuming everything and leaving only ashes. And bones. She shivered. "Do you want to take the day off? We could go for a ride or something—something to take our minds off the fire." She wiped her face with a crumpled tissue she'd found in her pocket.

"Thanks," he said, gently caressing her shoulder. "I'd rather work. I've got some old ceiling tile upstairs that has to come down. Today seems like a good day to rip a building apart."

"Just be sure you stop with the ceiling tile," said Lucy, attempting a feeble joke. "I don't want you to tear down the whole place."

"I'm not guaranteeing anything," said Bill, pulling a crowbar out of his toolbox and picking up the battered old tape player he kept on the job. "You'd better get out of here if you don't want Zoe to wake up. I'm gonna play some AC/DC—real loud."

"Be careful," cautioned Lucy. "We don't need any broken bones."

"See ya later," he said, mounting the stairs.

Back in the car, heading for home, Lucy could think of nothing but the fires. Sue was wrong. These fires weren't just happening. She was sure someone was setting them. But who? What sort of person would do such a thing? Did he stand in the dark, watching as the flames grew stronger, listening for the wail of the sirens? Why did he do it? Was he frightened, now that someone had died? Or was he thrilled by the fact that he had taken a human life? Would Monica's death spur him on to set more fires?

Pulling into her driveway, Lucy regarded her own comfortable home. A spacious white clapboard farmhouse, it had been built in the 1850s, just before the Civil War. The builder was known to have had strong abolitionist sympathies, and some people believed the house had been a stop on the Underground Railroad.

Lucy loved her house. She loved the fact that it was old, and the thought of the many generations it had sheltered reassured her. To her the house was a tangible link to the past, and a launching pad for the future. More than a wedding ring, or a big diamond, it was proof of the commitment she and Dill had made to each other. The house had been in terrible shape when they bought it, a real handyman's special, and they had labored together to make it a home.

We could be next, she thought, feeling very vulnerable. The house, after all, was nothing but wood. Mostly old wood. Like the others, it would go up in a flash. We're not safe. Nobody's safe, she thought, nobody who lives in an old house.

She shifted into park, switched off the engine, and began to unfasten the straps that held Zoe in the safety seat. Still sound asleep, Zoe didn't even blink. Lucy gazed at her beautiful baby and gently stroked her cheek. What if their house began to burn like the Hopkins Homestead? Would she be able to save Zoe?

She didn't want to find out. Whoever was setting the fires, this maniac, had to be found and stopped.

CHAPTER SIX

"Never, ever eat any of your trick or treat candy before your parents have a chance to look it over."

The next morning, Lucy kept her promise to Sara and visited the kindergarten. As she joined the other mothers in the back of the room, she felt remarkably light and unencumbered without the baby carrier strapped to her chest. She had taken Sue at her word when she insisted she would be happy to babysit and had left Zoe with her.

Lucy always enjoyed visiting the elementary school. Here, in the brightly decorated rooms, order prevailed. The children marched in lines, two by two. They practiced their round letters on lined paper. The answers were right, or they were wrong. There was none of the conflict and confusion that reigned in the real world. Here, for just a few minutes anyway, she could push the fire and Monica's death to a dark, back corner of her mind.

Catching Officer Barney Culpepper's eye, she gave him a little wave. He was standing in the front of the room, surrounded by the entire kindergarten class who were sitting cross-legged on the floor. At six feet, with a stocky build, he seemed enormous compared to the children. Lucy looked for Sara and found her in the front row, next to her best friend, Jenn Baker.

A hand shot up, and Culpepper leaned forward.

"Joey Wade, do you have a question?"

"What if my mom eats all my candy?"

The question set off a chorus of anxious laughter; Joey had voiced a shared concern.

"If you ate all your trick or treat candy yourself you'd probably get an enormous stomachache," said Culpepper, grabbing his beer belly and groaning. "I hate it when that happens, don't you?"

The kids laughed and nodded, and a few of the more active boys imitated him, grabbing their stomachs and groaning.

"John, Peter." The names were accompanied by a stern look from teacher Lydia Volpe, and the boys settled down. Lydia was a pro, she had been teaching for years. She had also taught Toby and Elizabeth.

"There's a reason why your parents should check your candy. They want to make sure it's okay for you to eat, that it hasn't been opened, and there are no germs." Officer Culpepper was doing his best to warn the kids without frightening them, thought Lucy.

"My cousin got an apple for Halloween and he bit into it and there were pins inside," volunteered a blond little girl dressed all in pink.

"My cousin bit into an apple and there was a razor blade," added a little brunette, already accomplished in the art of one-upmanship.

A general buzz ensued in which Lucy heard poison, thumb-tacks, and broken glass mentioned. She was shocked. Where did five-year-olds hear these things?

"Now, children," reminded Mrs. Volpe. "Officer Culpepper hasn't finished. He has more to tell us." Her dark eyes flashed. "We listen with our ears, not our mouths."

"Some of the stories you hear about Halloween aren't

true," advised the policeman. "But it's better to be safe than sorry." He turned the page of an oversized flip chart. "These are my safety tips for Halloween. Number one: Never go trick or treating alone. Who are you going with, Joey?"

"My brother."

"That's good. How about you, Heather?"

"With my mom."

"And you, Billy?"

"I don't know yet."

"Well, be sure you don't go alone," said Culpepper. "Here's tip number two: Don't wear a mask that covers your eyes and makes it hard to see. What can you use, if you're not wearing a mask? Samantha?"

"Makeup?" Samantha was enchanted with the idea.

"That's right. Makeup is better than a mask. Now for tip number three. If you go out after dark, carry a flashlight. Why should you carry a flashlight, Billy?"

"So you can see where you're going?"

"You got it. And so the drivers of cars can see you. Ready for tip number four? Here it comes. You've heard it before. Have your parents check your candy before you eat it. Only one tip left. Sara, can you guess what it is?"

"You shouldn't smash pumpkins or throw eggs or things like that," said Sara, nodding virtuously. She obviously remembered an unfortunate incident last Halloween, when Toby had been caught toilet-papering the principal's hedge. Lucy felt a blush rising from her turtleneck and studied her shoes as her cheeks reddened.

"That's very true," agreed Culpepper, winking at Lucy. "Trick or treating is more fun if you leave out the tricks." He flipped to the last page, where a glowing jack-o'-lantern had the letters HAVE FUN carved into its face. "Tip number five is to have fun. Everybody, what are you going to do on Halloween?" he asked.

"Have fun!" the children chorused back.

"Thank you, Officer Culpepper, for visiting our class,"

said Mrs. Volpe in her teacher's voice. "Class, how do we thank Officer Culpepper?"

"Thank you, Officer Culpepper," they shouted in unison.

"We have a Halloween treat for Officer Culpepper and our other visitors today," announced Mrs. Volpe. "If Officer Culpepper will go to the back of the room with the others, the children can stand in the front."

Culpepper joined the handful of mothers in the back of the room, placing himself next to Lucy, while Mrs. Volpe quickly arranged the children in front of the blackboard. "First, we have a finger-play. Ready?" The children raised their hands in front of their faces. "Begin."

"Five little pumpkins sitting on a gate," chanted the children.

"The first one said." They each raised a finger. "My, it's getting late."

"The second one said." Another finger went up. "I hear a noise."

"The third one said." Three fingers were now up. "It's only some boys."

"The fourth one said." Only the thumbs were folded. "Having Halloween fun."

"The fifth one said." Out popped the thumbs. "Let's run, let's run!"

"When, OOH went the wind, and OUT (here they all clapped) went the lights, and away they all RAN (the hands went behind their backs) on Halloween night!"

The mothers applauded, smiling and beaming with pride.

"Now for our song." Mrs. Volpe clapped her hand once and the children began singing to the tune of "Frere Jacques."

"Pumpkin moonshines, pumpkin moonshines,
Where are you? Where are you?
Here I am this evening.
Boo, boo, boo! Boo, boo, boo!"

* * *

The mothers all laughed and clapped enthusiastically. Lucy caught Sara's eye and gave her a wave and a smile.

"That's the end of our program, thank you for coming," said Mrs. Volpe, indicating the door.

Leaving the room, Lucy walked down the corridor with Officer Culpepper. They had been friends for a long time, and they'd gotten to know each other when they had served together on the Cub Scout Pack Committee.

"So, Barney, what can you tell me about the fire?" asked Lucy.

"Not much," he said, smoothing back his hair and setting his cap on his head. "The chief's taking this kinda personal. He likes to think he's got a quiet, law-abiding town. The fires are bad enough, but now that nice lady Mrs. Mayes got herself killed. He's doubled nighttime patrols—we've got two cruisers out instead of one—and he's got the state troopers helping out. But arson's tough. You can't prove anything unless you catch 'em in the act. We don't have enough manpower to cover every building in town."

"Come on, Barney. That's the official line. I want to know what you really think."

"Trouble is, nobody thought too much about it at first. Just figured it was kids."

"You don't anymore?"

"Nope. School started for one thing. Vandalism always drops once they go back to school. Don't have as much time to get into trouble. Fires oughta stopped, but they didn't. If anything, they've been coming closer together. The frequency is increasing."

"What does that mean?"

"It means we've probably got a nut on our hands. A pyro."

"That's what I think," said Lucy. "And he seems to go for old buildings. It makes me nervous. After all, our house is pretty old."

"I wouldn't worry too much. Guy from the fire marshal's office said he thinks we'll get this nut pretty soon. The more fires he sets the more likely he is to get careless. He'll make a mistake and we'll catch him."

"Somehow that doesn't make me feel a whole lot better. How many fires is it going to take? And it won't bring Monica back."

"That was a real shame," said Barney, holding the door for her.

"It sure was. See you around, Barney."

Lucy paused on the steps and watched as Barney climbed in his cruiser and pulled out of the school driveway. The holiday program hadn't taken long, it was only ten o'clock. There was no need for her to hurry back; Sue wouldn't mind keeping Zoe a bit longer. Making up her mind, Lucy crossed the street to the Broadbrooks Free Library.

The library had changed quite a bit since Miss Tilley's retirement. The polished wood floors that creaked whenever anyone moved, earning the transgressor a baleful stare from Miss Tilley, had been covered with carpet. Fluorescent lights had been installed, and it was now possible to read the titles in the stacks; readers no longer had to guess which was the right book and then take it to the window to check the title. These changes were all instigated by Miss Tilley's successor, perky little Bitsy Howell.

"My replacement" as Miss Tilley insisted on calling her, was breezy and casual. While Miss Tilley had emphasized order, and tolerated nothing out of place, Bitsy thrived on chaos. Her office was a mess, overflowing with papers and books waiting to be cataloged.

Bitsy greeted everyone who came in the door cheerfully, waived overdue fines with abandon, and resolutely ignored the three-book limit. Under her management, circulation had dramatically increased, donations were up, and a building drive was underway.

"Lucy, I haven't seen you for a while. We have some

wonderful new children's books—I'm sure Sara would love them."

"I'll have to bring her in," promised Lucy. "I'm doing some research today. Tell me, do you keep old copies of *The Pennysaver?*"

"Sure do. All the way back to 1837. It was called the *Advertiser* in those days. Fascinating reading, if you've got the time."

"I'm only interested in some recent issues. The last few months."

"Sure. They're right here," said Bitsy, ushering Lucy into a workroom. "I'll just move these out of your way," she said, scooping up some magazines, "and you can sit right here. The most recent papers are in this box—we send them to be microfilmed at the end of the year. You're welcome to help yourself, just put them back the way you found them, okay?"

Pulling out a stack, Lucy thumbed through the old newspapers until she found the July 9 issue. Her eye immediately fell on the dramatic page one photo of the old movie theater, which had gone up in flames on Sunday, July 5, providing a fiery climax to the holiday weekend.

Ted's story emphasized the heroism of the firefighters, who had managed to save much of the grand old movie palace. Winchester College had been planning to restore the gilded walls, red plush seats, and ceiling murals to create a performing arts center.

"We're grateful to the wonderful volunteer firefighters," said College President Gerald Asquith. "This terrible fire has delayed the restoration project, but we plan to go forward as soon as additional funds are raised."

There was no suggestion that the fire had been deliberately set. Everyone Ted interviewed agreed the fire was an unfortunate tragedy, probably due to a faulty electrical connection, or perhaps a holiday firework that landed on the wood-shingled roof.

Flipping through the papers, Lucy soon found the story about the second fire. BARN BURNS, blared the headline of the August 28 issue, nearly two months after the first fire. This time, firemen were unable to save the building.

"The structure was fully involved when we arrived," Fire Chief Stanley Pulaski was quoted as saying. "A decision was made not to put any of our personnel at risk, our objective was simply to confine the fire and let it burn itself out."

In other words, thought Lucy, they watched it burn. Again, there was no hint that the fire might have been deliberately set. Spontaneous combustion of new hay was given as the likely cause.

The third fire occurred only a month later, in late September. Fortunately, when the old powder house went up in flames it was quickly discovered, and the antique building, which dated from the Revolutionary War was saved. As Barney suggested, this fire was blamed on youthful vandals.

"I want to make one thing absolutely clear," warned Police Chief Oswald Crowley. "This sort of destructive behavior will not be tolerated in Tinker's Cove."

His warning went unheeded, thought Lucy, grimly noting that the Homestead burned barely three weeks later. This time there was no doubt that the fire was set. ARSON CLAIMS LIFE! declared the headline of the most recent issue. The headline was printed above a stark photo of the Homestead chimney, all that was left after the fire.

The story went on to say that fire officials were now taking a second look at the earlier fires, which seemed in retrospect to be the handiwork of the same deranged individual. "We're determined to catch this perpetrator before he takes any more lives," proclaimed Chief Pulaski.

A related story chronicled the amazing feats of Sparky, the accelerant-sniffing dog. "He's not just my pet," his handler was quoted as saying. "He's my partner."

As she replaced the papers in a neat pile, Lucy recited the dates of the fires. July 5. August 28. September 26. October

19. There didn't seem to be a pattern to the fires, except for the fact that they were coming closer together.

Leaving the workroom, Lucy wandered over to the non-fiction section. There, among the self-help books she found a thick volume on abnormal psychology. A glance at the index revealed an entire chapter devoted to "Pyromania and Related Disorders."

Bitsy smiled brightly as Lucy approached the desk.

"That's really heavy reading," she joked, taking the hefty volume. "Sure I can't interest you in something lighter? We have some brand-new mysteries."

"I don't have much time to read anymore with the baby. I'm just doing a bit of research."

"We have some excellent material on postpartum depression," offered Bitsy, determined to be helpful.

"I'm fine, really," said Lucy. "Just curious about something."

Bitsy couldn't resist. "Curiosity killed the cat. Now, why do people say that? Curiosity is wonderful, isn't it?"

"Sometimes. Sometimes it gets you in trouble." Lucy took the book and tucked it under her arm. She knew from experience that asking questions could be dangerous.

Not this time, she thought, as she left the library and headed for Sue's house. She was determined to find out who was setting the fires, but, she promised herself, she was going to be careful. Very careful.

Besides, she didn't really have enough time to get into too much trouble. Before she started investigating, she had to bake some cupcakes. How many had she promised Sue? Two dozen?

CHAPTER SEVEN

"*Twelve dozen?* I said I'd bake twelve dozen cupcakes? I must have been out of my mind." Lucy was sitting at the huge scrubbed pine harvest table in Sue's kitchen. Sue was always remodeling her kitchen—it had gone from cluttered country to fifties kitsch and now had a definite English accent. A plate rack hung near the sink, a Welsh cupboard hugged one wall, and a cobalt blue Aga stove was her pride and joy.

"You were kind of distracted," admitted Sue. "Forget it. Two dozen will be fine."

"Oh, no," said Lucy. "I'll manage." She knew she owed Sue a favor for taking care of Zoe, and she wanted to even the score as soon as possible. "Did the baby give you much trouble?"

"No. She's a little angel," said Sue. "She fussed a little bit when she realized I wasn't her mommy, she tried the bottle and didn't like it, and gave up and went to sleep. It's a shame to wake her— want some lunch?"

"Sure," said Lucy.

"I've got some leftover Cornish pasties."

"Sounds great," said Lucy, who hadn't the faintest idea what a Comish pasty was, but was always hungry.

"That was terrible about Monica, wasn't it?" said Sue, popping the meat pies into the microwave.

"I'm still having trouble believing it really happened," admitted Lucy. "What was she doing at the house this time of year, anyway? She only came in the summer." Lucy looked away, staring out the window.

"She had kids, didn't she?"

"All grown up, thank goodness." Lucy's voice quavered, and Sue quickly changed the subject.

"I called the Body Shop. They do have child care, and we can take one free class to try it out. Whaddya say we go over after lunch?"

"Today?"

"Sure," said Sue, slipping a steaming plate in front of Lucy. "These things are full of carbohydrates and fat grams and I don't know what all. Positively deadly."

"Delicious," said Lucy, savoring a mouthful.

An hour later, with Zoe safely installed in the child care center at the Body Shop, Lucy was calculating her chances of surviving the "Basic Body" class.

"Now that's five, and four, and only three more," said the perky blond instructor. They had been at this for forty-five minutes and Vicki had never stopped smiling, never stopped bouncing. Lucy had never seen anyone so completely fit— even Vicki's ponytail was perfectly conditioned. "Okay, now it's time to cool down. Take a deep breath. In, hold it, and out. That's right. Doesn't that feel good?"

Lucy stared at her reflection in the mirror that covered the wall. No doubt about it, she definitely needed this. She had borrowed an old leotard from Sue, and the tight spandex revealed a doughy stomach, flabby arms and thighs. Even her face was puffy. How had this happened? She used to have so much energy, she used to run miles every week. Now, it was all she could do to get up the stairs. And truth be told, she was still wearing her maternity clothes because her old things didn't fit. She either had to get back in shape or buy a whole new wardrobe.

"Okay, ladies, you're done. Now, don't you feel great?"

Lucy laid back on the wood floor, trying to find the energy to get up.

"Come on, lazybones," said Sue, extending a hand. She looked fresh as ever, much to Lucy's disgust.

Lucy took Sue's hand and pulled herself to her feet. Her legs felt wobbly underneath her. But, standing in the shower a few minutes later, she had to admit she felt better than she had in a long time. As the hot water poured over her tired body, soothing her aches and pains, she was aware of herself in a new way. There were muscles under that flab. She decided to sign up for a membership.

Refreshed and dressed, checkbook in hand, she approached the front desk.

"Hi, I'm Krissy. May I help you?" asked another bright blonde, displaying a dazzling smile.

"I'd like to sign up for the introductory special," said Lucy, glancing at a banner hanging on the brick wall.

"Super! You won't be sorry—it's an investment in yourself. Now, if you'll just fill out this form . . . sorry, I better get that phone." She slipped a sheet of paper in front of Lucy, handed her a pen, and picked up the phone, all in one smooth motion.

Lucy began filling in the blanks, while Krissy took the call.

"Body Shop . . . where fitness is fun. Oh, hi." From the change in tone, Lucy guessed this was someone special.

"What news? I've been so busy with opening the studio that I haven't had time to read the paper or anything. A fire?"

Curious, Lucy glanced at Krissy in time to see an expression of satisfaction flicker across her features. Then, she heard her murmur, "I just can't believe it. I'm so sorry. I'm here for you, you know that."

Krissy hung up the receiver and turned her attention to Lucy. "Sorry about that—my business partner just lost his wife. In a fire. Absolutely awful."

"That's too bad. It wasn't Monica Mayes, was it?"

"Did you know her?" Krissy's eyebrows shot up in surprise.

"A little," said Lucy.

"Of course. Everybody knows everybody in a town like this. I'm not used to it—I'm from the city. Now, that'll be twenty-nine dollars, and the membership is good for a month. You can take any regularly scheduled classes, use the showers. There is an extra charge for sessions with a personal trainer, massage, things like that. Child care is included. Any questions?"

"No," said Lucy, handing over her check. She was struck by the sudden change in Krissy's attitude. The smile was gone and she was all business. Lucy wondered if she was imagining it, or if Krissy really couldn't wait to get rid of her.

Turning to go toward the nursery, she saw Sue coming out of the dressing room.

"This was a good idea—I got a membership," she said, flashing her brand-new card. "How about you?"

"Me? I'm going to think it over. I'm not sure exercise is for me." Sue puckered her face with distaste and lowered her voice. "It made me sweat."

"That's the point. You're supposed to sweat."

"Oh." Sue tapped her pearly pink lips with a perfectly manicured finger, polished to match, then tucked a lock of her shining black Dutch-boy hair behind one ear. "I'd like to keep you company, Lucy, but I don't really think I have the time. I'll let you know."

Lucy watched as her friend hurried out the door. If Sue wasn't so nice, it would be easy to hate her. She always looked terrific, and she never gained a pound no matter how much she ate. Lucy shook her head and gave a little shrug, then headed for the nursery to retrieve Zoe. She didn't think Sue would have to think it over for very long—she seemed to have already made up her mind.

CHAPTER EIGHT

A tapping at the kitchen door startled Lucy. Exhausted by the workout, she had been dozing in Bill's recliner chair. The psychology book lay on the floor, where it had fallen. She rubbed her eyes and stretched, then hurried to the door. She blinked in surprise, recognizing Monica's husband.

Dr. Roland Mayes was the sort of man who always wore a suit and tie, and looked uncomfortable in casual clothes. On his infrequent visits to Tinker's Cove his polo shirts were obviously brand-new, straight out of the package, and his casual slacks were crisply creased. Today, however, Roland didn't look band-box fresh. His suit was rumpled as if he'd worn it for several days, and he had a dark five o'clock shadow.

"Come in, come in," said Lucy. She gave him her best smile, hoping he wouldn't realize how desperately she wished he hadn't come. She had never liked him very much. On the rare occasions when she had spoken with him she had gotten the distinct impression that she was boring him. But now, she told herself, the poor man was bereaved. She had a duty to try and comfort him.

"Take a seat," invited Lucy.

Roland staggered slightly as he headed for the chair, causing Lucy to look at him more closely. His face was pasty gray; he looked as if he was going to faint.

"When did you eat last?"

"I don't remember," he said, sitting down heavily at the table and placing a package in front of him. "I'm not hungry."

"You have to eat," she said. "You need to keep up your strength. How about a sandwich?"

"I could use that," he said. Lucy busied herself mixing up some tuna fish and laying slices of bread out on the counter.

"Bill and I both want you to know how sad we are about Monica," said Lucy. Once again, tears were welling up in her eyes. Fortunately, she had her back to him and was able to brush them away. It wouldn't do to inflict her own grief on this unfortunate man.

"It never should have happened," he said, shaking his head as Lucy set a plate and mug of tea in front of him. "Tuna salad," he said, looking up. "I haven't had this in years."

"Tuna's a staple around here," said Lucy, taking a sip of her own tea. "I suppose you've been to see the police and all. Are they making any progress in the investigation?"

"None, none at all," he answered, taking a bite of his sandwich. "They're absolute incompetents as far as I can tell. I've lost my house, and my wife, and they don't seem to care." His tone was belligerent, almost angry.

"I'm sure that's not true," said Lucy, in a soothing voice.

"Then why did that idiot police chief, Growley or Crowley or whatever his name is, keep me waiting forty-five minutes before he'd see me? And then he gave me the brush-off." Outrage burned in his eyes.

Lucy ventured to guess that Roland knew a brush-off when he encountered one. As a successful doctor, he cer-

tainly knew the value of his time. He was most likely an experienced practitioner of the very tactics he deplored in
Chief Crowley.

"He's just a small-town cop," said Lucy. "The state police are probably in charge of the investigation."

"I don't care who's in charge. I want some answers.
Somebody's gonna have to pay for this," he asserted, slamming his fist on the table and making the crumbs on his plate
jump.

"This must be absolutely horrible for you," sympathized
Lucy.

"Horrible doesn't begin to describe it." He shook his
head. "And it couldn't have come at a worse time. My nom-
ination for the Danforth prize was announced last week, you
know."

"I didn't know. Congratulations." She paused. "I'm not
familiar with the Danforth. What's it for?"

"The medical society's most prestigious award. It's between me and Feldman, the gastroenterologist. This won't
do me much good, I can tell you. The society are a pretty
conservative group. They simply will not tolerate the least
whiff of scandal."

"How could they hold something as tragic as this against
you? I should think you'll get a huge sympathy vote. After
all, none of this was your fault."

"You're absolutely right about that. Monica was so stubborn. She always had to have her own way. She wouldn't
listen to me. Oh, no! If this was anybody's fault, it was
hers."

"Her fault?" Lucy was puzzled. The conversation seemed
to have taken a strange turn. Perhaps Roland wasn't quite as
distraught as she had first thought.

"She took one look and went running off—wouldn't even
wait for an explanation. That would have required rational-
ity, something Monica didn't have a great deal of."

"She was upset about something?"

"You could say that. What the hell? Everybody has fights, right? We'd been married for a long time. Thirty years."

"That is a long time," agreed Lucy.

"Hey, murder only gets you twenty, twenty-five years in this state, right?" It was an old joke, one he told automatically.

"I guess," said Lucy, trying not to be judgmental. Grief took everyone differently, she reminded herself.

"I gotta get going. Hey, I almost forgot. I stopped by to give you this," he said, rising and shoving the package across the table. "It's a scrapbook Monica kept during the renovation."

"Really?" Lucy was delighted, and deeply moved. "How thoughtful of you to think of us. We'll treasure it always."

"What was I gonna do with it?" he said, as she opened the door for him. "Right now, the fewer reminders I've got to deal with, the better."

CHAPTER NINE

Later that evening, supper over, Lucy gave the kitchen counter one last wipe with the sponge and tossed it into the sink. For the first time since she'd come home from the hospital with Zoe, the kitchen was neat and tidy. The sink was empty of dirty dishes. The counter was clear of clutter. The stove top gleamed. Two dozen Halloween cupcakes, complete with orange icing and candy corn decorations, sat on the kitchen table, ready to be packed in a plastic container and hidden on the top shelf of the pantry.

It was the same with every baby, she thought smugly. The first weeks were always chaotic, the baby's needs came first and everything else was pushed aside. Bit by bit, however, order and routine returned and things fell into place.

The one thing Lucy had worried about most hadn't happened. She had feared that the other children would be resentful of the baby. To her surprise, however, they had taken the new arrival in stride. Toby and Elizabeth were too busy with their friends and school work to be jealous, and Sara was enjoying her new role of big sister. She had even taken photos of the baby to school for show and tell.

All in all, Lucy thought things had turned out better than she had expected. Refusing to think of the unmade beds upstairs, or the piles of dirty laundry in the basement, she congratulated herself for managing so well. Bill was out at his first historical society meeting, Sara was minding Zoe in the family room while she watched TV, Toby and Elizabeth were doing homework at the dining-room table. Deciding she deserved a reward, Lucy pulled a chocolate bar out of the secret stash she kept in the freezer and dialed Sue's number.

"Hello," said Sue.

"Mmmph," responded Lucy. She was working on a rather large chunk of frozen chocolate.

"You'll never lose those extra baby pounds if you don't stop stuffing your face all the time," scolded Sue.

"I was treating myself. After all, I did work out this afternoon," said Lucy, defending herself. "So how's the party coming along?"

"Not bad. Pam Stillings is going to make her famous black punch and she's going to freeze gummi worms in an ice ring."

"Sounds delicious."

"The art classes at the high school are carving pumpkins and making decorations. The Junior Woman's Club is organizing games, and the football boosters are lending us their popcorn machine. The Rotary are handling the apple bobbing—apparently Andy Brown, the guy who owns Farmer Brown's fruit stand, is one of their members. It's all coming together. This Saturday the Scouts and the cheerleaders and anybody else who wants to help are cleaning out the mansion. Can you come, and bring Bill with his hammer, in case there are any loose boards or anything?"

"Sure. What time?"

"Ten?"

"That's good. Sounds like you're really working hard on this."

"Mostly phone calls. I'm delegating. Everybody seems eager to help. Nobody's turned me down. In fact, people have started calling me and offering to help."

"That's great. You'll never guess who paid me a surprise visit."

"Monica's husband?"

"How'd you know?"

"I've been on the phone all afternoon," Sue explained. "I heard he was in town. Pam said he looks terrible. He must be taking this very hard."

"That's what I thought at first, but now I'm not so sure. He seemed more inconvenienced than grief stricken. I got the impression he and Monica hadn't been getting along lately."

"Really?"

"He came right out and told me that he and Monica had a fight, and that's why she was at the Homestead."

"Could be. It's too bad they didn't have a chance to make up."

"Maybe Roland didn't want to make up. Maybe he wanted her out of the way."

"Lucy! How can you think something like that?" Sue was shocked.

"Nine times out of ten it's the husband. He's the one who gave me the idea. He said he'd been married for thirty years and murder only gets you twenty."

"He said that?"

"I think it was a joke he was used to telling at parties—it just came out."

"The poor man probably doesn't know what he's saying. Besides, what about the other fires? Somehow I can't picture him starting all those fires."

"Me, either," agreed Lucy, thinking of the thwarted, repressed individuals the book portrayed as typical arsonists. "Maybe he knew about the fires and planned the murder hoping the police would include it with the others. Kind of a cover-up."

"It must be awful to have a mind like yours—always suspecting the worst."

"Well, my suspicions are not exactly unfounded. When I was buying my gym membership today a funny thing happened. Krissy, you know, the woman who owns the studio, got a phone call. It was from Dr. Mayes, telling her about Monica's death. She didn't look exactly heartbroken."

"Krissy knows Dr. Mayes?"

"Evidently. She said her business partner's wife died in a fire and I asked if it was Monica and she said it was."

"Dr. Mayes is her business partner?"

"That's what she said, but I wouldn't be surprised if he is something more."

"You're disgusting. It's always sex with you, isn't it?"

"Not often enough, according to Bill."

Sue hooted. "Men! You have a baby, and ten minutes later they want to start another one."

"Well, at least Bill has something to keep him occupied. Miss Tilley's got him on the historical commission."

"That's good. About time we got somebody sensible. You know, I think Miss Tilley's losing it. Yesterday I saw her drive right through the stop sign on the corner. She almost hit Franny Small's little blue Dodge!"

"Is everybody all right?"

"I think so. Franny had slowed down to turn the corner. I don't think Miss Tilley saw her. She didn't stop, just went sailing through in that huge car of hers. She came that close—it could have been a real tragedy."

"She knocked over my mailbox the other day. Never even noticed."

"That woman's dangerous. Somebody ought to have a talk with her and get her to give up her license. She shouldn't be driving. It's just a matter of time before someone gets hurt."

"You're right. I'll ask Barney. Maybe she'll listen to him."

"Maybe." Sue was doubtful. "She's awfully stubborn, and determined to be independent. Get this—Karen Baker who works at the bank told me she never cashes her social security checks. The social security people even called to find out if she was dead—Miss T. thought it was a tremendous joke and told Karen all about it."

"Sounds typical. Listen, Sue, I gotta go. Zoe's fussing. I'll call you tomorrow, if I can find a free moment, that is. Between baking cupcakes and working out at the gym I'll probably be very busy."

CHAPTER TEN

Ted Stillings entered the downstairs meeting room at Town Hall and glanced around. The board members were already seated at a long table, which was placed on a slightly raised dais A small audience had gathered, comprised mainly of applicants and a few Town Hall regulars who never missed a meeting. With a smooth, practiced motion he pulled his reporter's notebook from his back pocket and sat down.

Waiting for the meeting to begin, he tapped his pen lightly against the notebook. Despite the fact that this was his third evening meeting this week, he was looking forward to it. The TCHDC was fast becoming the best show in town. For years, when Miss Tilley and her Gang of Four were in charge, commission meetings were dull and predictable. Although Ted attended faithfully, he didn't have to. He could always predict exactly what the commissioners would say and how they would vote.

When Doug Durning and Jock Mulligan came on board, however, things changed. Stalemated, the commission members vented their frustration by raking one another, and the applicants, over the coals. Their scathing comments made good copy, and circulation always jumped a bit after a TCHDC meeting. Catching his friend Bill Stone's eye, and giving him a big grin, Ted wondered if he knew what he was getting into when he agreed to serve on the board.

"Let's get started," said Miss Tilley, banging her gavel. "This meeting of the Tinker's Cove Historic District Commission is now called to order. Mr. Brown, what can we do for you?"

Andy Brown stood up, hooked his thumbs around the straps of his overalls, and ambled to the front of the room. Considering that Brown was one of the most successful businessmen in town, Ted thought he was carrying the farmer act a bit too far.

"As you prob'ly know, I've got a little farmstand out on Route One. We have a cider press, and we let folks pick their own pumpkins from Farmer Brown's Pumpkin Patch. We've done pretty well, if I do say so myself."

Brown was being deliberately modest, thought Ted. He had discovered gold in those pumpkins, and every year the farmstand grew a bit bigger. This year he had added a haunted hay ride, and the spooky music, groans, and screams that emanated from the cornfield at night had prompted several angry letters to the editor.

"We're all familiar with your farmstand," said Miss Tilley.

"Well, what I'd like to do, y'see, is put up one of those portable electric signs, so folks can find the place a mite easier, 'specially at night."

"I find it hard to believe that anyone who is not completely deaf and blind would have the least difficulty finding your establishment," Miss Tilley stated. "Even an electric sign would hardly help such a person. Board, are we ready to vote?"

"Hold yer horses a minute," Brown protested. "My place brings lots of business to this town. Seems to me you could bend the rules, considering how the pumpkin patch extends the tourist season."

"Mr. Brown does have a point," admitted Jock Mulligan, owner of a rather adorable bed and breakfast. "We get quite a few families down from Boston and thereabouts who come especially to visit the pumpkin patch. Grandparents, even, bring the little ones."

"How heartwarming," observed Miss Tilley, with a sneer. "Exactly how large is this sign?"

"It's twelve feet long and eight feet high, and it lights up."

"The sign code clearly forbids lighted signs, and the outside limit is four square feet."

"I know. That's why I'm applying for a variance. This is a portable sign, it will be gone the day after Halloween."

"I don't see any harm in the sign," ventured Doug Durning. "They have something similar for the Blueberry Festival every summer."

"The Blueberry Festival takes place on the other side of town, and it's a fund-raiser for the rescue squad. This is right smack in the center of the historic district," observed Hancock Smith. "You've already got lights strung up all over the place, not to mention that monstrous great pumpkin thing and the sound effects. I agree with Miss Tilley—you couldn't miss the place if you tried."

"Bill, what have you to say?" asked Miss Tilley, giving him an encouraging wink.

"My kids love the pumpkin patch—we go every year," began Bill, giving Brown a nod. "But I have to say the place is pretty eyecatching already. I can't see any need for this additional sign."

"Application denied." Miss Tilley grinned broadly and brought down the gavel. "Next we have Miss Katz."

"It's Kurtz, Tammy Kurtz," corrected an attractive young woman, dressed in a stylish cashmere tunic and pants outfit. "I'm the owner of the Greengage Cafe. As you know, we're located in the rear of the Village Marketplace shopping complex. Under the sign code, we're only allowed one sign, a single board on the large sign that serves the entire complex. Our customers tell us they have trouble finding us, so tonight I'm asking for a variance so we can put up a second sign on the building. I've brought a drawing of the proposed sign with me. As you can see, it's quite attractive and understated."

"That's for us to decide, Miss Kootz," said Miss Tilley, reaching for the sketch with a clawlike hand.

Ted noticed a stiffening of the back under the cashmere, as Tammy stepped forward to hand up the paper.

"This looks very straightforward to me," said Miss Tilley, passing the sketch along. "The sign code clearly specifies that there shall be only one sign for a shopping complex. I will entertain a motion to deny the variance."

She glanced at Hancock Smith, who immediately cleared his voice, obediently preparing to make the motion.

"Not so fast," said Doug Durning. "This lady is trying to run a business, and she's asking us for help to solve a problem. I don't see the harm in one little sign."

"I might point out that if we make an exception for Miss Skootz, we'll have to make an exception for everybody," Miss Tilley huffed. "Why have a sign code at all, if we're not going to enforce it?"

"I've eaten at the Greengage Cafe," offered Jock Mulligan. "I can't remember if I had the Trout en Paupiettes or the Salmon Timbales on a bed of arugula, it was absolute agony deciding, but I will never forget the Mixed Berry Tiramisu, it was mar-r-rvelous," he said, leaning forward and rolling his eyes. "My congratulations to the chef."

"I don't see what the menu has to do with this matter," said Miss Tilley.

"Oh, but it does. The Greengage Cafe is attracting notice. People come from all over to eat there. It's bringing a very nice class of tourist to our town. Upscale. Just look at the cars in the parking lot. I think we ought to do all we can to help Miss Kurtz succeed."

"It's obvious we have two for and two against," said Miss Tilley. "What does our newest member have to say?"

Bill shifted uncomfortably in his seat as all eyes were focused on him.

"I think that sign at the Village Marketplace complex is confusing. You can't tell what's in there. I'm for granting the variance, and maybe even taking a look at the sign code with an eye to revising it."

"Variance granted, Miss Slutz," said Miss Tilley, banging down the gavel. She looked as if she had a mouthful of tacks, as she flapped the sketch back and forth.

Miss Kurtz smiled sweetly as she stepped forward to retrieve it. "Thank you, Miss Silley," she said. Turning to leave, she gave Ted a wink.

"Next we have Wilpers," said Miss Tilley, frowning as she consulted the agenda. "Anybody named Wilpers here?"

"That's us," said a clean-shaven young man, dressed in a blue oxford cloth shirt and khaki pants. His red face appeared painfully well-scrubbed; the comb tracks were still fresh in his hair. His young wife stood beside him, dressed in a flowered dress with pearl buttons and a lace collar. "We got a notice of violation."

Miss Tilley's eyes widened and she smacked her lips. Scenting blood, Ted thought to himself.

"I believe you're painting your house an unapproved color," she said.

"The house was very run-down when we bought it," said Mrs. Wilpers in a soft voice. "But Buddy and I have worked hard weekends and nights, and it's really starting to come together. It's a Greek Revival style, and we chose a historic color, Woodleigh Sage. I don't know why it's a problem. All the neighbors love it."

"The problem is that your house is in the historic district, and the only approved colors are white, light gray, light yellow and light tan," said Miss Tilley. "You will have to re-paint."

Mrs. Wilpers gasped. "But we're almost done. We've been working on this for months."

"You should have checked with us before choosing a color. I've seen it. That house is aqua."

"It's not aqua. It's a historic color. Woodleigh Sage," insisted Mrs. Wilpers.

"Everybody knows that historic houses should be painted white," said Hancock Smith. "That's the way the old-timers did it. That's what looks best."

"Actually," said Bill slowly, "our ancestors used more colors than most people think. White was popular, but green was also used a lot. A much brighter green than you would expect."

"I'm in the real estate business," said Doug. "I know nothing brings property values down faster than allowing people to paint their houses any old color. Next thing you know you've got flamingo pink and the neighborhood's gone to the dogs."

"That's not necessar-r-rily true," said Jock. "If it's used well, color can bring life to a neighborhood."

"This discussion has gone on long enough," said Miss Tilley, sensing rebellion in the ranks. "Who'll give me a motion?"

"I move a finding of fact, that indeed a violation has occurred, and must be rectified within thirty days or the building inspector will issue a fine of fifty dollars per day until said violation is rectified," said Doug Durning.

"All in favor?" Miss Tilley nodded with satisfaction as Durning and Smith raised their hands. "Three to two, the motion passes."

"You have the right to appeal," advised Jock Mulligan. "The regional board is somewhat more . . ." he paused, searching for the right word. *"Au cour-r-ant,"* he finally decided, gave him a chance to show off his French and roll his Rs.

"Next on the agenda," said Miss Tilley, with a bang of her gavel. "We have Mr. Lenk. Good evening, Randy."

Randolph Lenk had not bothered to dress for the occasion, observed Ted. He was still wearing the same oil-stained work clothes he had worn all day. In fact, he had probably worn the same clothes all week. A three-day stubble revealed he hadn't shaved recently, and the lines and creases in his hands were filled with grease. Lenk owned a small, ramshackle Northstar gas station that had been an eyesore on Main Street for years.

"The fellas at the comp'ny say I gotta remodel," began Lenk. "They've drawn up plans—even want a canopy and a convenience maht. They say I gotta do it, or I can't sell their gas anymore."

"I, for one, am glad to hear it," said Doug Durning. "It's long overdue. That place of yours is an embarrassment to the town. Damned valuable property, too. Are those plans you've got there? Let's see 'em."

Lenk shuffled forward and handed up a roll of papers. Durning took them and eagerly began unrolling them, distributing them to the other board members.

"My, my, my," said Jock Mulligan, clucking his tongue.

"It looks like a spaceship!" Miss Tilley shrieked.

"There does appear to be an awful lot of plastic and glass," said Hancock Smith, shaking his head. "And that sign. It could be seen for miles."

"That's the idea," agreed Lenk. "Cut down a few of these trees, and folks'll be able to see it from the Interstate."

"You're planning to cut trees?" Miss Tilley was aghast.

"You know," said Bill, "there's a new appreciation among preservationists for vernacular architecture. It may well be that Mr. Lenk's existing gas station is worth saving. I'd be very surprised if it wasn't a good example of roadside construction from the early Age of the Automobile."

Miss Tilley's eyes widened and she gave Hancock a wry

smile. She was beginning to suspect that Bill's appointment might not work out the way she had hoped.

"Since this is such a large project, and it affects so many people, I think we really ought to hold a public hearing," Miss Tilley said. "As proposed this will really change the appearance of the whole town. Especially if trees are cut."

"Are you saying I can't cut trees on my own prop'ty?" Lenk was ready to defend his rights as a landowner.

"We're not saying anything, Mr. Lenk," observed Hancock Smith. "What Miss Tilley has suggested, very wisely, I might add, is that the entire matter be discussed in a public forum. That way, all the interested parties can be heard."

"Who's interested? It's my land. I can do whatever I want." Lenk was beginning to get agitated.

"Your land is in the historic district," explained Doug Durning. "Special rules apply."

"I've got rights," insisted Lenk, raising his voice. 'I'm payin' taxes on that land. What happened to democracy?"

"Mr. Lenk," began Jock Mulligan. "Let me assure you that America is, indeed, still a democracy. What we must do here is weigh the rights of the individual against the r-r-rights of the community. Your neighbors also pay taxes, and they have an interest in the appearance of their town. Do you understand?"

"Can I tell Northstar to go ahead, or what? 'Cause if you say no, you're all gonna be sorry. Real sorry." Lenk was at the end of his rope; he was bouncing nervously on the balls of his feet, and rhythmically clenching his hands.

"Nothing will be decided tonight," said Miss Tilley, in the voice that had maintained silence in the Broadbrooks Free Library for more than thirty-five years. "We'll schedule a hearing for next week. Is the board agreed?" Miss Tilley received nods of assent from the other members. "We'll see you next week, Mr. Lenk. Bring whomever you want. Lawyers, company representatives, plans—we'll go over everything. Understood?"

Lenk nodded.

"A word to the wise," she said, leaning forward and waving a gnarled finger at him. "Don't make any changes to that property until you have a certificate of appropriateness from this board. I'm warning you. This board takes violations very seriously."

From the expression on Lenk's face as he headed for the door, Ted was pretty sure the commission was going to have one hell of a fight on its hands.

"Anything else? If not, meeting adjourned," Miss Tilley decreed without calling for a vote. "Oh, Bill, do you have a minute? I have a few thoughts I'd like to share with you."

Poor Bill, thought Ted, standing and slipping his notebook into his pocket. He looked as if he had been caught stuffing overdue books into the Book Return slot. Even though Miss Tilley could no longer charge overdue book fines, she would undoubtedly find some way to make him pay for his insubordination.

CHAPTER ELEVEN

"**D**id you tape *Seinfeld?*" Bill asked at breakfast the next morning.

Lucy put down the piece of toast she was about to bite and shook her head. "I forgot."

"How could you forget?" demanded Bill.

"Well . . ." said Lucy. "The evening started out peacefully enough but pretty soon the baby began fussing and then Toby couldn't find his gym shoes and Elizabeth needed help finding out why Connecticut is called the Nutmeg State and somehow it was too late and the show was over when I remembered. I'm sorry."

"I only asked you to do one simple thing," continued Bill, unwilling to drop the matter.

"It was only a TV show—it will be rerun before you know it. How was the meeting?" Lucy had been asleep when Bill came home.

"I should never have said I'd be on that damn commission." Bill shook his head and sat down with a cup of coffee.

"That bad?"

"Worse. Miss Tilley was not pleased with me. She told me independence of spirit is a fine thing, but not if it has a negative effect on the community. She also said I was a show-off."

"You? You're usually so quiet."

"I voted to let this couple paint their house green. I told them that early houses were often painted in bright colors but they didn't like it. The approved colors are white, off-white, and gray. Maybe yellow, if it's not too bright."

"It's bound to be a little awkward at first. You all have to get used to one another."

"They brought me on because I'm a restoration carpenter, right? I know about this stuff. It's how I make my living. But they don't want to listen to me. They've got some half-assed idea of what historic means, and they don't want to hear anything different. To them, a house is colonial if it's white and has shutters. They don't even care if the shutters are the right size for the windows. As long as it's a shutter, it's okay."

"Maybe you need to compromise a bit, too," said Lucy. "Nobody today wants to spend a lot of money on authentic shutters they'll never use."

"That's my point. They don't care if it's right. They might as well call it the Pseudo-Historic District, the Disney District. I think I'm gonna resign."

"You can't resign after one meeting."

"Why not? Besides it's gonna take a lot more time than I thought. You wouldn't believe the pages and pages of zoning bylaws she gave me. I'm supposed to 'familiarize myself' with them by the next meeting."

"It'll work out. You'll see. They really need you."

"I doubt it."

"Well, at least give it a while longer. You wouldn't let Toby quit Little League last spring, even though he wanted to. What did you tell him. Only quitters are losers?"

"That's the worst thing about being a parent," said Bill, grinning for the first time that morning. "Your words come back to haunt you."

"That's for sure," said Lucy, getting up to fetch Zoe, who was demanding her breakfast. "Was I the one who said another baby would be no trouble at all?"

Later, after Bill had gone to work and the kids had left for school, and Zoe had been bathed and fed and put down for her morning nap, Lucy got out Monica's book and set it on the table.

It was a wire-bound sketch book, which Monica had covered with blue Waverly plaid fabric. Lucy recognized the pattern, Monica had chosen it for the homing room curtains. She ran her fingers over it, and then opened the book.

The first page had several photographs of the house as it was when the Mayes bought it. Overgrown bushes covered the windows, there was a hole in the roof, and the original pine clapboards were covered with crumbling asphalt shingles.

"My heart stopped when I saw it," Monica had written in bold black ink. "Somehow I knew that this house would be mine. It was the house I'd always dreamed of having."

The statement gave Lucy pause; never in her life had she decided something should be hers simply because she wanted it. For her, life was a constant juggle of too little time, too little money, and too much to do.

Turning the pages, Lucy saw photos chronicling every stage of the restoration process. The plaster was stripped away from the walls, revealing the aged wood lath underneath. The chimney was torn down and rebuilt. The roof was replaced with bright new cedar shingles.

Lucy smiled to see snapshots of Bill and herself. He looked impossibly young. She, pregnant with Toby, was absolutely huge. There were also photos of Monica's teen-aged children, tan in swimsuits, scraping the paint off a door. Their names were obligingly penned in beneath the pictures: Rally, Mira, and Tiny. Monica, Lucy remembered, had a penchant for nicknames.

Once the house had been made sound and weathertight, Monica had focused her attention on decorating it. There were pictures of furniture found at auctions, paint chips, and fabric scraps. Sketches showed how each room was arranged. Once she had made a decision, recalled Lucy, Monica never changed her mind. She was not one to spend an afternoon rearranging the furniture.

Closing the book, Lucy clutched it to her chest. She leaned back in her chair and stared at the ceiling. She tried to guess how much the restoration had cost, but couldn't even remember how much Bill had charged.

Curious, she climbed upstairs to the little attic room he used for an office. There, under the slanted ceiling, he had set up a drafting table and a couple of file cabinets.

His files, as she discovered when she pulled out a drawer, were neater than she would have expected. She had no trouble at all finding the thick folder for the Hopkins Homestead. Lucy sat down at the desk and pushed aside the big stack of zoning bylaws Bill had left there. She opened the file; right on top was the estimate he had drawn up—labor and materials came to nearly one hundred thousand dollars.

Lucy whistled softly under her breath. She had no idea. And this was more than ten years ago—it would be a lot more at today's prices. Bill's figures didn't include the cost of the property itself, or what Monica had spent to furnish or decorate the place. Lucy wouldn't have been surprised if Monica's little project—the house she was determined to have—had cost Roland close to a quarter of a million dollars. Lucy even remembered Monica joking about it, she had once said Roland would have to deliver a lot of babies to pay for it.

Thinking back, Lucy couldn't recall even one picture of Roland Mayes in the scrapbook. It was a real old-fashioned marriage, thought Lucy. He made the money, and Monica spent it.

Closing the file to replace it, Lucy's eyes fell on a penciled phone number. Monica had given it to them a few years ago, when she had taken a trip. They had agreed to keep an eye on the Homestead, and if anything happened, they were supposed to call Mira. She was married, now, and lived in a Boston suburb with her husband and baby. Impulsively, Lucy reached for the phone, then hesitated. She certainly didn't want to add to the woman's grief by asking a lot of questions. On the other hand, she rationalized, it wouldn't hurt to let Mira know that others shared her grief.

"Mira? This is Lucy Stone, in Tinker's Cove. I wanted to call and let you know how sorry I am about your mother."

"Lucy, thanks for calling. It's so sweet of you."

"It's the least I could do. I feel absolutely awful about the fire."

"I don't think I've really taken it in yet. I keep expecting Mom to call and ask how I'm feeling." Mira paused. "I'm pregnant again, you know."

"I didn't know," said Lucy, thinking how sad it was that Monica would never see her second grandchild. "When are you due?"

"In about a month."

"And how old is the baby?"

"Freddie's almost two."

"You'll have your hands full." What a shame, thought Lucy, for Mira to lose her mother just when she needed her so much.

"I sure will," said Mira, her voice trembling.

"I don't want to keep you," said Lucy quickly. "I was just wondering when the service will be. I didn't see anything in the paper."

"I know." Mira fell silent. "I'm ashamed to say we haven't planned anything yet. It's all been so sudden. We're still in shock. You'd think something like this would make us all closer but instead it's ripping the family apart."

"Oh, Mira, every family's different. There's no right way to deal with death." Lucy hesitated a moment, then plunged ahead. "I saw your dad yesterday. He came by the house. He seems to be taking it pretty hard."

"Harder than I expected, that's for sure." There was an edge to Mira's voice. Lucy wondered how much Mira knew about her father and Krissy.

"Well, as you said, it was very sudden."

"Very convenient if you ask me." There was no mistaking the anger in Mira's voice. "He'd told Rally he was thinking of divorcing Mom. There was somebody else."

"Oh, no. Did your mother know?"

"I don't know how she could have missed it. Everybody knew. I used to see his Mercedes and Krissy's Fiero parked side by side all over town." Mira sniffled; Lucy was pretty sure she was crying. Suddenly, Lucy was ashamed of herself. She didn't want to add to Mira's pain.

"I'm sorry, Mira. I shouldn't have called "

"I'm glad you called," sobbed Mira. "I've felt so alone, like I'm the only one who loved her. It really helps to know that you cared about her, too. I'll let you know when we decide on a time for the service."

"Oh, Mira," said Lucy, her voice breaking. "Bill and I both loved her. She was very special to us. If there's anything we can do to help, please let us know." Lucy wiped her eyes and hung up the phone. Suddenly shaky, she sat down at the kitchen table. She crossed her arms across her stomach and hugged herself, waiting for the sick feeling to go away.

This was ridiculous, she thought. Mira had confirmed her suspicions about Dr. Mayes and Krissy. She was right after all. So why did she feel so horrible?

CHAPTER TWELVE

"**O**h, Mrs. Stone. Back already?" Krissy looked up from the class schedule she was decorating with little jack-o'-lanterns. "Vicki may have forgotten to mention it, but it's better to wait a day or two between sessions."

"Really?" said Lucy, feigning disappointment. "That's too bad. I was really counting on another workout before the weekend."

"I wouldn't advise it," said Krissy, staring right through her. The dazzling smile was definitely gone, Krissy seemed almost hostile. Lucy wondered why. Was it because Lucy had told her she knew Monica?

"Oh, well, there's something else I wanted to talk to you about." Lucy glanced around the counter area that was open to the public. "Is there someplace a bit more private, like an office, where we could talk?"

"I'm afraid not," said Krissy flatly.

"I suppose you haven't even finished unpacking yet," said Lucy, refusing to be deterred. "Never mind," she said, leaning over the counter and lowering her voice. "A group of us mothers are putting on a Halloween party for the kids. To try and keep them off the streets, you know. We're cleaning up the old Hallett house this weekend. Would you like to help?"

"I'm afraid I couldn't possibly. Allergies."

"Oh, I didn't mean for you to help with the cleaning," said Lucy with a little laugh. "A lot of businesses in town are making donations."

"A donation?" Krissy looked relieved. "Sure. Is twenty-five dollars okay?"

"More than okay. Terrific," said Lucy, accepting the cash. "Thanks so much."

"No problem," said Krissy, dismissing her and turning back to the schedule she was decorating.

"So, what made you decide to open a studio in Tinker's Cove?" Lucy asked, ignoring the cue.

"I was tired of working for other people. I tried giving private lessons, but, well, the customers kind of got on my nerves."

"Like Monica?" Lucy smiled slyly, and leaned forward slightly. She wanted to give Krissy every encouragement to discuss her rival.

"Oh, that's right. You said you knew her." Krissy was wary.

"My husband did some carpentry work for her." Lucy lowered her voice. "Very demanding. A real pain in the you know what."

"Tell me about it," said Krissy, succumbing to temptation. "She had nothing to do all day, she didn't work or anything, but she still had to keep changing appointments. Sometimes ten minutes before she was due I'd get a call. Can we make it tomorrow instead? So inconsiderate. Never occurred to her that my income depended on a full schedule. And my other clients didn't appreciate getting moved all around to accommodate her. But that was the least of it. She was so rude to me. Treated me like I wasn't as good as her. Nobody was, not even her husband. She was really nasty to him. She really didn't understand him."

Some things never change, thought Lucy. "Sounds typical. A lot of summer people are like that. They think the town was created for them. Never occurs to them that we were here first. So how do you like Tinker's Cove?"

"Everybody's so nice. Just folks. And the ladies seem real pleased to have a place of their own to work out."

"You've really made it attractive." Lucy waved an arm, indicating the mauve carpeting and freshly sandblasted brick walls. "Nobody would guess they used to can sardines here. Not a trace of the old smell."

"We have a really good ventilation system," said Krissy. "And you wouldn't believe the amount I spend on air freshener."

"I've heard it's really hard for women to get small business loans. Did you have any trouble?"

"Not really. I have a partner—he invested some of his own money and arranged for me to borrow the rest."

"Oh, that's right. Didn't you say Dr. Mayes is your partner?"

"Did I say that?" At least Krissy had the decency to blush.

"Yes, I think you did. You said your partner's wife had been killed in a fire and I asked if it was Monica and you said . . ."

"I may have," Krissy interrupted, glancing at a couple of women who had just entered. She greeted them and they gave her a wave, proceeding on into the dressing room. "I don't think he wants it widely known. He's kind of a silent partner—really just doing me a favor. He's such a sweet guy."

A real philanthropist, thought Lucy. "He dropped by at my house the other day. He seemed pretty upset."

"Oh, yes," agreed Krissy. "He's devastated. That fire was some shock."

"They say it was arson. Do you have any idea who could have set it?"

"No." Krissy shook her head. "Some maniac, I guess."

"Lots of times it's the owner."

"Dr. Mayes would never do a thing like that. He's a healer, he helps people."

She was partly right, thought Lucy. He was a heel, at any rate. "Just between you and me . . . do you think he'll re-marry? He's quite a catch."

"I wouldn't be surprised," said Krissy, giving Lucy a small, conspiratorial smile.

"Listen, I'm really stiffening up since my workout yester-day. Do you think I could use the exercycle?"

"That's probably not a bad idea," said Krissy, happy to oblige her new friend.

As Lucy pedaled she allowed her mind to drift, thinking over her conversation with Krissy. She didn't like to label people, but Krissy seemed like a classic bimbo. She hadn't come right out and admitted she was Dr. Mayes's lover, but she had implied it. And there was no love lost between her and Monica. She certainly stood to benefit from Monica's death. Now Roland was free to marry her. Could she have somehow lured Monica to the Homestead, and set the fire?

Lucy doubted it. Krissy didn't seem like the kind of girl who would handle the dirty work herself. Not if there was a man she could convince to do it for her.

CHAPTER THIRTEEN

The weekend did not start well. Lucy had no sooner poured herself a cup of coffee on Saturday morning when the phone rang. It was Lorna Phipps, Stubby's mother.

"You have simply got to get control of that son of yours," began Mrs. Phipps, in her usual tone of righteous indignation. Her son, Stubby, had been the class scapegoat since kindergarten, and she had plenty of practice.

"What's he done, now, Lorna?" asked Lucy.

"Well, Toby and those friends of his, Eddie Culpepper and Rickie Goodman and Adam Stillings, tossed my Stubby's gym shoes up in the air until they caught on the electric power line. I had to call the electric company to get them down."

"I do apologize. I'm sure it wasn't intentional, it must have been an accident."

"Accident, my eye. Of course they did it on purpose. They had no business taking Stubby's sneakers in the first place. They're always teasing and tormenting him."

Lucy knew this was true. Stubby, overweight and with an overprotective mother, was a natural victim. When Lucy had been the boys' Cub Scout den mother, her biggest challenge each week had been trying to think of something for the boys to do that was more interesting than picking on Stubby.

It had been an almost impossible task. Stubby seemed to invite abuse. He stood a little bit too close, he asked stupid questions, he picked his nose. That didn't excuse his tormenters, however.

"I'll talk to Toby," promised Lucy, as a horrifying scene right out of *The Lord of the Flies* played in her mind. "They didn't actually take the shoes right off him, did they?"

"No. They were his gym shoes. They offer no support whatsoever. Dear Stubby has flat feet, you know, and has to wear good, sturdy oxfords. So difficult to find nowadays."

"I bet they are," said Lucy, her heart going out to poor Stubby. With a mother who insisted upon dressing him in sensible shoes and a bow tie for school, he didn't stand a chance.

"Perhaps if you let him dress more like the other boys, they wouldn't tease him so much," she ventured.

"How dare you, Lucy Stone! Just because I refuse to let Stubby dress like those young hooligans, your son included, I might add, that's no excuse for them to tease him."

"Of course not," agreed Lucy. "You're absolutely right."

"And you haven't heard the last of this, I can tell you that. All this happened at the school bus stop, and I am going to make sure the principal hears about it. Those boys could lose their bus privileges, you know."

"I know," admitted Lucy, wondering how she was going to find time in her morning schedule to chauffeur Toby to school.

As soon as she had hung up, she yelled up the stairs. "Toby, get down here this instant."

"Sure, Mom, what's up?" From his sheepish expression, it was clear he knew exactly what was up.

"What's all this about Stubby's shoes?"

"We were just playing keep-away and Eddie tossed 'em up and they got stuck on the wire. Kind of a freak accident."

"You boys have got to stop teasing Stubby. It's mean. Why do you do it?"

"I dunno." Toby looked at his feet.

"How would you like it if the boys did it to you?"

"Not much, I guess."

"Well, stop doing it, okay?"

"Okay." He silently observed a moment of penance, then looked up. "Mom, what's for breakfast?"

Lucy poured herself a big glass of orange juice and joined him at the table. As she watched him wolf down a huge bowl of cereal, and then pour himself a second, she wondered if she had been stern enough with him. He didn't seem to be taking this very seriously. What else had he been up to?

She studied her son, thinking that in many ways he was already a stranger to her. Teetering on the brink of adolescence, his face still pudgy and round, she thought of the pending onslaught of hormones that would carry him even further away from her. Had it already started? What did he do when he was out with his buddies? Could they have set the fires? On a dare, maybe. Or carried away on a sudden surge of testosterone? The thought gripped her, filling her with anxiety.

"Mom, are you okay?" asked Toby. "Why are you looking at me like that?"

"Oh, nothing," she said, giving him a hug. "I was just thinking how fast you're growing up. It's kind of scary."

"Oh, Mom," he groaned, wriggling away and heading for the stairs.

It was a few minutes past ten when Lucy loaded the kids into the Subaru for the short drive to the Ezekiel Hallett house. When they arrived, the ramshackle old mansion was already abuzz with activity. The lawn was filled with cars and trucks; it seemed as if the entire town had turned out to help.

"Hi, Lucy. I see you brought the whole crew," said Sue, trotting up to the car and checking her clipboard. "Where's Bill?"

"He's working this morning. He'll be over later. I've got his lunch."

"I knew I could count on you," said Sue with a smile. "Okay, Toby, you can help the boys carry out trash. Girls, find Miss Perry, the high school art teacher—she's in charge of making decorations. Lucy, I know you've got the baby. Could you sweep and keep an eye on the kids?"

"Sure. I even brought my own broom."

"Great. Oops, I see some more new arrivals. Gotta go."

Lucy watched the busy scene for a minute, thinking how nice it was to see people rally for a common cause. Then, she transferred Zoe from the car safety seat to the red corduroy pouch she wore on her chest. Toting her dustpan and broom, she climbed the hill to the mansion.

"Oh, Mrs. Stone, can I see the baby?"

"Sure," said Lucy, pausing so Jennifer Mitchell could stroke Zoe's cheek. Jennifer, now a junior in high school, occasionally baby-sat for the older kids, but so far Lucy had been reluctant to leave Zoe.

"Isn't she adorable? How old is she now?"

"Six weeks," said Lucy.

"Is she heavy? I know a lot of mothers use those carriers—is it comfortable?"

"You get used to it," said Lucy. "Babies love them. They like being close to Mommy."

"Look at those bright eyes," cooed Jennifer. "She's watching everything."

"She'll doze off pretty soon. Listen, Jennifer. Have you done much sitting for babies?"

"Oh, yeah. I worked all last summer as a mother's helper for Mrs. Cunningham. She had twins—Bridget and Brendan. They were premature and had apnea monitors for a while. They needed special formula, too, and were on a high-frequency schedule. Plus the meds, of course."

Lucy was impressed. "I guess you could manage Zoe, then. She's a normal, full-term baby."

"That'd be great. I've missed playing checkers with Sara."

"How about next Thursday? I want to go to that gas station hearing. It shouldn't be too late, but it'll give you a chance to get acquainted with the baby."

"Sounds super," said Jennifer, with a huge smile.

"I'll pick you up around six-thirty?"

"You don't need to do that. I can drive, now," said Jennifer, beaming with pride. "I passed my driver's test on the first try."

"Congratulations," said Lucy, who still remembered bursting into tears when she failed her first attempt. "Have you got a car?"

"I do. I bought it with my baby-sitting money. It's that little red Toyota." She pointed to a tiny Tercel, rather the worse for wear. "It doesn't look like much, but it runs good. And it goes forever on a tank of gas."

"That's terrific. I'll see you a little before seven on Thursday?"

"You can count on me," said Jennifer, running off to help her friends, who were struggling to carry a mildewed old mattress to the Dumpster.

Lucy's progress up the hill was slow. She kept meeting people who hadn't seen her since Zoe's birth and wanted to peek at the baby. Finally, making her way into the entrance hall, Lucy paused to examine the plans Sue had tacked to the wall. Games would be located in the ballroom, and refreshments in the drawing room and parlor, while the stairs and a few upstairs rooms would be transformed into a "Trail of Terror" by the high school drama club.

"Whaddya think?" asked Sue, materializing beside her with two styrofoam cups of coffee.

"I think it's going to be a great party," said Lucy, accepting a cup.

"I didn't bring you any donuts—Jake's donated them—because I know you're trying to lose those extra baby pounds," reminded Sue.

"Thanks, so much," said Lucy, who was starving and could have eaten half a dozen. She consoled herself by nuzzling the baby's head with her chin.

"I have your best interests at heart," Sue assured her. "Are you sure Bill's coming? I need someone to tighten up the banister—I don't want any accidents."

"I'm absolutely, one hundred percent sure he'll come. I told you, I've got his lunch."

"Pretty clever. And I thought he was a conscientious, helpful sort of guy."

"He is," admitted Lucy. "Not like some men." She took a sip of coffee.

"Are you thinking of anyone in particular?" Sue leaned against the stained plaster, and settled in for a chat. It had been a long morning and she was ready for a break.

"Monica's husband. He *was* having an affair. With Krissy, just like I thought."

"How do you know?" Sue wasn't convinced.

"I called Monica's daughter, Mira. She told me. Then I happened to see Krissy at the gym and asked a few questions. It all adds up to a pretty big motive, if you ask me."

"Lucy, you're taking this stuff too far. If you keep poking around in other people's business you're going to get in trouble. In fact, someone's staring at you in the weirdest way right now."

"Who?" Lucy whirled around and saw Lorna Phipps

peering at her from a doorway. She gave her a cheery wave, but Lorna did not return it.

"That's just Stubby's mom—she disapproves of me," said Lucy, with a wave of her hand. "That has nothing to do with this. Don't you see? If he was having an affair, that would be a motive, wouldn't it? Say he wanted to marry Krissy."

"You've never heard of divorce?"

"You've never heard of alimony?" Lucy shot back. "Maybe he wanted to get rid of her and keep his money. Maybe he was afraid Krissy wouldn't be interested in him without his dough."

"It seems pretty risky to me. What if he got caught? Then he wouldn't be able to enjoy Krissy or his money,"

"Well, he's gotten away with it so far. And if it hadn't been for the dog, the body might never have been discovered," Lucy pointed out. "It was almost a perfect murder."

"What about the car?"

"You've got me there," admitted Lucy, running out of answers. "He should have gotten rid of it."

"See. It was an accident. Monica was in the wrong place at the wrong time."

"Maybe," agreed Lucy, draining her coffee and tossing the cup in a convenient trash barrel. "Time to get to work," she said, taking up her broom and beginning to sweep.

"Let me know as soon as Bill comes, okay?" Sue made a note on her clipboard and hurried off.

Buckling down to her job, Lucy soon had a sizable pile of dirt in the middle of the floor. Moving awkwardly because of the baby carrier, she was bending down to sweep it into the dustpan when she was almost knocked off her feet by Toby and Eddie, who were running through the foyer.

"Hey, watch it," she said sharply. "You're gonna hurt somebody."

"That's right, boys. Slow down," roared Barney, clamping his hands on Eddie and Toby's shoulders and stopping them in their tracks. "What's the idea, anyway?"

"We're helping," offered Toby.

"What's that you got there?" demanded Barney.

"It's a walkie-talkie. Rickie got 'em for his birthday."

"Where's Rickie?"

"We're trying to find him and Adam."

"That's how you're helping? You're running all over, chasing your buddies?"

"I guess."

"Gimme that," ordered Barney, taking the toy. "I'll find them. You find Mrs. Finch and she'll tell you how you can help. Okay?"

"Okay," agreed Eddie and Toby.

Barney pushed down the button on the walkie-talkie. "Boys, this is Officer Culpepper. Get your butts in here this minute and report to Mrs. Finch. Got that?"

A high squeaky voice came through the static. "Got it."

Lucy laughed. "Those boys are driving me crazy. Did you hear about Stubby's shoes?"

"Marge mentioned it." Marge was Barney's wife. "I had a little talk with Eddie."

"I had one with Toby. Do you think it will do any good? Is this thing out of control?"

"I don't think so. Kids tease each other. It's not nice, but it's normal. To tell the truth, Stubby kinda asks for it."

"I know. Somebody ought to tell him how to stick up for himself."

"That's a good idea, Lucy. I think I'll have a little talk with Stubby myself."

"Don't let Lorna catch you. She's determined Stubby won't be a hooligan like our boys."

"I can tell her a thing or two about youthful offenders—real sickos—that'll keep her awake at night."

"That reminds me—any progress on the fires?"

"Well, the fire marshal's office had us bring in anybody with a previous record of arson—arrests, mind you, not convictions. Computer gave us eight or nine names, but it turned out none of them could've set all the fires. The fires were started the same way, according to the state fire marshal, so they're pretty sure it's the work of one person. Could be somebody new, just discovered he likes to play with matches, or could be the fires are a cover-up for some other crime."

"Like murder?"

"Could be murder, could be insurance fraud, could be a nut. They're looking at everything. The word I've heard is that this case is going to be cracked in the lab."

"What do you mean?"

"They've got solid evidence of some kind—DNA, fibers, I dunno. Nobody's talking. They've really clamped a lid on it."

"Did they question Dr. Mayes? His daughter told me he was having an affair. He might have wanted Monica out of the way."

Barney nodded. "Oh, sure. He was the first one they questioned. Had an ironclad alibi. In surgery or something."

Lucy was disappointed. "Oh. Maybe he hired somebody."

"Maybe. If he did, we've still gotta figure out who it was. We're back at square one."

"I guess so." Lucy sighed. "There was something I wanted to talk to you about, but I can't remember what it is. Darn. I hate it when that happens. They say the short-term memory is the first to go."

"Give me a call when you think of it." He fingered the toy walkie-talkie he had confiscated from Toby. "I think I'll see if I can find Stubby. That boy needs a little man-to-man advice."

Maybe Toby does, too, thought Lucy, deciding to ask Bill to have a little talk with him.

CHAPTER FOURTEEN

Zoe was getting restless inside the baby pouch, so Lucy decided to go back to the car to change her diaper and let her nurse. Lifting the hatchback, she spread out a quilt and laid Zoe on her back. While the baby kicked her arms and legs, Lucy stretched a bit and arched her back.

When Bill slipped his arms around her from behind and nuzzled her neck with his beard, she was momentarily startled.

"What if my husband sees us?" she teased, covering his hands with her own.

"I don't care. I love you more than he does. I have to have you, Lady Dolores."

"Lady Dolores? Can't you do better than that?" teased Lucy. Actually she was delighted by his playfulness. Lately, it seemed he was either installing fire extinguishers or studying those darned zoning bylaws.

"I'm just a poor, humble carpenter," he said with mock humility. "So, what do they want me to do?"

"You better check with Sue. She said something about making sure the stairs are safe."

"Sounds like a good idea. Have you got anything to eat?"

"Sandwiches. PB and J, or tuna?"

"Tuna."

Lucy produced a couple of sandwiches, and a can of soda, and he settled in the way-back to eat while she changed the baby's diaper. That job finished, she sat down beside him to nurse the baby and eat her own lunch.

"Have you ever been unfaithful to me?" asked Lucy.

"What?" sputtered Bill, spraying soda. "What kind of question is that?"

"I just wondered. What makes a man have an affair?"

"Don't ask me. I'm a good boy."

Lucy raised an eyebrow. "Really?"

"Really. It isn't that I haven't been tempted, it's just that I'm usually too tired."

Lucy gave Bill a light punch on the arm. "Thanks a lot."

"Serves you right. Say, don't we have some children? Don't they want lunch?"

"There's a ton of donuts and soda and snacks inside. They probably pigged out as soon as they got here."

"Oh." Bill knew that a steady diet of balanced meals featuring whole grains and plenty of fresh vegetables had left his children extremely susceptible to the attractions of junk food.

"I'm worried about Toby." She looked up at Bill.

"He seems pretty healthy to me, but you could give him vitamins or something."

"Not his diet," said Lucy, smiling and shaking her head. "I'm worried he's going to get into trouble. Serious trouble. Last year he pulled that toilet paper stunt, and Mrs. Phipps told me he and the other boys have been playing cruel tricks on Stubby. I just wonder if he's getting a little wild. And Halloween's the time for it."

"I'll talk to him," said Bill, standing up and stretching. "Well, I guess the faster I get that staircase fixed, the faster I can get home and watch the game."

That will be nice, thought Lucy, watching him trudge up

the hill with his heavy toolbox. He'd been so down in the dumps since the fire. Maybe he'd watch with Toby, and they'd drink sodas and eat chips and roar their approval when Notre Dame or Florida State got a touchdown.

Lucy stayed at the car, nursing the baby. Zoe was in no hurry, so Lucy made herself comfortable and reached for another oatmeal cookie.

Looking up at the mansion, Lucy thought how different it looked today. No longer empty and deserted, it seemed to be coming to life once again, thanks to the vitality and energy of the volunteers. Windows were thrown open, voices were heard in the empty rooms, doors slammed as people came and went.

The whole town seemed to have turned out for the cleanup. The ladies from the women's club had arrived early, bringing donated baked goods. "Just something in case people get hungry," said Irma Stout.

All the scouts were there, as well as the high school soccer team and the Alpha club. "The football team had a game," explained Karen Baker, whose oldest son was a defensive end, "or they would have been here, too."

A lot of local businessmen had donated their services; Sue could be very persuasive. Lucy saw the Baxter Electric truck; Larry Baxter must be setting up temporary wiring, she guessed. Harry Potts had stopped by, too, checking out the best location for his Porta-Potts. Ted Stilling had been busy all morning, snapping pictures and getting quotes.

There must be some way to save this building, thought Lucy. A theater? A restaurant? A bed and breakfast? Maybe the party would attract some entrepreneur, someone who would see the wonderful potential of the old place. Some fresh paint and wallpaper could do wonders.

Enjoy Victorian elegance at the Hallett House, thought Lucy, picturing a tasteful magazine advertisement, complete with a pen and ink sketch of the Italianate tower. She looked up to the roof, where a flight of curving steps round the tower led to an octagonal platform, where eight pillars supported a roof topped with eight decorative wooden urns.

Bats in the belfry, was probably more like it, she thought, taking a closer look. A few minutes later, her attention was drawn to the arrival of the fire chief when he pulled up in his bright red sedan. Rearranging her clothes and strapping the baby pouch back in place, Lucy hurried up the hill to hear the results of his inspection.

Entering the hallway once again, she joined the group of anxious volunteers. "He better pass it," whispered Karen Baker. "I hope I didn't get this backache for nothing."

"Yeah," agreed Lucy. "It would be a shame if we couldn't have the party after everyone did so much work."

They all watched as Chief Pulaski came down the stairs. There was a hush as the volunteers waited for his announcement.

"I don't have any problem issuing a temporary occupancy permit," he said, "for one night only—October thirty-one."

The group joined in a collective sigh of relief.

"But," he added, raising a cautionary finger, "there will be absolutely no open flames—no candles, no jack-o'-lanterns, nothing like that. I'm satisfied with the temporary wiring—so let's use it. The last thing we need is another tragedy." Everyone nodded agreement.

"That said, looks like it's gonna be a great party." He signed the certificate with a flourish, and presented it to Sue.

"Happy Halloween, everybody!" she exclaimed, waving it high above her head in triumph. The mothers and fathers, the high school kids, the scouts all smiled and cheered and congratulated one another.

"Party on, dudes!" shouted Rickie Goodman, and everybody laughed, even Stubby Phipps. Stubby, Lucy couldn't help noticing, had abandoned his bow tie, and was clutching a walkie-talkie. Not a toy like Rickie's; this was an official police issue hand radio. It looked like Barney had made his first move in the campaign to make Stubby socially acceptable.

Lucy rounded up the kids and herded them toward the car, thinking of the chores that awaited her at home.

"Girls, how would you like to bake some cupcakes this afternoon?" she asked, as she made sure everyone was safely strapped in.

"Yeah," said Sara, her eyes brightening at the thought of licking the icing bowl.

"Do we have to?" protested Elizabeth.

Lord, give me strength, prayed Lucy silently, as she started the engine. Backing the car around, she glanced up at the Hallett house one more time. If that psychology book was right, she thought, the towering mansion would present an irresistible temptation to a pyromaniac. Steering the car down the dusty driveway, she couldn't help wondering if the old house would still be standing for the party next weekend.

CHAPTER FIFTEEN

Lucy was juggling the baby and a cup of coffee on Monday morning when the phone rang and Bill answered upstairs. He was grinning like the proverbial Cheshire cat when he appeared in the kitchen a few minutes later.

"We won the lottery?" she asked.

"Not quite—but almost. That was Shelburne Village."

"No." Lucy's tone was suitably reverent; Shelburne Village was the premier restoration project in New England, maybe the entire country.

"Yeah. That was them. They saw my letter in *Architectural Heritage* magazine, and they want me to take a look at a door. They want to know if it's as old as they think it is."

"Wow. That's great. What an honor."

"They want me to come today. It's awfully short notice and I'll have to spend the night. Can you manage all alone?"

"Sure. I'm a big girl."

"Three kids and a baby—it's an awful lot."

"I'll manage just fine," insisted Lucy. She would never have admitted it, but she secretly enjoyed Bill's rare absences. It was a chance to relax the rules a bit—instead of cooking meat and potatoes for supper she was already planning to mix up big bowls of macaroni and cheese for the kids to eat in front of the TV. After the hurly-burly of the weekend she was looking forward to having the house, and the baby, to herself.

So, after the kids left for school, and Bill finally finished packing and left for his trip to Vermont, and Zoe settled down for her morning nap, Lucy fixed herself a cup of decaf mocha and tackled the bills. If only the kids would turn off the lights once in a while, she thought, writing out a check for $87.73 for the electric company. The phone bill wasn't too bad, only $37.16 including the weekly long-distance chat with her mother in New York. The heat bill, $154.65 on something mistakenly called the budget plan, sent her scurrying to turn down the thermostat. If they wore sweaters and drank hot liquids, sixty-two degrees would be plenty warm enough.

Preparing to write out a $390 check for homeowner's insurance, thankful that it came only once a year, she noticed the house was valued at $165,000. That was a lot of money, she thought.

Insurance fraud, she remembered Barney saying, was a possible motive for the fires. Certainly not for the barn, or the powder house. Possibly for the theater, though Lucy doubted the very respectable members of the board of trustees at Winchester College would stoop to such a thing. That left the Homestead.

It must have been insured for a pretty penny, she guessed. If replacement value was the guide used by insurance companies, it would certainly be very expensive to accurately reconstruct an antique house like the Homestead.

She knew it represented a sizable investment on the part of Dr. Mayes, something in the neighborhood of a quarter million dollars. That was a lot of money, especially if you weren't getting any return on it. Lucy knew that Dr. Mayes had little interest in the house, it had been Monica's project from the start. She hadn't even referred to it as "theirs" remembered Lucy, it was always "her" house.

Suddenly Dr. Mayes seemed to have plenty of reasons to burn down the house. Not only would he get rid of Monica, and conveniently dispose of her body at the same time, but he would also get back the money he had invested in the house. Add to that the fact that he wouldn't be faced with a messy and expensive divorce, and it seemed more than likely that Dr. Mayes was responsible for the fire.

That meant the fire was premeditated; he had to have carefully planned the whole thing. Maybe the three earlier fires had given him the idea. What an opportunity—investigators would assume the Homestead fire was just another arson, not a murder. All he had to do was lure Monica to the Homestead. Then, once she was there, it would be simple enough to set the fire. End of Monica.

Lucy shivered, suddenly chilly, and wrapped her arms across her chest. He had lived with Monica for thirty odd years. They had raised a family, they had shared the same bathroom, eaten meals together, slept side by side. And then at some point, perhaps when she was leafing through a magazine or sipping her morning cup of coffee, he had decided to kill her.

Lucy reached for the phone and dialed the police station. She asked for Officer Culpepper and was surprised when she was connected; usually she had to leave a message and wait for him to call back.

"Barney, why aren't you out keeping the streets of Tinker's Cove safe for honest citizens?"

"Paperwork," he grumbled.

"Listen, Barney, I've got an idea about the fires."

"I'm listening."

"Well, it just occurred to me that Dr. Mayes had an awful lot of reasons to burn down the Homestead. One, he could get rid of his wife without paying alimony; two, he would be free to do whatever he wants with Krissy; three, he would get insurance money for the Homestead. . . ."

"Who's Krissy?"

"Don't you know? She opened that new fitness studio in town—she's the other woman in Dr. Mayes's life, and he's part-owner of the studio."

"Where'd you hear this?" asked Barney.

"You mean you didn't know?"

"Of course we know," said Barney, defending the department. "What I asked is how did you find all this out?"

"I've heard things here and there."

"Lucy, you better mind your own business. I'd hate to see you end up like Mrs. Mayes."

"Barncy, you're just trying to scare me. I'm not going to end up like Monica if you guys do your job and arrest Dr. Mayes."

"It's not that simple." Lucy heard Barney sigh.

"How much more do you need? He's got motives on top of motives!"

"That's not enough. Just 'cause he's got a motive doesn't mean he murdered her. Lots of people have got motives—all sorts of motives. That doesn't make them criminals."

"Oh."

"And besides, there are the other fires. The modus was the same. This is basically an arson case."

"Maybe he set all the fires, to cover up the murder," suggested Lucy.

"Lucy, I gotta go," said Barney, running out of patience. "And remember what I said. This is one case you should leave to the professionals."

"Okay, okay," said Lucy, tired of the same old refrain. "Bye now."

As she replaced the receiver Lucy wondered if Dr. Mayes had set all the fires. He was a surgeon, a methodical man. One fire resulting in a death would have been considered murder. A rash of fires, on the other hand, would make it seem as if poor Monica was simply in the wrong place at the wrong time. But could he have done it? Barney had said something about an alibi—he was supposed to be in surgery or something.

What about the other fires? She remembered seeing him at the Fourth of July parade, wondering what had brought him to Tinker's Cove. While Monica always attended, she had usually come with a group of houseguests, Lucy had never seen Dr. Mayes with them. The movie theater had burned that weekend, on July 5. Perhaps that was what brought him to town.

And the second fire, on August 28? Could he have set that one, too? Checking the calendar, Lucy saw that August 28 was a Friday. Was he in his office, she wondered, or was he skulking around Bumps River Road, setting a fire in the old barn?

Grabbing the phone, she called information and got his number. She dialed, then waited for his receptionist to answer.

"Dr. Mayes's office."

"This is Gloria at Blue Cross/Blue Shield. I need to verify a patient claim for a D and C supposedly performed by Dr. Mayes on August 28."

"Patient's name, please."

"Kenmore, Joyce," improvised Lucy, happening to spot the brand name on the refrigerator. "Birthdate, June 6, 1963. Social security number . . ."

"That won't be necessary. I'll just check the book." After a pause, she continued. "There must be some mistake. The office was closed that day. I checked our files, too. We have no patient by that name."

"I suspected as much. I knew there was something funny about this one. Thank you for your cooperation. Fraudulent claims cost us all money."

"You're welcome," replied the receptionist. Something in

her voice made Lucy wonder if she'd gone a bit over the top. It was so hard to get these impersonations just right.

Encouraged by her discovery, Lucy checked the calendar. September 26, the day the powder house burned, was also a Friday. But how could she find out if Dr. Mayes had an alibi? She could hardly call the office again.

Hearing Zoe fussing upstairs, Lucy reluctantly abandoned playing detective. Besides, she realized, as she climbed the stairs, Dr. Mayes would hardly shut his practice so he could set fires. Most likely he hired a professional. Much less risky. Especially when you considered how the Medical Society deplored scandal.

Back to the drawing board, thought Lucy, settling down in the recliner to nurse Zoe. Where did I leave off, she asked herself, opening up the psychology book and propping it on Zoe's hip.

"Sexual malfunction is almost always associated with the development of the arsonous personality," she read. "Impotence, in particular, often plays a contributing role."

Somehow, she thought with a sigh, that just didn't sound like Dr. Mayes.

CHAPTER SIXTEEN

After lunch, Lucy had planned to take her aerobics class, but first she stopped by at Doug Durning's real estate office on Main Street. She had promised to pick up some information about the upcoming gas station hearing for Bill. Fortunately, there was an empty parking spot right in front.

As Lucy hurried up the front walk, carrying Zoe in her arms, she noticed how similar this building was to the Hathorn-Pye house. Another big, four-square Georgian with a huge center chimney. Opening the front door, however, she was momentarily taken aback. Instead of the big center hallway she had expected, she found herself in a cramped entry, confronted with three doors.

Which one led to the office? Opening the middle one, she found herself looking at a jumble of old office equipment. The faintest whiff of a pungent scent reminded her momentarily of starchy plaid dresses with white collars and her fingers wrapped clumsily around a big yellow pencil.

Closing that door, she opened the one to the left. This was obviously Durning's office, but no one was there. Checking her watch she saw it wasn't quite eleven. When she had called, asking on Bill's behalf if he had any TCHDC min-

utes or records on Lenk's gas station, he had told her to
come by around eleven.

Deciding he would probably be along soon, Lucy went
back outside. It was a sunny, crisp fall day, too nice to be inside. Lucy set Zoe back in her safety seat and leaned against
the car, looking up and down Main Street. It was the sort of
day New England was famous for. The sky was bright blue,
the leaves on the maple trees lining the street were bright
yellow. The ground was covered with them. Lucy gave a
kick, sending up a small shower of rustling gold.

Regarding the stately old homes that sat well back from
the street, surrounded by generous yards, Lucy appreciated
the value of the commission. Tinker's Cove was a handsome
town, thanks in large part to the fine homes built by merchants and sea captains in the last century. Prosperous, and
proud of it, they spent their fortunes building large, stately
houses.

The age of sail hadn't lasted, of course, and the sea captains eventually fell on hard times, taking the rest of the
town down with them. There wasn't any money to add on to
the houses, or change them, so they stayed the way they
were. A few had been cut up into apartments or rooming
houses, but from the outside the street looked much as it had
looked a hundred years ago. Although the road was now
lined with parked cars, there were still a few mounting
blocks and hitching posts, Lucy noticed. Remnants from another age.

She liked that. In New England, people respected the past
and were slow to change. She'd visited relatives in the Sun
Belt and been shocked at the raw, utilitarian ugliness of the
buildings. The buildings were low and squat, with flat roofs.
There were no lofty steeples, no pitched roofs angled against
the blue sky. Without the garish, plastic signs, you couldn't
tell a store from a church or a house. There was no history;
everything was new.

Thanks to the recent recession, of course, there hadn't

been much new development in Tinker's Cove. Now that the region once again seemed headed for economic recovery, some people claimed the commission stifled initiative and new development. People like Randolph Lenk, for instance.

"Hi, Lucy. Sorry I'm late, I got held up at town hall." Doug was a bit out of breath, as if he'd been hurrying.

He was a good-looking man, not too tall, a touch of gray at the temples. There was something a bit battered, a bit world-weary about him that Lucy found appealing. She gave him a big smile.

"No problem. I've just been enjoying this beautiful day."

"Come on in and I'll see what I've got for you. You know, Lucy, Bill is a real addition to the commission. He knows his stuff, but he's not fossilized like the others. He knows what it's like to try to run a business and pay the bills."

"He sure does," said Lucy with a smile. "I just have to get the baby, okay?"

Toting the heavy, plastic seat, Lucy followed Doug into the rather bare reception area. A deacon's bench sat under one window, a couple of captain's chairs were pulled up to a desk.

"Sally's only part-time," he said, waving his hand at the empty desk. "I think she keeps the commission stuff in here." He opened a file drawer and began searching. "Hmm, this may take a minute or two. Go on in and sit down in my office—the chairs there are more comfortable."

Still carrying the sleeping Zoe, Lucy went into Doug's office and sat down in an upholstered wing chair. She tried to imagine what purpose this room must have served when the house was built and failed; it seemed too small to have been a parlor or dining room, too large to be a pantry.

Spotting a framed plan, she got up to examine it, and all was made clear. The old house had been completely remodeled inside and the original four rooms and a hall had been transformed into three office suites. The plan was surrounded by a display of photographs, and Lucy was intrigued.

There was Doug shaking hands with Larry Bird, there was a signed photo of hockey great turned businessman Bobby Orr, and a group photo that included Doug, George and Barbara Bush, and five or six others. Leaning closer, Lucy tried to identify the people in the other photos. Except for one rather notorious grouping, a savings and loan president now in jail along with a former state representative currently under indictment, she didn't recognize anyone.

"Here you are, Lucy. She had it filed under *T*; I can't imagine why."

"Thanks. Bill will really appreciate having some background information. I know he felt a bit at sea at the last meeting."

"It takes a while to get up to speed."

"I'm sure. This is a wonderful collection of photos." Lucy couldn't resist asking, "How did you happen to meet Larry Bird? What's he like?"

"Real nice. I actually had dinner with him." Doug was on the verge of boasting, but caught himself. "Me and a lot of other people. It was a business thing—a long time ago." He shrugged. "Seems like another life—the fabulous eighties. Those were the days. You could sell anything, for any price. Everybody had money to burn. Not anymore."

"Never, for me," admitted Lucy. "Seems like I've always been pinching pennies. That reminds me. I'm supposed to ask if you could make a donation to the Halloween Party."

"Oh, sure," said Doug, promptly sitting down at his desk and opening a massive checkbook. "That's a great idea, doing something for the kids at Halloween. Keep 'em out of trouble," he said, writing out a check and handing it over.

"Thanks," said Lucy, stuffing the check in her pocket. "I hate asking for money."

"Think nothing of it. It's for a good cause."

"Well, thanks again, for everything. I'll see you at the hearing."

Once again, Lucy picked up the heavy baby seat and

lugged it out to the car. Why, she wondered, did Zoe insist on sleeping when it was least convenient? Later, when they got back home and Lucy had dishes to wash and rugs to vacuum and cupcakes to bake, she would be wide awake and demanding attention.

Lucy strapped the car seat in place, and slid under the wheel. Remembering the check in her pocket, she pulled it out and looked at it. Ten dollars. She shook her head. She was going to spend more than that in cupcake mix. What was all that about worthy causes? she wondered, as she turned the ignition. Of course, she admitted with a shrug, with these Yankees you could never tell if they didn't have any money, or just didn't want to spend it.

CHAPTER SEVENTEEN

When Lucy arrived at the Body Shop she discovered she only had a few minutes before her one-thirty class. She quickly dropped Zoe at the child care center and hurried into the locker room to change. Then, taking a place at the back of the room she threw herself into the lesson. As she followed Vicki's instructions, amplified over the thumping beat of a rock song, she imagined the fat melting and slipping off her body, revealing firm, shapely muscles beneath. She lifted her legs and raised her arms, ignoring the aching, burning pain and concentrating on the firm, slim body she was determined to have.

When the class was over she felt a bit light-headed and wobbly so she headed for the juice machine. Sitting on a bench, she sipped a raspberry-kiwi concoction and waited for the sugar to take effect.

"Oh, good," said Vicki, sitting beside her and taking a long drink from a bottle of spring water. "I thought you looked a bit pale. I was going to suggest you have some juice or something."

"How do you do this all day long?" Lucy asked.

"You get used to it," said Vicki, shrugging a smooth bronze shoulder. "So, how do you like the class?"

"Fine, I guess. How long does it take before you notice a difference in your body?"

"After about six weeks you'll begin to see some changes."

"That long?" Lucy was disappointed.

"It takes time—think how long it took for you to get out of shape."

"Getting out of shape was a lot easier than getting back in," said Lucy. "Do you like working here?"

"It's great. I knew Krissy from Boston and I was real excited when she asked me to come up here. I was sick of the city—high rents, dirt, the crowds on the T, the homeless people lying on the sidewalks. Too depressing. Here, everything's clean and pretty."

"Wait till winter," warned Lucy. "There isn't much to do."

"That won't bother me," said Vicki, with a toss of her ponytail. "I'll just curl up by the fire with a good book."

"Have you known Krissy for long?" inquired Lucy.

"We worked at some of the same places, you know. The fitness world is kind of small—you keep running into the same people. But I didn't really know her well until I came here. We worked together all summer, getting this place ready."

"You did?" Lucy was interested. It seemed Krissy had been in Tinker's Cove longer than she thought.

"Yeah. We rented a floor scraper and we nailed up sheetrock and painted it. Krissy even did the electrical wiring."

"You're kidding." Lucy was amazed. Apparently Krissy wasn't quite the dumb blonde she had assumed.

"No, it's true. She knows all about this stuff. She helped her father remodel their house when she was a kid. I just did what she told me but it came out pretty good, don't you think?"

"It really did," agreed Lucy. "But isn't wiring kind of

tricky? I mean, what if she made a mistake and crossed some circuits or something?"

"Then we'd have a big problem, I guess. But everything seems to be working just fine. Sound system, ventilation, lights, you name it. Listen, I gotta go. My body sculpting class is waiting for me." She paused for emphasis. "Those girls are serious, believe me."

Lucy glanced at the clock, shocked to see how late it was. She had better get moving, she decided, tossing her juice can in the recycling bin next to the machine. She was supposed to pick up the kids at school and meet Sue for a trip to Andy Brown's pumpkin patch. She quickly showered, passed the blow dryer over her hair, threw on her clothes, and headed for the nursery where she found Zoe fussing in a crib.

"I tried everything I could think of," apologized the attendant. Lucy knew from the sign on the door that her name was Peggy and she was a nursing student at the community college. "I finally put her down, hoping she'd go to sleep."

"That's okay," said Lucy, "I think she's working on a tooth or something." She picked up Zoe and tucked her under her chin for a cuddle. Zoe gave a little snort, sighed, and promptly went to sleep.

"I guess that explains it. She just wanted her mommy," said Peggy.

"It's wonderful to be needed," Lucy said, hurrying off. She was halfway down the hallway, past the office, when she heard Krissy's voice.

"I can't believe this," Krissy sobbed. There was a pause. When she spoke again, she sounded angry. "Not after all I've done for you. Doesn't that mean anything to you?"

Lucy stepped closer, straining to hear. Then Zoe stirred against her chest and began to fuss. "Shhh," she whispered, rubbing her chin against Zoe's head.

Zoe was not about to be soothed. She took a deep breath, winding up for a full-blown cry.

Reluctantly, Lucy pulled herself away from the doorway and hurried down the hall. "It's okay," she murmured, patting the baby's back and gently bouncing her. She pushed open the door and crossed the parking lot toward her car.

At first she didn't notice anything wrong. It was only when she reached for the door handle that she saw the damage.

A long, jagged line of black paint had been sprayed along the side of her car.

CHAPTER EIGHTEEN

"I guess Halloween came early this year," said Sue, eyeing the damage a few minutes later. She licked a finger and rubbed the black streak. "Lucky for you, it seems to be water soluble."

"I'll try the car wash. Hop in, I'm running late. The kids got out of school five minutes ago."

Sue hopped into the car next to Lucy, and fastened her seat belt. "So, how's the investigation going?"

Lucy didn't need much encouragement and started right in. "I was pretty convinced it was Dr. Mayes—after all, ninety percent of the time it's the husband. But now I'm beginning to think Krissy might have done it. It turns out she's very handy. Vicki told me all about how she spent the summer wiring the gym."

"You think Krissy set the fires?" Sue was intrigued.

"She was here, and she knows all about electricity. And once she got Monica out of the way she'd have Dr. Mayes all to herself. But I'm not convinced. I've been reading this psychology book and it says arson is predominantly a male crime."

"Most crimes are," said Sue. "But don't forget, this is an

equal opportunity society. Girls can do anything boys can. Personally, I wouldn't put anything past her. She's entirely too . . ." Sue paused, looking for the right word. "Fit."

"By the way, I haven't seen you at the gym," said Lucy, pulling up in front of the school.

"I haven't had time."

"Excuses, excuses," said Lucy, shaking her head. "Hop in kids—Toby, you'll have to get in the wayback."

"You were late, Mom," said Elizabeth, climbing into the back seat. "We had to wait forever."

"Who painted the car?" asked Sara.

"Bad boys, most likely," said Lucy, catching Toby's eye in the rearview mirror. "I hope none of you would ever do such a thing."

"Mom, wash it off! It's bad enough I have to ride around in this beat-up old Subaru . . . what if somebody sees me?" Elizabeth was acutely self-conscious.

"Somebody like Matt Price?" teased Toby.

"No-o-o." Elizabeth's voice was scornful. "I don't care if Matt Price sees me."

"Who, then? Stubby Phipps? He told me he likes you."

"Stubby is disgusting. Almost as disgusting as you."

"Stop bickering, or we won't go to the pumpkin patch," warned Lucy. "We'll go straight home."

"Mom, are we almost there?" asked Toby. "It's not very comfortable back here."

"Almost," answered Lucy. "It's just down the road a little bit."

Even though the farmstand was on the outskirts of town, it was still in the historic district. Wary of commercialization, the town had voted to extend the district along Main Street to the town boundary.

"Can we go on the haunted hayride?" asked Elizabeth.

"That's at night. We're only here to get a pumpkin. A perfect pumpkin."

"What's a perfeck pumpkin?" asked Sara.

"We'll know when we see it," said Lucy, spotting a sign for Farmer Brown's Pumpkin Patch. "I think we're getting close."

Coming around a bend, Lucy couldn't help gasping as the full glory of Farmer Brown's was revealed to her. The farmstand itself was an old barn, painted the TCHDC-approved shade of yellow, but outlined with strings of orange lights. Constrained by the stringent sign code, Andy Brown had not hesitated to improvise. He had constructed a platform above the barn entrance, and arranged shocks of corn, bales of hay, and numerous harvest figures made from stuffed overalls with pumpkin heads. To the left of the barn another platform had been erected, this was a shrine to the 775-pound winner of Farmer Brown's annual contest for the biggest pumpkin.

Acres and acres of pumpkins, still clinging to their withered vines, surrounded the farmstand, along with acres and acres of parking. Hay wagons, pulled by small red tractors ferried customers from their cars and out to the farther roaches of the pumpkin fields. Judging from the number of cars in the parking lot, Andy Brown was certainly doing something right.

Opening the car door, Lucy heard recorded wails and shrieks, punctuated by Vincent Price's voice.

"It's the Monster Mash," a delighted Elizabeth cried.

"Hurry up, Mom," urged Toby. "We'll miss the wagon."

"There'll be another one," said Sue. "Your mom has to get Zoe and Sara."

After Lucy had zipped Zoe into the corduroy pouch, and released Sara from her booster seat, they all clustered around a bright orange post with a sign proclaiming PUMP-KIN PATCH EXPRESS and waited for the wagon.

Soon one trundled up and they were greeted by the cheery young driver.

"Climb on," he said. "I'm your driver, Brad, and we're off to the pumpkin patch!"

Lucy and Sue climbed on awkwardly and seated themselves on bales of hay, holding on for dear life as the wagon lurched into motion. The girls shrieked with excitement, and even Toby was having a hard time maintaining the sophisticated, world-weary attitude he adopted when he was out in public with his mother.

"Now, when you see the pumpkin you want, don't hesitate to holler. We can stop as often as you want," advised Brad.

"We want a perfeck pumpkin," piped up Sara.

"Well, you've come to the right place," said Brad. "We've got twenty acres of pumpkins. This is the biggest pick-your-own pumpkin patch in the state of Maine, maybe in the entire United States."

"I don't doubt it," said Lucy. "What do you think of that one, over there?"

"Ick," said Elizabeth. "I want a round pumpkin. That's a tall pumpkin."

"There's a nice round one," said Sue. "See it?"

"That's too small," said Toby.

"I don't know if we have room in the car for a really big one, Toby," reminded Lucy.

"That's it!" shrieked Sara. They followed her little pointed finger, and spotted a lovely, round pumpkin.

"Stop!" Toby bellowed, jumping off the wagon and leaping over pumpkins and vines. He hoisted the pumpkin in triumph, and then dropped it. "Uggh," he exclaimed. "It was all squishy."

"Sometimes they get that way," Brad admitted.

"What about that one next to it?" Lucy asked.

Toby approached it cautiously. "It looks okay."

"Knock on it," Lucy said.

Toby gave it a rap; it sounded like he was knocking on a door.

"Bring it over," Lucy ordered, with a wave. Seeing Toby struggle, Brad jumped down to help him lift the pumpkin and hoist it onto the wagon.

"That looks good, what do you think? Besides, it's getting cold."

"Hot chocolate, cider, and donuts inside," Brad recited, climbing back onto his seat and setting the tractor in motion. "Also, don't miss the chance to visit the House of Horror. Today, we also have a pumpkin carving seminar with lifestyles expert Corney Clark."

"Sue, don't you want to get a pumpkin?" Lucy asked.

"I'm going to get a white one. They have them inside."

"I never heard of such a thing."

"I saw them in a magazine," Sue explained. "You carve them with an Exacto knife. Something a little different, more like a lantern."

"Really?" Lucy was skeptical, as she climbed down from the wagon and followed Brad to the cashier's counter. "I guess we'll stick with the traditional version. How much do I owe you?" She asked the cashier.

"Sixteen dollars and forty-two cents."

"Are you sure?"

The cashier nodded her head. "Yes. It weighs thirty-three and a half pounds, at forty-nine cents a pound."

"Okay," Lucy agreed. This was highway robbery, but she couldn't disappoint the kids. "Will you take a check?"

"Certainly. We also accept Visa, Mastercard, and American Express."

"Cancel that sale," said Andy Brown, materializing behind the cashier. "Bill Stone's money isn't any good here," he said, with a big smile and a wink.

"What do you mean?" asked Lucy, puzzled.

"A free pumpkin's the least I can do for my buddy Bill," said Andy. "Just to let him know there's no hard feelings because he voted against my sign."

"Oh," said Lucy, as the light dawned. Andy was offering a small bribe because Bill was on the commission. "There was nothing personal in his vote. Bill will always vote his conscience, you know." She reopened her checkbook. "Now, how much was that pumpkin? Sixteen forty-two?"

Andy shrugged, and nodded to the cashier, who rang up the sale.

"I'm hungry," Elizabeth said, with a meaningful glance at the snack bar in the corner.

"Here's five dollars," Lucy said. "You guys get what you want. I'm going to watch this demonstration with Sue."

She waited a minute to make sure that Toby and Elizabeth didn't run off without Sara, and then joined the group of women clustered around Corney Clarke.

"We don't need to carve pumpkins a certain way, just because we've always done it that way," advised Corney, with a flip of her blond pageboy. "Pumpkin carving is yet another opportunity to explore our creativity, to express ourselves, each in our own unique way."

Zoe was getting restless in the pouch, so Lucy began rocking her back and forth, while she listened to Corney.

"You might choose to express your feminine side, your love of lace and crystal, with a white pumpkin like this." Corney displayed an intricately carved creation that looked more like a piece of delicate porcelain than a pumpkin. The women oohed.

"Or perhaps you'd like to express your whacky sense of humor," said Corney, grinning mischievously. She uncovered an enormous blue hubbard squash, with B-O-O carved in it. The last O contained the small figure of a ghost. The women chuckled.

"Or, perhaps you really want to scare someone." Corney paused dramatically, then uncovered a pumpkin with a spider carved into its side. Little black plastic spiders had been artistically placed to augment the effect. The women squealed.

"As you can see, there is no right way to carve a pumpkin." Corney leaned forward and nodded reassuringly at the women.

"There is only the way that is right for you. You must reach deep down inside yourself and find the wellsprings of your creativity. Then, you must look at your pumpkin. Go beyond the surface. Release the spirit within your gourd."

A wail from Zoe broke the awed silence with which the women were receiving Corney's every word. Lucy decided it was time for a strategic retreat.

"Catch you later," she told Sue, and headed over to the snackbar.

"Coffee, black," she told the girl behind the counter. Then, carrying her cup over to a table, she joined the kids, discreetly lifting her sweater so Zoe could have a snack, too.

"Whaddya think, guys," she observed, taking in the elaborate decorations and the frenzied commercialization of Farmer Brown's farmstand, "is it me, or is Halloween getting out of control?"

CHAPTER NINETEEN

L ater that evening, after supper, Lucy wondered if she had been too hasty when she encouraged Bill to go to Shelburne Village. Maybe I should have fallen on my knees and begged him to stay home, thought Lucy, plunging her arm up to the elbow in pumpkin guts.

"It's a shame Dad's missing this," she told the kids, who were gathered around the newspaper-covered kitchen table. "He would've loved it."

"We didn't wanna wait," Toby said. "It's almost Halloween."

"Only four more days," Elizabeth said.

"I can't wait," Sara squealed. "Trick or treat!"

Propped in her baby seat, Zoe did not seem very excited about pumpkin carving, or Halloween. If anything, her expression seemed to indicate some internal discomfort. She gave a little hiccup, and then started to cry.

"I have to feed the baby. Toby, can you finish cleaning out this pumpkin?"

"Sure." He started to reach into the pumpkin.

"Roll your sleeves up," Lucy advised.

"Oh, yeah."

Lucy kept an eye on him as she rinsed her hands, dried them, and picked up the baby. "No funny stuff," she warned, just as he picked up a handful of stringy seeds and hurled them at Elizabeth.

"That's it," she told Elizabeth, who was scooping up a handful herself in order to retaliate. "It stops here."

"That's not fair! He gets away with everything!"

"He's not getting away with it. I'll punish him later. Right now, let's concentrate on finishing up this pumpkin."

"How are you going to punish him?" asked Elizabeth, as Lucy settled Zoe at her breast.

"I don't know. I'll think of something."

"You should ground him," Elizabeth suggested with a malicious grin.

"That's not fair! You get grounded for something real bad, like stealing," Toby protested.

"I haven't decided, yet. Just remember, you owe a debt to society, young man. So, what kind of eyes are you going to give it?"

"Two triangles," said Sara.

"You don't have to make triangles. You can be creative. How about big, spooky circles?"

"Triangles," Toby said.

"Triangles," Elizabeth agreed.

Lucy sighed. "Okay, make triangles." Sometimes Lucy wondered about her children. They were so conservative. They never wanted to try anything new. "Be careful with that knife, Toby."

"How do you want the nose?" Toby asked. "Triangle?"

"Triangle," Sara said.

"Triangle," Elizabeth agreed.

"You know, I saw somewhere, how they made the pumpkin seeds dribble out of the jack-o'-lantern's mouth, so it looked like throw up," Lucy suggested, propping Zoe on her shoulder and patting her back. "It looked kinda neat, if you like that sort of thing."

"Yuck," Toby said, grimacing.

"That's disgusting," Elizabeth observed, as Zoe upchucked all over Lucy's shoulder.

"It's only spit up," said Lucy. "I hope she isn't coming down with something."

"She sure knows how to come up with something," volunteered Toby, pleased at his cleverness.

"Make the mouth smile," Sara said.

"A big grin with lots of teeth," Elizabeth added.

"What did you think of Mrs. Finch's white pumpkin?" Lucy asked, gently rocking Zoe.

"It's just not Halloween," said Elizabeth. "This pumpkin's right for Halloween."

Toby placed a flashlight inside the pumpkin and turned it on. Then he switched off the kitchen light, and they all admired the jack-o'-lantern. It had two triangle eyes, a triangle nose, and a big toothy grin. It was perfect.

"Okay, Toby. For punishment you can clean up. I'm going to put Zoe in her crib and see if she'll go to sleep."

"Aw, Mom, do I have to?"

"Yes, you have to. If you throw stuff around and make a mess, you get to clean it up. That's how it works, and I don't want to hear another word about it."

Surprised at her tone, Toby glanced at his mother. Lucy raised her eyebrows, and he decided that further argument would not be in his best interest. Instead, he reached for a sponge.

Coming back downstairs, Lucy listened to Zoe's crying and wiped up the table. Toby had done his best, it was just that when Toby cleaned up, somebody had to clean up after him. The baby wasn't really wailing, her crying was more in the nature of a complaint. Lucy decided to wait a bit and see if she'd go to sleep, so she opened the refrigerator and pulled out the salad greens.

Even after she'd made the salad, and boiled the water for the macaroni, Zoe was still crying.

"Elizabeth, could you get the baby? I'm making supper."

"Do I have to?"

"Yes. You can sit in the rocking chair with her."

"What if she throws up on me?"

"Then we'll clean you up. Do you want to eat tonight? I can cook, or I can rock the baby."

"I have to do everything around here," Elizabeth complained, mounting the stairs.

"Right," said Lucy, mixing up the cheesy sauce. "She has to do everything."

"Mom, the baby feels hot," Elizabeth said, when she returned to the kitchen with the baby.

"She's been crying," said Lucy, bending down to kiss Zoe's forehead. "Maybe she has a little fever."

"What if she's sick?"

"I'll get a cool washcloth. You can wipe her face, see if she cools down."

All through supper, which they ate in front of the TV as a special treat, Lucy laughed along with the kids at a silly sitcom rerun and refused to admit how worried she was about the baby. Zoe wasn't interested in nursing and only stopped wailing when Lucy held her against her shoulder. Finally, Lucy gave her a tiny dose of fever medicine, and she drifted off to sleep.

Returning to the kitchen, Lucy loaded the dishwasher and wiped off the counter. Then, deciding she still had a tiny bit of energy left, she mixed up another two dozen cupcakes and set them in the oven. While they baked, she thought about calling the doctor.

No point, she decided, at this hour she would only get the answering service. Zoe probably had a little cold, nothing to worry about. She was well-nourished, well-hydrated, full of maternal antibodies. If she wasn't better tomorrow morning, Lucy decided, she'd call the doctor then.

* * *

By the time Lucy got the older kids settled down, and had changed into her nightclothes herself, it was ten o'clock. Zoe kept waking and fussing, nursing a bit and spitting up. Lucy tried bathing her to bring down the fever, but Zoe cried so much she abandoned the idea. Dressing her only in a diaper and shirt and wrapping her in a light receiving blanket, Lucy held her against her shoulder, and sat in the rocking chair. Rocking was the only thing that seemed to soothe the baby, which meant going to bed was out of the question.

Lucy rocked back and forth. She listened to the dishwasher go through its cycle. She listened to the hum of the refrigerator. She heard the click of the thermostat, and the whoosh of the furnace. She closed her eyes and told herself that resting was almost the same as sleeping.

A second later the phone rang.

Startled, she jumped to her feet, clutching the baby. She picked up the receiver.

"Hello," she said, expecting to hear Bill's voice.

She didn't hear anything, just the sound of someone breathing. That was followed by a hoarse, male voice. "You can't stop me."

Then, far away in the distance, she heard the fire horn, and the wail of sirens.

CHAPTER TWENTY

Had he made a fool of himself? Driving back home the next afternoon, Bill wasn't sure. This consultant stuff was harder than he had expected. He hoped the Shelburne Village people weren't disappointed in him.

He'd done his best. The door was atypical. Quite unique. He'd never seen anything like it. Some features were eighteenth century, others nineteenth. Faced with the curator's puzzled expression, he'd finally ventured a guess that it was made in the nineteenth century by a very old craftsman using his father's tools.

It wasn't that far-fetched, he told himself. Even today, in remote pockets of New England, there were people repairing chairs and building stone walls and making baskets just the way their parents or grandparents had taught them.

Turning onto Main Street, he sighed. No use crying over spilt milk. What was done was done. Either they were impressed with his honesty and frankness, or they figured he was a fool. In the big scheme of things it hardly mattered. He had plenty of work to keep him busy and put food on the family table.

Slowing for a traffic tie-up, Bill was surprised to see a

cop directing traffic. Given the time of year, Tinker's Cove only had traffic problems in the summer, this was unusual. Curious, he pulled over and got out of his truck. He had only gone a few feet down Main Street when he saw the blackened remains of Doug Durning's real estate office.

"What the hell," he said under his breath, joining the group of curious onlookers along the yellow tape.

"Our arsonist at work again," said Ted Stillings, returning his camera to its case.

"When did it happen?"

"Last night. It was some blaze. Chief called for mutual aid from companies as far away as Gilead and Wilton. Twelve engines, thirty-five firefighters, it was quite a show. Where were you?"

"I had business over in Vermont. I'm just getting back." Bill shook his head. "This is an awful shame. That was a nice old house."

"Yeah. Was is the operative word. Chief says it's a complete loss. There's Doug, now. Excuse me, I've got to get a statement."

Bill watched as Ted approached Doug, notebook in hand.

"I'm sorry to bother you at a time like this," he began. "I just wondered if you have anything to say for *The Pennysaver?*"

"I sure do," Doug began. "I'm mad as hell." His face was red and his gestures were choppy. Bill wondered if he'd been drinking; he wouldn't have blamed him if he had. "What's it gonna take? How many buildings have to burn before they catch this guy? Is he gonna burn the whole goddamn town down before they get him?"

Suddenly deflated, Doug paused for breath and staggered. Ted took him by the arm and steadied him.

"This was my life," he said, shaking his head. "I took some hits in the recession, but business was picking up. I was one of the survivors—I thought. Now it's all gone. I've lost everything."

"Was the building insured?" asked Ted, scribbling away.

"Yeah, but not enough. Not near enough. I'd cut back, trying to save money."

"That's too bad," said Ted, momentarily at a loss for words. He always found it hard not to identify with the people he interviewed, and this cut close to the bone. He could put himself in Doug's place all too easily, and knew how devastated he'd be if the Pennysaver Press burned. "Hang in there, man," he said, giving Doug a pat on the shoulder.

Standing a few feet away, Bill also sympathized with Doug.

"I'm sorry," he said, stepping up and clasping his hand. "Anything I can do?"

Doug stared hollowly at the burned-out building that had been his livelihood, and gestured emptily with his hands. Blinking furiously, he turned away and headed down the street. Bill watched him go, then climbed in his truck.

It was time to go home.

When he pulled into his own driveway, however, he was surprised to see a police cruiser parked by the back door. Hurrying into the kitchen he was relieved to see it was only Barney, sitting at the kitchen table with a mug of coffee.

"Hi," he said, pouring himself a cup, giving Lucy a peck on the cheek, and joining them at the table. "Guess you guys were busy last night, huh?"

"You could say that," agreed Barney.

"I saw Doug. He's taking it pretty hard."

"I was just there the other day. I was thinking what a nice old place it is . . . was," said Lucy.

"I gotta finish this report, Lucy," Barney said, reluctantly drawing her attention to the form on the table in front of him.

"There isn't much to tell," Lucy began. "The phone rang around ten. I picked it up. There was a breathing sound, then someone said, 'You can't stop me.' Then I heard the sirens."

"When was this?" demanded Bill.

"Last night."

"Are you telling me the arsonist called here?" demanded Bill, looking at Barney.

"We don't know who called," admitted Barney. "The timing could have been a coincidence."

Bill turned to face Lucy. "How come you didn't call the police right away? Why'd you wait til now?"

"Calm down," she said. "I called first thing this morning and Barney got here as soon as he could. I thought about calling last night, but I could hear the fire horn and I knew everybody'd be busy. It wasn't an emergency—it was just a phone call. A scary phone call. I figured it was a Halloween prank, like the paint on the car. Actually, I was more worried about the baby."

"What's the matter with the baby?"

"Ear infection. I took her to the doctor this morning. She'll be fine."

"I hate this," said Bill, fingering his coffee mug. "I go away for one night and all hell breaks loose."

"Not quite," said Lucy, patting his hand.

"What did he say? It was a man?"

"Definitely a man. He said, 'You can't stop me.'"

"Have you made any enemies lately?" asked Barney. "Had an argument with someone, made anybody angry?"

"It's the commission," said Bill, smacking his forehead with his hand. "I never should've agreed to join that thing. Doug's a member, and look what happened to him. All you do is make people mad. The couple with the green house, Andy Brown, Lenk—any one of them could be pissed off at me."

"Not the couple," said Lucy.

"Right. I voted for them."

"People do take this stuff more seriously than I thought," said Lucy, thinking of the free pumpkin Andy Brown had offered her.

"Sure they do," said Bill. "That commission is powerful.

If I had to paint my house all over again, I might make an anonymous phone call or two myself. Maybe I'd even be mad enough to set a fire."

"Hold your horses, Bill. You're kinda jumping to conclusions, here. We don't know who made the call," said Barney. "Most likely Lucy's right and it's a Halloween trick."

"Arson and anonymous phone calls kind of go together," said Lucy, thinking of the description of the typical arsonist in the psychology book. She had been so sure that Krissy and Dr. Mayes were responsible for the fires, now she wasn't so certain. Maybe there was a pyromaniac loose in Tinker's Cove.

Or, maybe that's exactly what Krissy and Dr. Mayes hoped everyone would think. Maybe this fire was carefully planned to divert attention away from Monica and bolster the theory that she was truly a hapless victim who was just in the wrong place at the wrong time.

Or, thought Lucy, her mind racing, maybe the fire was supposed to send a message to Doug. Did he know something he shouldn't? Had he stumbled on some bit of evidence? Did they need to get him out of the way, too? Lucy's heart skipped a beat. What if they knew she suspected them and had been asking questions? Would they come after her next?

"Are you okay?" Bill asked, interrupting her thought. "You're awfully quiet."

"You look kinda pale, Lucy." Barney furrowed his brow in concern, looking a bit like a huge St. Bernard.

"Maybe this is more serious than I thought," Lucy admitted. "The paint, the phone call—maybe somebody is trying to warn me off."

"What do you mean, Lucy?" Bill asked. "Warn you off what?"

Lucy held her breath, waiting for Bill to draw the inevitable conclusion.

"Have you been investigating these fires?" Bill looked her right in the eye.

Lucy looked at the salt and pepper shakers on the table. "Not really."

"What does 'not really' mean?"

"I think . . . I thought it might have been Dr. Mayes, especially after I learned about him and Krissy. I was asking some questions around the gym."

"I wish you'd mind your own business, Lucy," said Bill.

"You should leave this investigation to the police," advised Barney.

United in agreement, Bill and Barney sat back and lifted their coffee mugs.

"What about those Patriots?" began Bill.

"I think I hear the baby," said Lucy, glad to escape the male chauvinists in the kitchen. But as she tended to the baby one fact became very clear to her. If the arsonist was threatening her there was only one thing she could do. She had to catch him before he had a chance to hurt her, or her family.

As much as she liked Barney, she had to admit he didn't exactly inspire confidence in the investigative abilities of the Tinker's Cove Police Department. It was time to consult an expert. Fortunately, she had made the acquaintance of a state police detective a few years ago when she was working for the Country Cousins catalog store and found the body of the owner, Sam Miller, in the parking lot. She decided to give Detective Horowitz a call.

CHAPTER TWENTY-ONE

Glancing around the kitchen the next afternoon, Lucy wondered how things had degenerated so fast. The sink and counter were littered with dirty dishes, the garbage bin was overflowing, the tablecloth was stained and full of crumbs. Was it just a few days ago that she had been congratulating herself on managing so well?

It was the cupcakes, she decided. Twelve dozen cupcakes was the straw that broke the camel's back. If it wasn't for the damned cupcakes, she told herself as she reached for a bowl and box of cake mix, she would have time for everything else. At least she had reached the halfway mark—when these were done she would only have six dozen to go. Six dozen, three more days until Halloween, that was two dozen a day. No problem. The trick, of course, was to keep the kids from finding them. That's why she had to get this batch baked, cooled, iced, and hidden on the top shelf of the pantry before the school bus arrived. It was one o'clock—she had almost two hours, plenty of time as long as Zoe didn't wake up early from her nap.

Hearing the crunch of tires on the gravel driveway, Lucy went to the window to see who it was. Seeing the familiar unmarked blue Ford, Lucy smiled. Detective Horowitz was as good as his word.

"Hi," she said, opening the door for him. "It's good to see you—it's been a while."

"That's right, Mrs. Stone." Horowitz was a serious, formal man with a long face and rabbit lips. He always looked tired.

"Can I get you some coffee?"

"No, thanks. If I have too much I can't sleep at night." He pulled out a chair to sit down, and picked up the large sneaker that was resting on it.

Lucy took it from him, and tossed it in the corner next to its mate. "Toby—he's eleven."

"Big feet," he said, sitting down heavily.

"You detectives are so observant." Lucy took a seat at the table opposite him.

"It's our job, ma'am," said Horowitz, with the slightest hint of a smile. "So what seems to be the trouble?"

"You know about the fires? Are you working on them?"

"Not directly, but I'm familiar with the case."

"Well, I'm worried someone may be threatening me—but maybe it's just Halloween. There was paint on my car, I got a phone call, and I found this in my mailbox this morning." She slipped a small piece of paper across the table.

Horowitz looked down at it, but didn't touch it. It was a piece of cheap, lined notepaper crudely ripped from a spiral pad. Little square bits of paper clung to the top, and the right corner was missing. A black marker pen had been used to write the brief message in childish block letters: MIND YOUR OWN BIZNESS OR BURN.

"Have you been investigating the fires?" he asked, raising his pale eyes to meet hers.

"A little bit here and there—I don't have much time. I have a new baby, you know." Lucy stood up. "Do you mind if I do some cooking? I have to bake some cupcakes for a Halloween party."

"Not at all." Horowitz studied the note. "What are your thoughts on the fires, Mrs. Stone?"

"I'm no expert," began Lucy, switching on the oven and setting paper liners in the cupcake pans. "I don't know anything about accelerants or stuff like that, but I can't help thinking Dr. Mayes had an awful lot to gain from burning down the Homestead." Lucy paused and began ripping open the box of cake mix.

"Go on."

"He got rid of his wife, no divorce, no alimony, and he'll get a big insurance settlement. You know about the girlfriend, right?"

Horowitz nodded.

"So you agree with me? He is a suspect then?"

"Was. He couldn't have done it."

"What about Krissy? They're more than lovers, you know. He owns part of her business."

Horowitz looked interested, in spite of himself.

"You didn't know that, did you?" crowed Lucy.

"I told you, I'm not directly involved in this case. But I hadn't heard that. Are you sure?"

"Yup." Lucy cracked an egg on the side of the bowl. "She told me herself. I joined the gym, you know, to get back in shape after the baby." She switched on the mixer.

"I'll pass it along," promised Horowitz. "Mind if I take the note?"

"Please. I'll be glad to get rid of it."

"Did you handle it much?" he asked, slipping it carefully into a plastic bag.

"Probably. It was under the mail. I flipped through the letters and stuff before I even found it."

"I don't think this note is connected with the fires," said Horowitz.

"Why do you say that?" asked Lucy carefully, pouring the batter into the cupcake pans. Then she slid the pans into the oven.

"The only reason I'm telling you this is because I don't want you to worry. They're very close to making an arrest in this case. I'm no expert in accelerants either, but they tell me that the same accelerant was used in every fire. They're all the work of the same individual, they know that because he has certain signature behaviors. He doesn't write notes." Horowitz took a packet of photographs from his pocket. "These are between you and me and nobody else, okay?"

Lucy nodded eagerly and leaned across the table.

"Fire one, the theater." He spread out three or four photos.

Lucy was shocked and fascinated by what she saw. A row of red plush theater seats with blackened, burned centers. A cot in a dressing room, covered by a neat plaid spread. Only the center was burned. The stage, completely ruined by flames.

"You can see how he splashed accelerant around, but not enough to do the job. Real amateur. He did better with the barn."

Horowitz handed her another photograph. This one showed the one remaining corner of the barn, the wood blistered and scarred by the fire.

"This time he used enough accelerant. The conditions were in his favor. The wood was old and dry, there hadn't been rain for a couple of weeks. The barn was a total loss. Not the powder house. It was barely touched," he said, passing her another photo. "Too public, he probably got scared away. Then the Homestead, and Durning's place." He flipped down the photos as if he were dealing cards. "He's hit his stride. He knows what he's doing. Complete losses, both of them. He probably thinks there wasn't any evidence left, but there was. A lot of evidence. The lab guys are real happy with this one. I wouldn't worry if I were you. This guy doesn't write notes or make phone calls or anything like that. All he cares about is making a nice, big fire."

"This is creepy," said Lucy, gathering up the pictures and handing them back to Horowitz. "He's crazy."

"A sick puppy. But he's not Dr. Mayes, and he's not Dr. Mayes's girlfriend whatever her name is, and he's probably not even aware of your existence so don't worry anymore, okay?"

"Okay," said Lucy, opening the door for him.

"On the other hand, I wouldn't dismiss this note," he said, patting his pocket. "It's pretty good advice, if you ask me. Leave the investigating to the experts, Mrs. Stone." He paused and sniffed, wrinkling his nose. "Do I smell something burning?"

"The cupcakes!" cried Lucy, dashing for the oven.

CHAPTER TWENTY-TWO

"What happened to you?"

Slipping into a seat beside Sue at the TCHDC hearing Thursday evening, Lucy couldn't help noticing the Band-Aids on her fingers.

"I'm a victim of Corney Clarke."

"Corney Clarke did that to you?"

"Not directly. I did it to myself. I was overambitious. I reached for the stars. I wasn't happy to have a regular orange jack-o'-lantern like everybody else. Oh no. I had to have a white pumpkin, artistically carved to look like lace."

"It was tougher than you thought."

"I'll say. The damn thing was like cement. I used Sid's woodcarving tools, but I couldn't make a dent in it. I sure made a mess of my hands, though."

"That's terrible," said Lucy, unable to control her laughter as she pictured Sue hacking away at the little white pumpkin.

"It's not funny," Sue sniffed indignantly. "I could've bled to death or lost a finger."

"I'm sorry," Lucy said, adopting a serious tone. "I guess the spirit of your gourd wasn't ready to be released yet."

"You could say that gourd was not afraid to defend itself," Sue said. "It was one spirited squash. But I got it in the end."

"You did?"

"I ran over it."

"With the car?" Lucy asked incredulously.

Sue nodded her head proudly. "Yup."

"Didn't that make an awful mess?"

"Sure did. I'm not proud of it, but I did it. I squashed that squash."

"The hearing will now come to order," announced Miss Tilley with a bang of her gavel.

Silence was not immediate. The hearing room was packed and it took a while for everyone to quiet down. In addition to Ted, the cable TV station had sent a crew, and several local radio station reporters were also present. Such extensive coverage wasn't really necessary; it seemed that everyone who was interested was already there.

"This is a public hearing on the application of Randolph Lenk for a certificate of appropriateness for alterations to an existing structure in the Tinker's Cove Historic District. Mr. Lenk, I understand you have legal representation tonight?"

"Whuh," said Lenk, arching an eyebrow. He hadn't gone to any trouble for the hearing. He was dressed in his usual grimy work clothes, and had a two-day stubble of beard.

"I am representing Mr. Lenk," volunteered a tall young man dressed in a pinstripe suit. "I am Fred Carruthers from the legal department at Northstar. I would also like to introduce Dave Anderson, vice president in charge of development, New England, Stan Lepke, head of our design department, and Cindy Josephs, from our public relations department."

The three didn't need to stand. Their sober business suits and professional demeanor set them apart from everyone else in the room. Cindy smiled brightly, but it was clear that she was a strange fish in these waters, with her crisp navy suit, pantyhose, heels, and perfectly coiffed hair.

"Can you imagine dressing like that?" whispered Lucy, crossing her blue jean–clad legs.

"Only for a funeral," answered Sue, slipping out of her barn jacket.

"I understand you have a presentation," Miss Tilley said, once again banging her gavel for order.

"That's right," Carruthers answered. "First, we have a brief history on the development of the concept. Dave Anderson will handle that."

"If I may," said Mr. Anderson, stepping forward. He shifted his shoulders in his navy jacket, and smoothed his red print tie.

"The design we are proposing for Mr. Lenk's station was developed in response to several factors." He walked over to an easel set to one side and pointed to an architect's drawing of a futuristic gas station.

"First, we must meet federal and state safety requirements. This is not voluntary. We must have a vapor recovery system and a fire suppression system." He waved a laser pointer in the direction of the canopy.

"Second, as a business, we are interested in responding to the expressed needs and demands of our customers. Consumer polls tell us that our customers want self-service pumps that accept charge cards. They want to get their gas and get back on the road as fast as they can." He pointed to the gas pump.

"Convenience is important to our consumers. They appreciate being able to pick up cigarettes, a gallon of milk, a cup of coffee, when they get gas. So, we've added convenience markets to our stations to meet that need.

"We have also added complimentary car washes. This is a feature consumers really appreciate—a free car wash with a purchase of eight or more gallons. This is especially popular in northern areas like yours. I don't have to tell you the damage road salt can do to the finish on your cars and trucks.

"I'm giving you this background so you'll understand

some of the factors that led to the development of this particular design. Now, I'm going to turn things over to Stan."

Stan Lepke stood up and approached the easel. He was a few inches shorter than Dave Anderson, his hair a few shades lighter. He, too, shifted his shoulders in his dark gray jacket and smoothed his red print tie.

"This design," he began, indicating the easel, "is something Northstar is very proud of. We believe it combines form and function in the best tradition of modern design, meets all safety regulations, and is appealing and attractive to customers.

"Furthermore, we have adapted this design to complement the architectural styles of the various regions of our great country."

He flipped a page. "In the Southwest we use simulated stucco."

He turned the page. "In the Pacific Northwest, notice the totem pole theme.

"On the next illustration, we show the barn theme used in the Midwest. In the South, these one hundred percent vinyl pillars are reminiscent of the great plantations. And here in the Northeast, you'll notice I've saved the best for last, our simulated clapboard and cedar shingles are almost indistinguishable from the real thing."

"Why don't you use the real thing?" came a voice from the audience. There was a murmur of agreement from the crowd.

"Order," said Miss Tilley, banging down her gavel. "We will take questions from the floor later. Right now, if you are done, Mr. Lepke, I think the board has some questions for you."

"Fine," said Mr. Lepke. "I may not have all the answers but I'll do my best."

"I have a question," said Bill. "I think the man in the audience had a valid point. Why don't you use real clapboard and cedar shingles?"

"Maintenance," answered Mr. Lepke. "Gas stations are dirty, it's a dirty business. Car exhaust, road dirt, you know what I'm talking about. These simulated materials can be washed and hosed down."

"Why does the station need to be so large?" asked Miss Tilley. "Mr. Lenk's present station is often empty, and he has two pumps. Why do you need to add six more?"

"I'll pass that question on to Mr. Anderson," said Mr. Lepke.

"That is a good question," began Mr. Anderson. "It comes to me because as vice-president responsible for development, it has fallen to my division to implement our corporation's strategic plan for right-sizing. To boil down this rather complicated effort to maximize profit and improve service, we are reducing the number of service sites in this particular facet of the corporate structure." He blinked furiously as he ended his spiel.

"If I understand you correctly," said Hancock Smith, a retired corporate vice-president himself, "Northstar is closing a number of stations, hoping to redirect business to a smaller number of better-equipped stations?"

"That's right." Mr. Anderson swallowed hard, and smoothed his tie.

"So Mr. Lenk's station has been chosen for improvements, while other Northstar stations in surrounding towns will be closed?"

"Right, again." Mr. Anderson nodded his agreement.

"That will mean increased traffic," observed Miss Tilley.

"Increased traffic is not necessarily bad," observed Jock Mulligan. "It could bring more people to the other businesses in town. People have to come to get gas, so they also do their grocery shopping or banking. However, I do have r-real r-r-reservations about this design. It's absolutely atrocious."

"I tend to agree," said Bill. "This is an historic area, and this design looks like a misplaced space station."

"I think we've heard from everyone except Mr. Durning," said Miss Tilley. "Do you have anything to add, Doug?"

Doug, who had been listlessly shuffling through his packet of papers throughout the meeting, shook his head.

"I will now open this up to the floor," said Miss Tilley. "The chair recognizes Fred Tibbett."

Fred, a gray-haired man dressed in the Tinker's Cove uniform of khaki pants, plaid flannel shirt, and windbreaker, stood up.

"Goes to reason," he said, "if you fellas are investin' a whole lotta money in this here station, you'll wanna get some kind o' return. Does that mean you'll be raisin' the price of gas?"

"I guess that question is for me," said Cindy Josephs, jumping to her feet. She shifted her shoulders inside her neat navy jacket and tossed her blond hair.

"The price of Northstar gas is figured based on a number of factors that include our costs, taxes, the price our competitors are charging, and what we call the value factor. That is, what consumers are willing to pay for our particular gasoline. Have I made myself clear?"

"Nope," said Fred.

"What she's trying to say, or trying not to say, is that if they think they can get more, they'll charge more," said Hancock Smith, much to the amusement of the crowd. Cindy shrugged and sat down.

"The chair recognizes Dotty Cooper," said Miss Tilley.

Mrs. Cooper, a gray-haired woman dressed in wool slacks and a sweater, stood up.

"As most of you know, I live opposite Mr. Lenk's station. I have no problem with the station as it is now. It's a quiet little country gas station. I get gas there myself. Mr. Lenk is open from seven or so in the morning until six in the evening, he's not open at night. If my guess is right, this thing will be brightly lit twenty-four hours a day and all sorts of people will be coming at all hours of the day and night. I really object to it. I think it would have a negative effect on the neighborhood."

"Very well said, Dotty. You can be sure the board will take your comments very seriously." Miss Tilley nodded her head and banged down her gavel. "Joe Marzetti."

"You all know me," began Joe, the owner of the local IGA. "For more years than I like to count I've been doing my best to provide good food at good prices. I'm the only grocery store in Tinker's Cove—if I went out of business you'd have to go quite some ways to the superstore. I'm telling you, I'm not getting rich at this. There's not a heck of a lot of business in this town, especially in the winter. What I don't need is a gas station cutting into my milk and bread business—I think Northstar should stick to selling gas."

Miss Tilley nodded and recognized Jonathan Franke, executive director of APTC—the Association for the Preservation of Tinker's Cove.

"I see a lot of APTC members here tonight," began Franke. He had recently trimmed the wild beard and long hair that had been his signature in favor of a more conservative, professional look. "In the past few years I think there's been a recognition that the environment is the basis of our economy here. Let's face it, people are not going to come and vacation here if the water is polluted and the trees are all dead. My concern about the Northstar plan is the proposed car wash. If a car wash is to be included, we have to make sure that the water is recycled, and that any runoff is contained and treated appropriately before it is allowed to return to the aquifer. This water could be a real toxic brew."

"I would like to answer that," said Mr. Carruthers, rising to his feet. "You can be sure that Northstar will comply with all EPA regulations. We are as concerned about the environment as you are—we all share the same planet."

"Then why does your company routinely use single-hulled tankers?" demanded Franke. "What about the North

Sea oil spill? You had no part in that? You're still fighting for reduced damages in court!"

The gavel came down. "Thank you, Mr. Franke. You can be sure we all appreciate your efforts on our behalf," said Miss Tilley.

"Are there any more questions?" She scanned the audience, apparently failing to see a number of raised hands. "Since there are no more questions, I would like to suggest a course of action for this commission. I propose we continue this hearing at a later date. Furthermore, I suggest Northstar withdraw their application without prejudice, and come back with a more appropriate plan. Is everyone agreed?"

Seeing no disagreement, Miss Tilley continued, shaking a bony finger at the corporate executives. "It's obvious this plan simply will not do. Not in Tinker's Cove. I suggest you gentlefolk go back to the drawing board. Surely a company with your resources can come up with something simple, unobtrusive, and tasteful. Here in New England, we are proud of our heritage. We value the buildings constructed by our ancestors, we still hold the same values they did. We have a sense of place. We don't want to look like New Jersey, do we?"

"Hey, what's this mean? You tellin' me I can't fix up my station?" Randy Lenk was on his feet, gesturing angrily with his fists.

"Mr. Lenk, I have explained this to you before. Your station is in the historic district. You can make alterations, but they must be approved beforehand by the historic commission—that is this board. If your proposal is approved by this group of five people you see sitting here tonight, then you can go ahead." Miss Tilley spoke clearly and slowly, as if to a first grader who insisted on talking in the library.

"Has it been approved?" asked Lenk.

"No, it hasn't."

"Well, take a vote right now. I want it approved."

"We understand that. However, Mr. Lenk, the proposal we saw tonight does not stand the least chance of being approved by this board. You have heard the expression about an ice cube in hell? This proposal has less chance than that. However, we are allowing you to withdraw this proposal without prejudice, and come back with a new one. We're doing you a very big favor."

"You're not doing me any favor," he shouted angrily. "Who do you think you are? I can do what I want with my land. You can't stop me. It's mine. I can do whatever I damn well please with it. Ain't that right?"

Lucy jerked to attention. What was that Lenk had said? *You can't stop me.*

Miss Tilley banged down her gavel. "Do I hear a motion to adjourn?"

Wasn't that what the anonymous phone caller had said? While the board went through the business of voting to adjourn, Lucy studied Randolph Lenk. Was he the one who made the phone call?

She grimaced with distaste as he ran his black, grimy fingers through his greasy hair and shook his fist at the board members. "It's my property," he yelled, revealing uneven broken teeth. "I can do what I want!"

"Meeting adjourned," announced Miss Tilley, pointedly ignoring him and banging down the gavel.

CHAPTER TWENTY-THREE

Driving home after the meeting, Lucy turned to Bill. "I think Randy Lenk made that anonymous phone call."

"I think so, too. Seems he called the other commission members. Said the same thing to everyone. 'You can't stop me.'"

Lucy shook her head. "What a weird thing to do."

"He's a pretty weird guy. You know that ugly sandpit on Bumps River Road."

"Mmm."

"That's his. It didn't used to be a pit like that. It was a nice piece of woods. He cut all the trees and stripped off the soil."

"Why would he do that?"

"Sold the timber and the top soil. Made a pretty penny, I guess. But he made the town so mad they passed a tree-cutting bylaw at the next town meeting. Now you have to get a permit from the conservation commission before you can clear-cut your property."

"That's good," Lucy said, nodding.

"Most people think so. But not Lenk. He was so mad he went out to another piece of land he owns—his family's been around forever and he's got a lot of land—and he ringed all the trees so they'd die. You've seen it, that sick-looking woods behind the dump."

"I thought it was toxic runoff from the dump or something."

"Nope. Lenk, making a point."

"Seems kind of crazy to me," Lucy said.

"Miss Tilley says it runs in the family," explained Bill. "According to her, his father was a pervert who got sent to jail and got himself killed. Apparently he set his bedding on fire as some sort of protest but nobody noticed until it was too late and he died. She said he died of stupidity."

"That's awful," Lucy said, wrapping her arms across her chest.

"Miss T. said it was the nicest thing he could have done for his family."

"She would." Lucy chuckled. "I wonder if he was a mental masturbator."

"You don't get sent to jail for crimes of the mind," said Bill, turning into the driveway and braking. He reached over and took Lucy's hand. "What did you think of your husband, the commissioner?"

"I thought you looked very handsome and important." Lucy squeezed his hand. "I was proud of you."

"I saw you, sitting next to Sue."

"Oh, yeah?" Lucy tilted her head. "What did you think?"

"I thought you looked pretty cute." He bent down and kissed her.

When they went into the house a few minutes later, they found Jennifer sitting in the rocking chair with Zoe sound asleep in her arms.

"How did everything go?" asked Lucy.

"Fine. She took a little bit of the milk you left, but she didn't seem very hungry."

"She's still not quite herself. Did you give her the medicine?"

"Yup. Went down with no problem."

"You're amazing, Jennifer. It's wonderful to be able to go out for an evening and know the kids are in such capable hands."

"I love kids, especially babies," she said, carefully passing Zoe over to her mother.

"Can you sit for us a week from Saturday? I'll call with the details," asked Lucy, handing her a ten-dollar bill.

"Sure. I'll look forward to it," said Jennifer, bouncing out the door.

"Isn't she cute?" Lucy asked Bill. "She just got her driver's license—she's got a little car of her own. Wouldn't it be great to be sixteen again?"

"I remember my first car. It was a big old Dodge Dart. Gosh I had good times in that thing, until I hit an icy patch and slid into a light pole. I thought my father was going to kill me." He paused, and put down a stack of papers next to his chair. "There's something I want to check in the bylaws. I'll be up in a minute."

"Okay," said Lucy, taking the baby upstairs and gently placing her in her bassinet. Thoughtfully, she stroked Zoe's soft, fuzzy head with her index finger. She traced the roundness of her baby's head, and her cheek; she sniffed the sweet baby smell.

We all start out the same, she thought, how does a perfect little baby turn into a pathetic specimen like Randy Lenk? Once upon a time he must have been a lovely little baby. Though with a father like that, he certainly didn't get off to a very good start.

A pervert. Trust Miss Tilley to use a horrible word like that. An old-fashioned word. Today he'd be what? A child molester. An abusive parent. Lucy shuddered.

Suddenly, she wondered if Lenk could be the arsonist. Didn't he fit the profile in the psychology book? According to the learned author, arsonists frequently had difficulty accepting authority. They were often survivors of childhood sexual abuse. They also indulged in other antisocial behaviors, such as making anonymous telephone calls and writing hate letters. And even if he didn't have a justification for his behavior in the beginning, he certainly did now. He could have burned Doug's place as a warning to the other members of the historic commission.

Now that she thought about it, it seemed unlikely that Dr. Mayes was responsible for the fire at Doug's place. Having already achieved his objective, it would have been foolish and risky. Maybe Krissy did it, she thought, remembering how angry she had been with Dr. Mayes. Setting another fire would let him know that he couldn't control her, that she was dangerous when she didn't get what she wanted.

Lucy rubbed her temples. No doubt about it, she was getting a headache. She had been so sure that Dr. Mayes had set the fires but now she had her doubts. Instead of becoming clearer, this situation was getting murkier by the minute. She headed for the bathroom, thinking of a commercial for a painkiller she had seen on TV. "Yes," she said out loud to herself as she opened the medicine cabinet and reached for the familiar bottle, "I do get really tough headaches."

CHAPTER TWENTY-FOUR

The next morning, as soon as she had the house to herself, she picked up the phone and dialed. While it rang, she looked out the window at the red and yellow trees bordering the yard. She loved the way the garden looked in the fall, a bit tousled and blowsy, the sharp edges of summer blurred by frost. Brown leaves blew this way and that, the flowering annuals that had been so green and bright a few months ago now sprawled black and exhausted in their beds. She really needed to get out there with a rake and tidy up.

"Barney? I had an idea."

A low groan came through the receiver.

"Don't be like that. I think I may be on to something."

"Okay, shoot."

"Well, I think Randy Lenk might be the arsonist."

"Congratulations. You and everybody else."

"He was already a suspect?" Lucy was disappointed.

"You could say that. A prime suspect. Suspect number one."

"Well, how come he hasn't been arrested?" Lucy pulled a chair out from under the kitchen table and sat down, leaning her elbows on the table.

"He's been brought in for questioning, but we always had to let him go."

"Why?"

"Not enough evidence."

"Can't you stake him out or something?"

"We've been watching him, but somehow he always manages to slip away."

"That doesn't say much for the Tinker's Cove P.D.," Lucy teased, sliding down in the chair. "He's supposed to be real dumb."

"Dumb like a fox. It's like a game with him. He knows he's being watched, y'see. So he sets up little decoys and distractions. Took the boys a while to figure out he's got his lights on a timer. It looks for all the world like he's watching TV, then the downstairs lights go out and the bedroom light goes on for about fifteen minutes. Then it goes off. We thought he was sound asleep in bed till an off-duty cop spotted him at the pool hall in Gilead. And I'll tell you somethin', Lucy. The more I know about this guy, the creepier he gets."

"Really?" Lucy sat up straighter.

"Yeah. We tried searching his house, but it was pretty near impossible. He's got stuff piled up all around, and little pathways in between to get from room to room. He could have anything in there, buried under the boxes of newspapers and crap.

"And the kitchen. Lucy, I thought I'd seen dirty, but I was wrong. His was the worst I've ever seen." Barney's disgust came through the telephone line. "Except for his bathroom. I'm not sure he doesn't wash engines in his bathtub. Or keep pigs there. Gives the word filth new meaning."

"Couldn't the board of health condemn it or something?"

"Turned out they couldn't. DA said the ACLU'd be on it faster'n a tick on a dog. Individual rights, or some nonsense or other."

"Oh. What about Monica's rights?" Lucy was indignant. "The rights of the people whose property he burned?"

"I guess the ACLU doesn't care about them. Don't worry, Lucy. We're keepin' an eye on him. Sooner or later he'll screw up. Lab says he's using alcohol to start the fires and it's a piss-poor accelerant. If it hadn't been so dry lately, the buildings wouldn't even've burned. We'll get him. It's just a matter of time."

"I guess you're right. You know, Barney, every time I talk to you I get this nagging feeling that there's something I should tell you."

"About the kids?"

"No, that's not it. It'll come to me, but it's driving me crazy. I just haven't been the same since the baby. I keep forgetting things."

"I guess that's to be expected," said Barney indulgently. "You've got a lot on your mind. If you think of it, give me a call. Okay?"

"Yeah. Bye."

Lucy lifted the last sack of groceries from the cart and put it in the wayback, then slammed down the hatch. She returned the cart, then slipped Zoe out of the corduroy carrier and strapped her into the safety seat. Relieved to be unburdened, Zoe seemed to be gaining so fast, she slipped behind the wheel of the Subaru and turned the key in the ignition.

Checking the gas gauge, she decided to stop and fill the tank before going home. Lenk's Northstar, she remembered was just down the road.

Pulling into the rather ramshackle station, she wondered what the Northstar people saw in it. The paving was old and worn, the two pumps were dented, and the building needed paint. Of course, they planned to replace all that. But why this station? Did they really think Lenk would keep the new station up to their standards?

Not likely, she decided. Most probably they were using Lenk as a front man, while the project gathered the necessary permits and approvals. Local boards would find it harder to turn down one of their own, where they wouldn't hesitate to refuse a big corporation eager to cash in on the tourist economy. Once the project was approved, Lucy guessed, Northstar would buy out Randy Lenk. No wonder he got so mad at the hearing. He probably stood to gain a lot of money from this deal.

"Fill it up, please," said Lucy to the kid manning the pump. "Do you mind if I look around?" she asked, waving a hand at a pile of junk next to a shed. "I lost the cap to the tank on my snowblower. Maybe you've got one that'll do."

"Sure," said the kid with a shrug.

He looked up as Miss Tilley zoomed into the space on the other side of the pump, and rolled down the window of her huge Chrysler Imperial.

"Nice car," Lucy heard him say in an admiring voice as he went to wait on her.

She lifted Zoe out of the baby seat, and zipped her into the corduroy carrier she wore on her chest. Not quite sure what she hoped to find, Lucy began sifting through the pile. There were bits and pieces of all sorts of machinery, car parts, a snowplow, even a sewing machine. Just the sort of stuff that might come in handy, she thought wryly, especially if you were going to be very rich.

I wonder what he'll do with his money, she thought. Buy a big mansion and surround it with odds and ends in his best backwoods fashion. Maybe better grade car parts, she chuckled to herself. BMW hubcaps. Mercedes-Benz mufflers. Rhino guards from Range Rovers; also handy for moose.

Standing on tiptoe, she grasped the windowsill and tried to peek in. The window was filthy, and the sun was too bright. She couldn't make out a thing. The shed could be filled with cans of alcohol and she'd never know.

Why alcohol, when he had all this gas? she wondered. Why not? It was probably supposed to fool the cops. Just the sort of reasoning someone like Lenk would use.

"Whaddya think you're doin?"

Lucy jumped and wrapped her arms protectively around the baby. She turned slowly, reluctant to face Randy Lenk. His dirty hair fell into his eyes and he had a three-day stubble of beard. His teeth, she was appalled to see, really were green.

"What the hell do you think you're doin'?" he growled.

"By any chance," she said politely, "do you have a cap that would fit the gas tank of a Toro snowblower? I somehow lost mine."

"Nope." His voice was flat.

"Could I just take a peek in the shed?" persisted Lucy. "You've got so much stuff around here—I bet you've got something I could use. I'd be happy to pay for it."

Lenk narrowed his eyes and stepped closer. Lucy could smell his sour scent.

"If you know what's good for you, you'll get outta here," he snarled.

"Fine. No problem," said Lucy, stepping backward. Not too hasty, she told herself. Stay calm. Don't panic. Back to the car.

"How much do I owe you?" she asked the attendant once she reached her car.

"Ten," said the kid.

"Here you go. Thanks."

Lucy repeated the business of strapping Zoe into the car seat. Then she started the ignition and pulled up behind Miss Tilley, who was signaling to turn left.

That Chrysler certainly was some car, she thought, as she waited her turn to exit. Acres of solid black hood and trunk were trimmed with massive chrome grilles and heavy bumpers. There was no plastic on this baby. Everything was shining, gleaming metal. It was easily twice as big as her Subaru. What had Bill told her? It was the favorite model of demolition derby drivers.

"Those things are built like tanks," he'd said. "They just don't make 'em like that anymore."

Too bad, thought Lucy. That car had certainly given Miss Tilley good service. She'd had it forever. Of course, she had taken good care of it. There wasn't a speck of rust on it.

Sensing movement ahead, Lucy automatically flipped the signal stick, and shifted into first, ready to follow the Chrysler. Instead of accelerating gradually, however, Miss Tilley's Chrysler suddenly lurched ahead, apparently out of control.

Careening wildly into oncoming traffic, the huge black car smashed head on into a tiny red Toyota Tercel.

CHAPTER TWENTY-FIVE

The sickening thud of the collision was still echoing in Lucy's ears when she remembered what she had meant to tell Barney. She had wanted to discuss Miss Tilley's erratic driving, in hopes of avoiding an accident like the one she had just witnessed.

Fighting off shock and willing her wooden limbs to move, Lucy hurried up to Miss Tilley.

"Are you all right?" she demanded, yanking the door open.

"I seem to be," answered the old woman. Her voice was shaky and uncertain, and her eyes weren't quite focused.

Giving her hand, which was still clutching the steering wheel, a quick pat, Lucy rushed over to the red Tercel.

The damage was worse than she thought. The entire front hood had crumpled under the force of the impact, it was simply gone. The tiny naked wheels were askew; the windshield was smashed; the doors deeply dented.

"I can't get the door open," panted the gas station attendant. For the first time, Lucy noticed that the name embroidered on his shirt was Rob.

"Did somebody call rescue?"

"Yeah. The boss." He grunted, straining to wrestle the twisted metal open.

"I think they'll have to use the jaws of life or something," said Lucy. "Who's the driver?" Leaning forward she peered through the crackled side window.

"Oh, no." Her legs buckled under her in shock as she recognized the driver. She stumbled forward, catching herself on the tiny car. "That's Jennifer."

"Yeah. She don't look too good, either."

Jennifer was unconscious, her face cut and bleeding. But that wasn't what worried Lucy. With no airbag to protect her, Jennifer must have been thrown against the steering wheel, suffering internal injuries. The way the car folded in the crash, Lucy knew the weight of the engine would be crushing her legs and feet.

"When are they going to get here?" Lucy moaned, growing frantic at the delay.

"I hear a siren," said Rob.

Lenk appeared next to them, carrying a filthy old quilt. Lucy took it with shaking hands and went to help Miss Tilley out of her car.

"Help is on the way," said Lucy, swallowing hard to avoid sobbing. "Here, let me help you out of the car. We'll put this blanket around you and you can sit in my car."

Miss Tilley didn't respond, so Lucy took her elbow. Moving slowly and stiffly, she allowed Lucy to help her out of the big old Chrysler. As far as Lucy could see, except for a smashed headlight and a few dents, the car was undamaged.

"Who's in the other car?" asked Miss Tilley, as Lucy put the nasty quilt around her shoulders.

"Jennifer Mitchell."

"Is she all right?" Lucy felt Miss Tilley's hand tighten on her arm.

"I don't know. We can't get the door open."

Lucy got Miss Tilley settled in the passenger seat of the

Subaru, then climbed in behind the wheel. She wanted to move the car out of the way, to give the arriving rescue workers plenty of room to work. Her hands trembled as she turned the ignition key; she wanted to drive away as fast as she could.

She couldn't do that. She had witnessed the accident; she had Miss Tilley in her car. She was sure they would have to answer some questions. She shifted the car into reverse and parked in the corner of the gas station.

Realizing that Zoe was fussing in her car seat, Lucy got out of the car. She unfastened the straps holding the baby and lifted her up, pressing her tiny body against her chest. Holding Zoe against her shoulder, and patting her back, Lucy paced back and forth alongside the passenger side of the car.

"I hope she isn't hurt," said Miss Tilley.

Not much chance of that, thought Lucy, drawing Zoe closer. She was supposed to be consoling the baby, but instead, she was drawing strength from Zoe's regular breathing and sweet warmth. Instinctively rubbing her chin against Zoe's fuzzy head, she tried to reassure Miss Tilley.

"She's in good hands."

They watched as the rescuers went about their work. An ambulance and a fire engine were on the scene, police cruisers had arrived and officers were directing traffic away from the wreck. Rescue workers, dressed in fire hats, slickers, and boots went back and forth between the vehicles and their truck, getting supplies and equipment. Lucy heard the whine of power machinery, and the ever-present cackle of the radios.

A fireman was pumping white foam out onto the road, and Lucy belatedly realized there was a chance of the whole mess exploding and going up in flames.

"Oh, God, please let Jennifer be okay," she whispered, closing her eyes as tears rolled down her face. "Please, please, please."

"I just have a few questions I need to ask you," said a young officer, approaching her.

Lucy brushed away her tears, and focused hard on his nameplate. "Kirwan, T." it read. He must be one of Dot Kirwan's boys, she thought, placing him. Dot Kirwan was a cheerful, gossipy lady who cashiered at Marzetti's IGA—several of her children worked in the police and fire departments.

"Did you witness the accident?" he asked, producing an accident report form.

Lucy nodded.

"Miss Tilley was driving the Chrysler?"

"Yes."

"Can you tell me what you saw?"

"All of a sudden her car started moving—fast," remembered Lucy.

"Do you think the brakes failed?"

"She didn't brake," said Lucy, picturing the rear end of the car. "The brake lights never went on." Lucy sniffled. "Is Jennifer going to be okay?"

For a moment, the young officer's true emotions broke through his professional demeanor, and Lucy caught a glimpse of ragged grief. He quickly caught himself, his back straightened, and he answered in clipped tones.

"They're doing everything they can, but I don't want to mislead you. It doesn't look good."

Lucy swayed a bit, catching herself against the Subaru.

"Can I take Miss Tilley home? She's very old. I'm worried she'll go into shock."

"Sure," he said. "Someone'll be in touch with you later."

After she had returned Zoe to her car seat and was back in the driver's seat, she turned to face Miss Tilley.

"I'm going to take you home."

"We mustn't leave."

"The officer said we could. They'll follow up later."

"I want to make sure Jennifer is all right. I remember when she got her first library card. Such a bright little girl."

"They'll soon have her out of the car and off to the hospital," Lucy lied. "Everything's going to be okay."

"Don't patronize me," snapped Miss Tilley. "Anyone can see she must be severely hurt. We must stay and make sure she's properly cared for."

"Trust me, they're doing everything they can," Lucy said, with a sudden flash of temper. Miss Tilley had been bossing people around for too long, she decided, starting the car. "We're in the way here."

Miss Tilley put up no further opposition as Lucy drove her home. By the time they arrived at her little half-Cape house, Lucy was beginning to regret her outburst. The poor old woman was doubtlessly carrying a heavy burden of guilt and grief, as well as the shock of the accident.

When Lucy helped her out of the car she noticed that her wrists stuck out of her coat sleeves like sticks, and she stood unsteadily for a minute until Lucy took her arm and helped her up the walk. She was probably living on nothing but tea and toast, guessed Lucy, as she went back for Zoe.

Lucy soon had Miss Tilley installed in her usual armchair, snugly wrapped in a soft afghan. Folding Lenk's filthy quilt, Lucy set it outside on the back porch. Returning to the kitchen, she sniffed. The house smelled stale, something she had never noticed before.

She put the kettle on to boil and looked for something for lunch. As she had guessed, the kitchen was poorly stocked. The refrigerator contained nothing but a stick of butter, a tube of hemorrhoid ointment, a bottle of lemon juice, and a bag full of flashlight batteries.

Shrugging, she turned to investigate the pantry, but found little there except a few cans of soup and vegetables. Standing on the floor, however, were quite a few empty sherry bottles. There was one on the shelf, half full, and she helped herself to a swig. Feeling its warmth spread through her, she took another.

Lucy popped the last four slices of bread in the toaster and dumped a can of cream of mushroom soup in a saucepan. She stirred in a bit of milk, and added some canned asparagus.

When she took the plates and cups out of the cabinet, she noticed that although they were neatly stacked, they were not very clean. Was it failing eyesight, she wondered, or too much sherry?

Lucy quickly washed the dishes and made a tray for Miss Tilley. Perching opposite her, with a plate balanced on her knees, Lucy quickly devoured her meal. She hadn't realized how hungry she was, or how tired. The morning's events had sapped her energy.

Zoe, also, was ready for lunch. Lucy picked her up and settled back in the couch to nurse and sip her tea.

Miss Tilley, she observed, was only playing with her food.

"You should try to eat."

"It's the speed," said the old woman, shaking her head. "These young people drive too fast."

"What do you mean?"

"If that young woman hadn't been driving so fast, I would have seen her."

Lucy sputtered in her teacup. "Are you saying the accident was Jennifer's fault?"

"Of course. It couldn't be my fault. I've been driving for seventy years, and I've never had an accident. I have a perfect driving record."

"What about my mailbox?" Lucy reminded her. "You knocked it right over. And Franny Small? You nearly smashed into her last week."

"Franny is notoriously absentminded. She shouldn't be allowed to drive."

"And my mailbox? Did it leap in front of you?"

"Well, it is in an awkward location . . ."

"Nonsense. It's precisely where it's supposed to be. And it's high time you stopped blaming everybody and everything for your own mistakes. You're too old to drive."

As soon as the words were out Lucy regretted them. Miss Tilley looked as if she'd been slapped in the face.

"I am not too old to drive. My father drove until the day he died. He was ninety-four."

And he probably died in one hell of a crash, thought Lucy, propping Zoe on her shoulder and burping her.

"Everyone is different. Don't forget the roads are busier now." Lucy laid Zoe down on the couch and began to change her diaper. "I think you should consider giving up your license. If you don't, after what's happened, I'm afraid they'll suspend it."

"Even though the accident wasn't my fault?"

"Enough," said Lucy, firmly snapping the diaper cover in place. "I saw everything. The accident was definitely your fault."

Miss Tilley poked at a piece of toast with her fork. Honestly, thought Lucy, she was as stubborn as a two-year-old.

Miss Tilley looked up. "If I surrender my license, I'll lose my independence."

"You could ride the Senior Shuttle," said Lucy, referring to a van service provided by the local Senior Council.

"With all those doddering fools and half-wits? And you can't go when you want. You have to make an appointment."

"Take a taxi, then."

"Think of the expense! Not to mention having Billy Smits knowing all my business."

"It's time to face facts. You need some help. To be honest, it seems to me you're not doing such a great job of housekeeping."

"Too busy." She waved a large, bony hand.

Lucy sat Zoe in her lap and held her tiny chest with one hand while she gently patted her back with the other.

"The house is dirty, you're not eating properly, you need to make some changes."

"Hmmph," said Miss Tilley, looking right past her head and out the window. "Look at handsome Mr. Bluejay, at the bird feeder."

Lucy turned and saw a bit of blue plastic bread wrapper caught on a twig.

"That's not," she began, but seeing the rapt expression on her old friend's face, she paused. "He is a handsome fellow, isn't he?"

CHAPTER TWENTY-SIX

Ted was just wrapping up an interview with Don Swazey, the owner of an impressive matchbook collection, when his pager went off. Glancing at the number, he asked permission to use the phone.

"It's me," he said to Phyllis, the imperturbable woman who answered the phone, took the classified ads, maintained the subscription list, and proofread all the copy.

"Oh, Ted, I think you better get over to Lenk's gas station. The scanner's been going crazy. Sounds like a bad accident."

"Damn," said Ted, who hated covering accidents. "I'm on my way," he said, and replaced the receiver. "Mr. Swazey, I'm afraid I've got to go. Do you mind if I take your picture for the paper?"

"Not at all. How about if I hold this one? It's the jewel in the crown of my collection," he said, proudly displaying an aged matchbook printed with palm trees.

"Fine," said Ted, raising the camera. "Now, where's that one from?"

"The Coconut Grove nightclub in Boston."

"You don't say," said Ted, reaching for the proferred bit

of cardboard. Everybody knew about the tragic Coconut Grove fire; Ted had recently seen a piece about it in *New England Life* magazine, complete with photos of charred victims, still seated at their tables. The fire was thought to have started when some paper palm-frond decorations caught fire in the popular night spot that was packed with soldiers celebrating the end of World War II. The fire grew very quickly, consuming all the oxygen, so that those who hadn't burned to death had suffocated. Only a handful of the hundreds who packed the club that night had survived.

"I was one of the lucky ones," Mr. Swazey said.

"You were there the night of the fire?" Ted asked.

"Nope. The night before. We were going to go the night of the fire, but my date had to work. She was a nurse. So we moved it up. I proposed to her that night. Pretty lucky, hunh?"

"I'd say so," Ted agreed. "Thanks for the interview. I'm sorry I've got to run."

Fires, thought Ted. These days it always seemed to be fires. At least an auto accident would be a change, he thought, as he drove to the scene. A nice spectacular crash for page one. Something where the car was a total wreck, but the driver walked away without a scratch. That way he wouldn't have to call the grieving family for information about the deceased.

"Some life this is," he muttered, as the cop directing traffic away from the accident waved him through. Maybe it was time to give up small-town news and go into public relations.

Approaching the little Tercel, Ted swallowed hard. This looked like a bad one. Rescue workers had removed the roof of the little car, but were still unable to extricate the driver.

"Jeesus Christ," swore Fire Chief Pulaski. "Closest air bag's over at Wilton. Goddamn town meeting!" he exploded. Catching sight of Ted, he added, "And you can quote me on that!"

Ted nodded grimly, as the chief stormed past. Last spring Pulaski had asked town meeting voters to approve the purchase of a heavy-duty rescue air bag and they had turned him down. Now he had to borrow one from a neighboring town, losing precious time.

"Who's in the car?" he asked the kid who worked at the gas station.

"Jennifer Mitchell. The Medflight helicopter is on the way, but they can't get her out. Her legs are caught under the engine block."

Ted nodded. No wonder Pulaski was so upset. His daughter, Molly, played on the high school field hockey team with Jennifer. Ted usually covered the games, and had often seen Pulaski there, cheering the girls on. Ted remembered Jennifer running down the field in her regulation kilt, long blond hair streaming behind her, to score a goal.

That was the trouble with small towns, he remembered a state trooper telling him. You knew everybody—the crooks, the troublemakers, and the victims. He was sick of writing about the people he knew, his friends, and the horrible things that happened to them.

"Copter's landed on the football field," he heard a firefighter tell the chief.

"Damn," said Pulaski. "Where the hell is Wilton?"

"Out of my way, Stillings." Ted recognized Police Chief Crowley's gruff voice, and turned to face him. He was carrying a large aluminum case.

"Wilton broke down coupla miles from here," said Crowley. "Fella said you wanted this."

"Right," said Pulaski, reaching for the case. "C'mon, boys, let's get this thing under the engine."

As the men busied themselves positioning the airbag and starting the compressor, Ted began snapping pictures. He finished off one roll of film and reloaded, watching breathlessly as Pulaski gave the order and the airbag began to inflate.

At first, it seemed as if the weight of the engine block was too much for the bag; nothing moved. The compressor continued hissing and the bag grew larger and larger, until finally the crushed metal yielded, groaning in protest.

"Hold it there!" shouted Pulaski.

The fireman who was manning the compressor adjusted a valve, and the bag stopped growing. Ted held his breath; it seemed incredible that air pressure was powerful enough to lift the engine and keep it from crashing back down.

In a matter of seconds the medics had Jennifer out of the car and into the ambulance. Minutes later, Ted saw the helicopter rise into the sky and fly off toward the trauma unit at the hospital in Portland.

"That was pretty amazing," Ted said to Crowley.

"Nah," he answered. "Modern technology."

"Actually, I meant what you did. If you hadn't brought the airbag that girl would still be stuck in the car."

"It was nothin'," said Crowley. "I heard it on the radio, and happened to be in the vicinity."

"It's your day off," Ted persisted.

"What are you? Some kinda wiseass, know-it-all reporter?" Crowley's voice was just as gruff as ever, but Ted noticed a gleam of amusement in his eyes.

"You're damned right I am," he shot back. Ted gave him a quick salute and hurried back to his car. He had to get to the office. He had a story to write.

CHAPTER TWENTY-SEVEN

Leaving Miss Tilley's, Lucy also saw the Medflight helicopter, rising above the trees. She sent a little prayer along with it, as it banked and whirled off to the trauma center, the same prayer she had been repeating ever since the accident. Please, please God, let Jennifer be okay.

The poor girl must have been trapped in that car for at least an hour and a half, thought Lucy, as she started up the Subaru. That couldn't be good. Everything she knew about first aid stressed the fact that minutes could mean the difference between life and death. At least Jennifer had youth on her side, and was strong and healthy.

Miss Tilley, on the other hand, was old and weak, much weaker than anyone guessed. Now that she thought about it, Lucy could see a pattern of increasing intolerance. Miss Tilley had always been something of a character, but lately her tongue had been sharper and her wit more scathing. Lucy suspected this was her way of compensating for her increasing frailty.

The old woman had no family that Lucy knew of. Dear Poppa, as Miss Tilley always referred to her father, had died during the second Nixon administration. Miss Tilley always maintained that the shock of learning a Republican could be involved in something as disgraceful as Watergate had killed him.

With no family to take charge, Lucy knew she would have to assume the burden of making sure her old friend got the help she needed. There wasn't anybody else. Lucy decided to call the Senior Council as soon as possible to find out what resources were available.

Stopping at the traffic light on Main Street, Lucy spotted Toby and his constant companions, Eddie Culpepper, Adam Stillings, and Rickie Goodman. Stubby Phipps was trailing along after them, and if he didn't quite seem to be part of their group, they were tolerating him. Barney's social rehabilitation program seemed to be working.

They were probably headed to the scene of the accident, in hopes that the wrecked automobiles hadn't been towed away yet. She wondered if she should stop them. She could order them into the car and take them home, get out some board games, and cook up some popcorn in the microwave.

No, she thought. They might as well see. Maybe they would remember when they were driving themselves. Not, she thought with a sigh of relief, for at least a few more years.

Driving down Main Street, she passed the movie theater that had burned in July. The facade was boarded up with plywood, but the marquee bravely proclaimed the upcoming opening of an art exhibit.

COMING SOON it read in big black letters. COLLEGE ARTS COMPLEX. Smaller letters were arranged in the bottom row. "Premier show: The Red Zone."

A bit farther along the road, Lucy saw the ruins of Doug Durning's real estate office. Like the Homestead, it had burned completely. Looking at the pile of charred timbers that remained, surrounded by official yellow tape, Lucy felt sick. It had been a beautiful old building, a real treasure, and now it was gone. What a shame. If this kept up the town wouldn't have any old buildings left.

"Oh my God," she said aloud, remembering the groceries in the wayback. At least there was no ice cream, she thought, grateful for small favors and crisp fall temperatures. Everything was probably fine.

By the time she got home she was so tired she was tempted to leave the groceries in the car for Bill to unload. Zoe didn't wake, however, when she lifted her out of the safety seat, so she decided she might as well get it done.

She was putting two boxes of instant oatmeal in the pantry, a buy one-get one-free special, when the phone rang.

"Lucy, it's Mira."

"Oh, hi," said Lucy. "How's everything?"

"Okay, I guess. I take one day at a time." Mira's voice sounded small.

"That's all you can do," said Lucy sympathetically.

"I wanted to let you know about the memorial service we've planned for Mom. It's Sunday, at First Parish here in Brookline. Two o'clock."

"Thanks for calling," said Lucy. "We'll be there."

But when she hung up, Lucy realized she didn't want to spend an hour thinking about poor Monica, burned to cinders in her bed. She didn't want to think about Jennifer, fighting for her life in a Portland hospital. And she didn't want to think about Miss Tilley, slowly decomposing in her musty, dusty old house.

Up until now, she thought, she'd been concerned with conceiving and planting and growing. That was her job—tending the garden, keeping the house, and raising the children. She had nothing to do with death. Even her father's sudden passing from a heart attack hadn't really touched her. She'd been so busy taking care of the details and helping her mother that she had barely noticed her loss.

But now, more than anything, she missed her father. She

wished he could come back and sit in his favorite spot at her kitchen table. She remembered him there on Sunday mornings, with a mug of coffee and a cigarette, tackling the *Times* crossword puzzle.

He was gone. Sometimes she thought she saw him, an old guy in a plaid shirt jac and a tweed driving cap; sometimes she got a whiff of wool and cigarettes that reminded her so strongly of him, but it never was.

She brushed away a tear, feeling suddenly much older, and she knew she had crossed some invisible line. She heard a late autumn bluebottle fly buzzing at the window, and watched as it faltered, searching for an exit. There was only one way out—for the fly, for her, and even for baby Zoe.

CHAPTER TWENTY-EIGHT

Promptly at ten on Halloween Lucy met Liz Kelly, the outreach worker from Senior Services in front of Miss Tilley's house. Liz was much heavier than Lucy expected, but she had given Lucy reason to be optimistic during their brief phone conversation the day before.

Liz hadn't hesitated to schedule an outreach meeting for Saturday morning. After hearing Lucy describe Miss Tilley's situation she had agreed it required immediate action.

Today, however, Lucy was having doubts. As she watched Liz square her shoulders and march up to the front door, for all the world like a soldier going into battle, she wished she were certain this was the right thing to do.

"Good news," chirped Miss Tilley, as she opened the door. "The man from the auto body shop called and said my car will be just fine. There was no mechanical damage. He says it will be good as new once he pops out a few dents and slaps on some paint. His choice of words, not mine."

Lucy felt a small bubble of anger welling up in her throat, and she swallowed it down. Scolding at the old woman wouldn't accomplish anything. It certainly wouldn't help Jennifer.

"That's all well and good then," said Liz, carefully lowering her rather ample bottom onto Miss Tilley's prize Windsor chair. It squeaked a bit, but held, much to Lucy's amazement. She had expected the chair to splinter under Liz's weight. "You'll be able to get a good price when you sell it."

"I don't plan to sell it," said Miss Tilley.

"Of course you're going to sell it," said Liz, with all the subtlety of a bulldozer. "You can't continue to drive after what happened."

"I certainly can. If I stop driving I'll lose my independence. It would be like giving up and dying."

"That's ridiculous," said Liz flatly. "Besides, they'll probably revoke or suspend your license. You'll be lucky if you don't go to jail. I heard the police are considering manslaughter charges, maybe even vehicular homicide, if Jennifer dies."

"Is that true?" Miss Tilley turned to Lucy. "Is she going to die?"

"I don't know," Lucy answered. "I called the hospital this morning and they said she was in intensive care. She's listed in poor condition."

"Well, there's no use crossing that bridge until we get to it," said Liz brightly. "And if the need arises, Senior Services has free legal counseling. In fact, I think you'll be amazed at the range of services we offer. I like to tell people it's like an all-you-can-eat buffet. You take all the services you want and leave the rest."

Lucy doubted Miss Tilley had ever attended an all-you-can-eat buffet; in fact, she suspected her old friend would find the very idea repulsive.

"I think I'll put the kettle on," said Lucy, rising. As she puttered about in the kitchen, she listened to the conversation in the other room.

"We have Meals on Wheels," said Liz. "Delicious hot nutritious meals brought right to your home every day."

"Macaroni and cheese in tin foil," snorted Miss Tilley.

"We have trained home care aides, to help you with light housekeeping and personal care."

"Snoops and busybodies." Miss Tilley waved away the brochure.

"We have friendly visitors, volunteers who will pay you a visit to brighten your day."

"Ghouls," Miss Tilley snapped. "Waiting to snatch the silver."

"What shall I put you down for?" asked Liz, licking her pencil.

"You can get lead poisoning doing that," said Miss Tilley. "Not to mention that it's a very unattractive habit." She folded her hands in her lap.

"Maybe you'd like to think about it for a bit," Lucy suggested, bringing in the tea tray. "She doesn't have to decide today, does she?"

"Oh, no," Liz agreed. "Give me a call anytime. Actually," she checked her watch, "I have to scoot, or I'll be late for a meeting."

"Don't let me keep you," said Miss Tilley.

"I can see what you meant when you called yesterday," Liz whispered as Lucy showed her to the door. "She's a stubborn old dear, but she'll come around. They all do. They fight it at first, but eventually they realize that they need help."

"We'll work something out," said Lucy. "Thanks for coming." Standing in the tiny hall with Liz, Lucy felt smothered.

"Some of these old folks live in shocking conditions, but this is the worst I've seen in a while." Liz raised an eyebrow. "Not even a TV."

"Oh, that's because . . ."

"I'm sure we can find her a used one. And that furniture! Absolutely filthy. Needs a good scrubbing if you ask me."

"Maybe a bit of lemon oil," said Lucy, imagining Liz taking a sudsy sponge to Miss Tilley's priceless antiques.

"Don't you worry, we'll soon have everything ship-shape." Liz patted Lucy's hand and clumped down the path in her sensible shoes, clutching her flowing Guatemalan wrap around her bulky form.

"What a remarkably ugly woman," said Miss Tilley, when Lucy returned. "Why doesn't she get that huge hairy mole removed?"

"Beats me," said Lucy. She took a sip of tea. "Is it true that you don't cash your social security checks?"

"That's rather a personal question, don't you think?"

"I was thinking that if you cashed them you could hire some one to help out a couple of hours a day. Cook a hot meal for you, and drive you wherever you wanted to go."

"Like Cynthia Durning?"

"Who?" Lucy was distracted, today she didn't have the patience to listen to one of Miss Tilley's stories. She couldn't help worrying about Jennifer.

"Douglas's mother. She kept house for Wilfred Peters for years. Some people said she did more than keep house." The old woman cackled wickedly. "That's why old Peters left her his house. Too bad it's gone, now."

"It's too bad," Lucy repeated.

"That's right. Used to be Mr. Peters's house. People talked, of course, but I thought it was fitting, really. He didn't have any family except for that daughter of his who ran off with Rupert Lenk. After that Mr. Peters wouldn't have anything to do with her, and I think he was absolutely right. He warned her she was throwing her life away, that Lenk was trash. And he was."

"Who was Rupert? Randy's father?" Lucy snapped to attention. This was getting interesting.

"That's right. He was a vicious sort of man, and never took care of anything. He would have let it fall to rack and ruin, of course. When Randy was a little boy I wouldn't even let him in the library, he was so foulmouthed and dirty.

Just like his father. Douglas, on the other hand, was such a nice, polite boy. I felt badly when he brought that project of his before the commission and we had to turn him down. It didn't set well with a lot of people."

"What project? Do you mean Doug Durning's place?"

"That's right. The old Peters house." Miss Tilley was growing impatient. "He wanted to remodel that lovely old house into an office complex. It was quite grand, with a gazebo and an ATM machine. But it wasn't very well thought-out. He was going to rip off that fine pine clapboard and stick in a stainless steel machine!"

"Really?" Lucy sighed. She couldn't spend all day sitting around with Miss Tilley. She had to get ready for the Halloween party tonight. Not that she felt like going to a party.

"It was one of the first cases that came before us," reminisced Miss Tilley. "In fact, he just missed the deadline. If he'd submitted his plans a day or two earlier, he wouldn't have needed commission review." Miss Tilley gave a big yawn. "I'm tired today. I didn't sleep very well last night."

"Why don't you take a little nap?" Lucy suggested, rising. "I'll clean up the tea things." She had to get moving, she had a million things to do.

Lucy took the tray into the kitchen and began filling the sink. The trash was full so she carried it outside to empty into the barrel that stood on the back porch. As she lifted the lid she noticed Lenk's quilt on the bench, where she'd left it the day before.

It always seemed to keep coming back to Lenk, she thought. What had Miss Tilley said? Doug Durning had inherited a house from Randy's grandfather. Was it his office? she wondered. Was that what it was all about? Had Randy been simmering with jealousy all these years, and finally decided to do something about it? Something spectacular that everybody would notice?

Lucy picked up the quilt and fingered it thoughtfully. It

wouldn't hurt to stop off at Lenk's gas station to return the quilt. Maybe this time she would find a clue, something that would connect Lenk to the fires.

She went back inside and finished washing the tea things, leaving them to dry on the drainboard. Tiptoing, so as not to disturb Miss Tilley, she went into the front room to retrieve her purse.

"I'm not asleep," said the old woman.

"I have to go," Lucy said.

Miss Tilley nodded, and grasped Lucy's hand. "I've been thinking. I've decided to surrender my driver's license."

"I think that's the right thing to do."

"Did you notice that young man who works for Lenk?"

"Rob?"

"He seemed awfully taken with my car. I bet he'd enjoy driving it around town, even with me in it."

"That's a good idea."

"Who knows? If he really likes my classy chassis, I might even leave it to him."

"You're a filthy old witch," said Lucy fondly, placing her hand on Miss Tilley's shoulder and bending down to kiss the top of her grizzled head.

"I know," said Miss Tilley.

CHAPTER TWENTY-NINE

Lucy wished she had thought to put Lenk's quilt in a bag; it was so saturated with oil and grease that it left her hands feeling dirty.

Nothing the matter with a little dirt, she told herself, taking the quilt out of the car. You can always wash your hands.

She crossed the gritty asphalt of the service station and opened the office door.

"I'm returning your blanket," she said, cautiously poking her head in.

Lenk stared at her, and his little piggy eyes were hostile.

"I'll just put it down here," said Lucy, abandoning her plan of looking for clues in her hurry to escape.

"Not so fast," he growled. "You're married to Stone, ain't ya?"

"I'm married to Bill Stone, if that's who you mean."

"That's the guy. I want you to tell him about this," said Lenk, waving a piece of limp letterhead in front of her face.

Lucy stepped forward, reaching for the letter, and heard the office door thud shut behind her. It was broad daylight, she was in a public place, so why did she feel trapped? Was it the confined space of the office, the clutter of papers, and the stacks of dusty old cardboard boxes that climbed the walls?

"I'll tell him," said Lucy. "What is it?"

"That's for me to know and you to find out," teased Lenk, sensing her discomfort.

"I'm outta here," said Lucy, turning to go.

"There a fire or something?" he asked, putting a hand on the door and holding it shut. "It's from Northstar, that's what it is. They don't want my station anymore—they're not renewing my contract."

"Let me see that," said Lucy.

The letter was short and to the point. Following the meeting with the historical commission, Northstar's marketing department had reviewed the situation and determined that an alternative location would be preferable for their full-service station. In line with the company's current marketing policies, they would be unable to renew Mr. Lenk's contract as a dealer. They were grateful for Mr. Lenk's years of participation as a member of the Northstar team and wished him all the best in the future.

Lucy had a sinking feeling in the pit of her stomach. She slowly raised her eyes and met Lenk's.

"It's because of the commission. I lost my chance to fix up the station—'cause o' your husband!" He shoved his face right in hers, giving her the full benefit of his foul breath.

"It wasn't just Bill," said Lucy, standing her ground. "They didn't even vote. They asked Northstar to come back with an improved plan, that's all."

"Big companies like Northstar ain't gonna waste time on a bunch o' small-town cranks. They can go anywhere. They sure don't need me. They'll put whatever kinda station they want out on the highway—they'll put an igloo out there if they want."

"You're right," said Lucy, sympathizing with him in spite of herself. "Can't you become an independent dealer? Get some no-name gas?"

"Lookee here, missy," he said, pointing a blackened finger at her. "This here's all your fault, you and that husband o' yours. Think you can move in and tell people what to do. That commission wrecked the best deal I was ever gonna get."

Lenk was working up quite a head of steam and Lucy decided the office was definitely too small for both of them. The pungent smell of gasoline and assorted engine fluids, not to mention Lenk himself, was overpowering. Her head began to swim.

"Who's gonna make that up to me, hunh?" he demanded, stepping closer to her. "Nobody, that's who!" His face was just inches from hers. "I got screwed, and I know who did the screwing."

Lenk paused for breath, and Lucy took the opportunity to slip through the door. Her heart was pounding wildly as she gulped great mouthfuls of fresh air. Hurrying to the car, she quickly climbed inside, half expecting him to follow her. He didn't, however. In fact, when she looked back and saw him standing in the doorway, she could have sworn he was laughing at her.

CHAPTER THIRTY

"I don't like it one bit," Lucy complained to Bill. "He's really got a grudge against you, you know. I wouldn't be surprised if we came home tonight and found the house burned to a pile of cinders."

"Chief Crowley promised to put on an extra patrol—said he's aware of the situation and keeping an eye on things."

"Why doesn't that make me feel a whole lot better?"

"Do you want me to stay home? I could borrow a shotgun from Mr. Sanford." The Sanfords were the Stones' nearest neighbors on Red Top Road, and Mr. Sanford was always taking potshots at the groundhogs that raided his garden.

"And miss the party? We'll just have to hope for the best," Lucy grumbled, slipping the last of the dinner plates in the dish washer and shutting the door. "Now, would you please get down those boxes on the top shelf."

"Sure. What's in them?"

"Cupcakes. Twelve dozen."

"When did you have time to bake cupcakes?"

"In batches. I got the last two dozen done this morning. Zoe didn't go back to sleep after her midnight snack so I baked cupcakes."

"In the middle of the night? You're nuts," said Bill.

"Who needs sleep, anyway?" Lucy said, yawning.

"I'll take everybody out tomorrow so you can have a nice long nap," said Bill, slipping his arms around her. "It's a promise."

"Really?" Lucy turned her face up to his.

"Yup." He bent down to kiss her.

"Mom, Elizabeth's hogging all the makeup!" Sara burst open the pantry door.

Startled, Lucy turned.

"Sara, you look great!" Sara was already in her costume, the pink tutu she'd worn in the ballet recital last spring.

"This turtleneck itches," she complained, scratching her neck.

"You'll need it, though. It's cold tonight," said Lucy. "And it really doesn't show too much."

Elizabeth, she saw, was seated at the kitchen table surrounded by every cosmetic Lucy owned.

"Mom, don't you have any eye shadow?" Elizabeth was also wearing her tutu, but she'd added a plaid flannel shirt and a pair of clunky black oxfords.

"Is that your costume?" asked Lucy.

"Yup. I'm a punk ballerina."

"That's kind of cute. Want me to pierce your nose for you?"

"That's not funny, Mom." Elizabeth's tone was withering. "What I really need is a tattoo."

"I think we've got some. The kind that wash off."

"Yeah. Right." Elizabeth was skeptical.

"In a cereal box." Lucy went back in the pantry and emerged triumphant with a huge box of crispy flakes. She dumped the contents into a bowl, plucked out the cellophane-wrapped sheet of tattoos, and then carefully poured the cereal back into the box.

"You have to eat this stuff up, you know."

"Thanks, Mom. I will," said Elizabeth, studying her face

in the mirror she had propped up. "Where should I put it? On my cheek?"

"On your neck?"

"Neat. Say, Mom, what are you going as?"

"Myself."

"You've got to wear a costume!"

"That's right," agreed Bill. He had stuffed himself into Lucy's black maternity tights, added a yellow and black striped T-shirt, and topped off his ensemble with a bobbing antennae headband.

"What are you supposed to be?"

"A bumblebee. I thought it was obvious."

"I get it," said Lucy, stifling a giggle. "You just took me by surprise."

"I need a stinger. Got any ideas?"

"Aluminum foil?"

"Great." Bill ripped a big sheet off the roll, sat down, and began shaping it.

"Mom, I can't find one of my hairy hands," bellowed Toby from upstairs. "The left one."

"Did you look under your bed?"

"I can't find it anywhere," he insisted.

"I'd better help him," said Lucy. "Not too much makeup, okay, girls?"

"Sara, why don't you try this Very Berry lipstick," offered Elizabeth, in a rare display of sisterly helpfulness.

Lucy ran upstairs to Toby's room. As always, it was a mess, with clothes and books and athletic gear strewn everywhere. She sighed.

"Toby, it's no wonder you can never find anything. You have absolutely got to clean this room tomorrow."

"Oh, Mom," he groaned. "You should see Rickie's room. My room is neat compared to his."

"Right." Lucy didn't believe a word of it. She knelt down, lifted the dust ruffle, and peered under the bed. She reached in and shoved a few books aside. She pulled out the hairy hand glove.

"I looked, Mom. I swear."

"Oh, you looked all right. You just didn't move things around. Listen, I'm serious about this. Inspection is at fifteen hundred hours tomorrow, that's three o'clock. If you don't pass, you're grounded. This room is unhealthy. It's an accident waiting to happen. It's a fire hazard."

"So, how do I look?" Toby turned to face her. He resembled a very short Lon Chaney, in his werewolf mask and gloves, plaid shirt and jeans.

"Aaaah," screamed Lucy, running from the room and clatter- ing downstairs. "Run for your lives! It's the wolfman!"

Bill and the girls looked up.

"Mom, where's your costume?" asked Elizabeth.

"I told you. I'm not wearing one."

"You'll have more fun if you do," coaxed Bill.

"I haven't given it any thought."

"You could be a fairy princess," offered Sara. "Or Wonder Woman."

"Or a witch," suggested Elizabeth.

Lucy rolled her eyes at Bill.

"I know," he suggested brightly. "I bet Toby's baseball uniform would fit you."

Lucy went back upstairs and pulled the uniform out of Toby's bottom drawer. She took it into her room and tried it on. Standing in front of the mirror, she decided she looked like a stuffed sausage. So much for all that exercise at the Body Shop.

Bill appeared behind her and wrapped his arms around her.

"This makes me look awfully busty," complained Lucy.

"I noticed," said Bill, nuzzling her neck. "You look great."

"I do?"

"Mmm," said Bill, turning her around to face him. They

kissed, and Lucy felt something inside her stir that had been dormant for a long time. Bill led her to the bed.

"We can't do this," she protested. "The kids will come looking for us."

"The girls are so absorbed in making themselves up that they wouldn't notice an atom bomb. Toby's so scattered he never notices anything. Sometimes I worry about that boy," said Bill, pulling her down beside him.

"Mom, we're gonna be late," called Elizabeth. "What are you doing up there?"

"Your mother is putting on her costume, and I'm helping her. We'll be right down," said Bill. He grinned wickedly at Lucy.

"I've never done it with a bumblebee before," said Lucy. "How was it?"

"Sweet, like honey," she said, hooking her bra and pulling the baseball jersey over her head.

Detouring to Toby's room she found a baseball cap and slapped it on her head backward. Then she scooped up Zoe, who had been sleeping in her bassinet, and carried her downstairs.

"Have we got any black greasepaint?" she asked.

"Here," said Elizabeth, passing her a tube. Lucy bent down to see her face in the mirror, and drew a line across each cheekbone, under her eyes.

"Hey, Mom, you look pretty good," said Elizabeth. "Want some lipstick?"

"Okay."

"We've got Mostly Melon, Misty Mauve, Very Berry, and Great Grape."

"How about Misty Melon Mauve, or whatever."

"Great Grape is good. It's not as dark as it looks."

"Okay," said Lucy, smearing some on. She eased Zoe into the baby carrier and fastened the straps. "Have we got everything?" she asked, grabbing the diaper bag. "Everybody take a box of cupcakes. Don't drop them. Don't eat them," she added, as an afterthought.

As the family straggled out and headed for the car, Lucy set a bowl of candy out on the porch and dropped a lit flashlight into the jack-o'-lantern.

"That's in case there are any trick or treaters," she said, hopping into the passenger side front seat.

"Don't sit on your stinger," she cautioned Bill.

He carefully folded his shirt up, tucking the foil stinger against the small of his back, and slid behind the wheel.

"Have we got everything?" he asked. "Cupcakes?"

"I think we're all set," said Lucy, patting Zoe who was nuzzled against her chest. She glanced at the house. She had left the kitchen light burning, and the porch light. The jack-o'-lantern glowed, grinning a holiday welcome.

She thought of all the treasures the house contained. Her grandmother's silver. Old family photographs. Love letters from Bill. The kids' report cards. If it burned, all those things would be lost.

She couldn't bear to think about it. Tonight she wasn't going to worry about fires or death or car accidents. Tonight she was going to have fun.

CHAPTER THIRTY-ONE

Light was pouring from the windows of the old Hallett House when they pulled up under the porte cochere, and music could be heard from within. Night concealed the cracked clapboards and peeling paint—this was probably how the mansion had looked to guests arriving a hundred years ago.

"I'll let you out here," said Bill. "Looks like I'm going to have to park the car out in the field." He waited while Lucy and the kids scrambled out. When all was clear, Lucy gave him a little wave. "See you later," he said, as he slipped the Subaru into gear and drove off.

Climbing the steps, and approaching the heavy oak double doors, Lucy savored the moment. Maybe she was dressed in a ridiculous baseball costume, but she felt for all the world like a rich lady arriving at a magnificent mansion.

Entering the foyer, she paused. Black and orange streamers hung from the ceiling, artificial spiderwebs adorned the doors and windows. The room was packed with people, in all sorts of costumes, and at first Lucy didn't recognize anybody.

"Hi, guys, let me take those cupcakes," said a woman dressed exactly like Morticia Addams.

"Sue, I didn't recognize you!" Lucy exclaimed. "You look fabulous. Is that a wig?"

"One hundred percent polyester," said Sue, fingering her long, wavy black locks. "It's machine washable—if you believe labels. You look pretty cute, yourself."

"Cute's a curse," muttered Lucy. "I've finally got boobs, but nobody ever gets to see them. The baby carrier covers them up."

"Refreshments are in here," said Sue, indicating the way with a tilt of her head.

Lucy followed Sue and her trailing bits of costume. Together they arranged the cupcakes at the end of a long table covered with an orange cloth.

"This is terrific," said Lucy, surveying the table laden with food, the decorations, and the crowd of happy faces. "You did a great job."

"It all came together, didn't it?" Sue smiled proudly. "Look, that's Marge Culpepper." She indicated a large woman in a witch costume.

"And that's Barney, dressed in a prison uniform. Pretty clever."

"There's Rachel Goodman—quite the femme fatale."

"Wow," agreed Sue. Rachel, Rickie's mom, was wearing a sensational movie star dress made of clingy gold lamé, which she had topped with a wavy blond wig and a pair of oversized sunglasses.

"Hi, guys," she said, hurrying over. "This seemed like a good idea but my underwire bra is killing me —I'd forgotten what a girdle feels like, not to mention high heels. I'm in agony."

"Well, you look mahvelous." Lucy turned to Sue. "Doesn't she?"

"Absolutely mahvelous. Want a cupcake?"

"Couldn't. Can't even breathe."

Three high school girls Lucy recognized as friends of Jennifer Mitchell's tottered over—they were wearing platform shoes from the seventies, miniskirts, crocheted vests, floppy hats, and granny glasses.

"How do we look? Did we get it right?" asked Biz Henderson.

"Disco . . . that was before our time, wasn't it?" Sue was all innocence.

"Definitely," agreed Lucy. "I, myself, was only a babe in arms. But from the little I remember, I'd say you look great."

"Thanks." The girls all smiled. "We're so happy tonight," continued Biz. "Did you hear? Jen is out of intensive care. Her mom says she's gonna be okay."

"That's great news," said Lucy. "When will she be coming home?"

"Not for a while. She has to have lots of rehab and stuff, but she isn't going to die or anything," said Biz.

Lucy pasted on a smile and tried not to think of the accident; how afraid she'd been that Jennifer wouldn't survive.

"We're going to visit tomorrow," added one of the other girls.

"Meanwhile, we're supposed to keep an eye on Jeff Ryan for her. He's her boyfriend and we don't want anybody else to grab him while she's in the hospital."

"You'd better get busy," said Sue. "Isn't that him, dancing with Laurie Frye?" Laurie was notorious.

"Do you believe her? Jen's in the hospital," muttered Biz, as the girls hurried off.

"Aren't you glad you're not sixteen?" asked Sue.

"No," confessed Lucy. "I think I'll circulate, and see what the kids are up to."

Strolling into the ballroom, where the games were set up, Lucy spotted Toby in the group clustered around the apple-bobbing tank.

The girls, she guessed, would not be interested in getting their faces wet and messing up their makeup. Sure enough, she soon found Sara engaged in a lively game of Duck, Duck, Goose. Elizabeth was standing in a corner, preening and gossiping with her friends.

Noticing that Zoe was becoming increasingly restless in the baby carrier, Lucy looked for a quiet corner. She found it in the drawing room, where tables and chairs had been placed. A coffee urn sat in the corner, surrounded by a tempting assortment of snacks donated by Tammy Kurtz at the Greengage Cafe.

Lucy poured herself a cup of hazelnut coffee, put a few of the chocolate-pecan treats on a paper plate, and headed for a shadowy corner. There she could enjoy her snack, and nobody would notice if she nursed Zoe, too. She slid the diaper bag under a chair and sat down.

A sense of well-being crept over her as Zoe began to suck and her milk let down. She smiled to herself and gently stroked the baby's plump little cheek. She took a sip of coffee, and followed it with a bite of cookie. It was delicious, and she tried to guess what the ingredients were. There was a shortcake base, a layer of nuts and caramel, and the whole thing was topped with a drizzle of dark chocolate. Without exact proportions, it would be hard to duplicate, she decided.

"Let's sit over here," she heard Doug Durning say, and looked up. She wouldn't have recognized him—he was dressed in black tie and tails, had slicked his hair back, and was wearing vampire teeth.

"Excuse me," he said to his companion, as he slipped the teeth into a white handkerchief. "That's better."

He was with Krissy, of all people. Well, she wasn't wasting much time, thought Lucy. Krissy was dressed in flowing white draperies that showed off her figure, and had frosted her hair. Lucy had no idea what her costume was. A fairy of some sort? A Midsummer Night's Dream? Maybe an early frost, she guessed, spotting some blackened leaves pinned to her shoulder.

"I just love this house," said Krissy, giving Doug a flirtatious smile.

Oh, ho, thought Lucy. Krissy must have given up on Dr. Mayes and was looking for somebody new. No doubt about it, Doug was attractive and he could stand a little attention. He'd been through a lot lately, with the fire and all.

"It would be such fun to fix it up. I'd use black and white in the foyer—keep it formal. But I'd go wild with color in the rest of the rooms. Red for the dining room, pink and gold for the ballroom—can't you just see it?"

"Sure," said Doug, popping a cheese puff into his mouth. "Sounds great. It would take a hell of a lot of cash, though."

"I suppose it would," said Krissy, drawing her finger around the rim of her coffee cup, and lifting her eyes to meet Doug's.

This is so funny, thought Lucy, stifling a giggle. The woman was clearly signaling her availability. She wished she could see Doug's reaction but his back was to her.

"This old building is in pretty bad shape," said Doug, eager to display his expertise. "The sills are probably rotted—there's a lot of water damage. The land is probably worth more without the house than with it."

"How can that be?" asked Krissy, slipping her finger in her mouth and sucking it.

Did I ever stoop to tricks like that? wondered Lucy. She and Bill had been together for such a long time that she really couldn't remember what it had been like to be single and seeking a mate.

"Because of the hysterical district, that's how. Anybody buying this land with the house would have to pour a ton of money into restoring it. If the house was gone, you could put anything you wanted here. It's a prime location, with a water view. Somebody'd snap it up, believe me."

"Business is way over my head," confessed Krissy, making her eyes very large. "I can't even balance my checking account."

Lucy almost snorted in disbelief. If the Body Shop's success was any indication, Krissy was an extremely shrewd business-woman.

"Say," said Doug, with studied casualness. "Whaddya say we split? Find someplace that serves something a bit stronger than coffee?"

"Sounds good to me," said Krissy, rewarding him with a sexy smile.

"So here you are," said Bill, joining Lucy at the table. "I've been looking for you everywhere. Having a good time?"

"I sure am," said Lucy, grinning. "I've been people watching. I just saw true love, or maybe it was true lust, bloom."

"Yeah?" said Bill, leaning across the table. "What happened?"

"Well, first she went like this," said Lucy, running her finger around the cup. "And then she did this." She put her finger in her mouth.

"That's pretty good," said Bill. "I'm interested. Wanna dance?"

"With the baby?"

"Sure."

"So, you like kids?" said Lucy, leading the way to the dance floor.

CHAPTER THIRTY-TWO

A few days after Lucy had given birth to Zoe, a sock hop had taken place at the elementary school. Lucy hadn't gone, of course, but she'd heard nothing but raves about the dance, and the terrific deejay, Sammy Witherspoon.

Sammy was spinning the platters again, tonight, and Lucy could understand why the dance had been such a success. He chose classic rock songs that everybody knew, and that were appropriate for the whole family.

Lucy was having a grand time, and so was everybody else. They did the bunny hop and the electric slide, everybody sang along to the Beatles' "Yellow Submarine." Sammy pulled out funny old songs Lucy hadn't heard in years, like "Yellow Polka Dot Bikini" and the one about putting chewing gum on the bedpost overnight.

Age didn't seem to matter. Biz Henderson and her friends were dancing, so was Dotty Cooper, along with her grandson, Billy. Everybody was smiling, their faces shiny with perspiration and their eyes sparkling under the mirrored disco ball.

"Everybody having a good time?" asked Sammy.

"Yes!" the crowd shouted back.

Lucy took Bill's hand and made her way to the wall, so she could rest her back. Zoe seemed to be getting heavier in the baby carrier as the evening went on.

"Great! There's gonna be more music later, but right now I've been asked to announce the winners of the costume contest. May I have the envelope, please?"

Sue scurried forward and presented Sammy with a crumpled piece of paper. He raised his eyebrows.

"Our accountants at the firm of Price and Pimplemousse do not vouch for the accuracy of these results," he said, smoothing out the paper. Everybody laughed.

"In the preschool category, the winner is . . . drumroll please . . . Emily Ford!"

Propelled by a push from her mother, Emily stepped forward to receive her trophy. She was dressed in a beautiful Cinderella costume. Lucy had heard it was a joint effort by Emily's mother and her grandmother, and that they had worked on it for weeks. Noting the shining hand-sewn beads and ribbon trim, Lucy didn't doubt it.

Sammy presented Emily, who was a bit overwhelmed by the crowd, with her trophy. She clutched it to her chest and ran back to her mother, earning a round of applause.

"Next, is the elementary school category. I've been told the judges had a particularly tough time deciding," said Sammy. "They were able to come to a decision, however, and the winner is . . . Jared Kirwan."

Jared raised his hands above his head in a victory sign and dashed forward, throwing in a karate kick for good measure. He was dressed in a bright blue Mighty Morphin Power Ranger suit, and was clearly living the role. He grinned boldly when he received his trophy, revealing a mouth full of mostly missing teeth. The kid was an imp, a real crowd-pleaser, and everyone clapped for him, including his grandmother, Dot.

Recalling Dot Kirwan's excellent connections—her son was a police officer and her daughter was the dispatcher at the fire department—Lucy sidled over to her.

"What a cute kid," she said.

"Oh, Jared's a handful. I don't know how you youngsters manage. This must be the new baby," she cooed, slipping her finger inside Zoe's clenched fist.

"She's been awfully good tonight, but I have to confess my back is killing me," Lucy said with a sigh.

"Those baby carriers are great, though. I wish we'd had them," said Dot.

"I don't know what I'd do without it," agreed Lucy. "Listen, Dot, what do you think about all these fires? Have you heard anything?"

"Actually," said Dot, leaning closer, "I think they're close to solving the case."

"Really? That would be such a relief. I've been so worried, especially since Doug's place burned. You know all the members of the commission got threatening phone calls?"

"Well, I don't want to mention any names," she nodded knowingly, "but I don't think you have to worry anymore."

Lucy was about to answer when she heard Stubby's name called.

Kicking the floor bashfully with his toe, Stubby stepped forward. He was dressed in one of Barney's old uniforms, cut down to size, Lucy guessed, by Marge. His heavy utility belt was complete with genuine handcuffs, a toy pistol, and a walkie-talkie.

"This prize is for the most authentic costume," said Sammy. "Say, officer, don't arrest me, okay?"

"You're under arrest!" yelled Stubby, reaching for the handcuffs.

"Whoa," said Sammy. "If you handcuff me I won't be able to give you your prize."

He presented Stubby with a handsome trophy, and raised his hands over his head. "I give up, officer," said Sammy. "Please, don't shoot."

Stubby pulled out his gun, waved it, and returned to the little gang of boys. They clustered around him, examing his prize. Lucy was smiling her approval when she heard Bill's name called.

"This prize is for the adult who absolutely does not care how ridiculous he looks, and I think you'll all agree that Bill Stone took a bit of a fashion risk tonight," said Sammy.

Everyone laughed as Bill stepped forward.

"Man, you are one ugly bumblebee," said Sammy. "I'd sure hate to meet you in the flower garden."

"You don't have to worry. My buzz is a lot worse than my sting," said Bill, turning to model his aluminum foil stinger.

Everybody clapped and cheered as he accepted his trophy, and gave the crowd a wave.

"Well, that concludes this portion of the program," said Sammy. "Let's party!" He flipped a switch, and the performer who used to be called Prince began encouraging everyone to "Party like it's 1999."

"Shall we dance?" asked Bill.

"I'm bushed," said Lucy. "I'd like to go home."

"Okay," he said. "You find the kids and I'll get the coats. Meet you in the foyer."

Lucy beckoned to Elizabeth and Sara, and led them to the hall, where they met Toby, along with Eddie, Richie, Adam, and Stubby.

"Toby, it's time to go."

"Aw, Mom, I don't wanna go home yet."

"It's late, and I'm too tired to argue . . ."

"It's not late," replied Toby. "It's not even nine o'clock."

"Don't talk back to me. It's time to go." Lucy was exhausted and she was in no mood for a discussion. "Get a move on," she snapped, not caring that she was embarrassing Toby in front of his friends.

"Leaving already?" asked Barney.

"I'm trying," said Lucy.

"That's a shame," said Barney. "The party's not over, and I promised the boys I'd take them trick-or-treating for a bit."

"Oh, I don't know," said Lucy, sensing that the battle had turned and she was losing.

"What's up?" asked Bill, materializing with his arms full of coats and jackets.

"Toby wants to stay and go trick-or-treating with the boys," explained Lucy. "What do you think?"

"No problem," said Bill. "Be home by ten at the latest, okay?"

"Sure, Dad," said Toby. "I promise."

"Relax, Lucy," said Barney. "I'll keep an eye on them. They won't get into any trouble."

"Okay," said Lucy, with a sigh of resignation. She'd heard that line before, last year, when the boys decorated the middle school principal's hedge with toilet paper. Toby had narrowly escaped suspension; he was lucky to get off with two weeks of after school detention.

"I thought the whole point of this party was to keep kids off the streets," complained Lucy to Bill as they strolled down the hill to the car. "That way, they could have a safe Halloween, and have fun, too. And parents wouldn't have to go out of their minds worrying."

"Lucy, he'll be fine," said Bill, opening the car door.

"I'd feel a lot better if he was coming home with us," said Lucy, climbing in.

"Girls, what did you think of the party?" asked Bill, starting the engine.

"It was fun," said Sara.

"I don't see why Toby gets to stay and I have to go home," complained Elizabeth.

"I don't either," said Lucy, in rare agreement with her daughter. "It's too bad the weather's been so dry. If we'd had rain tonight, the boys wouldn't be able to stay out."

"Lucy, stop being a spoilsport. You can't keep him tied to your apron strings forever. A boy's got to have some freedom. What's the world coming to if a kid can't have a few adventures on Halloween?"

"I guess you're right," Lucy said, thinking that she would feel a whole lot better if Toby was coming home with the rest of the family.

Looking out the car window as they drove along, Lucy noticed shadowy figures flitting from door to door. Passing one house, she saw a group of costumed children gathered on a brightly lit porch, where the festive decorations promised a generous welcome. Little white ghosts dangled from the porch roof, and a string of glowing pumpkin lights had been wrapped around the railing. Cornstalks stood on either side of the door, sporting cheerful orange ribbons. A stuffed scarecrow lounged on the porch swing. The door opened and the group surged forward, eager to receive the treats a plump, grandmotherly woman was distributing. It could have been a scene from a Norman Rockwell painting.

She couldn't help smiling. Trick-or-treating was lots of fun, and where could it be safer than in a small New England town like Tinker's Cove?

CHAPTER THIRTY-THREE

When they got home, Lucy took baby Zoe upstairs and laid her down in the center of the big bed, still zipped in the corduroy baby carrier. She was sleeping soundly and Lucy didn't want to risk waking her.

She bent over the bed, arranging the baby, then straightened up. Arching her back and stretching, she tried to work out the kinks. Her back ached from wearing the baby carrier for such a long time.

"Did you have a good time, girls?" she asked, poking her head in the bathroom. Sara and Elizabeth were washing their faces.

"I would have had a better time if you didn't make me come home early," whined Elizabeth. "Toby gets to do whatever he wants. It's not fair."

"Life's not fair," said Lucy, picking up a brush and combing out her oldest daughter's hair.

"I don't see why Jared Kirwan won for his costume," fumed Elizabeth. "It was store bought. Mine was more original."

"What about you, pumpkin," said Lucy, turning to Sara. "Did you have a good time?"

"Daddy was funny," she said with a big smile. Her face was bright pink from the energetic scrubbing she'd given it. "I liked when he got the prize."

"Yeah, that was okay," Elizabeth agreed.

"Into your pajamas," Lucy urged, shooing them out so she could take possession of the bathroom. "I'll be in to kiss you good night."

She pulled off the baseball cap and shook out her hair. Then she washed her face with cool water. She hoped the baby would sleep well tonight, she could really use a good night's sleep. Tomorrow would be a long day—they were planning to attend the memorial service for Monica in Brookline. If there was time, she thought, maybe they could stop in at the hospital on the way home and visit Jennifer.

The girls were already in bed when Lucy went in to them. Elizabeth was reading Roald Dahl's *Witches*, but she put it down and climbed in bed with Sara when Lucy opened up Tasha Tudor's *Pumpkin Moonshines*. Both girls listened raptly as Lucy read the the story of a little girl's adventures with a huge jack-o'-lantern.

"I wish I could have a dress and bonnet like Sylvie," sighed Sara, pointing to one of the charming illustrations of Sylvie in her old-fashioned clothes.

"I wish I could paint my fingernails black," said Elizabeth.

"Time to go to sleep," said Lucy, closing the tiny book. She leaned over and kissed Sara on the top of her head. Sara reached up and wrapped her arms around her in a tight hug. Lucy squeezed back, glad that Sara was still a little girl who loved to hug her mommy. "Nighty-night," she said, tucking the covers around her. "Sleep tight."

"Can I read for a while?" asked Elizabeth, who had returned to her own bed.

"It's past your bedtime."

"It's Saturday. I don't have school tomorrow."

"It will disturb your sister."

"I'll use a flashlight."

"Okay," Lucy said, reaching down and caressing her cheek. "Not too late, now," she said, giving her oldest daughter a quick peck on the cheek. "Good night." She turned out the light.

Closing the girls' door, Lucy leaned against it for a minute. The party had thrown off her usual evening routine, and she wasn't quite sure what to do. Zoe was still sleeping soundly and she hated to disturb her. On the other hand, if she changed her diaper and nursed her now she might sleep through the night.

She was still weighing the decision when a whimper from the bedroom made it for her. She went into the nursery to get a diaper but discovered the basket was empty. With all the baking and planning for the party she had gotten behind in the laundry. She would have to get a disposable from the diaper bag.

Where had she left it? It wasn't on the kitchen chair where she usually dropped it. Was it in the car? With a flash of clarity she remembered shoving it under her chair when she had coffee at the party. It was probably still there.

"Bill, I left the diaper bag . . ." she began, intending to ask him to retrieve it for her. But Bill was sound asleep in his recliner, the zoning bylaws still in his hand.

"I might as well go get it myself," she decided, checking the baby who had settled back into a deep sleep. "I can be back in ten minutes," she said to herself, throwing on a jacket and grabbing the car keys.

CHAPTER THIRTY-FOUR

The Hallett House was dark and empty when Lucy arrived; it was the very image of a haunted house. She found this a bit disconcerting. She had expected to meet a few lingering party-goers, or at least the cleanup crew. Maybe even Toby and his band of trick-or-treaters.

She checked the dashboard clock and saw it was later than she thought, past ten o'clock. That explained it, she reasoned. Those with kids had taken them home to bed, and the serious party types had gone on to the scattered nightspots in the area that featured local bands and cheap drinks.

She hesitated, figuring the old house was probably locked up tight. Besides, the huge hulk of a mansion was not inviting as it loomed above her. This is too spooky, she thought, deciding to pick up a box of disposables at the Quik Stop.

Don't be ridiculous, she argued with herself, reaching for the flashlight she kept in the car. It was worth a try. Going to the Quik Stop would take at least twenty minutes more, and she was afraid Zoe might wake up.

As she climbed out of the car the full moon suddenly appeared from behind a cloud and the hill was flooded with light.

A good omen, she thought, as she hauled herself up the steps to the big front door and reached for the knob. To her surprise, it turned.

Lucy smiled. Thanks to someone's carelessness she would be able to grab the diaper bag and return home before she was missed.

Inside, the foyer was pitch black. Moonlight could hardly penetrate where bright sunlight never reached, blocked by the dilapidated porch and gloomy stained-glass windows. Lucy switched on the flashlight and cast the beam around the room. The floor was littered with discarded cups, and crepe paper streamers dropped from the ceiling. Sue must have decided to put off the cleanup until tomorrow.

Lucy heard a scuttling noise from one of the rooms beyond and shuddered. Probably mice, or even rats, after the crumbs. She didn't want to know which, she wanted to turn around and run out the door as quickly as her legs would take her.

Instead, she stepped forward and hurried through the empty rooms, determined to find the bag and return home to her hungry baby. She could hear squeaks and groans, the old house seemed to have a life of its own. It certainly wasn't empty, it had plenty of inhabitants. And now that the party was over and the humans had left, they were reclaiming their territory.

Lucy paused at the parlor door and explored the cavernous room with her flashlight, praying she would not encounter any pairs of glowing eyes. All clear. She was about a third of the way through the room when she heard something and instinctively stopped in her tracks, straining her ears.

Nothing. She must have been mistaken. She advanced a few steps, and she heard it again. A crunching noise, like footsteps on gravel. It seemed to be coming from outside.

She pointed the flashlight at the long windows, but the blank glass only bounced the reflection back at her.

Lucy took a few more steps toward the drawing-room door on the opposite wall, and again heard the noise. When she moved, she heard the steps. When she stopped, they stopped. It was almost as if someone on the outside of the house was following her movements inside. She began to shiver and she felt the little hairs on the back of her neck stand up. Lucy could hear herself breathing; her breaths sounded loud, like roars. Her heart was pounding in her chest. She couldn't move, she couldn't even scream.

Then she heard a sound she recognized—Toby's giggle.

"Cut it out!" she yelled, as the adrenaline drained away in a great wave of relief. "Toby, I know it's you out there!"

There was no answer, but after a minute or two she heard the boys running away. Great, she muttered to herself. So much for Barney's promise to keep an eye on the boys. It was getting late and they ought to be home in bed.

Finally reaching the doorway, she paused and cast the light over and under chairs and tables, searching for the pink gingham diaper bag. She found it in the corner, exactly where she had left it, and dashed into the room to retrieve it. She was bending to pick it up when she sensed a presence behind her. She whirled around, fully intending to give the boys a scolding.

"You boys should be ashamed . . ." she began, when there was a sudden explosion of bright, white light

CHAPTER THIRTY-FIVE

L ucy loved sniffing the clean scent of duplicating fluid, and she loved running her fingers over the slick smoothness of the paper. In a moment, when Mrs. Birchall gave the signal, she would open her eyes, turn over the paper, and begin work on the quiz.

Always a good student, full of curiosity and eager to learn, Lucy enjoyed the challenge posed by tests and quizzes. A bright child, she had soon discovered that even if she didn't know the answer she could usually figure it out, or make a good guess. But what was taking Mrs. Birchall so long? Lucy opened her eyes a crack to take a peek.

Something was wrong. She wasn't in Mrs. Birchall's third-grade classroom. Even with her eyes wide open she couldn't see a thing. It was too dark. And her head throbbed. She probed cautiously with her fingers, and discovered a huge lump on her temple.

She had been dreaming. That explained it. She was flat on her back, in the dark, and she had a wicked headache. What she needed was some aspirin, and a big drink of water. Still groggy, she tried to sit up, but the effort made her head spin. She felt queasy. Her breasts tingled as her milk let down, and she reached for baby Zoe.

There was no baby beside her; Bill wasn't there, either. There was only emptiness. She was lying on something hard, and gritty. She smelled dust, and something else, the reek of duplicating fluid. Panicking, she felt around with her hands. It was a dirt floor, a hard-packed dirt floor. Where was she? Why wasn't she in bed?

Once again she tried to sit up, and this time she succeeded. She was dizzy, but she could manage. She reached out with her arms and her hand met a rough wooden wall. She shifted herself around and leaned against it, trying to push down her fear and sort out her thoughts.

The last thing she remembered was returning to the Hallett House and searching for the diaper bag. Poor Zoe. She must be frantic with hunger by now. She had to get back to her.

Lucy pulled herself to her feet and began feeling her way along the wall. Wherever she was, she had to find a way out. She came to a corner, turned, and then found another. It was hard to judge distances, but she seemed to be in a rather small shed, or maybe a closet. Groping with her fingers, she found the door. She reached for the knob, but found an old-fashioned latch, instead. It lifted, and she pushed against the door, but it didn't open. She was locked in.

She leaned against the door, resting her forehead against it. This whole thing was crazy. Someone had knocked her on the head, and locked her in something that seemed to be Ezekiel Hallett's retreat, the old cabin he had insisted on preserving inside his fancy Victorian mansion.

Was this a joke, a prank of some kind? Certainly the boys would never do anything like this. Lucy pounded on the door with her fist. "Let me out!" she screamed. "Let me out!"

She coughed, choking on dust and fumes. The duplicating fluid. Alcohol. Smoke.

Her heart raced. She began to pound harder on the door. Her head was clear now; she knew she had to get out. Her fear gave her strength, and she beat her fists against the plank door as hard as she could.

"Help! Help!" she yelled, at the top of her lungs. Pounding on the door didn't help, so she kicked at it. Coughing and sputtering, she pulled her shirt up and held it over her mouth. It was getting very smoky. She had to get out. She only had minutes.

Stay low, she remembered. Crouching, she threw her whole body against the door, desperately trying to crash through. She did it again and again. Her shoulder throbbed. She was getting dizzy. She collapsed against the door. There was no air. She had to get out. She had to get back to Zoe, and Bill. She sobbed. One more time. She had to try one more time. She couldn't give up.

She tried to gather her last bit of strength for one more assault on the door, but she couldn't move. It was so hot, and there was no air. Something was pressing on her chest, getting tighter and tighter, and she couldn't get her breath. If she could just get one breath she could try again.

The door shuddered. There was a splintering, ripping noise, and chunks of wood crashed around her.

"Breathe in," barked a male voice, as something was placed over her nose. Sweet, fresh air. She sucked it in.

CHAPTER THIRTY-SIX

A noisy cart, rattling down the hallway, woke Lucy around seven o'clock. She knew right away she was in the cottage hospital, where her babies had been born, but couldn't remember how she got there.

Her mouth was dry, and she had a raging sore throat. She spotted the water pitcher on the bedstand, but was unable to reach it. Her left arm was taped tightly to her chest, and her right hand was encumbered with an IV tube. She leaned back against the pillow and took inventory. Her head throbbed and she was sore all over, but her most immediate problem was with her breasts. It had been quite a while since she had last nursed Zoe and they were painfully full.

Poor Zoe must be starving, she thought. She had to get home. She looked for a call button, found it safety-pinned near her pillow and rang for the nurse.

"How are we doing this morning?" inquired the nurse. She was a brisk woman in her early fifties, whose short gray hair was cut in a no-nonsense style.

"Thirsty," croaked Lucy, surprised at the sound of her voice.

"I'll bet you are," said the nurse, as she raised the bed to a sitting position and rolled the tray table closer to Lucy. She poured a glass of water, and held it for Lucy. "Sips, dear, tiny sips."

She let Lucy take five or six sips, and then set the glass on the table. Lucy immediately reached for it, but a deep, racking cough shook her body and filled her mouth with phlegm. The nurse handed her a tissue, and Lucy spat out a wad of gray-tinged mucous.

"Ugh," said Lucy, rather alarmed.

"From the fire," the nurse explained. "You inhaled quite a lot of smoke."

"What happened?" asked Lucy. "I don't remember a fire. Are the kids all right?"

"I don't really know the details," said the nurse. "I only came on duty a few minutes ago. You'll have to talk to the doctor."

"I have a little baby. I need to get home to her," said Lucy.

The nurse shook her head sympathetically. "The doctor will be in soon. Meanwhile, you're supposed to take these." She held out a cup containing two white pills. "For pain."

Lucy obediently took the pills in her mouth and swallowed them down with a swig of water. The nurse patted her hand, and left the room. Lucy closed her eyes and hoped the pills would work soon.

She started to drift off, when a startle reflex shook her body and jerked her awake. Fire. The nurse had said fire. Her stomach felt hollow and she began to breathe rapidly. Where was the fire? Why hadn't they told her? What were they keeping from her? She had to know what happened, and whether Bill and the kids were all right.

She reached for the call button, but fell asleep before she could ring.

*　　*　　*

When she woke a few hours later Doc Ryder was standing over her. "Up to your old shenanigans," he said, waggling a finger at her. An old-fashioned country GP, Doc Ryder had delivered Lucy's babies, stitched up Toby's foot when he cut it on a broken bottle while swimming at the lake, and prescribed countless bottles of sticky pink antibiotic syrup for ear infections. He flipped open Lucy's chart and reviewed it.

"Looks like you'll live," he said. "But you're going to feel pretty miserable for a couple of days. You've got a concussion there, and a dislocated shoulder. We've got that strapped up, should heal nicely. Smoke inhalation's tricky, though. Don't want you to get pneumonia, got you on antibiotics through the IV."

"Can I go home?" asked Lucy.

"We're just going to take things one day at a time," he said. "I want to keep an eye on that concussion. Give you a chance to rest."

"The baby needs me," said Lucy.

"Now, now," he said, patting her hand. "Why don't you let us take care of you for a change?"

She wanted to tell him that a nursing mother and baby needed to be together, bound as they were by the law of supply and demand, but she couldn't summon the energy to argue before he was gone. All alone, she tried to remember what had brought her to the hospital. The nurse said she had been in a fire, but she couldn't remember when or where. And why was Doc Ryder so evasive when she asked if she could go home? Did she still have a home, or had it burned down? And why couldn't she have the baby? Was Zoe all right?

Spotting the telephone on the bedstand, she pulled herself up until she could reach it. Her first attempt to punch in the number failed, and she blinked back tears of frustration. Taking a deep breath she tried again, but only got a busy signal. Relieved, she dropped back onto the pillows. Everything must be okay if somebody was talking on the phone, she decided. Reassured, she closed her eyes to go back to sleep. She was so tired. Between sleep and consciousness she heard the insistent beep of the busy signal. She saw the wall phone at home; the receiver was dangling.

She started, suddenly wide awake. The busy signal didn't mean anything, she realized. All it meant was that the receiver was off the hook. For all she knew, the house could have burned down around it. She remembered Lenk sneering at her. "This is all your fault," he'd said. "You and that husband of yours." She wanted to try calling again, but didn't have the energy to reach for the awkwardly placed phone. She felt tears pricking her eyes and lifted her hands to brush them away, but her hand dropped to her chest as she fell asleep.

Waking a few hours later, Lucy once again assessed her condition. Her headache had subsided; it was still there but it was manageable. The same with her throat. It only hurt when she swallowed. Breathing was a bit of a problem; her breathing passages were raw and she was painfully aware of each breath. Her breasts were tender and a constant reminder of how much she missed her baby.

"So, how's Sleeping Beauty?" inquired the gray-haired nurse with a warm smile.

"Better," she said with a wan smile. "Could you hand me the phone?"

"First things first," said the nurse, producing a thermometer. "Open wide."

Conversation was temporarily shut off as the nurse tended to Lucy's needs. Finally, she tucked the sheet around her and pulled out the thermometer.

"Hmm," she said, making a notation on Lucy's chart.

"What does that mean?" asked Lucy.

"Looking good," said the nurse, with a grin. "I'd tell you

if I could, but it's against hospital policy. Only the doctor can discuss your condition with you."

"Can you tell me anything about last night? About why I'm here? I'm so afraid something has happened to my family."

The nurse shook her head sympathetically. "I don't know, but I'll see what I can find out. Meanwhile, why don't you call?" She placed the phone on the bed, next to Lucy.

"Thanks," Lucy said. She punched in the familiar numbers, but all she got was the same busy signal. She tried Sue's number, but there was no answer. In desperation she dialed her mother's number, long distance to New York, thinking she would have heard if there was a tragedy. She let the phone ring and ring, she counted thirty times, and then gave up.

She was sitting, staring at the phone in her lap, when the door opened. An orderly brought in a lunch tray, set it on the table in front of her, and lifted the cover.

Lucy leaned forward; she was hungry and eager to see what was for lunch. There was milk, in a little carton, and a plastic cup of tea. Also a small container of orange juice and two slices of white bread in plastic wrap with a pat of margarine on top. The entree appeared to be a slice of meatlike substance smothered in thick pinkish-tan gravy, surrounded by rounded humps of red cabbage, instant mashed potatoes, and a tiny bowl of stewed tomatoes. Dessert was a bowl of applesauce.

Lucy took a sip of tea and a spoonful of applesauce. It was unsweetened. She looked for sugar, but there wasn't any. She poked at the mystery meat with her fork but the thought of eating it made her nauseous. She pushed the tray away and sank back onto the pillow.

She punched out her number on the phone and again got the busy signal. She couldn't stand it; she had to know what had happened. She felt incomplete without her family, especially the baby. Her little round head, her fuzzy hair, her fat baby cheeks. They had rarely been apart—Lucy was used to nursing whenever and wherever Zoe seemed hungry. Zoe spent a good part of the day in the baby-carrier, nestled under Lucy's chin.

She felt much stronger, she decided, wiggling her toes. There didn't seem to be anything the matter with her legs. She bent her knees, and stretched her legs out. The movement hurt. She flexed her ankles, and walked her feet up and down the bed, trying to work out the soreness.

She eyed the IV tube in her hand. The needle, she saw, was held in place by a big piece of tape. She raised her hand to her mouth and took hold of a corner of tape with her teeth. She gave a little tug and it pulled away. In a matter of seconds she had peeled the tape off.

She looked at the needle sticking into her hand. Carefully, she bit down on the plastic collar that connected the needle to the tubing and gave her head a quick jerk. The needle came out smoothly. Lucy watched a bead of blood well up, and licked it away. No more blood appeared.

She swung her legs over the side of the bed and stood up, feeling an immediate draft on her bare backside. So far, so good. She wasn't even dizzy. She opened the bedside stand and found a plastic bag containing her clothes.

Opening it, she grimaced. The baseball shirt and pants. What had she been dressed for? A costume party? She wrinkled her nose. They stank of smoke. Too bad, they would have to do.

Getting dressed with only one arm was a bit tricky, she discovered. Leaning her fanny against the bed she pulled on the tight pants, first tugging one leg and then the other. Socks didn't seem worth the trouble; she jammed her bare feet into her sneakers. The bra would be impossible so she ignored it and pulled the striped shirt over her head, leaving the left arm empty. She sat for a minute on the chair, holding her purse in her lap. Then, taking a deep breath she stood up and headed for the door.

Hearing voices approaching, she froze in her tracks. Thinking quickly she climbed back in bed and pulled the covers up over her. The johnny was on the floor but it was too late to do anything about it. The door was opening.

"Oh, didn't I put this in the laundry?" asked the nurse, picking it up. She shook her head. "Sometimes I think I'd forget my head if it wasn't fastened on! I forgot your meds— here you go."

She held out the little white cup with two pills and Lucy tossed them back, following with a swallow of water from a second cup.

"I'm so sorry," said the nurse. "I hope you weren't too uncomfortable."

Lucy shook her head. "I'm feeling much better."

"Not much appetite, I see," she said, indicating the tray.

"I just can't," Lucy said apologetically.

"Never mind. I'll take this away and let you get some rest." She picked up the tray and swept out of the room.

Lucy waited for a few minutes after the nurse left, then got up very cautiously. She tiptoed to the door and peeked out. The hall was empty, blocked by double doors at either end. A clutter of wheelchairs and a meds cart at one end seemed to indicate the nurses' station, so she went the other way.

Pushing through the doors she found a staircase. She went down a floor, backtracked through another hallway, and found herself in the lobby. She sat down in an armchair and considered her next step.

Call a taxi? She checked her wallet. Two bucks. No problem, they probably took VISA. She spotted a pay phone and stood up. The room whirled around her. Maybe she wasn't in such good shape after all. She waited a minute or two and the dizziness subsided. Careful not to move too fast she made her way to the phone. The number for the taxi company was conveniently printed on a sign above the phone. She was rummaging for a dime when she heard a voice.

"Lucy! What are you doing here?" It was Doug Durning.

"I don't really know," said Lucy. "They said I was in a fire."

"Really? The Hallett House burned down last night. Were you there?"

"I guess I must have been," said Lucy, as memories of the party flooded back. She looked down at the baseball outfit. "I wore this as a costume."

"That was some costume Bill wore—a giant bumblebee. He's got some balls, that's all I can say."

"Was anybody hurt in the fire—besides me, I mean?" Lucy grabbed his hand. "Is my family okay?"

"Sure," Doug said. "Why wouldn't they be?"

"I don't know," Lucy admitted. She couldn't help smiling foolishly; she felt light-headed with relief. 'They wouldn't tell me anything here. I got a little crazy, I guess. I just want to go home."

"Can I give you a lift?" Doug's brow was furrowed with concern. "You look a bit shaky to be out on your own."

"I feel a bit shaky," confessed Lucy, gratefully taking his arm. "This is really nice of you."

"No problem," said Doug, carefully supporting her as he led her out to his car.

CHAPTER THIRTY-SEVEN

Seated in Doug's aging Saab, Lucy felt unaccountably weepy. Embarrassed, she brushed away her tears.

"I'm sorry," she said. "I'm an awful mess."

"It's probably the medication," said Doug, starting the engine.

That was probably it, thought Lucy, wondering what they had been pumping into her. Whatever it was, it was taking her on an emotional roller-coaster ride. "Thanks for the lift," she said. "I can't tell you how much I appreciate it."

"It's nothing," said Doug, turning smoothly out of the parking lot. "So, what happened to you?"

"I don't know. I really can't remember much. They said I was in a fire."

"Like I said, the Hallett House burned down last night. It was a total loss."

"Oh." Lucy sat stunned. Poor Monica had died in a fire . . . the same thing could have happened to her.

"A bunch of kids discovered it. They called the fire department. Probably saved your life."

"I was lucky," said Lucy, wondering what she had been doing at the mansion. She should have been home.

"Yeah," said Doug. "Say, why don't we take a look at the place? Survey the damage. It's right off this road."

"I don't want to go there," said Lucy, as her stomach gave a lurch. "Could you take me home first? It's just a little bit farther."

Doug's hand tightened on the steering wheel. "This'll only take a minute," he said, making a sharp turn. They bounced along the rough dirt road and pulled up in front of the blackened pile of rubble that had once been the magnificent Hallett House, the finest house in Tinker's Cove.

"Oh, my God," gasped Lucy, shocked at the sight. "I can't believe I survived that."

Absolutely nothing was left, even the chimneys had cracked from the intense heat and collapsed. It was all gone—the fanciful pillared tower, the widow's walk, the ornate portico. Everything was reduced to soot and cinders, surrounded by a thin ribbon of yellow tape.

"It was quite a fire," said Doug. There was an odd note of satisfaction in his tone. "You should have seen it," he said, nodding. "Flames forty, fifty feet high. It was something." He gestured excitedly with his arms, and Lucy caught a whiff of something pungent. What was it? she wondered. It was so familiar.

A small group of bystanders had gathered. They stood, exchanging only brief bits of conversation, occasionally shaking their heads.

"They had to call in fire companies from Wilton and Gilead and even Rockland," said Doug. "But even with all that extra help they couldn't save it."

"You sound almost pleased," said Lucy.

Doug jerked abruptly and looked sharply at her; she wondered if she'd said something wrong.

He shrugged. "The town's better off without it. It was an eyesore." He started the engine.

"I guess," said Lucy, yawning. She was very tired. She

was having trouble keeping her eyes open. She leaned back and closed them, just for a minute. She felt the car begin to move. Soon she would be home.

A jumble of images crowded her mind. She could hear Zoe crying, but she couldn't find her. She was stumbling through a maze of rooms that opened before her, tilted at crazy angles like a carnival fun house. She was running uphill, then downhill and someone was pursuing her, laughing. It was Mrs. Birchall, her third-grade teacher. There was a horrible, choking smell. Mimeo fluid. She opened her eyes.

She was still in the car, but she was lying across the front seat. Through the window she saw dark green—balsam and fir trees—and blue sky. They were parked somewhere in the woods.

She felt a rush of cold air as the car door opened. She tilted her head to look behind her. She saw Doug. His face was red and angry. He was holding a length of two by four. "Nosey bitch," he said, raising his arm.

Instinctively, Lucy rolled away as Doug slammed the wood down on the seat where her head had been. Grabbing the dashboard with her good arm she pulled herself upright. Turning, she spotted Doug outside the car and watched him warily, waiting for his next move.

To her surprise, he dropped the two by four and fumbled in his pocket. Pulling out a book of matches he carefully and deliberately tore one off and struck it, then tossed it in the car. Lucy followed it with her gaze and saw it land in the back seat, which, she discovered, he had loaded with firewood and scrap lumber. The reek of mimeo fluid filled the air.

As she watched, the orange flame of the match grew larger. It turned blue, spreading along a piece of scrap wood, then leaped onto a branch of dry tinder that caught immediately with a snapping sound. A whitish gray column of smoke formed and began filling the car. Durning slammed the door and stepped back. His eyes were wide open, his expression eager with anticipation. He licked his lips.

Lucy reached for the door handle on the passenger side but couldn't find it. Blinking, her eyes already smarting, she discovered it was broken. Through the smoke she saw Durning laughing. Coughing, she grabbed the steering wheel and pulled herself toward the driver's side door. The horn blared. Awkwardly, she fumbled for the lock with her right hand. The back seat was now fully ablaze, the car was like a furnace. The smoke was so thick that she could no longer see. Groping with her fingers, she found the latch. She pushed against the door and the lock finally yielded; she fell out of the car onto her knees.

Retching and choking, still blinded by the smoke, she tried to crawl away from the heat of the fire. Durning stopped her, grabbing her by the hair and pulling her to her feet.

"What's your hurry?" he asked. "Don't you like the pretty fire?"

"Let me go!" she screamed. "You're crazy! You're going to get us both killed!"

"Not both of us," he said, shoving her back toward the car and raising his arm to hit her. Staggering, she threw up her good arm to block the blow, but it never came. Instead, she saw Bill materialize in the smoke and grab Durning by the shoulders, throwing him back against a tree. He hit him twice in the stomach, and then punched him in the face. Durning's head snapped back and he slid to the ground. Bill stood over him, fists clenched, breathing hard. His eyes were narrow slits, and his jaw was clenched. Lucy could see a vein in his neck pulsing.

A sudden roar made her turn her head, and she saw the Saab disappear in a rush of bright orange flames. Black smoke filled the air. Bill grabbed her arm and dragged her away from the burning car.

"Oh my God," she said, feeling her knees start to buckle underneath her. He caught her in his arms. Lucy leaned against him, drinking in his strong, sweaty smell. She nuzzled her face against his beard, and felt the smooth flannel covering his chest under her fingertips. He tightened his arms around her.

"I want to go home," whispered Lucy.

CHAPTER THIRTY-EIGHT

Being home was bliss, thought Lucy later that afternoon as she looked down at Zoe's sweet little head. She was sitting sideways on the couch, with her legs stretched out. Zoe was propped on pillows, because of Lucy's taped arm, and was enthusiastically making up for missed meals. Edna, Bill's mother, hovered nearby, ready to assist.

"Would you like some more juice?" she asked. "How about some lemonade?"

"That would be great," said Lucy. She had an enormous thirst; she couldn't drink enough.

Edna bustled off, pleased to have an errand.

"I told Bill," she said, when she returned. "I told him the hospital wouldn't know what to do with you. Bring her home, I said, so she can be with the baby. If Lucy takes care of the baby, we can take care of Lucy. That's what I said."

"All I could think of was getting back home," said Lucy, after she'd gulped down half the lemonade. "I felt like one of those trapped foxes that chews off its leg to get back to her babies."

"It's mother love, dear."

"It's instinct," said Toby. "Learned about it in school."

"It's probably a little bit of both," said Lucy, reaching for Toby's hand. "Is everything okay? You look worried."

"You're gonna be okay, aren't you, Mom?"

"Sure," said Lucy.

Toby shifted nervously from one foot to the other. "Are me and the guys in trouble?" he asked.

"What do you mean?" asked Lucy. "Sit down and tell me about it." She patted the side of the couch.

"Are they gonna think we started the fire?" he asked, perching next to her.

"Why would they think that?" A horrible thought flitted through her mind. "You didn't, did you?"

"No. We wouldn't do anything like that. But last year, remember the toilet paper? Everybody thought me and Eddie put it on Mr. Reid's hedge, but it wasn't us. It was really Tim Rogers. He said we'd be real sorry if we told."

"This is different," said Lucy, covering his hand with her own. "This isn't kid stuff."

"I was scared," confessed Toby. "Really scared."

"Me, too," said Lucy. Now that she remembered what had happened last night she didn't want to think about it. She pushed the dark thoughts away, and smiled at Toby. "You boys really gave me a fright."

"Yeah, that was funny. You jumped a mile. You yelled at us and we ran behind some bushes. We heard some footsteps and we thought it was Officer Barney, coming to take us home. We were gonna make him look for us, and then jump out and scare him. But it wasn't Barney—it was some guy. He started carrying cans into the house and we figured he was the one setting the fires. Stubby called the fire department on his walkie-talkie."

"He knew what to do?"

"Sure. Officer Barney lent him a real police radio for his costume. Showed him how to use it and everything."

"I'm surprised the dispatcher believed you—didn't he think it might be a Halloween prank?"

"Yeah." Toby nodded. "He took our names and said we'd be in serious trouble if it was a false alarm. That scared us a little bit, because we waited and waited and nothing seemed to happen. Then the guy ran out and drove away, and still nothing happened. Richie and Eddie said maybe we ought to go home and tell our parents, but I didn't want to leave you there. Then it started to smell like the charcoal fire when Dad lights it, you know there's a fire in there but you can't see much. That's when I really got scared. I wanted to go in and get you, but the guys wouldn't let me. We looked through the window and there were blue and orange flames racing around, up and down the walls and across the floor. They'd start up and go out. It was weird.

"That's when the fire truck came. They made us stand back and we saw them go in with oxygen tanks on their backs. They went in and then the whole place seemed to explode. There was a big whoosh, and all at once it was really on fire. That's when the fireman carried you out. I saw him in the doorway, with the red flames behind him."

"Wow," said Lucy, reaching up and pulling his head down for a quick kiss. "You boys did the right thing. You were really brave."

"I'm just glad you're okay. You really are okay, aren't you?"

"Yeah," said Lucy. "I'm gonna be fine."

"That's good," said Toby, " 'cause Mom, you don't look too good right now."

"I don't feel too good, either," admitted Lucy. "I wonder where your dad is with those prescriptions."

Lucy ached all over, her throat was raw and she was uncomfortably aware of her chest as she breathed. Her shoulder throbbed, and her head was pounding.

"You look bushed, Lucy. Let me take the baby and put her down in the crib," offered Edna. "She's sleeping like an angel."

Toby wandered off, and Edna carried the baby upstairs,

leaving Lucy alone. She glanced around the room—it was getting a bit shabby. The couch was worn, the rug needed a cleaning, the pictures were just a bit askew. Magazines were piled in an untidy heap on the lamp table, a pair of Elizabeth's shoes lay forgotten under the coffee table. It had never looked better.

"So, how ya doin'?" asked Bill, appearing in the doorway.

"Fine. It's great to be home. Baby's sleeping."

"About time," said Bill, sitting down heavily in the recliner, still holding a plastic shopping bag.

"Did you get everything?"

"Yup." He began unpacking. "Antibiotics, pain killer, ice bag, heating pad, disposable diapers. You know, I couldn't find a single diaper anywhere in the house!"

"I know—that's why I went to the Hallett House. I left the diaper bag there."

"I knew there had to be a reason. I thought you might have gone after Toby. That was some night." He shook his head. "Phone call woke me up, I didn't know what was going on. Girls were frantic, baby was soaking wet and screaming, cops brought Toby home, you were at the hospital. It was crazy."

Lucy nodded. She was content to look at Bill. Always the same outfit—jeans, plaid flannel shirt, work boots, beard. Except in summer. Then it was shorts, T-shirt, work boots, and beard. He never changed. He was steady and reliable. Strong. Always gentle with her and the kids. In all the years they'd been married she'd never seen him strike anyone, until today.

"I didn't know you could fight," said Lucy.

"Neither did I. Pure adrenaline." Bill's cheeks reddened and he fingered a brown plastic medicine vial. "I didn't want to stop hitting him. I coulda killed him."

"How did you find me?"

"Mom sent me to the hospital to bring you home. I saw

you getting in the car with him. I called your name, but I was too far away and you didn't hear me. I decided to follow. I couldn't figure out what was going on. Why did you leave with him?"

"Nobody would tell me anything and I was going crazy— I thought they were keeping something from me. I was afraid Lenk had burned the house down and I was the only one left. I had to get home and find out what had happened."

"Why didn't you call?"

"I tried and tried but all I got was a busy signal."

"Oh." Bill blushed. "I was on the phone for quite a while trying to get things organized, and as soon as I got off the phone the kids took over."

"I should have thought of that," said Lucy.

"Anyway, I pulled into the parking lot and saw you getting into Doug's car. I figured he was just bringing you home, but I didn't feel good about you being in the car with him. I don't know why— I just felt uneasy. I started thinking as I was following you and it was pretty clear that he had the most to gain from the fires."

"He did?"

"Sure. Because of the bylaws. Getting rid of his house gave him a clean slate. He could pretty much build what he wanted, long as it was white and had shutters."

"The Red Zone!" exclaimed Lucy. "I can't believe I was so dumb."

"I don't get it."

"It was on the movie marquee. *The Red Zone.* I looked right at it."

"Zoning by fire," said Bill thoughtfully. "That's what he was doing. Come to think of it, I heard something about him buying the Hallett House."

"I heard him talking to Krissy at the party—all about how the property was worth more without the building!"

"That's right. Burning it down gave him a very nice piece of commercial property. It was a pretty clever plan—everybody thought there was a pyromaniac loose. Then Lenk started spouting off and everybody thought it was him."

"I think it started out as a rational plan," Lucy said, "but it got out of control. He liked setting those fires. I'll never forget the expression on his face when he started the fire in the car. It was creepy."

"I think he had some idea of killing you at the Hallett House but there were too many people so he headed off down that old dirt track into the woods. That was scary. I couldn't get too close or he'd see me but I was terrified of losing him. I called the cops on the phone in the truck and decided to follow on foot. Then I saw the smoke and panicked— I was afraid I was too late. When I saw him trying to hit you it was like a movie or something. I didn't even realize what I was doing."

"You were great," said Lucy.

"I wouldn't want to make a career of it," said Bill, flexing his hands and massaging his knuckles. "Thank God for cell phones I was real happy when the cops came and took him off my hands." He reached for the remote control and pushed the chair back so the leg rest came up. He flipped through the channels until he found the NFL game.

In her nest of pillows and blankets on the couch, Lucy snuggled down and closed her eyes. She started to drift off, then jerked awake. She blinked. She was home. She could hear the girls' arguing upstairs. Edna was running the mixer in the kitchen. Bill was snoring in the chair, a shaving cream commercial was playing on the TV. Everything was fine.

EPILOGUE

Outside, a fine dusting of snow, the first of the season, was softly falling.

Inside Miss Tilley's house a fire was burning brightly, the tea was hot, and the scones were dripping with butter. Lucy reached for another, and Sue's eyebrows shot up in disapproval.

"I can't help it," said Lucy. "I'm hungry all the time. I think it's from working out. I haven't lost any weight, but I feel great."

"Isn't it about time to wean that child?" asked Miss Tilley. "Franklin Delano Roosevelt's mother nursed him until he was two, you know. Look how he turned out." Miss Tilley had regained much of her snap and vigor, and about ten pounds, since she had arranged for Rachel Goodman to come in for a couple of hours every day.

"You mean how he became President of the United States?" asked Rachel, her eyes sparkling mischievously.

"Rode into office on Teddy's coattails," said Miss Tilley, with a wave of her hand. "He was always a mamma's boy, and he packed the Supreme Court with Communists and tried to destroy the free enterprise system." She took a healthy bite of scone and chewed happily; once again the Republicans were in charge and the nation was back on course. "And that wife of his," she paused and rolled her eyes. "Eleanor!"

"My grandfather didn't think much of her, either," admitted Lucy. "He used to say Eleanor Roosevelt and John Dewey practically ruined the country."

"Sound man," said Miss Tilley, nodding. "Is he . . . ?"

"No." Lucy shook her head. "He's been dead for quite a while, but he always used to say that he liked Ike."

"We all did," said Miss Tilley, smiling at the memory of the Supreme Allied Commander turned politician.

"So, Lucy, how are you feeling?" asked Rachel, bringing in a fresh pot of tea.

"Fine. Krissy and Vicki gave me some special exercises. I'm sure I recovered faster because of them. My shoulder's a little stiff, but that's all."

"You were lucky," said Rachel. "I didn't want the boys to stay out after the party, but it was a good thing they did. Imagine what could have happened if they hadn't been there. . . ."

"I know," said Lucy. "It's still hard for me to believe it all wasn't a really bad dream. A nightmare. He tried to kill me twice. I never suspected him for a minute. I thought he was a nice guy. I was grateful when he offered to give me a ride home from the hospital."

"You kept telling me it was poor Dr. Mayes," said Sue.

"Well, I did suspect him at first, especially when I learned about Krissy," admitted Lucy. "I think even his daughter, Mira, had her suspicions. I'm glad it wasn't him. And then I was sure it was Randy Lenk, and the police thought so, too. He was making those anonymous phone calls and his father died in a fire and he lives in that weird house full of junk. But when I opened my eyes and saw Doug holding that two by four over my head, well, that convinced me he was the arsonist. Plus, the fact that he'd filled the car with firewood and soaked it with mimeo fluid was also a clue."

"He was going to burn you up?" Rachel's dark eyes were huge.

"In the car, after he'd bashed my head in." Lucy shuddered. "He was trying to make it look like an accident."

"A very wicked man," said Miss Tilley. "Now that I think of it he was a sneaky little boy. I used to find him in the adult book section, sneaking peeks at *Peyton Place*."

"You allowed a book like that in the library?" Lucy was surprised.

"I did. Of course, nobody had the nerve to take it out."

The women laughed.

"And how is Jennifer? She always reminded me a little bit of Alison in the book," said Miss Tilley.

"So you read *Peyton Place?*" Lucy pounced on her.

"Of course. I used to read all the books that I bought for the library before putting them out on the shelves."

"Jennifer's home," said Rachel, who lived across the street from the Mitchells. "She's one brave little girl. She's got pins in her legs—it looks dreadful—but she's absolutely confident that she'll walk again. I saw her playing field hockey in the garage in her wheelchair with a bunch of her friends the other day."

"That was a terrible accident," said Lucy, who immediately wished she could take the words back. Miss Tilley had fallen silent, and was staring at the window.

"Just look at that snow," said Sue, changing the subject. "Isn't it pretty? Soon it will be Christmas!" She loved all holidays, but especially Christmas when she decorated her house lavishly and set up three Christmas trees.

"What will happen to Doug?" asked Rachel.

"They have to decide if he's crazy," said Lucy. "He's been sent to the state hospital for psychiatric tests."

"I don't think an insanity defense will play very well,"

said Sue, tapping a scarlet nail against Miss Tilley's blue Canton china cup. "He had a solid financial motive, and the fires were all carefully planned."

"That's right," agreed Miss Tilley. "He was determined to develop that property. When the commission said no, he decided to take matters into his own hands and burn it down. Such a shame."

"I don't understand," said Rachel.

"Neither did I," said Lucy. "Until Bill explained the bylaw to me. As long as Durning's antique house was standing, the commission would only let him make changes that were appropriate to the period it was built. But once the house was gone, he had a valuable piece of commercially zoned property right in the center of town. He could build pretty much whatever he wanted, as long as he followed the commission's style guidelines."

"That's right," said Miss Tilley. "That house was a fine old captain's home built in 1830. He wanted to remodel it into an office complex. It was quite ambitious. There was even a bank, with an ATM machine and a drive-through window. There was going to be a big parking lot—the entire character of the house would have been destroyed."

"So you turned him down?" asked Rachel.

"Of course. We had no choice. But the bylaw did create a dangerous situation, although we didn't realize it at the time. If a historic building was destroyed—by fire or hurricane or Act of God—and couldn't be repaired, then the owner would have a lot more leeway. The commission standards for new construction aren't nearly as strict."

"The ATM would have been okay?" Sue asked.

"As long as it was painted white and had shutters," said Lucy, echoing Bill.

"That's right," agreed Miss Tilley.

"But why all the other fires?" asked Rachel. "He burned down half the town."

"Camouflage," said Sue, with a knowing nod.

"Barney said they're investigating to see if he had financial interests in some of the other buildings. The Hallett House was owned by a realty trust—it's complicated but they suspect Durning would have profited from that fire, too."

"One person who hasn't made out very well is Randy Lenk," said Rachel. "I met Ted at the bank and he said state inspectors found gasoline leaking from his underground tanks. He's going to have to pay for a very expensive cleanup."

"Don't bet on it," said Sue derisively. "When I stopped in for gas the other day, he tried to sell me the station. At a bargain price. Nice of him, don't you think?"

"Not very . . . you would have got stuck with the cleanup," said Lucy.

"That's the plan. I bet he'll find some poor sucker who thinks he's getting a deal. Lenk wants to move to Idaho or someplace. Said he's sick and tired of the government poking into everything, and there's some other folks out there that think like him. They're forming some militia or something, they're going to reclaim the government for the people, he said."

"Well, they better make him general," said Miss Tilley. "He can't abide taking directions from anyone. Never could."

The women fell silent, and Rachel got up to put a fresh log on the fire.

"I bet you haven't heard," said Sue. "The selectmen have appointed me to the Recreation Commission."

"Congratulations," said Lucy, "That's the perfect job for you."

"I think so," Sue agreed. "In fact, I'm already making plans for a big town picnic in the spring. Lucy's prime suspect, Dr. Mayes, has donated the Homestead property to the town, for a conservation area. Isn't that neat?"

"That's a wonderful way to remember Monica," said Lucy.

"I think so. We're going to put up a nice sign, you'll have to help us with the wording, okay, Lucy?"

"Sure."

"And maybe you could make some cupcakes for the picnic? Say, six dozen?"

Lucy met Sue's eyes, and she smiled. "I'll donate soda, paper plates, napkins, whatever you need. I'll even bake brownies, but cupcakes?" She gave her head a little shake. "Never again."

WICKED WITCH
MURDER

PROLOGUE

Mind the witches' rede ye must,
in perfect love and perfect trust.

Diana Ravenscroft was shivering but told herself it was not fear, but simply excitement. She had absolutely nothing to dread from the people standing in the circle, waiting for her. They were all Wiccans and had pledged perfect love and perfect trust. No, it was excitement . . . and the cool weather.

Spring comes late in Tinker's Cove, Maine, and it was decidedly chilly on the last day of April, and even cooler as darkness fell. The full moon was shining brightly and the trees' budding branches were a tangle of black scribbles against a navy blue sky. Her senses were sharper than usual, and she was aware of the cool breeze that fluttered her sacred garments, the salty tang of the coastal air, the prickly grass beneath her bare feet. The earth felt ripe to her, ready to burst into leaf and flower, as she approached the magick circle.

It was fitting, she thought, that Lord Malebranche had chosen this night, Beltane, for the ritual that would raise her to the third degree as a high priestess in the coven. Only a witch can make a witch and only a high priest can make a high priestess, and Diana had been his student for months now. It had been a demanding apprenticeship, and she had struggled to memorize the chants and magickal properties, the spells and rituals, all of which had to be performed precisely, because a simple mistake could unleash powerful destructive forces.

But the craft, as any witch would tell you, wasn't about destruction. It was all about the five elements in nature: fire, water, earth, air, and spirit. The practitioners sought ecstatic union with the forces of the universe and tried to live in harmony with natural laws. And now, just as she had spent the last months in quiet study and meditation in preparation for this night, so had the natural world been resting and gathering strength for the great season of rebirth, renewal, and growth that was to come.

Diana felt she was on the brink of something, and she hoped she was ready, worthy of taking the next step. Because tonight, for the first time, she would be celebrating the annual Beltane sabbat skyclad, demonstrating the commitment the craft demanded. And there was more. Until now, the mystic union of male and female had only been symbolized by the dipping of a finger in a chalice of water or by slipping an athame, the ritual dagger, into a cup of wine. But tonight it would be the real thing: Lord Malebranche would consummate her ascension to the high priesthood before the entire coven.

And now they were gathered, a small group to be sure, but they were none the less fervent for that. Lady Sibyl was casting the circle, clearing it of all maleficent forces and preparing this forest clearing for the midnight ritual. Diana took her place in the circle, planting her feet in the good earth and raising her palms and face to Goddess Moon. Then, with a flash of light, the great Beltane fire was alight and Lord Malebranche stood before her, magnificent in his horned nakedness. The members of the coven began chanting and drumming, and with a snap of his fingers, Lord Malebranche released the shoulder clasps of her ritual garment and it fell to the ground, around her ankles. He then took her hand and drew her toward the flickering fire in the center of the circle, her white body bathed in moonlight. When she arose, she would be Lady Diana, High Priestess of the Silver Coven.

I
FIRE

The Ordains have spoken:
When winter's icy grasp is broken,
When the warming sun returns,
Let the Beltane fires burn.

CHAPTER ONE

She didn't believe in any of it, not for a minute, thought Lucy Stone. She was a hardheaded reporter for the *Pennysaver,* the local weekly newspaper in Tinker's Cove, Maine, and being skeptical was part of her job. No wonder, then, that all this nonsense about second sight and spells and magical powers didn't impress her in the least. It was all fakery and trickery; you couldn't fool her. So when Pam Stillings announced she'd made an appointment for them all to have a psychic reading after their regular Thursday morning breakfast, she'd been less enthusiastic than the others but didn't want to be left out either. But as far as she was concerned, the only reason she was going along with her friends on this late June morning to Solstice, the new shop in town owned by Diana Ravenscroft, was to see if she could figure out how it was done. That was the only reason. Period. She was happily married, had four well-adjusted children and an adorable grandchild, and she wasn't at all interested in meeting a tall, dark stranger or going on a long trip. And so far, none of her dear, departed relatives had tried to contact her, and that was the way she liked it.

"I've been dying to come here, ever since it opened," said

Pam as she slipped her aged Mustang into a parking spot in front of the little shop. "It's so cute." Pam was married to Lucy's boss, Ted, and still retained the enthusiasm she'd displayed as a high school cheerleader.

The shop was cute; there was no denying that, thought Lucy, reaching for the car door handle. It was located in a quaint antique building that used to be a shoe store, with a little studio apartment upstairs. It was a bit like a child's drawing, a cockeyed little square with a triangle perched on top. Even though it was at least a century old, maybe more, it had gone largely unnoticed, tucked behind an overgrown garden, until Diana moved in and painted it lavender with purple trim. The rampant vines and weeds had been tamed, window boxes overflowing with petunias accented the mullioned display windows that were filled with crystal pendants that caught the light, an assortment of bath and body products were arranged in pyramids, and there was a smattering of books and hand-made jewelry. A black cat was curled up on a thick green velvet cushion, asleep in a patch of sun.

"This ought to be a hoot," said Sue Finch, flipping down the sun visor and checking her lipstick in the mirror before opening the door and gracefully exiting the car. Sue was the only woman in the little seaside town who consistently wore high heels, and she got her hair done in New York City when she visited her daughter, Sidra, who was an assistant producer for *The Norah! Show.* "I hear psychics are all the rage now. All the stars have their favorite fortune tellers, and Sidra says Norah's even doing a show on them."

"That doesn't surprise me one bit," said Rachel Goodman with a nod that sent her black-rimmed glasses sliding down her nose as she scrambled out of the backseat. "There are mental forces we don't understand. The mind is very mysterious." Rachel had been a psych major in college and had never really gotten over it.

"It's just a lot of hooey," muttered Lucy as they trooped

through the shop door. "Unhappy, desperate people will cling to anything."

"If you really believe that, then why did you come?" asked an ethereal voice, coming from above.

Lucy followed the sound and found Diana Ravenscroft perched atop a tall ladder in the corner, watering a hanging plant. Her long hair flowed over her shoulders in a tumble of auburn waves, and she was dressed in a form-fitting velvet gown the color of a fine aged wine. A graceful alabaster arm extended from the loose sleeve as she tipped the watering can and released a stream of silvery water into the hand-crafted pot containing a lush fuschia dripping with purple and magenta flowers.

"Why not?" responded Lucy, rising to the challenge. "Are you afraid I might see through your tricks?"

Diana smiled sweetly. "Not at all," she said, descending with a light step and setting the watering can on a table, beside a display of variously colored candles. "I'm the genuine article, a high priestess in the Wiccan religion. I even have a title: Lady Diana."

Give me a break, thought Lucy.

"You actually consider yourself a witch?" asked Rachel.

"Oh, yes," said Diana. "I've even got a familiar, my cat. His name is Piewocket."

"Do you belong to a coven?" asked Pam.

"I do, but not all witches belong to covens. There are a number of solitaires, who practice alone."

Sue, ever the shopper, was examining a display of gemstone and silver jewelry. "How do you become a witch? Is it something you can learn, or are you born with it?"

"A little of both," said Diana. "I always knew I was a bit different. They called me 'sensitive' as a child. I remember bursting into tears one time, apparently for no reason at all, and then we got a call that my brother had been hit by a car while bicycling and was taken to the hospital."

"Oh, my goodness," gasped Pam.

Diana smiled. "He was fine, just a broken arm." She paused. "But it made me wonder about myself. And then when I heard about Wicca, I began to read and study and eventually found others like myself. I guess I have always been a witch, but I've been in the coven for only a few years now."

"And are there a lot of witches around here?" asked Lucy, sensing a possible story for the *Pennysaver.*

"The ordains, the rules of the coven, prohibit revealing the identity of other witches," said Diana. "I'm sure you understand, since witches have often been persecuted by those who fear the craft." She smiled, making eye contact with each of them in turn. Lucy was surprised to feel a sense of warm relaxation when Diana's gaze met hers. "There's nothing to fear," continued Diana. "The first and last rule of witchcraft is 'An ye harm none, do as ye will.' So, shall we begin the readings? I can do them individually or as a group."

"Group?" asked Pam, checking with the others. Receiving nods all around, they followed Diana toward a curtained doorway in the rear of the shop. When she pushed it aside, they stepped into a small circular space hung all around with richly colored curtains in red, green, blue, and silver. A round table stood in the center, containing a crystal ball. The sight made Lucy giggle; it was such a cliché and she'd expected Diana to be a little more original.

"You're laughing at my crystal ball?" asked Diana, amused.

"I'm sorry," said Lucy. "It just struck me as corny."

"I know," admitted Diana. "But I'm fond of it. It was a gift from someone who is terribly dear to me." Her back was to them as she busied herself at a small table covered with a cloth and two tall white candles at each corner, like an altar. A green candle stood in the center, along with two bowls. "I use a variety of methods: cards, palms, tea leaves. Whatever seems appropriate." She turned and faced them, holding a dagger in one hand and a bowl in the other. "Seat yourselves and I will begin by casting a magick circle."

The four friends obeyed, glancing at each other.

"Please join hands," instructed Diana.

Lucy linked hands with Sue on one side and Rachel on the other; she smiled across the table at Pam, then turned to watch Diana.

"Watery cradle of life, bubbling source of creation, cleanse this space of any and all impurities and evil," recited Diana, dipping the dagger into the water. Then she replaced the bowl on the altar and picked up another bowl containing salt. "Salt born of sea-water, allow only good and beneficent forces to enter here and aid me in my work." She dipped the dagger into the salt, then raised it. "So mote it be!"

Replacing the bowl of salt on the altar, she proceeded to walk clockwise in a circle around the table, holding the dagger. "I conjure and create this circle as a sphere of protection, free from all evil and negative forces. I now bless and consecrate this circle to be a place of peace, love, and power." Then, taking her place, she set the dagger on the table and gazed into the crystal ball. Placing her hands over the ball, she made circular motions, then turned them palm sides up. "Visions now appear to me; only true ones will I see."

She remained still, eyes closed, for a long few moments, then turned to Pam. "I see money. You're anxious about money."

Pam chuckled. "I think this recession is making everyone a bit nervous. We're seeing all these foreclosures; the stock market is down; gas and groceries are up."

Silently, Lucy agreed. Everybody was concerned about money; it was a sure bet for a so-called psychic.

"No, this is something to do with your husband. Perhaps he's made an unwise investment?"

"Only if you call a newspaper an unwise investment," replied Pam.

"No, not the newspaper. A car."

Not exactly rocket science—everybody had a car, thought Lucy, but Pam was impressed.

"The hybrid?" she screamed, raising her eyebrows. "He just bought a hybrid!"

Diana shook her head. "I see him, parked on the side of the road, with the hood up. And there's an odd sound, like clucking. Birds, maybe chickens." She shrugged. "I'm not at all sure what this means."

In spite of herself, Lucy felt the hairs on the back of her neck rising. "Ted was going out to Clark's Chicken Farm to do a story about the rising price of eggs," she blurted out. She stared at Diana. "How could you know that?" she asked, then quickly supplied an explanation. "You ran into him earlier, didn't you? He must have told you!"

Diana smiled. "I haven't left this building all day, but you don't have to believe me." Once again, she leaned over the ball and repeated the words: "Visions now appear to me, only true ones will I see." She stared into the ball for a long time, then raised her head and looked at Sue. "I see worry and dollar signs and small children."

Lucy's skepticism returned as she thought she detected a method in Diana's readings. The setting and the mumbo jumbo set the mood, and then she threw out some general ideas and waited for her clients to respond. But Sue, Lucy noticed, wasn't playing along.

"What else do you see?" she asked.

"Another woman, a younger woman. She's knocking on a door. It's the door to a bank."

"I don't know how you could possibly know this," mused Sue. "Chris went to the bank to apply for a loan this morning." Chris Cashman was Sue's partner in Little Prodigies Child Care Center, and they'd recently had a cash flow problem.

Diana smiled at her. "It's just a temporary situation," she said. "You'll be able to pay off the loan in six months, and all will be well."

Once again, Lucy found her skepticism returning. It was no secret that Sue was part owner of Little Prodigies; her photo was in every ad. And as for money troubles, the recession had hit a lot of families hard, and it was only to be expected that some would be struggling to meet their child care expenses.

Sue, however, had no such doubts. She seized on the good news, letting out a big sigh and laughing. "I can't tell you what a relief this is. I was really worried."

"No need to worry," said Diana, bending once again over the crystal ball. "Mmm, this is odd," she said, bending closer, then looking up at Rachel. "I see a very old woman, but she's no relation of yours. A friend, perhaps?"

Rachel nodded. "I provide home care for an elderly friend."

"That explains it," said Diana, returning to the crystal ball. "Your friend is very old, right?"

Rachel nodded. "I worry about her. She's well over ninety and increasingly frail."

"No need to worry—she's a tough old bird," said Diana. "She's going to be around for quite a while."

Rachel pressed her hands together and beamed at Diana. "That is wonderful news. Thank you."

Lucy, however, wasn't convinced. Women their age were usually caring for at least one elderly person; it was yet another safe guess for Diana.

"Now for my doubting Thomas," said Diana, repeating her invocation over the crystal ball. "Visions, now appear to me, only true ones will I see." Then she opened her eyes, stared into the ball, and recoiled as if she'd been stung. She repeated the process, but it didn't seem to work. Whatever she was seeing was still there, and Lucy knew it wasn't good. "I don't like what I see," said Diana, pulling a pack of cards from beneath the table and shuffling them. "I'm going to try a different method—the tarot," she said, laying out five cards and turning the first one over to reveal a figure hanging upside down. "The Hanged Man, Le Pendu."

"That sounds ominous," said Lucy.

"It's not bad," said Diana. "It means devotion to a worth-while cause, but you might find that circumstances are turned upside down for a bit. Change is in the air."

Lucy nodded and watched as Diana turned over the next card, revealing a knight on a handsome white stallion. *This must be something wonderful,* she thought. Her knight had come to rescue her. But Diana's face was grave.

"Le Mort, Death," she said, sighing. "Of course," she added, "it can mean the end of a phase, not necessarily the end of life."

"Absolutely, the end of a phase," said Lucy, determined not to let this nonsense rattle her. "Let's look on the bright side."

But the next card, which pictured a blindfolded and caged figure, didn't seem to offer much hope.

"The Eight of Swords. It generally indicates major diffi-culties and adverse circumstances," said Diana.

"Well, I've still got two more," said Lucy.

Diana revealed the fourth card, which showed a lively figure in medieval garb who seemed to be dancing. "This is better," she said. "The Fool. I see energy and optimism, per-haps the beginning of a journey or an unexpected happening that will challenge you."

"I'm up for it," said Lucy, laughing, as Diana reached for the fifth and final card, which pictured a group of figures battling with staves.

"Five of Wands, the Lord of Strife," said Diana, sounding disappointed. "I'm glad you're ready, because it looks as if trouble is coming and it can't be avoided." She looked at Lucy. "I'm sorry. I wish I had better news for you."

"Oh, well," said Lucy, shrugging. "I don't suppose it matters, because I don't believe in this stuff anyway."

Diana pressed her lips together, as if debating with herself. After a moment or two, she spoke. "I think you need to be careful."

Her tone was so serious that it gave Lucy pause. "What did you see in the crystal ball?" she asked.

Diana's face went pale. "I didn't want to tell you—that's why I used the cards. I was looking for more information so I could understand it better, perhaps find a broader context." She paused and reached for Lucy's hand. "It was fire," she said, "and that's not all. There were screams . . . screams in the night."

Lucy considered for a moment, then smiled. "Well, as it happens, I put new batteries in the smoke alarms last week. So I think we're covered."

"I hope so," said Diana, smiling back. Then, signaling that the reading was over, she covered the crystal ball with a cloth and collected the tarot cards. Rising from her seat and holding the dagger, she walked counterclockwise around them. "O mighty circle that has preserved and protected us, I now withdraw your force and release thee. So mote it be."

Understanding that the session was now concluded, Sue asked how much they owed her for the readings.

"I cannot request or demand payment," she said. "That is not the way of the craft. But if you would like to offer me something in return for my time, I would be honored to accept it."

The four friends looked from one to the other, unsure what to do next. Finally, Rachel spoke. "Is there a customary offering?"

Diana produced a printed card. "Here are some guidelines," she said, handing it to Rachel and then withdrawing through the curtain to the front of the shop.

Rachel held the card and they gathered around, looking over her shoulders at the neat list. In addition to readings, they saw that Diana offered spells, charms, and potions.

"Maybe you should get a protective charm, Lucy," advised Pam. "They're only fifteen to thirty dollars."

"Everything is fifteen to thirty dollars," observed Sue.

"Let's give her twenty apiece and be done with it," said Lucy. "As far as I'm concerned, it's all a big scam. She scares you and then offers protection—just like the Mafia!"

CHAPTER TWO

The *Pennysaver* came out on Thursdays, so that was always a light day for Lucy, who took the morning off but usually went in for a few hours in the afternoon to help Phyllis, who handled reception duties as well as the listings and classified ads.

"So how was the reading?" asked Phyllis, who was sitting at her usual spot behind the reception counter. She had recently lost quite a bit of weight and had given up her colorful muumuus in favor of more sedate clothing that showed off her figure, but she still dyed her hair a bright tangerine color and wore multicolored reading glasses. And her nail color changed weekly—this week it was lime green.

"She's good, I'll give you that. I don't know how she does it, but she was right on target. She told Sue that her money troubles with Little Prodigies will clear up, told Rachel that Miss Tilley will be around for a good long while, and, you won't believe this, told Pam that Ted was having car trouble out by the chicken farm."

Phyllis's jaw dropped. "That's amazing. He called, just a minute or two before you came in. That expensive newfangled hybrid of his wouldn't start when he finished interviewing Bruce Clark!"

Lucy took a minute to absorb this information. "There must be some rational explanation," she said.

"What about you?" asked Phyllis. "What did she predict for you?"

"Nothing good," said Lucy. "She said she saw fire and a lot of disruption in my life."

"Oh, dear," said Phyllis, handing her a stack of press releases to sort. "Are you worried?"

"I don't believe in it, so why should I worry?" she replied, seating herself at her desk and checking her e-mail. There was nothing but a few jokes from friends, so she settled down to the task at hand, filing the press releases according to date. She was just finishing up when the little bell on the door jangled and a middle-aged man with shoulder-length gray hair and a silver beard walked in and went up to the counter. Despite his unconventional haircut, he was dressed like most men in town—in khaki pants and a plaid sports shirt. Lucy recognized Ike Stoughton, whom she'd encountered at various county meetings.

She knew that Ike, a licensed surveyor, had built a sterling reputation with his title-search company. If the title to a piece of property was unclear—which was a common occurrence thanks to missing or damaged town records and ancient deeds that set boundaries by referring to long-gone landmarks such as "the large elm tree" or "the stone fence"—it was generally agreed that Ike was the man to call, even though he didn't come cheap. He had a gift for parsing ancient terminology and tracking down old wills and bills of sale to establish a single thread of ownership from a tangle of competing claims that had made him one of the county's most successful businessmen.

"Can I help you?" asked Phyllis.

"Why, sure," he said, producing a white business-size envelope. "I've got a letter to the editor."

"Ted's not here right now, but I'll make sure he gets it," said Phyllis.

"I'd really appreciate it," said Ike, looking around the office. "I was hoping to meet him. I just moved into town, you see."

Hearing that, Lucy got up and approached him, hand extended. "I'm Lucy Stone. I've covered a few county meetings where you spoke."

Ike took her hand. "Nice to meet you, Lucy."

"When did you move to Tinker's Cove?" she asked.

"I bought the old Whipple homestead back in April, but we moved in only a couple of weeks ago," he replied.

Lucy knew the Whipple place, an eighteenth-century house just down the road from her house, on the other side of the creek. She rarely went that way and hadn't noticed the long-vacant property was now occupied.

"That's a beautiful old place," she said. "I'm glad it's not going to be empty any longer."

"That's a real antique," said Phyllis, slipping the letter into Ted's mailbox.

"You said it," said Ike. "It needs a lot of work, but it's going to be worth it."

"Lucy lives out that way," said Phyllis.

"That's right, we're on Red Top Road. Our place was a wreck when we first bought it. It took a lot of work and a lot of money, but I wouldn't give it up now for anything."

"Are you in the old farmhouse on top of the hill?" he asked. When Lucy nodded, he continued. "I think my daughter Abby has met your girls. Sara and . . ."

"Zoe," said Lucy.

"That's right. Zoe. They're nice girls."

"Thank you," said Lucy, feeling slightly unsettled. How did he know her kids but she didn't know his? It was time to get better acquainted. "The folks on Prudence Path are holding a neighborhood potluck this Saturday. Why don't you come and bring the family?"

"That's mighty nice of you," said Ike. "I've been looking forward to meeting our neighbors."

"See you Saturday," said Lucy as Ike gave Phyllis a parting nod and left the office.

"Seems like a nice guy," said Phyllis as the bell on the door jangled behind him.

"I hope so," said Lucy. "You never know with neighbors."

Phyllis adjusted her glasses and peered at her computer screen. "Yup. I love my neighbors, the Reeds. They'd be just about perfect if it weren't for that noisy leaf blower."

Lucy chuckled and went back to her filing, popping the last few press releases into the folder. "Budget meeting tomorrow?"

"Nine o'clock," said Phyllis.

Lucy put on her jacket and slung her purse over her shoulder. "I'll be here," she said, and headed for the door. "Have a good evening."

"You too," said Phyllis as Lucy made her way through the office to the back door and the parking lot.

She was exiting onto Main Street when she remembered that she had planned to have strawberries for dessert, so instead of turning right, she went left, toward Rebecca Wardwell's little homestead on the other side of town. Rebecca kept chickens and sold a variety of produce that was far superior to the supermarket version.

The strawberries were also a lot more expensive than the ones at the IGA, she discovered when she handed over a ten-dollar bill for two pints and got only a dollar back.

"Your price has gone up," she commented, tucking the money in her pocket.

"My costs have gone way up," explained Rebecca. As always, she was dressed in an old-fashioned sprigged cotton dress with leg-of-mutton sleeves. A starched lace cap covered her fine white hair, which was twisted into a straggly bun, but her feet were bare. Though she was approaching sixty, her pink cheeks were as plump and round as they ever were, but a few lines radiated from her eyes when she smiled, which was often.

"Oh, well, they're worth it," rationalized Lucy. "They taste a lot better than the ones from California."

"I wait until they're ripe before I pick them. That's the trick," said Rebecca. "Want to see my garden?"

"Sure," said Lucy, jumping at the chance. She was an enthusiastic gardener, and Rebecca's little plot was legendary for its productivity.

Lucy followed Rebecca through the squeaky gate. "I have to fence it because of the woodchucks," she said. "Yesterday I left the gate ajar and look!" She pointed at a row of young pea plants, all nibbled down to nothing but stubs.

"It's early—you can replant," said Lucy, taking in the neat rows of vegetables interspersed with colorful cosmos, marigolds, and zinnias. "Your Swiss chard is ahead of mine," she observed. "But my lettuce is bolting."

"It has been awfully hot and dry this year," commiserated Rebecca. "I've had to water, which I don't like to do so early in the summer. It's not even July."

"Me too," said Lucy. "My tomato plants wilted so badly I had to rescue them by watering them in the middle of the day, which I don't like to do because they say it causes shallow root growth."

"Once or twice in an emergency is all right, as long as you don't make a habit of it," said Rebecca, sounding as if she equated daytime watering with alcohol or drug abuse.

"Oh, I wouldn't," vowed Lucy, bending down to examine a thriving young squash vine. "What's this? Zucchini?"

"Pumpkin. I saved some seed from last year and have high hopes for the giant pumpkin contest," said Rebecca. She was staring at Lucy with an odd expression.

Lucy ran her tongue over her teeth, wondering if a piece of spinach or a poppy seed from her lunch had gotten stuck. But that wasn't what was bothering Rebecca.

"You need to very careful for the next few days," she said in a very serious voice. "Check smoke alarms, wear your seat belt, keep an eye out for trouble."

"Why do you say that?" asked Lucy.

"No reason," replied Rebecca with a shrug of her shoulders, sharp and bony under the lavender and black sprigged cotton. "I say that to everybody. It's good advice. Trust me."

"Thanks," said Lucy, carefully carrying the strawberries, which were packed in recycled cartons without tops, back to the car. Twice now she'd been warned, in the same day. If this kept up, she told herself, she'd have to rethink her views about the supernatural.

But nothing happened on the way home. She had the road to herself. And the house too. Her husband, Bill, a restoration carpenter, was out on a job, and the two girls who were still home, Sara and Zoe, were volunteering at the Friends of Animals shelter. Toby, her oldest, was now married and lived with his wife, Molly, and baby son, Patrick, on nearby Prudence Path. Elizabeth, a senior at Chamberlain College in Boston, was spending the summer as an intern at a Cape Cod newspaper. Only Libby the Labrador was home, and she greeted Lucy enthusiastically with lots of tail wagging and attempts to lick her face.

"Down! Down!" ordered Lucy, holding the strawberries above her head, out of harm's way. "I'll take you for a walk, so calm down."

Hearing the word "walk," which was one of her all-time favorite words, Libby became more excited than ever, and Lucy opened the door, shooing her out of the house. Five minutes later, Lucy joined her in the backyard and they set off down the old logging trails that meandered through the woods behind the house.

Libby kept her nose to the ground, sniffing as she went, but Lucy was gazing at the cloudless blue sky and wondering when it was going to rain. Rebecca was right; it had been an awfully dry spring, and the summer ahead looked to be a scorcher. Fallen leaves and branches crackled underfoot, and the trees already had a forlorn, droopy appearance. It was so hot that even the birds were silent. Nonetheless, Lucy was enjoying herself. She'd had an especially busy week, with several nighttime meetings that ran late, and she needed to stretch out her muscles and use her body, even if it meant working up a sweat.

She put rather more energy into her walk than usual, and it wasn't long before she realized she'd gone farther than she'd intended, following a path that she rarely took. She was also aware of an unpleasant, acrid scent and had decided to turn back when she realized the dog had disappeared.

"Libby! Libby!" she shouted, but all she got was a sharp bark, as if the dog was summoning her. Lucy checked her watch. It was nearly three. She really needed to get back home and start that pot roast, and here the dog had gotten herself into trouble. Stuck in a bunch of brambles or something. So she trudged on, calling the dog and getting barks in reply, until she came out of the woods and found the dog standing in the middle of a circular clearing.

"What?" she demanded. "You couldn't come to me? I had to come to you?"

But the dog didn't come to her, even then. She remained in place, fixed on a tree with a blackened, bulbous trunk.

A fire? wondered Lucy, stepping closer for a better look until she was practically overcome by a powerful stench of decay. There was no doubt, she realized with horror as she discovered whitened bones and bits of charred cloth, that she'd stumbled upon the burned body of a human being.

CHAPTER THREE

B ent over double, Lucy stumbled to the edge of the clearing, where she was violently sick. Behind her, she could hear Libby barking frantically. When the retching stopped, she was still trembling, but she attempted to leash the dog. Libby, tail between her legs, was alternately darting at the thing on the tree and retreating. Once Lucy succeeded in fastening the clasp of the leash onto the dog's collar and had her firmly under control, Libby began shivering and whining and pulling at the leash.

Giving the leash a yank, Lucy turned her back on the dreadful sight and pulled her cell phone out of her pocket. It took a couple of tries before she managed to punch in 911. When the operator answered, Lucy could barely get the words out.

"A b-b-body, b-b-burned, in the w-w-woods," she stammered.

"Where is your location?" asked the operator in a crisp, unemotional tone.

"Th-the old logging road, off Red Top Road," she said. "This is Lucy. I was out walking the dog."

"Oh, hi, Lucy. Sounds like a hell of a thing," responded

the dispatcher. As a reporter, Lucy was a familiar figure at the police station. "Just stay put. I'm sending everything out there."

"That's not really necessary," said Lucy, but she could already hear the siren that summoned the volunteer firefighters wailing in the distance. They would answer the call as quickly as possible, but she knew she had a bit of a wait, being so far out in the woods, so she settled herself on the ground with the dog beside her. Holding tight to Libby's collar, she tried not to think of the gruesome scene behind her and focused on soothing the dog. It was about fifteen minutes later when the fire department's brush breaker came barreling down the dirt road. Libby, who was still a shivering heap of misery, was back on her feet, announcing its arrival with loud barks. Sirens could be heard in the distance, evidence that more rescue vehicles were on the way.

"The fire's out," said Lucy when the two firefighters jumped out of the heavy-duty truck. She indicated the tree with a jerk of her head but wasn't about to take another look.

"My God!" exclaimed one firefighter, taking in the horrible sight.

The other, younger man started to approach, then stopped when the stench hit him. "This is one for the medical examiner," he said, retreating.

"It's amazing the whole woods didn't go up," said the older man, studying the site.

"That tree's by itself," said the younger man, scratching his stubbly chin. "In the middle of this clearing. And it looks like whatever happened here happened a while ago."

"Yeah," said the older man, surveying the scene. "A lot of trees and brush have been cut. It's almost like it was prepared on purpose for something like this." He shivered. "This is an evil place."

It was true, thought Lucy. It was as if the sap rising in the trees that circled the clearing was tainted and bilious, as if the ground beneath her feet were seething with nests of twisting snakes, a place where monsters lurked and the trees came alive, whirling around her.

Next thing she knew, she was on the ground and one of the firefighters was wrapping her in a foil shock blanket and Libby was licking her face. "You didn't look too good there," he said, handing her a lollipop.

"I just want to go home," she said, obediently licking the pop and concentrating on the taste. It was grape, not her favorite.

"We'll get you home soon but first I have a few questions." Lucy sat up slowly and saw that the police and more fire trucks had arrived while she had been unconscious. Several cruisers with blinking lights were lined up on the dirt road, and a couple of officers were stringing yellow tape around the edge of the clearing. She recognized her questioner; he was one of the Kirwan boys. Todd, according to his nameplate. Dot Kirwan, who worked at the IGA, had produced a large brood of kids, most of whom now worked for the police and fire departments, including her oldest, who had recently been named chief of police.

"I don't know anything," said Lucy. "I was just walking the dog."

Todd nodded. "You live nearby. Did you hear anything?"

Lucy thought of Diana Ravenscroft, who'd looked in her crystal ball and saw fire and heard screams in the night. But Lucy hadn't heard any screams; she hadn't seen any column of smoke rising from the woods or noticed any fire. Or had she? Perhaps one morning, months ago, hadn't there been a smoky scent in the morning air that she'd attributed to a smoldering woodstove?

"Maybe, a couple of months ago, I thought I smelled smoke."

"Can you be more specific than that?"

"It was a foggy, misty morning. Still cold. April, maybe early May?"

Todd nodded. "Just one more thing. Did you touch anything? Did the dog?"

"No, no," said Lucy. "Once I realized what it was, I immediately leashed the dog. I was sick."

"No wonder," sympathized the officer. He wasn't very old, not yet thirty, with a blond crew cut and an unlined face.

"What do you think . . . Why would somebody do this? Who was this person?" asked Lucy.

Kirwan shrugged. "A drug deal gone bad, maybe a gangland killing. The body was probably burned to prevent identification."

Lucy had been a reporter for a long time, and as far as she knew, the little seaside town was a peaceful haven where people didn't bother to lock their doors and left the car keys in the ignition. "Here? In Tinker's Cove?" she asked.

Kirwan shrugged. "Up 'til now, when we got reports of a fire in the woods, it's always been partying kids. This is a new one for me." He looked solemn. "And I hope it's the last."

The cops gave Lucy a ride home. She got to ride in front, but the dog had to sit in the caged rear of the cruiser. She wished she could stay home—the empty house was sturdy and cozy and reassuringly normal with dog dishes on the kitchen floor and a couple of coffee mugs in the sink—but she knew the discovery of the burned body in the woods was big news, and she had to file her story. So she tossed some dog biscuits into Libby's bowl, gave her some fresh water, and headed out to her car.

It was a few minutes before five when she got to the office, and Phyllis was tidying up her desk, preparing to leave. Ted was seated at the old rolltop desk that had once belonged to his grandfather, a legendary small-town editor. He was on the phone with somebody, laughing it up.

"What are you doing back here?" asked Phyllis, peering at her over her harlequin reading glasses. Her rhinestone-studded tote bag and zebra-striped purse were ready on her desk.

"Big story," said Lucy. "I was walking the dog, and I found a body."

"You know, that's the reason I don't have a dog," said Phyllis, slinging her bags over her arm. "You're always hearing about people finding bodies when they walk the filthy beasts."

"A body?" inquired Ted, ending his call.

Lucy nodded, her expression grim. "It was burned. Tied to a tree and burned."

Phyllis stopped, her hand on the doorknob. "That's awful."

Ever the editor, Ted had a ghoulish appreciation for a sensational story, but even he was horrified. "Ohmigod. Who is it?" he demanded.

"They don't know," said Lucy, trying unsuccessfully to block the sight from her mind. "It was in a clearing off the old logging road behind my house. The cops think it was drugs, or maybe gang related. They think the body was burned so it couldn't be identified."

"Dumb," said Phyllis, who was a fan of *CSI.* "They never heard of dental records?"

"This happened here in Tinker's Cove?" wondered Ted.

"I wouldn't believe it if I hadn't seen it myself," said Lucy, suddenly feeling the need to sit down.

"Well, if you ask me, a lot of strange things have happened since that Diana Ravenscroft moved to town," said Phyllis. "She makes no bones about it—she comes right out and says she's a witch."

"Considering the fact that throughout history, witches got burned quite a bit, I think it's fair to assume that Diana is firmly opposed to the practice," said Ted, reaching for the phone with one hand and his pen with the other. "Just my luck," he muttered. "Why do big stories like this always have to break on Thursdays?"

"Well, I'll leave you two newshounds to it," said Phyllis, opening the door. "See you tomorrow."

There was always a chance of selling a breaking story to the Portland or Boston papers, so Ted and Lucy got to work calling every contact they could think of. The investigation was in such an early stage that they didn't get much information, except for learning that the state police would issue a statement sometime Friday.

"Great," muttered Ted. "There goes my scoop."

Lucy nodded in agreement. At best, they had enough for only a short brief that would be included in a regional news roundup. But tomorrow, once the official statement came out, the town would most likely be overrun with newspaper and TV reporters hunting a sensational story. She was shutting down her computer and tidying her desk, getting ready to leave, when Ted snorted and tossed a letter in the trash basket.

"I can't believe the stuff people expect me to print," he snorted.

Lucy was checking her bag, making sure she had pens and a notebook and an extra battery for her camera. "What is it now? Another please-scoop-your-dog-poop letter?"

"No. It's all about this so-called witch. Has that little purple shop."

Lucy put down her bag. "I was there today, and so was Pam. We went after our usual breakfast and had our fortunes told."

"Well, according to this guy, Ike something or other, you were consorting with a Devil worshipper."

"Let me see that." Ted retrieved the letter and passed it to Lucy, who found her suspicion about the author confirmed. It was the letter Ike Stoughton had delivered earlier that afternoon. "He dropped by earlier," she said, smoothing out the crumpled sheet of paper. "He's just moved into town, out by me. He bought the old Whipple place."

"Sounds like a nut," said Ted.

Reading the letter, Lucy had to agree. Ike not only accused Diana of worshipping the Devil but also claimed she was corrupting the town's youth and was responsible for the recent drought. He stopped short of suggesting that decent people ought to drive her out of town, but he did call for all God-fearing folk to boycott her shop. Finishing the letter, Lucy screwed up her mouth. "You're right. He's some sort of bigot. I wish I'd known."

"So he's your neighbor; you don't have to be buddies."

"My girls are friends with his daughter."

"So what? You say hi and good-bye and that's it."

"More than that, I'm afraid," said Lucy. "I invited him to the neighborhood potluck on Saturday night."

Ted was grinning. "Well, if I were you, I wouldn't mention your recent séance."

"You're right," said Lucy, crossing the office. "And it wasn't a séance. It was a psychic reading, and"—she stopped at the door—"Diana had some very interesting things to say about you!"

Then she was gone, leaving Ted to wonder what Diana had said about him. Lucy, however, was thinking about her new neighbor when she got in the car and started the engine. She was tired; it had been a long, emotionally exhausting day beginning with Diana's disturbing predictions, followed by the gruesome discovery in the woods, and ending with Ike Stoughton's letter. She couldn't understand why he found Diana Ravenscroft's presence so disturbing.

A honk reminded her that she needed to pay attention to the road. She was well below the speed limit, which sometimes happened when she was tired and distracted, as if it was too much effort to press her foot against the gas pedal. She gave her head a shake and stepped on the gas, looking forward to getting home.

Considering the events of the afternoon, pot roast was out of the question. Luckily, school vacation had started earlier that week, and she'd left a note explaining she'd had to go back to the office and instructing the girls to cook supper, maybe a simple menu of spaghetti and salad. While they prepared dinner, she planned on sipping a glass of wine out on the porch.

But the minute she pulled into the drive, she heard the piercing shriek of the smoke alarms and the frantic barking of the dog. Braking hard and pulling the key out of the ignition, she jumped out of the car and ran toward the house. There was no sign of fire that she could see, but she still hesitated at the door, remembering that you should never enter a burning building. There was no scent of smoke when she opened the kitchen door. The kitchen was cool and fresh from the breeze blowing through the windows. There wasn't even any sign of cooking in progress, although she could hear voices coming from upstairs, in between the strident wails of the smoke alarms.

Climbing the back stairway that led from the kitchen to the bedrooms, she became aware of a smoky scent, and she found herself taking the steps two at a time. What was going on? Had the girls been smoking and started a fire? Were they trying to put it out themselves?

In the hall the scent was even stronger; it was clearly coming from Sara's bedroom. Lucy pushed the door open and saw the room filled with a bluish haze. Sara, Zoe, and a third girl had opened the windows and were waving pillows around, trying to dissipate the smoke. Libby was following her, barking anxiously.

"Where's the fire?" demanded Lucy.

"No fire, Mom," shrieked Sara over the smoke alarms.

Lucy grabbed a chair and took it out into the hall, where she climbed up and disconnected the alarm. The sudden silence was a huge relief. She took a deep breath, then stepped down and marched back to question the girls. "Were you smoking?" she demanded angrily. Cigarettes were strictly forbidden.

"No, Mom," said Sara. "We were casting a circle."

"What? And who's this?" demanded Lucy, afraid she knew the answer. The girl was about Sara's age, fourteen or fifteen, wearing a long summer skirt that fell below her knees. She had her long, blond hair pulled back into a thick braid.

"I'm Abby Stoughton," said the girl, confirming Lucy's suspicion. "It's nice to meet you, Mrs. Stone."

"I met your father today. He said we're neighbors."

"That's right," said Abby. "We just moved into a new house down the road, on the other side of the bridge. Well, new to us. The house was built in 1799."

Lucy sat down on the bed, and Libby rested her chin on her knee. She was beginning to get the picture. The girls had apparently struck up a friendship with their new neighbor, they'd even met her father, but they hadn't bothered to inform her. She had the same unsettling feeling she'd first encountered when Toby, her oldest, began going to kindergarten and was occasionally greeted by people she didn't know. Her first reaction had been suspicion but they usually turned out to be parents of other students who'd visited the class. It was ridiculous, she thought, but she'd never quite come to terms with the idea that her children had lives of their own.

"So what set off the smoke alarms?"

"We were casting a circle," said Zoe. "We were going to make a spell."

Lucy's heart sank. "A spell?"

"To get rid of pimples," volunteered Zoe. "Abby's been collecting rainwater under the moon."

"Rainwater didn't set off the smoke alarms," said Lucy.

"No," confessed Sara. "First we burned a bundle of sage to clear the circle of evil forces."

Spells, circles, evil forces, thought Lucy. "This sounds a lot like witchcraft," she said.

Sara produced a well-thumbed paperback book with a gorgeous, raven-haired woman pictured on the cover. *Witchcraft for Teens* was the title. "I bought it at that new shop in town," she said. "And the sage bundle too."

Now, not only was Ike her neighbor, but also her girls had been practicing witchcraft with his daughter. Lucy sat there, stroking the dog and staring at the pink and green braided rug that covered the floor. It occurred to her that so far, Diana Ravenscroft's predictions had been right on target.

CHAPTER FOUR

"Now, Abby," said Lucy, looking the girl in the eyes, "it just so happens that I saw your father today, and he expressed his deep concern about the presence of Diana Ravenscroft in town. He's very much against any sort of witchcraft, as I'm sure you know. There's absolutely no way I can allow you to come here and do something that your father disapproves of, now, can I?"

"No, Mrs. Stone." Abby was hanging her head.

"Maybe you should see a dermatologist instead of fooling around with a lot of mumbo jumbo," suggested Lucy.

"That's just it!" exclaimed the girl angrily. She raised her face, and Lucy saw that her chin was indeed spotted with a few pink bumps. But it was her eyes that caught her attention. Fiercely blue, they were tearing up. "I've begged and begged but my parents won't let me see a doctor. They won't even let me use anything on my face except soap and water!"

"Pimples are just part of being a teenager," said Lucy. "You'll outgrow them."

"It's like being cursed," muttered Abby. "I feel like a leper having to go around like this."

"I think you're overreacting," said Lucy. "They're not that noticeable, really."

"They're disgusting," exclaimed Abby, beginning to sob.

"Mom's right," said Sara, handing her a tissue. "You can hardly see them."

"I hope I never get zits," said Zoe, getting a sharp look from her mother. "And you have really pretty hair," she added. "I wish Mom would let me grow my hair long like yours."

"No, you don't," said Abby, dabbing her eyes. "I wish I could have short hair, too, but my parents won't let me cut it. It's a pain, having to brush it all the time. It gets all snarly and it hurts."

"Well, pretty soon you'll be old enough to leave home and do what you want," said Lucy. "But in the meantime, you have to obey your parents. They're giving you a home and they love you."

"I know," grumbled Abby. "It's one of the Ten Commandments: Honor thy father and thy mother."

"That's right. And it's getting late, almost dinnertime," reminded Lucy. "Do you need a ride home?"

"No, I've got my bike," said Abby.

Lucy led the way and they all trooped downstairs. At the kitchen door, Abby paused. "I'm really sorry about the smoke alarm," she told Lucy.

"It's okay," said Lucy. "And you're always welcome here, as long as you don't do anything your parents would disapprove of." As soon as Abby was out the door, Lucy turned on her daughters. "What were you thinking?" she demanded. "Practicing witchcraft! You were supposed to cook supper, not some magic spell!"

"Sorry, Mom," muttered Sara, opening the refrigerator and pulling out the package of ground chicken.

While Sara emptied it into a bowl, Lucy poured herself a glass of chardonnay. "Set the table, Zoe," she ordered, seating herself at the kitchen table.

Sara added egg and breadcrumbs and shaped the mixture into little balls, which she set on a baking sheet. Lucy watched, wondering how involved the girls had become with Diana Ravenscroft.

"So how long have you girls been practicing witchcraft?" she asked.

"Not long," said Sara, keeping her back to Lucy as she worked.

"Weeks? Months?" persisted Lucy. She could hear Zoe thumping plates onto the dining room table.

"I've just gone to a couple of classes," said Sara.

"Classes?"

"Yeah, Lady Diana has classes for teens. On Wednesdays, after school. It's like a club, like Scouts or gymnastics."

Lucy was astonished. "I thought you were at track," she said. "You've been lying to me."

Sara was very busy with the meatballs, arranging them in neat rows on the pan. "I didn't lie—I just didn't tell you."

"But why?"

"I don't know." She turned around and opened the oven door, sliding the meatballs inside and setting the timer for ten minutes. Her face was flushed, and she seemed about to burst into tears. "It was fun having a secret, you know? And witchcraft isn't bad. It's all about appreciating nature and the life force and harnessing natural energy to live a harmonious, spiritual life."

Lucy bit her lip, thinking. It was obvious that Sara was deeply attracted to whatever Diana was offering, and she thought she understood why. Now that global warming and saving the environment had become such big issues, the girls had been involved in calculating the family's carbon footprint and suggesting ways to reduce it. But more than attempting to live in harmony with nature, Lucy suspected, casting spells and mixing up potions allowed Sara to feel as if she was powerful and could control her life. That was exciting stuff for an adolescent struggling to form her own identity and free herself from her parents.

"Well, I guess there's no harm in it," she announced. "As long as you keep your father and me informed. No more secrets, okay?"

"So I can join the coven?" exclaimed Sara, wiping her eyes and smiling.

Lucy's jaw dropped. "Coven? You said it was like Girl Scouts."

"It is," insisted Sara. "But Lady Diana says I'm really progressing, and soon I'll be able to join the coven and become a real witch. She says there's a vacancy in her coven. Ideally there should be thirteen people, and she'd like me to fill it."

"I'll have to talk to her," said Lucy, finishing off her wine. "Forget what I said. No more witchcraft. Everything's on hold until I get more information."

The oven timer began to beep, announcing it was time to turn the meatballs, but Sara ignored it, whirling around and stomping up the stairs. Lucy got up, resigned to the fact that she would be cooking supper. She hoped that Sara wasn't gathering up the hair from her hairbrush and searching her wastebasket for nail clippings to make an anti-mother spell.

On Friday morning, Lucy stopped at Solstice on her way to work. The shop wasn't open yet, but she'd called and made an appointment. Sure enough, Diana was waiting for her, standing in a long silky dress and holding the black cat in her arms.

"Thanks for seeing me so early," said Lucy, stepping inside the fragrant little shop.

"No problem," said Diana, scratching the cat behind its ears. "I'm a full-service witch, on call twenty-four seven. Isn't that right, Piewocket?" The cat closed its eyes slowly, basking in the attention. "So how can I help you?"

"I understand my daughter Sara has been coming here after school," began Lucy. The shop smelled lovely, but Lucy was determined not to be seduced by the charming atmosphere.

"Yes, Sara's a delightful girl, and she's definitely got the gift," said Diana, sounding like one of Sara's teachers. "She's made wonderful progress, and I think she's ready to join a coven."

"That's why I'm here," said Lucy. "She's much too young to do anything like that."

"Too young?" Diana sounded puzzled as she set the cat on its cushion in the window. "She's sixteen. Children much younger than that have their First Communion in the Catholic Church; Jewish children have their mitzvahs when they're thirteen; Protestants confirm twelve- and thirteen-year-olds. If anything, Wiccans tend to be conservative in these matters, waiting until an individual is mature enough to make a responsible decision."

"That's the problem. Sara hasn't been responsible. She hid her involvement with Wicca from her father and me, and even worse, she's been helping Abby Stoughton to deceive her parents. I don't know if you're aware of it, but Abby's father, Ike, is very upset with you—this is not the right time for these young girls to get involved with witchcraft."

"On the contrary, it's actually the perfect time. Tomorrow is Midsummer's Eve. We'll be holding our sabbat and celebrating the longest day of the year. Who could object to that?"

"Oh, I suspect quite a few people might not approve—especially Ike Stoughton," said Lucy. "He thinks you're worshipping the Devil."

"Well, I see that I have a lot of work to do. There is absolutely nothing wicked or sinful about Wicca. It draws on centuries of rich, wonderful cultural tradition beginning with the Celtic Druids. Does Ike Stoughton object to hanging mistletoe at Christmas or decorating a Christmas tree?"

"I don't have a clue about how Ike Stoughton celebrates Christmas, or if he even does. I'm not here to argue," said Lucy, growing impatient with Diana's attitude. "I'm here as Sara's mother, and I'm telling you that I am not allowing her to join your coven, period. End of story. I'm responsible for her, and I deeply resent the way you've insinuated yourself with her and encouraged her to keep secrets from her parents."

"I have not encouraged Sara to deceive you," declared Diana. "If she did not want to tell you how important her new beliefs are to her, it's because you don't encourage openness in your home."

"That's awfully presumptuous," said Lucy, reacting angrily. "My husband and I may not be perfect parents—I never said we were—but we are trying to bring our kids up to be responsible members of society, and witchcraft is too extreme."

"That's only because people don't understand it," insisted Diana, shaking her head sadly.

"My point exactly," said Lucy in a softer tone. She was already regretting her show of temper. "And until they do, I don't want my child to confuse religious conviction with her admiration for a glamorous and persuasive woman."

"This isn't about me," insisted Diana. "Wicca's a religion, not some cult of personality."

"I think you may be wrong about that, especially when it comes to impressionable teenagers. People are starting to talk about you," she added, remembering Phyllis's comment that Diana had brought trouble to town.

"So that's what you're worried about," crowed Diana with a tinkling laugh. "Well, let me assure you, witch hunts are a thing of the past. I don't think you need to worry about anybody persecuting Sara if she decides to become a witch."

"I thought I made myself clear," said Lucy, emphasizing every word. "Sara is not joining your coven. I forbid it."

"Take it easy," said Diana. "I understand." She drummed

her fingers on a table. "But it is a shame. Midsummer's Eve is a wonderful opportunity to witness a sabbat, and this is my first as high priestess. I really want it to be perfect, which means we need thirteen members. I wonder if Abby . . ."

Lucy looked at her, trying to decide whether the woman could possibly be this stupid. "Are you crazy?" exclaimed Lucy. "If I were you, I'd keep a low profile for a while—and I'd leave Abby Stoughton alone. Her father has some very strong convictions, and it's not just the purple paint that bothers him. He's very much against witchcraft."

"Well, thanks for the warning," said Diana, shrugging. "Now can I interest you in a protective charm? Perhaps a spell to drive the pests from your garden and help the plants to grow? I hear cutworms are a big problem this year."

"Not today, thanks," said Lucy, shaking her head. "My garden is doing just fine. But I think you better stay away from Ike Stoughton's daughter!"

Back in her car, Lucy felt uneasy as she drove on down Main Street to the *Pennysaver* office. She'd been a reporter for a long time now, covering the little town, and she sensed trouble ahead. Ike Stoughton and Diana Ravenscroft were polar opposites, and there was bound to be friction. Good, healthy controversy was one thing, but when emotions were running high, things could get out of control. She didn't want to see anyone get hurt, and she certainly didn't want Sara to get caught in the cross fire. Maybe, she thought as she parked the car in the little lot behind the office, she was overreacting. But she'd seen the body in the woods, as well as other terrible sights through the years, and she knew that ordinary people were capable of doing dreadful things to each other, especially when they were driven by the conviction that they were right.

"Goodness, you look serious today," said Phyllis when Lucy walked into the office.

"I was just thinking about the body in the woods," said Lucy. "Any news?"

"Not yet," said Phyllis. "Ted's at the press conference. He should be back soon with some answers. In the meantime, he left this for you." She plopped a thick sheaf of papers on her counter with a thud.

"What am I supposed to do with this?" asked Lucy, examining what appeared to be a highly technical study of the effect of rising ocean temperatures on lobster populations.

"Read it and weep," wisecracked Phyllis. "No. Read it and recap the information for the average reader."

"I think you had it right the first time," said Lucy, heading for her desk.

When Ted arrived an hour or so later, she knew more than she wanted to about the sex life of lobsters.

"How's it going?" he asked, seating himself at his desk and turning on his computer.

"Inconclusive," said Lucy. "Warmer water may make the lobsters mature sooner and thus reproduce at a faster rate, or it might encourage parasites and disease, which would have a negative effect. What about the press conference?"

"Inconclusive," replied Ted. "The body is male, but that's all they're about to say at this point. They're checking the missing persons, have some likely matches, but nothing definite yet."

"These things take time," said Phyllis, "especially if they have to use DNA."

"DNA tests are expensive. The ME said that's a last resort."

"It's so horrible," said Lucy, remembering the oppressive sense of evil she'd experienced in the clearing. "Nobody should end up like that, no matter who they are."

Saturday afternoon, when Lucy was picking lettuce for a salad to take to the annual neighborhood cookout, she noticed a number of newly planted tomato and pepper seedlings had fallen over and were wilting. When she took a closer look, she realized they'd been neatly nipped off at ground level. Cutworms! She'd never had a problem with them before. What was going on? Was there really a sudden infestation, and how had Diana known about it? And where had she gotten that bit about fire and screams in the night? How could she have known? It was enough to make you wonder, she thought, carrying her bowl of lettuce into the kitchen.

Lucy had been looking forward to the cookout all week. It was a chance to catch up with the neighbors, and her son Toby, his wife, Molly, and their baby son, Patrick, would be there too. Even though the young family lived on Prudence Path, just a hop, skip, and a jump away through a narrow patch of woods, she didn't get to see Patrick as often as she wanted, which was every minute of every day. Patrick was growing so fast and changed so much every time she saw him that she was afraid he'd be all grown up before she knew what happened. So when she and Bill and the girls arrived at the party, Lucy made a beeline for her grandson, scooping him up in her arms.

"He's so heavy and only three months!" she exclaimed.

"He's a real chowhound," said his beaming father.

"Fourteen pounds," said Molly, who looked tired. "When he hits fifteen, Doc Ryder says I can start solids. I can't wait—maybe then he'll sleep through the night."

"Are you waking your poor mommy up?" cooed Lucy, jiggling the baby and looking into Patrick's big blue eyes. "Are you a naughty boy?"

Patrick answered with a smile and a burp, or maybe just a burp, but Lucy was sure it was a smile. "Did you see that?" she exclaimed. "He smiled at me!"

But now the smile was gone. Patrick was beginning to fuss, and Lucy reluctantly handed him back to his mother. Molly retreated to a secluded porch swing to nurse him, and Lucy joined her neighbors Frankie La Chance and Willie

Westwood, who were arranging dishes on an improvised table made out of a door set on sawhorses. The party was actually taking place in the little cul-de-sac shared by five houses. Barbecue grills and picnic tables had been brought from individual yards and arranged together under a canopy improvised from a big blue tarp. Twinkling Christmas lights had been hung underneath the tarp, and soft rock music was playing on a donated stereo. Ice-filled coolers held an assortment of soft drinks, beer, and wine.

"Can I help?" offered Lucy.

"I think we're all set," said Frankie. "Everything looks delicious."

"I'm starving," said Willie, helping herself to a handful of potato chips. "I was at the barn all afternoon." Willie was a keen horsewoman who taught riding lessons; her husband Scratch was a vet. They had two kids—Sassie, who was Sara's age, and Chip, who was still in elementary school.

"The burgers should be ready soon," said Frankie, who was the primary organizer behind the annual cookout. She was a real estate agent and a single mom with one child, Renee, also Sara's age. "In the meantime, can I get you a glass of wine?"

Soon the three women were settled on lawn chairs, sipping their wine and swapping stories about their kids, their pets, and their neighbors.

"Did you hear about this awful thing in the woods?" asked Willie. "I heard about it on the radio."

"What thing?" asked Frankie.

"I was the one who discovered the body," said Lucy. "It was horrible."

"Whose body?"

"They don't know yet," said Lucy. "It was burned."

"Mon Dieu!" exclaimed Frankie.

"They said it was probably a drug deal gone wrong, something like that," said Willie.

"Maybe a gangland slaying. They burned the body so it couldn't be identified. That's the theory anyway," said Lucy.

"I can't believe anything like that would happen here," said Willie, sipping her wine.

"Me neither," said Lucy, eager to change the subject. "By the way, I invited our new neighbors, the Stoughtons. They moved into the place on the other side of the bridge."

"Ike Stoughton?" asked Frankie.

"Yup."

"He's a shrewd one. I bet he got that place for a song. It's been on the market for over a year."

"Speak of the devil. Here they come now," said Willie.

Lucy looked up to see the entire Stoughton clan advancing down the road. Ike was leading the procession, followed by two tall and muscular young men, presumably his sons, dressed almost identically in crisp blue jeans with tucked-in shirts and close-shaved haircuts. Abby and her mother, a painfully thin woman with graying hair fastened into a bun, trailed behind in their unfashionably long skirts, each carrying a covered dish.

"I'm so glad you could come," said Lucy, greeting them.

"These are my sons, Thomas and Mather," said Ike, "and my wife, Miriam, and daughter, Abby."

"I know Abby, of course," said Lucy, smiling hard, "and it's nice to meet you all. Shall I introduce you around?"

"That would be fine," agreed Ike as Frankie and Willie hurried over.

"Let me take those dishes off your hands," said Frankie, approaching Abby and Miriam.

"They smell delicious," said Willie, holding out her arms.

"It's an old family recipe for baked beans," said Miriam, her voice so soft she was almost whispering. "I cooked them in the bake hole next to our fireplace."

The women's eyebrows shot up in surprise. "My goodness, that must have been a lot of work," said Willie.

"My husband likes them that way," she whispered, with

lowered eyes as if imparting a shameful secret. "He says there's nothing like the taste of real, slow-cooked beans."

"I can't wait to taste them," said Lucy as Toby approached the little group, gripping a bottle of Sam Adams beer. She figured he would take Thomas and Mather off her hands.

"Hi!" he said, shaking hands with the menfolk. "I'm Toby Stone. Can I get you guys some beers?"

He didn't get the reaction he expected. Thomas and Mather stiffened their backs and turned to their father, who adopted a stern expression. "We do not drink alcohol," he said in a disapproving tone.

Lucy was pleased to see that Toby didn't miss a beat. "Well, there's plenty of pop too," he said.

"We prefer water," declared Ike. "That's the beverage the good Lord provides for us in abundance."

"We've got that too," said Toby, tilting his head toward the cooler and drifting away to rejoin his friends.

Willie and Frankie had also drifted off, leaving Lucy with the entire Stoughton clan. She dutifully took them around to meet everyone but was unable to get any sort of conversation going. Finally, having run out of people to introduce and finding little in common to talk about, she suggested they serve themselves from the buffet. Escape was not possible, however, as Ike reminded her she really had to try his wife's baked beans. She was just digging in when the fire siren went off, calling the volunteer firefighters, and she flinched at the sound. Now whenever she heard it, she was reminded of the dreadful scene in the woods.

Toby and a few others ran to their pickups, their radios already cackling with orders. "It's on the mountain!" yelled Toby, sticking his head out the window and pointing as he backed around and sped off.

They all looked at the range of hills that rose behind the town, and sure enough, there was a thick column of smoke rising from the tallest one, Hawk Mountain.

"It's been awfully dry," said Scratch, Willie's husband. "I hope it doesn't come this way."

"We're miles away," said Bill.

"I've seen fires like this out West," said Scratch. "If conditions are right, they can move really fast."

"Mark my words," said Ike, in a tone Moses might have used, "this is the work of that witch."

A few uneasy glances were exchanged before Frankie spoke up. "Diana's a charming woman," she said. "She would never harm anyone." She laughed. "And I adore her little shop."

"You have been deceived," said Ike, handing his plate to his wife for a refill. She quickly gave her own plate to Abby to hold and hurried over to the buffet table while Ike continued. "In time, her wickedness will be revealed. There are disturbing signs already—like that poor soul found burned in the woods."

His words cast a pall over the group, and conversation faltered as the smoke column grew thicker and darker as the fire spread through the dry woods. They were all keeping a nervous eye on the mountain as they filled their paper plates and ate their salads and hamburgers and watched the kids playing tag. Soon people began collecting their belongings and drifting along home. The Stoughtons were among the last to leave, so Lucy didn't even have the satisfaction of discussing their odd behavior with her neighbors.

CHAPTER FIVE

Lucy was wakened early Sunday morning by the phone. It was Ted, asking her to go to the crisis center at the police station. The fire was still raging, and he was out with the firefighters, covering the story.

"Have you been up all night?" she asked, grasping the situation.

"Yeah."

"This is bad," she said, her thoughts immediately turning to Toby. She sent up a quick prayer for his safety.

"Yup. They're evacuating some campgrounds, trying to notify people with cabins in the area."

"I'm on it," she said, throwing back the covers.

"I knew I could count on you."

Lucy was certain they would have been notified if they were in any danger from the fire, but she still went straight to the window, just to make sure. Smoke was still rising from the mountain, but the fire seemed to have moved to the other side, away from the town center. Somewhat reassured, she went into the bathroom to wash up. A few minutes later, she was leaving the house, carrying a commuter mug of coffee.

She noticed the smell of smoke the minute she stepped out the door—it irritated her nose and stung her eyes—and she hurried to the car, where she made sure the windows were shut tight and turned on the AC. It was still early and there was little traffic, which was normal for a Sunday morning, but there weren't even any joggers running along the road because the air was so bad. Lucy felt a sense of suspended animation, similar to the period of time after a storm warning was announced but before the storm watch actually began and people started boarding up their windows and pulling their boats out of the water.

When she reached Main Street, she saw the white satellite trucks that indicated the Boston and Portland TV stations were covering the fire. The parking lot at the police station was full, forcing her to park in the little lot behind the *Pennysaver* office. She felt a rising excitement as she hurried across the street and through the parking lot to the back door of the police station. The crisis center was located in the basement, a windowless area that was deemed secure from flood, wind, and reporters. A small group of newshounds, including several men with TV cameras, were gathered at the gray steel door.

"Nobody's getting in," said one guy with an NECN cap.

"There's not much room inside," said Lucy, who'd been given a tour when the crisis center opened. "And I suppose they've got more important things to do than talk to reporters."

"I've got to make a report in ten minutes," said a young woman in a WCVB Windbreaker. "What am I going to say?"

Lucy gave her a sympathetic smile, thinking that perhaps there were advantages to a weekly deadline. She didn't have to file her story on the fire until Wednesday morning.

It was then that the door opened just wide enough for an arm to protrude, and they all watched as a notice was taped to the outside, announcing a press conference in an hour.

"Might as well get some coffee," muttered one guy, and the crowd began to thin. Lucy lingered, trying to figure out her next step. Suddenly she spotted Todd Kirwan coming down the sidewalk and went to meet him. He was out of uniform, and as she got closer, she realized he was fresh from the shower, still smelling of shampoo, but his eyes were tired and red.

"Were you out all night?" she asked, with a nod toward the mountain.

"Yeah. I grabbed a half hour for a quick nap, but now I'm back on duty." He sighed. "This has been a hell of a week. First that poor devil in the woods and now this."

Lucy looked away, breaking eye contact and checking out the mountain. "I'm supposed to cover the response to the fire. Mind if I tag along?" she asked.

"Just keep a low profile," he said, politely holding the door for her. She followed him through the foyer and down the stairs to the crowded crisis center, where phones were ringing like crazy, radios were cackling, and everybody's attention was focused on a large map. She recognized most of the people, even if she didn't know them by name. There was fire chief Buzz Bresnahan; police chief Jim Kirwan; and Roger Wilcox, chairman of the board of selectmen.

"What's the status of the fire?" demanded a young woman Lucy recognized as a part-time dispatcher. "The governor wants to know."

"Tell the governor the fire is ten percent contained, but we hope to get to fifty percent by noon," replied Buzz Bresnahan.

Lucy didn't think that sounded very good. She had a million questions she wanted to ask, but she took Todd's advice and made herself small, sitting on a plastic chair shoved against the wall. As she watched and listened, she gradually made sense of the scene: Reports were coming in from firefighters on the front lines, the information was evaluated, and orders were issued for fighting the fire and evacuating people. The area was popular with hikers and campers, and there were also a number of summer homes; those people were taken to a temporary shelter the Red Cross was setting up in the high school gym. Lucy was considering going over to the shelter to cover that aspect of the story when somebody called for attention.

"We've got trouble," shouted a young officer. "A caller reports seeing a group of hikers near George's Falls."

The fire chief and a couple of others rushed over to the map. "That's the way the fire's moving," he said.

"Maybe we can get a National Guard helicopter?" suggested Wilcox.

"It's our only option—but I'd hate to be wrong," said Buzz. He raised his head, making eye contact with the young officer who was still on the phone. "How reliable is your caller?"

"Rebecca Wardwell? She's honest as the day is long."

"She knows the area," said a man in a Red Cross vest.

"Okay," agreed Bresnahan. "And it's gotta be fast. I think we've got a small window here—maybe thirty, forty minutes, tops."

From outside they could hear shouting and banging on the door. "What the hell?" demanded the police chief.

"Time for the press conference," said somebody.

"The hell with 'em," muttered the police chief, and Lucy concentrated hard on making herself even smaller. She couldn't help wondering about the hikers and whether they knew the danger they were in. She hoped they had some survival skills and would be making some sort of marker so they could be spotted from the air.

"They're giving us a Coast Guard heli," announced Chief Kirwan. "It's closer but it's smaller—they're gonna have to make a couple of trips. We need a landing spot."

Todd was already pointing at a spot on the map. "How about the outlet mall parking lot?"

"I need the coordinates, fast," snapped the chief.

Lucy didn't need the coordinates; she was a faithful customer at the outlet mall, and that's where she headed, arriving just after a couple of cops had finished marking off part of the lot with yellow tape. One of them was her old friend Barney Culpepper, and he introduced her to his young companion, Officer Jason Struthers. They could hear the copter approaching, and minutes later it broke through the smoke and clouds and landed. Four people were practically tossed out, and it took off as soon as they had scuttled to a safe distance.

The little group didn't look like hikers to Lucy; they were carrying baskets and tote bags instead of backpacks, and not one was wearing hiking boots. One woman, who was extremely overweight, was wearing a long, full skirt and had lots of chains and beads strung around her neck. Her long, gray hair hung loose from a central part and fell to her shoulders; large hoop earrings hung from each ear.

"Is everybody okay?" asked Barney, pulling out his notebook.

"Relatively speaking," snapped the large woman. "If you call being up all night in the middle of a fire okay."

"Lady, you're lucky to be alive," said Barney, producing his notebook. "Now, if you don't mind, I need your ID for my report."

Hearing this, the other three, a scruffy-looking man and two equally disheveled women, exchanged glances.

"ID? I didn't bring any. Will a library card do?" The woman was rummaging through a basket, tossing out a variety of brightly colored garments, some with mystical designs.

The young cop, Officer Struthers, turned to the others. "How about you?"

Reluctantly, they began producing their wallets and showing their driver's licenses. The fat lady triumphantly produced a paperback book. "Here! How about this? It's a book I wrote and has my photo on the cover."

The book, Lucy noted with interest, was titled *Modern Witchcraft,* and the author was Lady Sybil Wellington.

"This 'lady' part, is it a name or a title?" asked Barney.

"It's a title," said Lady Sybil, pulling herself up to her entire five feet.

"So you're some sort of nobility? Like from England?" asked Struthers.

"I am an initiated priestess of the Wiccan religion and the author of numerous books on the subject," declared Lady Sybil. "I am a United States citizen and live in New Hampshire."

Barney shrugged. "Okay, I'll take your word for it."

The helicopter could once again be heard approaching, and Lucy could hardly wait to see who emerged this time. She was certain the "hikers" were actually members of Diana Ravenscroft's coven, who had gone up the mountain to celebrate Midsummer Night. She wasn't disappointed when four more ill-equipped hikers scrambled out. This group included two men and two women, all middle-aged and mostly dressed in cheap tracksuits. Like the others, they were carrying an assortment of duffel bags and baskets. Lucy had just decided to approach them for an interview when she was interrupted by Lady Sybil.

"Where's Lady Diana?" she shrieked, addressing the new arrivals.

"She insisted that we go first," said a young man with a prominent nose and a receding chin. "She said that she's"— the fellow lowered his voice to a whisper —"she's the high priestess, responsible for everyone, and she should be the last to be rescued."

"So what exactly were you folks doing up on the mountain?" asked Barney, sounding suspicious. "You weren't starting any fires, were you?"

Glances were exchanged among the group members, and Lady Sybil finally spoke. "Fire is part of the Wiccan Midsummer Sabbat celebration," she admitted. "But we seek only to encourage the growth of crops and their ultimate fruition."

"So did you start a fire or not?" persisted Barney.

"You better discuss that with our leader, Lady Diana. She should be here shortly," said Lady Sybil.

"If they make it in time," said Struthers, who was checking the newcomers' IDs. In the distance, they could all see smoke rising from the mountain and the occasional burst of flame as the fire advanced through the pine woods. Everyone fell silent, listening for the sound of the helicopter. Seconds stretched into minutes. It seemed an eternity before somebody yelled, "I hear it!"

This time the helicopter landed and the pilot and copilot, dressed in orange jumpsuits, climbed out and helped the rescued hikers alight. The four ducked close to the asphalt and scrambled out from under the slowly whirring blades until they reached safety. Lucy recognized not only Diana Ravenscroft, but also Abby Stoughton. She was dying to talk to the girl but knew her job came first.

"How about a photo?" she suggested, producing her camera. "I'm from the local newspaper."

"I don't know . . . ," began Diana, scratching her arm.

"Good idea," said Barney, beginning to corral the group.

"Sure," said the helicopter pilot, smiling broadly. "My mom will put it in her scrapbook."

"My kid can take it in for show-and-tell," said the copilot, forcing the issue. The coven gathered reluctantly, lining up in front of the helicopter that rescued them, with the Coast Guard pilots at either end. Everybody said "cheese" as Lucy snapped the photo. When she asked for names, however, the group scattered, leaving only Diana and the helicopter crew members.

"What now?" asked Lady Diana, scratching her stomach as the helicopter lifted off. "Do we call some taxis?"

"Not so fast," said Barney, who had been reporting to headquarters on his radio. "The fire marshal has some questions for you. The mountain was posted you know—there were notices warning about the risk of forest fire. All fires were strictly prohibited."

"First things first," said Diana, coughing violently and scratching energetically. "I need to see a doctor."

Taking her cue, a couple of other members of the coven began coughing and complaining of assorted aches and pains.

"Should I request an ambulance?" asked Struthers, consulting Barney.

"Nah," growled Barney. "They might need it for people with serious injuries, like the firefighters. Get a school bus." He nodded his head sharply. "One of 'em small ones, to save gas."

While they waited, Lucy seized the opportunity to talk to Abby, who was looking extremely anxious, standing with the group but not really part of it. "Everything will be fine," she said, giving the girl a hug.

"I don't think so," said Abby. "My father's going to kill me when he finds out that I sneaked out last night."

"You'll certainly have some explaining to do," said Lucy. "But I'm sure he'll be relieved that you're safe and sound. Your parents must be worried sick." She pulled her cell phone out of her pocket. "Do you want to give them a call?"

Abby shook her head, and Lucy, dismayed, tucked the cell phone away. She understood the girl was trying to postpone the inevitable, but she believed she would be wiser to get it over with.

Minutes later, the school bus arrived and everybody climbed aboard. Lucy brought up the tail of the little procession headed to the cottage hospital, following the cruiser with its flashing lights and the bright-yellow minibus containing the coven. Arriving at the cottage hospital, she followed them into the emergency room waiting area and waited as they were examined one by one. Eventually, Diana and Abby emerged and Lucy approached them.

"I've got poison ivy," declared Diana. "The doctor said he'd never seen such a bad case. I've got it everywhere. He wanted to give me cortisone but I refused—that stuff's poison."

"Everywhere?" asked Lucy.

"I was skyclad for the sabbat," said Diana in a matter-of-fact tone.

Lucy didn't get it. "Skyclad?"

"Nude."

Lucy looked at Abby, doubtful that a young girl who was embarrassed about her pimples would strip in front of a group of strangers.

"It's optional," said Abby, "and I didn't look during that part."

Lucy nodded.

"Is this really going to be in the *Pennysaver?*" asked Abby.

"I don't know. I'm not the editor," said Lucy. "But there's no way you can keep this from your father. You're a minor and the cops will have to notify your parents."

Tears began to well up in the girl's eyes. "I didn't know I was breaking the law!"

Just then, Ike Stoughton came marching through the sliding glass doors, looking very much like a man with a mission. "I'm taking you home," he said, grabbing Abby by the arm and hauling her to her feet. "And you!" he declared, pointing his finger at Diana. "Leave my daughter alone! You are the Devil's playmate, and I will see you rot in hell!" Then, grabbing Abby by the scruff of her neck, he stomped out the door, dragging her with him.

"Really! That man is pathological," declared Diana, exhaling. "I worry for that girl's safety. I dread to think what goes on in that home."

Lucy was silent, imagining what her reaction would be if she were in Ike Stoughton's shoes. Or what her husband,

Bill's, reaction would be if one of his daughters had been taking part, skyclad or not, in a witch's sabbath. She had to admit her sympathy was with Stoughton. She thought Diana had been reckless and foolish at the very least.

"Lucy," said Diana. "Would you mind giving me a ride home after they question me?" She added a sardonic little snort. "If they don't throw me in jail, that is."

"Sure," she said, feeling a little bit sorry for Diana. She'd been irresponsible, that was certain, but she hadn't intended to cause trouble. Her intentions were good, but she'd landed herself in a big, boiling cauldron of trouble.

That trouble only increased when she emerged, white-faced and shaken, from her session with the assistant fire marshal. "It seems the fire was probably started by a cigarette thrown from a car," she reported as they walked to Lucy's car. "We did have a fire, but we put it out. I told him what we did, but he said sometimes fires travel through roots, underground, and if that's the case, I could be charged."

"How can they tell?" asked Lucy. "Doesn't all the evidence get burned up?"

"You'd think so," said Diana, "but they have their ways. Something about mapping incidences and quadrants and I don't know what all." She nodded somberly. "Lord Malebranche warned me, but I didn't understand: 'Now is the time to progress and grow. Light the fire and burn it slow.' That's what he told me, but I was nervous. I was uncertain of my power, and I tried to rush things. That was my mistake." She got in the car and looked in the distance, sighing and rubbing her arm. "He always spends part of the summer with a coven in England, but I really miss him this year."

"Things will work out," said Lucy mechanically. That was what you said when somebody had a problem, but she wasn't convinced it would be easy. What she didn't expect was the crowd of reporters gathered on Diana's front porch.

"Keep driving," ordered Diana, ducking down to hide her face.

"Okay," said Lucy, sailing right on by the little shop. "Where to?"

"I don't know," moaned Diana. "I'm exhausted, I itch all over, I've got an indictment hanging over my head, Ike Stoughton wants me to go to hell, and now I've got the media on my tail. Can I stay at your house?"

II
WATER

She is the Moon Goddess's most darling daughter
Chosen from the elements five,
Not a one can compete with water
The sparkling source of everything alive.

CHAPTER SIX

"Are you crazy?" The words popped out of Lucy's mouth before she had a chance to think.

"Just for a night or two," added Diana. "Until this blows over."

"I don't think it's a good idea," insisted Lucy. She wasn't comfortable with the idea of Diana being in such close contact with her girls, and she was sure Bill wouldn't like it either.

"Oh, you've got to help me," begged Diana. "I don't have anywhere else to go."

"What about the other members of the coven?" asked Lucy.

"Nobody lives close by. . . ."

"That might be a good thing."

"No, I need to keep an eye on my shop—and besides, I'm in no shape to travel."

It was true, admitted Lucy. Diana was a mess, with poison ivy blisters all over her body, and it was only going to get worse before it got better. She needed someplace quiet to rest and recuperate.

"Okay," said Lucy reluctantly, "but only if you promise not to involve my girls in any witchcraft."

"Absolutely not," agreed Diana. "You won't even know I'm there."

Bill and the girls were in the kitchen when they arrived; Bill was making himself a sandwich for lunch, and the girls were working on late Saturday morning breakfasts. They looked up in surprise at the unexpected visitor.

"Bill, this is Diana Ravenscroft," said Lucy, pulling out a chair for their guest. "She's temporarily homeless, and I've invited her to stay with us for a day or two." She gave the girls a warning look. "Maybe you two can double up for a night or two in Sara's room?"

The girls usually resisted sharing a room when their older sister Elizabeth came home from college, but today they were all smiles. "No problem," agreed Sara. "Right, Zoe?"

"I'll go and put clean sheets on the bed," volunteered Zoe.

Bill seated himself at the table and bit into his sandwich. "Did you lose your house because of the fire?" he asked, raising an eyebrow.

"Sort of," said Lucy quickly. "Any word from Toby?"

"Molly says he called a while ago. He's okay but they still need everybody they can get to fight the fire." He took a big swallow of Coke. "I'm going to cover at the fire station, soon as I finish eating." Bill had been a volunteer firefighter for a number of years, when the kids were small, and he was occasionally called to fill in during emergencies.

"I need to get over to the shelter at the high school and take some pictures," said Lucy. "Ted's out with the firefighters." She was thinking that she really didn't want to leave the girls home alone with Diana. "Diana was trapped on the mountain all night and got a terrible case of poison ivy—she really needs to rest."

Bill looked at her with new interest. "What was it like up there?" he asked.

"Hot and smoky and we were lost. It was really scary until the helicopter came."

"What were you doing up there?" he asked.

"Celebrating the summer solstice," said Diana.

Bill looked at her skeptically. "Pretty darn foolish of you," he said, shoving his plate across the table and standing up.

"I know that now," said Diana, shamefaced.

He was by the door, picking up the helmet, boots, and jacket he had piled on the floor.

"I don't know when I'll be home," he told Lucy. "Don't count on me for supper."

"Okay," said Lucy. "Be careful."

He nodded and went out the door.

Lucy watched him go and hoped he wouldn't be called into danger; she thought of Toby, who'd been out all night with the other volunteers. "I hate this fire," she said, to nobody in particular.

"It wasn't my fault, honest," said Diana. "We didn't start it."

Lucy looked at her with a serious expression. "Don't make any trouble here. I'm warning you."

"Oh, I won't. I promise," said Diana, looking hurt.

Lucy didn't believe her for a minute, but she had no choice; she had a job to do. The fire was a big story, and she had to help cover it.

Later that afternoon, tired and hungry, she checked in at the office. Nobody was there. Phyllis didn't work Saturdays, and there was no message from Ted. Lucy sat down at her desk and began transcribing her notes into the computer, adding her impressions while they were still fresh. Images flitted through her mind: the anxious faces of the evacuees as they arrived at the shelter; the intense, focused expressions at the crisis center; Lady Sybil's outrageous appearance as a most unlikely hiker. When she finished, she saved the file, then headed home. She was done for the day and had the luxury of going home, but the firefighters had no choice but to keep battling the flames. Her thoughts were with them, especially Toby, as she locked up and crossed the parking lot to her car. It was unusually dark for this time of day, late afternoon, and she attributed it to the smoke from the fire. But when she started the car, she noticed drops of water leaving grimy tracks as they dribbled through the soot on her windshield. Rain! It was raining!

She stuck her hand out the window, just to be sure, and felt the drops coming faster and faster. Soon it was a real downpour. A soaker. Thank heaven.

Flipping on her wipers and turning on the headlights, she headed home, praying that the rain would continue until the fire was completely doused. But when Monday dawned and it was still raining, Lucy was beginning to be sorry she got what she'd wished for. True, Toby and the other volunteer firefighters were able to return home. Only a handful of cabins were lost, and the evacuees were able to leave the shelter. Miraculously, no lives were lost and there were only a few minor injuries, but this unending downpour was too much. The streets were beginning to flood as storm drains backed up, creeks were rising, and moods were falling as people settled into sulks and depression. Even worse, Friends of Animals day camp, where both girls had summer jobs, was closed because of the weather, and Lucy had no choice but to leave the girls alone in the house with Diana. So far, the witch had been true to her promise not to practice witchcraft and had pretty much stayed in Zoe's bedroom, passing the time by watching Zoe's little twelve-inch TV. As much as Lucy would have liked to send Diana packing, her conscience wouldn't allow it until the rash subsided and she could take care of herself.

"First the fire and now this," grumbled Phyllis when Lucy arrived at the office on Monday morning. Lucy hung her dripping rain jacket on the coat rack and gave her umbrella a gentle shake, then propped it against the wall. She thumped across the room to her desk in her black and white polka-dot Wellies.

"I guess we're never satisfied," said Lucy, pulling off her boots and slipping into the pair of worn loafers she kept under her desk. "Just last week, everybody was complaining that it was too dry."

"Well now it's too wet," said Phyllis. "My lawn is getting all soggy. I could use a pair of boots like those. They're cute."

"My poor tomato plants are treading water," said Lucy, attempting a joke. "Where's Ted? Resting up after the fire?"

"No rest for the wicked," said Phyllis. "Press conference at the police station."

"About the fire?" asked Lucy, switching on her PC.

"Your guess is as good as mine," said Phyllis.

But when Ted came in an hour later, dressed like the Gorton's fisherman in bright yellow rain gear, it turned out the press conference hadn't been about the fire after all.

"The state police identified the burned guy," he said, carefully placing a handful of rain-splotched papers on Phyllis's counter.

"Who was he?" asked Phyllis, dabbing at the mess with a paper towel.

"Name of Malcolm Malebranche. He was a magician, worked at kids' birthday parties, stuff like that."

"Malebranche, that's an unusual name," said Lucy. She knew she'd heard it before but couldn't quite remember when.

Ted wasn't looking good; Lucy figured he was still tired from covering the fire. Being out there in all that smoke couldn't be good for a person. It was no wonder he had a nasty little cough and looked a little green about the gills.

"It's really horrible," he was saying, swallowing hard.

Lucy and Phyllis were all ears. "Yeah?" prompted Phyllis.

Ted sat down on one of the chairs in the reception area,

by Phyllis's counter. "The medical examiner says he was burned alive."

Phyllis's thin, pencil-line eyebrows shot up. "What did you say?"

"He was burned alive," repeated Ted.

Lucy had heard him the first time, and she was struggling to understand how something like that could happen.

"The ME thinks it might have been some sort of magic trick gone wrong, a Houdini-style escape that didn't work, something like that."

"He must've been really dumb to try something like that," said Phyllis.

"Nobody's that dumb," said Lucy, suddenly remembering where she'd heard the name. It was in the car, with Diana. She'd remembered something Lord Malebranche had told her. Diana knew him, and from the way she referred to him, Lucy suspected he was also a witch—and she wondered if his death was really a tragic accident or something more sinister.

"I'll be back," said Lucy, pulling on her boots. "I've got a lead I need to follow up on."

When she got to the house, she found the girls in the kitchen, making chocolate chip cookies for Diana. The kitchen smelled wonderful, rich and chocolatey, and Libby, the Labrador, was keeping an eye on the proceedings, ready to lick up any spills.

"Don't give her too many cookies or she'll get sick," warned Lucy, slipping off her rain gear and grabbing a cookie from the wire tray as she headed for the stairs. The cookie was at that perfect stage when the chocolate chips were still warm and gooey and the dough was crispy, but she didn't really enjoy it, because her mind was already on the conversation she was going to have with Diana. Swallowing the last bit, she knocked on the door.

"Diana, it's me, Lucy," she said.

"Come in." Diana's voice was thin and reedy.

When she opened the door, she found Diana in a cotton T-shirt and underpants, lying on the bed with the covers thrown back. The poison ivy rash was peaking, and the large pink blotches that spotted her body were blistered and oozing. She looked so miserable that Lucy found her defenses crumbling.

"Is there anything I can do for you?" she asked.

"The girls are taking good care of me," said Diana. An inflamed patch near her mouth made speaking difficult; another had nearly closed her left eye. "They keep bringing me cold drinks and things to eat."

"It will pass," said Lucy.

"I know, but it sure seems to be taking its own sweet time," complained Diana. "I know I promised not to practice witchcraft, but I really think a repelling spell might help, if you wouldn't mind." Seeing Lucy's lips tighten, she quickly added, "The girls wouldn't even have to know. I could be very quiet."

"Why don't you give the doctor a call and get some of that cortisone?"

"Filthy poison," snapped Diana. "I wouldn't pollute my body with that stuff."

"Maybe there's something else he could prescribe?"

"A prescription isn't going to do any good," said Diana. "What's going on here is much stronger than any little pill."

"It's worth a try," insisted Lucy. "I'm always amazed at the new stuff. . . ."

Diana sniffed. "I don't think pharmaceutical companies have come up with anything to counteract a maleficent spell."

Lucy blinked. "You think your poison ivy is the result of an evil spell? Is that what you're saying?"

Diana nodded.

"But you told me there's nothing wicked about witch-craft."

Diana shrugged. "It's like any other religion—there are always some who stray. Witches are people, too, and there are jealousies and rivalries, and when you have attained a certain level of expertise, it's tempting to use your powers in a negative way."

"Do you suspect anyone in particular?" asked Lucy.

"I think it was Lady Sybil," whispered Diana. "She was very upset when Lord Malebranche asked me to fill in during his absence."

"You mentioned Lord Malebranche before. . . ."

"He's the high priest of our coven. He's been called away."

"Who called him? Where did he go?"

"He always spends Midsummer in England, with a coven in the New Forest."

Not this year, thought Lucy, taking a deep breath. "They've identified the body in the woods—it's Malcolm Malebranche. . . ."

A deep shudder racked Diana's body, and Lucy quickly wrapped her in the comforter that had been tossed to the bottom of the bed. "No, no," moaned Diana, rocking back and forth. "Not Lord Malebranche."

"They think it was an accident, a magic trick gone wrong," added Lucy.

"Evil . . . evil is afoot," whispered Diana. "I have to take steps to protect myself and the others."

"You're safe here," said Lucy, trying to calm her. "It was an accident."

Diana shook her head; she was still shivering. "No accident." She seized a pen and notepad that were lying on the bedside table and began scribbling frantically. When she finished, she shoved the paper at Lucy. "You must get me these things. They're all at my shop."

Lucy took the paper and studied the list: black candles, salt, chalice, wine, athame, frankincense, onyx stone. "You promised," protested Lucy. "No witchcraft."

Diana had pulled her long hair down over her face, but her eyes glittered brightly through the tangled locks. "It's a matter of life and death," she said, her voice little more than a hiss. "You have to get these things for me."

This wasn't what Lucy had intended at all. She'd come back to question Diana about Malebranche, but all she'd found out so far was that he was the high priest of a Wiccan coven. "What can you tell me about Malcolm Malebranche?" demanded Lucy. "He was a magician, right?"

Diana wasn't yielding; her jaw was set, her hands curled into fists. "Get me the tools I need for the spell and I'll tell you," she said.

Lucy knew when she was beat. The woman was hysterical, crazy, totally insane, but she wasn't going to get another word out of her until she produced those black candles and all the rest. "All right," said Lucy.

"And don't delay," warned Diana. "Time is of the essence when evil is afoot."

"Righto," said Lucy, heading for the door.

Down in the kitchen, Lucy grabbed another cookie. It had cooled and wasn't as good as the first. That's the way it was with chocolate chip cookies, but it was still good, and she took another, chewing it thoughtfully.

"What's going on?" asked Sara, dropping the last balls of dough onto a cookie sheet.

"Diana's had some bad news. A friend died. She's pretty upset, so I think you should leave her alone until I get back. I just have to get some things for her. It won't take me long."

"Okay," said Sara, sliding the pan into the oven.

"We could make tea for her," suggested Zoe.

"Not just yet," said Lucy, reaching for her rain jacket. "Maybe when I get back, okay?"

Lucy was backing the car around when she noticed a little VW beetle turning into her drive. Probably one of Sara's friends, she thought, but when she pulled alongside the car, she discovered Rebecca Wardwell behind the wheel.

"Horrible weather," said Lucy by way of greeting. The two cars were side by side, and both drivers had rolled down their windows. "What brings you here?"

"I understand somebody at your house has a bad case of poison ivy, maybe one of your children?"

"No, well, yes," admitted Lucy, marveling at the efficiency of the Tinker's Cove grapevine to spread news. "It's not one of my kids; it's Diana Ravenscroft. She must have gotten into a patch. It's very bad."

"Poison ivy can be a real trial," said Rebecca.

"As a matter of fact, she wants me to go to her shop and get some candles and things so she can cast a spell to get rid of it," said Lucy.

"All this drama is so unnecessary." Rebecca sniffed, pulling a small bottle out of the large quilted bag she always carried. "I have a sweet fern solution here that I think she'll find quite effective."

"Thanks," said Lucy, reaching out the window and accepting the bottle. "It's very kind of you."

"Not at all," she said with a wave of her hand. "Now I'll be on my way."

And before Lucy could get her car in gear, Rebecca had backed out onto the road and was gone. Neat trick, thought Lucy, wondering where Rebecca had learned to drive. Her own driving, she admitted, tended to be erratic, mostly because she was trying to do so many things while she drove. Right now, for example, she was calling the office on her cell phone to let Ted know what she'd found out about Malcolm Malebranche.

"He wasn't just a magician—he was a high priest in the Wiccan religion. Diana Ravenscroft says he was the head of her coven, you know, those folks who had to be rescued from the forest fire. She said they thought he was in England, that he always went there every summer. Anyway, she's promised to tell me more about him, but first I have to get her some stuff so she can work a special protective spell because evil is afoot." Lucy let out a big sigh. "I can't believe I'm actually saying this stuff."

"Listen, whatever works," said Ted, chuckling. "Stick with it and get this story. It's hot stuff."

"Bad pun, really bad," snapped Lucy, ending the call.

CHAPTER SEVEN

Lucy didn't know what to expect at Diana's shop. She doubted very much that the reporters would still be gathered there; they wouldn't waste time hanging around when it was obvious Diana wasn't home. But then again they might, and there was a real likelihood that Ike Stoughton or his sons might be keeping an eye on the place, hoping to confront Diana. But when she did a slow drive-by to assess the situation, she found it deserted, although there was clear evidence that somebody had been there: a large pentagram had been sprayed on the lavender door in thick black paint.

Lucy took care to park her car at some distance from the shop and walked back, peeking out from under her umbrella and watching for trouble. However, when she approached the little shop, nobody seemed to be out in the rain except her. As she drew closer, she saw the sodden ground was littered with takeout wrappers, probably dropped by the reporters. Once she stepped on the porch, she discovered a couple of windowpanes had been broken. Peering through the window, she saw rocks lying in the display area. Probably the work of some of the town's dimmer youth, stoked by a few beers, but distressing evidence that public sentiment was turning against the witch, she thought, unlocking the door. Stepping inside, she found mail that had been shoved through the slot in the door lying on the floor. She picked it up after propping her dripping umbrella against the wall. As she gathered the envelopes, she found some letters that had not been delivered by the postman—they had no stamps or address, only the single word *WITCH* crudely scrawled in angry red capital letters.

One wasn't even in an envelope but was simply folded in half, and she was unable to resist the temptation to read it. The message was short and to the point: *BURN NOW OR BURN IN HELL.* The author had thoughtfully illustrated the letter with an amateurish drawing of red, yellow, and orange flames. Lucy quickly refolded the paper, wishing she'd never seen it, wishing she could throw it away and be rid of it. It made her feel queasy, and she desperately wanted to wash her hands, as if she could wash away the hate and anger. Increasingly uneasy, she quickly searched the store and made sure it was empty. It was, except for Piewocket. She found him hiding under the counter, tucked into a dark corner behind a trash basket. She gave him a little scratch behind the ears, but let him be for the moment, hoping he'd come out of his own accord.

Stuffing the mail into one of the lavender bags with the shop name, SOLSTICE, printed in gold, she gathered the things that Diana had requested. Diana had also asked her to bring some clean clothing, so Lucy had to go upstairs to the apartment. She climbed the stairs reluctantly, not exactly sure what she was afraid of. The sound of rain on the roof grew louder as she climbed the stairs.

But when she opened the door to the cozy little studio that was tucked under the sharply peaked roof, she found everything in order. The door opened to a basic kitchen area, with a counter and a couple of stools where Diana probably took her meals. It was very clean and neat. A row of glass canisters held staples like whole wheat pasta, oatmeal, and beans.

The living area contained a daybed with iron curlicues, neatly made with a purple coverlet and a number of brightly colored pillows. A big bentwood rocker and an old wooden trunk that served as a coffee table completed the furniture arrangement. A small bookcase held a number of books on witchcraft. A chest of drawers stood next to a closet, and a tiny bathroom with a claw-foot tub was tucked behind. Lucy found a big tote bag on the closet shelf and filled it with basics: underwear, T-shirts, shorts and jeans, a comfy hoodie. An empty cosmetics bag was in the tote, and Lucy filled it with the herbal shampoo, face cream, and deodorant she found in the bathroom—all products she'd seen downstairs in the shop.

When she finished packing and went back downstairs, Lucy found herself in a bit of a quandary. Piewocket had emerged and was sniffing at some broken glass on the floor. She didn't want to leave him, but she wasn't at all sure that Libby would welcome a feline guest. She quickly taped some of the SOLSTICE bags over the broken windows in an effort to keep the rain out, then decided to tackle the cat. Noticing Piewocket wore a collar, Lucy cut a length of ribbon and fastened it like a leash. The cat didn't seem to mind being touched, so Lucy scooped him up and tucked him under her arm and stepped outside, making sure the door locked behind her. Then she hurried down the street as fast as she could go with the squirming cat and the tote bag and the umbrella, eager to get back to safer territory. She was out of breath when she reached the car, yanked the door open, and tossed the bag inside. Still holding the cat, she seated herself in the driver's seat, setting Piewocket down on the passenger seat. He seemed content to sit there, but she tied the ribbon to the door handle so he couldn't wander around the car and get underfoot. Then she was off, cruising down the street, keeping an eye on the cat. It was only when she reached the stop sign on Main Street that she began to relax, realizing she had a decision to make.

She could go straight home and deliver the witching supplies to Diana, or she could go back to the office, where there was plenty of work waiting for her. It wasn't just her strong work ethic that made the decision easy—it was also the fact that if Diana had the supplies, she would undoubtedly use them, and Lucy didn't want her girls to take part in any spell-casting. But when she arrived with the cat in tow and told Ted about her errand, he was all over her.

"You have to write it up," he said. "It's a terrific feature story. 'My Bewitching Houseguest,' something like that. Readers will love it."

Lucy was horrified. "No!" she protested, putting down a bowl of water for Piewocket, who ignored it and focused his attention on Ted, rubbing his face against his legs. "Diana's got enemies—her shop was vandalized—I don't want them painting pentagrams on my house!"

"She'll be back home by the time the story comes out," said Ted, picking up the cat and setting it in his lap. Piewocket half closed his eyes as Ted scratched behind his ears. "And your story will show that Wicca is completely harmless and that there's nothing to fear from witchcraft, right?"

"Are you crazy?" asked Lucy "This guy who I now know was a witch was burned alive in the woods, I find a note that tells Diana to burn now or burn in hell, and you want me to write a puff piece on witchcraft? I don't think a cute story about casting spells to get rid of poison ivy is going to change anybody's mind, and I sure don't want some loony thinking that I'm allowing a witch to cast spells in my house." Lucy paused for breath. "And I have kids. I don't want my girls getting involved in this stuff."

It was then that her phone rang, and she snatched up the receiver. The caller didn't wait for her to identify herself.

"Ike Stoughton here," he began. "I've got a problem with your girls."

Lucy's heart sank. What were they up to? "What exactly—"

"They called my girl and invited her to a spell-casting."

Lucy could hear the anger in his voice—anger she shared. "That's outrageous," she said. "I absolutely agree with you. When is this, uh, event supposed to take place?"

"I'm not sure. They were going to call back with the details."

"I will talk to them," vowed Lucy. "They had no business involving Abby—"

"Is it true that witch, that Diana woman, is staying at your house?" he demanded.

"Well, yes," admitted Lucy.

"Your home is your castle, and I can't tell you who you can have as a houseguest—"

Lucy didn't like the way this conversation was headed. "That's right."

"But I have to warn you that she is a very dangerous woman. You'd be wise to make her leave."

"Thanks for the advice," said Lucy in a curt tone.

"I'm just warning you," he said. "I'd hate to see something bad happen to you or your family."

Lucy felt her hackles rise. "Is this a threat?"

"No, absolutely not," said Ike. "I have your best interest at heart."

"Point taken," said Lucy, ending the call.

"What was that all about?" demanded Phyllis, who, along with Ted, had been listening to every word.

Lucy was trying to sort out her emotions, a complex tangle of anger, disappointment, and fear. "It's Ike Stoughton, warning me about Diana."

"Did he threaten you?" asked Ted.

"Not exactly," said Lucy. "He says not but it felt like a threat. And after what I saw at Diana's place . . ."

"You have to write this story. It's the only way to let people know they have nothing to fear from Diana," said Ted. Piewocket had settled in on his lap and was purring, sounding like an idling engine. "The sooner the better. I'd like it for Wednesday. So mote it be."

"What did you say?" demanded Lucy.

"So mote it be. It's just an expression I picked up from Pam. It means—"

"I know what it means," said Lucy, booting up her computer. "It means I'm working for a warlock."

When Lucy got home around five that evening, she went straight to the family room, where the girls were watching TV.

"What on earth were you thinking? Abby's father called me—very angry—because you invited Abby to this spell-casting."

The girls glanced at each other; then Sara spoke. "We thought she'd want to be part of it."

"I'm sure she would, but her father has other ideas." Lucy paused. "She's already in trouble because of the Midsummer thing. Now you've made it worse for her."

"We didn't realize . . . ," said Zoe, shamefaced. "She said she couldn't come, anyway, 'cause her mom is sick and needs her."

"Are we still having the spell-casting tonight?" asked Sara.

"I'm afraid so," admitted Lucy, going back to the kitchen.

She was pulling the frying pan out of the cupboard when Diana came scrambling down the stairs to greet her. The poison ivy had spread, and she was covered with sores that made the least movement painful. "What took you so long?" she demanded. "I've been waiting all day!"

"I have a job, you know," replied Lucy, rather self-righteously.

"Did you get my stuff?"

"It's here, right here," said Lucy, handing over the bag. "And I've got your cat too. He's in the car. I wasn't sure how the dog would react." A sudden burst of barking sent her outside, where she found Libby jumping and barking at the cat, who was calmly perched on the back of the driver's seat. Lucy managed to drag the dog away and confined her in the garden shed. Then she carefully lifted the cat out of the car and carried him into the house.

Diana was looking in the bag. "Where's the jasmine? And the power oil?"

"They weren't on the list you gave me," said Lucy, handing over the cat and taking off her jacket. Something thunked against the wall as she hung her coat on the hook, and she reached inside the pocket, finding Rebecca's solution. "I do have this stuff that Rebecca Wardwell gave me, though."

Diana took the bottle and unscrewed the top, sniffing it suspiciously. "I think I better rely on my own magick," she said, handing it back.

Lucy set the bottle on the windowsill behind the sink. "Is there any chance that I could watch you cast the spell? Ted wants me to write a story about Wicca for the paper."

"I suppose that would be okay," said Diana, cuddling Piewocket. "Midnight is the most auspicious hour."

"I don't think you should wait that long," said Lucy, rinsing a potato under the tap. She was tired and had no intention of staying up late. "Nine is thrice three," she said, wondering where she'd picked up that particular phrase. "The power of your spell will be magnified three times.'"

"Good thought," said Diana, nodding seriously. "Nine it is."

At nine o'clock, Lucy and the girls met Diana in the backyard, under a starless, moonless sky heavy with clouds. The air was still and misty, but it wasn't raining. Diana had decided it was too cold and damp to go skyclad, and Lucy was grateful for small favors. Instead, she was wearing an old summer bathrobe of Lucy's.

"Blue symbolizes harmony, so I think it will work," she declared after the girls had ransacked every closet in the house, looking for appropriate garb.

"It looks fine," said Sara, who was setting up a card table to serve as an altar. She and Zoe were wearing a couple of Lucy's long skirts, remnants of the eighties, that they'd found in the back of a closet, and they'd draped themselves with scarves. Lucy hadn't dressed for the occasion; she was still wearing the jeans and polo shirt she'd worn to work, as well as the polka-dot boots.

"We need either a black or a white cloth," said Diana. She was obviously uncomfortable but determined to go through with the ceremony.

Lucy didn't have a black tablecloth, but she did have several white ones. Once the table had been covered, Diana carefully arranged her tools: a black candle and a white candle, a bowl of salt and one of water, a sheet of writing paper, the frankincense and onyx stone, and finally her athame.

"We are ready to begin," she said, taking a deep breath.

Lucy and the girls arranged themselves in a semicircle around the altar. Moving cautiously and carefully, Diana spread her legs wide apart, angled her head back, and raised her hands, palms up.

"Glorious goddess of the moon, I pray your heavenly presence grant me soon. As dark of night gives way to day, hear my plea and grant this boon."

Completing the invocation, she lit the candles, then sprinkled nine pinches of salt into the water. "Salt and water mix tonight, this I do with all my might, that dark and evil fade away and only good shall come this way."

She then placed the blade of the athame first in the flame of the black candle, then did the same with the white candle.

Using the heated blade, she inscribed a diagram on the sheet of paper; then she placed a bit of frankincense on the blade and held it in the flame of the white candle until its scent filled the air. She picked up the onyx stone and passed it through each flame and then through the smoke of the frankincense.

"Diana, goddess of the moon, hear my plea: Your love and blessings give to me. Take away my fearful sores, that they will trouble me no more. Thus protected I need not fear; peace and love be always near." Completing her spell, Diana folded the paper into a small square and placed the onyx stone on top. "We will leave the candles to burn for one hour, and then I will place these talismans under my pillow. In the morning, when I wake, the poison ivy will be gone, and I will be protected from those who would do me harm. So mote it be."

"So mote it be," chorused the girls.

Give me a break, thought Lucy.

The girls were excited about the spell-casting, and Lucy heard them chattering away when she went upstairs to bed. Bill was still awake, reading *Sports Illustrated,* and Libby was curled up on the floor beside the bed. She gave Lucy a resentful look, remembering her confinement in the garden shed.

"Did the spell work?" he asked.

"Not yet, but Diana's convinced it will," said Lucy, pulling her shirt off over her head. "By tomorrow she will be healed."

"And then she'll go home? And take her cat too?" asked Bill.

"I hope so," said Lucy. "The reporters are gone, and the spell will also protect her from those who would do her harm, so there's no reason for her to hang around here," said Lucy, dropping her nightgown over her head. "So mote it be."

"What?" asked Bill.

"Never mind." Lucy gave him a kiss and turned on her side, settling down to sleep. In a matter of minutes, she'd drifted off, dreaming of witches on broomsticks, riding through the night, all jumbled up with Ted and deadlines and snow that turned out to be copies of the *Pennysaver,* drifting down from heaven and catching fire as they fell.

Waking with a start when someone shook her shoulder, she discovered Diana bending over her in the darkness.

"Wake up, Lucy," she was whispering.

"Whuh?" asked Lucy, still caught in her dream.

"I need the solution Rebecca gave you," hissed Diana.

"What solution?" whispered Lucy. She was gradually waking up and didn't want to disturb Bill, snoring gently beside her.

"The stuff Rebecca gave you. I'm sorry to wake you, but this itching is driving me crazy. . . ."

"It's okay," said Lucy, throwing back the covers and getting up. She padded across the room and through the hall into the bathroom, where she'd stored the solution in the medicine cabinet. "Here it is," she said, heading back to bed.

"Thanks," whispered Diana.

But Lucy was already back in bed, spooning against Bill.

It was raining hard when Lucy woke the next morning, and Lucy was aware of the steady patter on the roof as she washed her face and brushed her teeth. Diana's nighttime visit seemed like a dream she hardly remembered, and she was surprised when she went down to the kitchen and discovered Diana was already up and had made a pot of coffee. She was sitting at the table, hidden behind the paper.

"Good morning," said Lucy. "Did you sleep well?"

"After I woke you and got Rebecca's solution," said Diana, lowering the paper and revealing her completely healed face.

"The poison ivy is gone from your face!" exclaimed Lucy.

"From everywhere," said Diana. "All gone."

"That's amazing," said Lucy, pouring herself a cup of coffee. She carried it over to the table and sat down, then took a sip. "I really can't believe it," she said.

"Neither can I," admitted Diana. "I never had a spell work that completely before."

"Are you sure it was the spell?" asked Lucy, eyeing the half-empty bottle of Rebecca's solution.

"I wish I knew," said Diana. "Whichever it was, it was some powerful magick."

Lucy took another swallow of coffee. She was happy for Diana—she was glad the poison ivy was gone—but she didn't like the way it went. She would have been a lot happier if Diana had just taken the cortisone pills the emergency room doctor prescribed. That was a cure she understood, created by scientists and tested in clinical studies, and much preferable to spells and incantations and bottles of mysterious healing solutions.

"Now that you're better," said Lucy, "I suppose you'll want to get back to your own place."

Diana's expression was serious. "Last night, when I couldn't sleep, I went through my mail," she said. "It was pretty scary, and I was wondering if you'd mind very much if I stayed a little bit longer? I know it's an imposition, especially with the cat, but I'll keep him in my room, with me."

Lucy did mind. She'd really had enough of Diana. But how could she send the woman away when she needed protection? She'd read the letter; she'd seen the pentagram painted on the door. "You can stay," said Lucy slowly, "on one condition: that you go to the police and show them the letters and tell them everything you know about Malebranche."

"I'll have to think about that," said Diana, rising and leaving Lucy alone at the table. The bottle of Rebecca's healing solution was still there, and Lucy picked it up and unscrewed the cap, sniffing it. It didn't have any smell. She

tipped the bottle and poured a drop or two on her hand, dis-
covering it wasn't greasy, and it didn't sting. It felt like nothing more than water.

More puzzled than ever, she screwed the cap back on and
left the bottle on the table. It was getting late and she had to
get to work.

CHAPTER EIGHT

The rain was really getting to be a pain, thought Lucy, letting the door slam behind her and dashing to the car, splashing through an enormous puddle that stretched from the back porch steps to the driveway. She was damp and uncomfortable as she started the engine, but that wasn't the only thing bothering her. Friends of Animals day camp had been canceled again because of the weather, which meant the girls were home alone with Diana. Diana had promised not to discuss witchcraft with the girls, but that sudden poison ivy cure was pretty spectacular, and she wouldn't be surprised if they pestered Diana until she gave in. On the other hand, she finally concluded as she eased into an empty parking spot in front of the newspaper office, if Diana could cast a spell to end the rain and bring the sunshine back, she was all for it.

Once inside, she shook out the umbrella, hung her rain jacket on the coat rack, and clomped to her desk. Today it seemed too much effort to take the boots off; the cool but muggy weather made her feel as if she had a fever, both overheated and chilled at the same time.

"Have you heard the forecast?" she asked Phyllis, who

was working her way through a big stack of press releases. "When's the rain supposed to stop?"

"Not anytime soon," said Phyllis gloomily. "It's getting me down."

"Tell me about it. There's no day camp again today, and the girls are home with Diana."

"It can't be much longer," said Phyllis. "She must be on the mend by now."

"She's cured."

Phyllis's eyebrows, actually thin penciled lines, rose above her colorful harlequin reading glasses. "No way!"

"She did a spell," said Lucy. "Last night. And this morning her skin is perfectly clear, like she never had poison ivy at all. Though I have to say, she also used some stuff Rebecca Wardwell cooked up. Whichever it was, she's all better."

"So how come she hasn't gone home?" asked Phyllis.

"She's afraid. This whole Malebranche thing has really shaken her up, and she's been getting some dreadful hate mail."

"Goes with the territory, if you ask me." Phyllis sniffed. "If you advertise yourself as a witch, you have to expect that some people aren't going to approve."

"The letters were really nasty," said Lucy, booting up her computer. "I can see why she doesn't want to be alone, even though she did cast a protective spell."

"If you ask me, Lucy Stone, I think she's got you bewitched."

"Maybe," admitted Lucy. "I'm not a complete pushover. I told her she can stay only if she tells the police everything she knows about Malebranche."

And just then, almost as if Diana had picked up her thoughts, the phone rang. Diana was ready to play "Let's Make a Deal."

"Lucy, I want you to know that I really appreciate everything you've done for me. I know I'm being a big baby, but those letters really scared me, and I'd like to stay with your family a bit longer, but it would be a violation of the ordains for me to talk about Malcolm with either you or the cops. You're really putting me in a bad spot."

Lucy decided to adopt Phyllis's line of thought. "This has nothing to do with me. You're the one who decided to become a witch. And what are 'ordains'?"

"Ordains are the rules all witches agree to follow. And you're absolutely right. I made my choice—nobody made me become a witch. But what I could do is give you the name of Malcolm's assistant—if you let me stay."

"His assistant?"

"Yeah, he knows everything about Malcolm. He can tell you whatever you want to know."

Lucy was tempted. The police hadn't released much information about Malebranche, and this could be a real scoop. She knew Ted would want her to go for it. "Just a couple more days, okay? Absolutely no witchcraft with the girls. And you've got to keep Piewocket in your room."

"Oh, I will, I promise. Thank you so much! You're a sweetie!" enthused Diana.

Lucy knew she wasn't doing this because she was a sweetie; she wanted to get the story. And she was uncomfortably aware that Bill was getting tired of having a houseguest. Just this morning, he'd been muttering about fish and company stinking after three days. "The name?" she asked.

"What name?"

"The name of Malcolm's assistant," hissed Lucy, somewhat irritated. "That's the deal, right?"

"Oh, yeah. It's Peter, Peter Symonds, and he lives over in Northboro, near the river."

Lucy was jotting down directions to Symonds's place when Ted arrived, dressed in full foul-weather gear. "I've been out at the river with the fire chief," he said, removing his sou'wester and setting it on top of the coat rack. "If this rain doesn't stop soon, we're going to get some flooding. Even the creeks are rising."

Lucy thought of Scorton Creek that ran near her house but decided it couldn't possibly be much of a threat. After all, the last time she'd crossed the bridge, it had been little more than a trickle. "I've got a lead on Malcolm Malebranche," she said, watching Ted unzip his yellow slicker. "His assistant."

"You could do a phone interview," suggested Ted when Lucy pushed back her chair and grabbed her bag.

"I think face-to-face would be better," said Lucy, slipping into her jacket. "And this way I can take him by surprise."

"Or you can waste a lot of time when it turns out he isn't home," said Ted, but Lucy was already out the door.

It was a fair distance to Northboro, and Lucy had to keep slowing to cautiously inch around the big puddles that were forming over every storm drain and low spot. It was warm and dry in the car, the wipers kept up a steady beat, and she had the radio switched to an oldies station. This was the part of her job that she liked best: tracking down a story that nobody else had. As she drove along, she was thinking of the questions she wanted to ask Symonds and the best way of posing them.

She found his house without any problem, thanks to Diana's directions, but there was no answer when she knocked. For a moment, she feared Ted's prediction that Symonds probably wouldn't be home was true until she noticed a car in the driveway and decided to try the back door. Maybe he was in the shower or had the TV on and couldn't hear her knocking. When she went around to the rear of the house, she spotted him, as thin and awkward as a scarecrow, standing in the backyard and watching the river, which was overflowing its banks and rising.

"I'm Lucy Stone, from the *Pennysaver*," she yelled, approaching him through the downpour and pulling her camera out of her bag. "Mind if I take some photos?"

"See that stick?" he yelled, pointing at a little nubbin poking out of the water about twenty feet from the water's edge. "That's where the water was when I woke up this morning, about four hours ago."

"Oh, my," exclaimed Lucy, checking the distance from the water's edge to the house, about fifty feet with a gentle slope. She raised the camera and framed her shot, featuring Symonds pointing to his stick. As she snapped the photo, she realized she recognized him: He was one of the members of the coven who had been rescued by helicopter, the guy with the prominent nose and receding chin.

"Hey!" he protested. "I didn't say you could take a picture."

"Oh, sorry," she said, lowering the camera and deciding to play it cool, leaving her reporter's notebook in her bag. "Do you have flood insurance?"

"No," he replied. "It's never done this before." He was wearing fisherman's waders and a camouflage slicker, and the rain had plastered his long, dark hair to his head. It wasn't a good look, emphasizing his rather large nose, small chin, and splotchy skin. "I suppose all this rain is a big story?"

"It is," said Lucy. "I'd love to interview you about it. Do you mind if we go inside?"

"I can't talk long. I have to start moving my stuff upstairs," he said, giving her a funny look. "Do I know you?"

"I get around, because of my job," she said, following him into the little bungalow. Once indoors, she saw the furniture and decor were dated, as if he'd inherited the house from an elderly relative. Interviewing him about Malcolm Malebranche wasn't going to be hard—a box full of posters and magic equipment was on a chair by the door. "Are you a magician?" she asked.

"I was Malcolm the Magnificent's assistant," he said.

"Why'd you stop?" asked Lucy, watching as he knelt down and began gathering books and photo albums from a bookcase and packing them in a cardboard carton.

"He died unexpectedly."

"I heard about that," said Lucy. "Were you close?"

Symonds shrugged, dropping a couple more books into the box. "We worked together for six years."

Looking around the place, which had a forlorn air, Lucy suspected it hadn't been a very lucrative arrangement. "Want me to carry this upstairs?" she asked, indicating the collection of memorabilia.

Symonds again gave her a funny look, a sideways glance, that made her regret her offer. "If you want," he muttered, sounding as if he was doing *her* a favor.

Lucy was halfway up the stairs when she heard Symonds behind her and found herself stepping a little quicker. She went into the first room she saw, a bedroom with a dingy chenille spread covering the sagging bed, and set the box on a tall dresser. "The water can't possibly rise this high," she said, turning to face him with an encouraging smile.

Symonds was staring at her, and she could practically see the lightbulb above his head switching on. "You were there, when we got off the mountain "

"Like I said, I'm a reporter. I get around."

"And you're here because of the storm?" he asked in a sarcastic tone.

"Well, yes, and I also wanted to ask you about Malcolm," said Lucy, perching uneasily on the edge of the bed and trying not to look as nervous as she felt, alone with him in this bedroom that was straight out of a horror movie. "The medical examiner thinks he died practicing some sort of Houdini-style escape trick."

Symonds sat beside her, leaning his hands on his knees and panting, and she resisted the urge to edge away from him. Up close, she decided he didn't look too healthy. He was very thin and his cheeks were sunken. "That's crazy," he said, with a hollow cackle of a laugh.

"Why do you say that?" asked Lucy.

"Have you ever seen the show?" demanded Symonds.

"I don't think so."

"Well, it was for kids. He pulled a lot of coins from behind little kids' ears. He made bunny rabbits disappear and come back again, stuff like that. When the routine was over, we made balloon animals for the kids."

Suddenly Lucy knew exactly who Malcolm was. She'd seen his show a number of times, performing at school fairs and church festivals. The kids were always amazed, the parents less so, despite the black cape lined with red silk and the top hat Malcolm always wore.

"We better get the rest of the stuff," said Lucy, standing up. "Well, what do you think happened if it wasn't a trick? Did he have any enemies?"

"Not that I know of, and that's what I told the cops. The state police were here and asked a lot of questions," replied Symonds, letting out a big sigh and standing up. "I don't like to think about it. I like to remember him the way he was before a show—you know, up and excited. He never lost that, no matter how many shows he did."

"Do you think he was burned because he was a witch?" asked Lucy, following him down the stairs.

Symonds turned and faced her. "Where'd you hear that?" he demanded angrily from the bottom of the stairs.

Lucy hesitated. She wasn't about to identify Diana as her source. "Around," she said with a shrug. "You know how these rumors get started."

"Well, that's just what it is, a rumor!" declared Symonds, opening the front door at the bottom of the stairs. "Thanks for your help. I can take it from here."

Lucy tried one last, desperate measure. "I was there at the helicopter rescue. I know you're a member of the coven, that you were all on the mountain to celebrate Midsummer Night."

Symonds laughed hollowly. "That's a good one. Me, a witch."

"This act of yours isn't very convincing," said Lucy. "And it's not going to help find Malcolm's killer either."

"Right now, all I've got on my mind is this flood," said Symonds. "If I were a witch, why wouldn't I just cast a spell and make the water go back, huh? Answer me that."

"Because witchcraft doesn't work like that," said Lucy.

"How do you know?" he demanded, narrowing his eyes. "Are you a witch?"

"I've done some research," said Lucy.

"It's time for you to go," said Symonds, reaching around her and grabbing the door, leaving her nowhere to go except outside.

"If you change your mind, just call me at the *Pennysaver.* Ask for Lucy."

"Don't hold your breath," said Symonds, slamming the door behind her.

The trip hadn't been a complete loss, thought Lucy as she drove back to the office. She'd gotten some good quotes and photos of the flood, and she'd gotten some good background on Malcolm the Magnificent. A lot of people would be shocked and surprised to learn that he was the victim of the burning in the woods; almost everyone in the area had seen his little magic show. It was too bad she hadn't dared to ask Symonds for a photo of Malcolm the Magnificent, but she was hopeful they had one on file.

As for Malcolm being a witch, well, that was a sensational twist that would certainly have surprised the folks who took their little ones to see his show. But she hadn't gotten either Diana or Symonds to admit that on record, so she couldn't print it. She could tell the police, however, and that's what she was planning to do when her cell phone rang. She pulled over to the side of the road to take the call. Sometimes she did talk and drive, but not today, when the roads were so treacherous.

"Mom!" wailed Sara.

Lucy imagined the worst: The puddle had spread; the kids were marooned in the house, which was going up in flames thanks to one of Diana's black candles. "What's the matter?" she asked.

"We're over at Abby's, and her mom fainted or something. What should we do?"

Lucy remembered how frail Abby's mother, Miriam, had appeared at the neighborhood cookout. "Get her head lower than her feet," she advised.

"She's flat on the floor," said Sara, "and she doesn't seem to be coming around."

"Call the rescue squad," said Lucy.

"Abby says we can't do that or her father will kill her. It's against their religion or something. Can you come, Mom? Please."

"What can I do? Call the rescue squad!"

"Mom, you gotta come. I'm really scared and Abby is freaking out."

"All right, I'm on my way." She was about to end the call when she remembered that Victorian ladies kept smelling salts on hand for their frequent swoons. "Try putting some ammonia on a tissue and holding it under her nose," she advised.

"Where would we get ammonia?"

Oh my word, thought Lucy. What was she raising? Idiots? "With the cleaning stuff. Under the kitchen sink, in a broom closet, someplace like that. Abby will know." Unlike her own daughters, who didn't seem to have a clue, she thought as she navigated around a small lake that had formed in the road. She was pretty sure none of her children could locate a light switch in the house they had grown up in, even if their lives depended on it, and they also had no clue how to operate a window shade or open a window. She had often come home from work to find them sitting in dark, stuffy rooms, mesmerized by the TV.

When Lucy arrived at the Stoughton homestead a half hour later, she found Miriam conscious and lying on the couch. "The ammonia worked," said Sara.

"I'm so grateful your girls were here," said Miriam in a weak voice. She was dressed in the sort of wraparound cotton housedress Lucy remembered her grandmother wearing, and her thin, bluish legs were propped on a pillow. With her thinning hair and sagging skin, she looked quite frail and elderly, much older than you'd expect for a woman whose children were still in their teens.

"Is there anything I can do?" asked Lucy, irritated that Sara hadn't called to tell her that Miriam had recovered. "Take you to the doctor?"

"Oh, no, I'll be fine," said Miriam.

Lucy didn't think she looked fine at all; her arms and legs were like sticks, she was trembling, and her lips were decidedly blue. "Abby, I think your mother could use a blanket," she suggested.

"Oh, don't bother her," said Miriam. "I'm fine. Really."

Abby scurried off and returned with a flannel summer blanket, and Lucy tucked it around Miriam. "Maybe some nice hot tea with sugar?" she suggested.

"I'll make it," volunteered Abby.

"I shouldn't be lying here like this," said Miriam, struggling to sit up. "What will my husband think?"

"I hope he'll think that you need to see a doctor," said Lucy. Sara and Zoe were standing awkwardly in the kitchen doorway, obviously eager to leave.

"My husband doesn't believe in any medicine except prayer," said Miriam, smiling. Lucy thought she looked like some of the sainted martyrs she'd seen in paintings, pictured just before they left their mortal coils behind and were welcomed by the heavenly host.

"I know prayer can be strong medicine," said Lucy, "but sometimes God needs a little help. Why don't I take you to see Doc Ryder right now, before your husband comes home?"

"You can't do that!" exclaimed Abby, dropping the mug of hot herb tea she was carrying. It splashed against her bare legs, but she didn't flinch. "Father would be furious," she added, reaching for a cloth to mop up the mess.

"Oh, dear, let me see your legs," said Lucy, rushing toward her. "Do you have ice?"

"I'm fine, I'm fine, and so is my mother," insisted Abby, dropping to her knees to wipe up the mess. "Father will be home any minute now, and I think it would be better if you left."

"Abby's right," added Miriam, throwing back the blanket and slowly swinging her legs off the sofa. "My husband doesn't like me to waste my time gossiping with visitors."

Looking at Abby's and Miriam's anxious faces, Lucy knew she'd seen that expression numerous times before. It was the same frightened look she'd seen in the county courthouse, when victim's advocates tried to get bruised and battered women to apply for restraining orders against their abusers—the same stubborn expression they wore when they were asked to testify against their abusers and refused. "It was just an accident," they'd insist. "I'm so clumsy. It was all my fault." No wonder the poor girl was drawn to Diana and her promise of personal power through witchcraft.

Lucy knew there was nothing she could do here, but she couldn't leave without throwing out a lifeline. "If you need anything, anything at all, give me a call," she said. "I'm just on the other side of the bridge."

"Oh, same here," chirped Miriam. "That's what neighbors are for, right?"

Lucy was shaking her head as they left the house and splashed across the squishy lawn, past the garden where everything seemed to be thriving. One particularly handsome plant caught her eye. She suspected it was an heirloom tomato, perhaps a potato. The contrast struck her: the healthy, green vegetation outside the house and the sickly woman inside.

In the car, the girls were quiet as they buckled their seat belts. Lucy called the office to let Ted know she was on her way back to work. He sounded put out, and she assured him she'd gotten solid information about Malebranche as well as some flood pictures. She then started the car and headed down the long drive, sending up waves of water as she drove through the puddles. The rain was still falling, the sky overcast with heavy clouds.

"Mom," said Sara, "I think Abby and her mom are afraid of her father."

"That's what I think too," said Zoe.

"I think you're right," said Lucy, braking at the end of the drive to check that the road was clear before making the turn. She switched on the turn signal, and that's when the car died.

"Mom! What are we gonna do?" wailed Sara.

"Maybe I gave it too much gas," said Lucy, remembering her father's warnings not to flood the engine when he was teaching her how to drive. That was when she was sixteen, though. She hadn't heard anybody mention that warning in quite some time. "We'll give it a minute and try again."

They sat for a while, just as her father had instructed all those years ago, and then Lucy attempted to restart the engine, being very careful not to press her foot on the gas pedal when she turned the key. She was rewarded with a click, nothing more.

"I think the battery is dead," she said, reaching for her cell phone. "Maybe Dad can come and give us a jump."

But when she called Bill, all she got was voice mail.

"We could walk home," suggested Zoe.

It was true; their house was less than a mile or so away, on the other side of the bridge over Scorton Creek. "I can't leave the car like this. It's blocking the driveway. And besides, it's raining hard."

"What if Abby's father comes home?" asked Zoe anxiously.

"Maybe he could help us," said Sara, sounding doubtful.

Lucy wasn't eager to encounter Ike Stoughton, but she didn't see any alternative. "Maybe he'll be a good Samaritan and help us," said Lucy, determined to be cheerful in the face of adversity. She didn't really think it very likely, especially since he knew that Diana was staying at her house. At the very least, he'd scold her for sheltering the witch; at the worst he'd . . . Well, really, what could he do? He couldn't attack her physically because he'd get in trouble. The worst he could do was yell at them. That cheered her until she realized that he would most likely take out his anger and frustration against her on his wife and daughter. Lucy gave the key another turn, hoping to start the car, but only got the click.

She decided her only option was to call for a tow. She reached for the glove compartment, where she had a business card from a towing service she'd used in the past. Suddenly, somebody started tapping on her window. Startled, she whirled around and made out Rebecca Wardwell's face through the steamed window. The power window didn't work, so she opened the door.

"Are you stuck?" asked Rebecca. She was wearing an oversized man's slicker, bright yellow, and had a soft cap dotted with a colorful assortment of flies for trout fishing on her head.

"I sure am," said Lucy, "I think the battery is dead."

"Pop the hood and I'll take a look," offered Rebecca.

Lucy did, then hopped out of the car to help lift the heavy hood. They stood side by side in the rain, and Lucy watched while Rebecca pulled out the oil stick to check it, and twisted this and that. "What are you doing out in this weather?" asked Lucy. "Though I'm awfully glad you came along."

"I was tickling trout over at Blueberry Pond. Rain is the best time—it gets them excited."

"Did you catch any?" asked Lucy.

"I got a nice big one for my supper," said Rebecca. "I almost hated to take him—he's so handsome, and he did so enjoy the tickling, but a body's got to eat." She looked skyward. "All this rain is too much. The pond's just about overflowing its banks."

"I'm not surprised," said Lucy, who was fascinated by the idea of tickling trout. "Do you actually tickle the fish?"

"Yup. I stick my hands in the water and call the fish. I don't have to call much because they really enjoy the tickling." She winked at Lucy. "It's kind of a mean trick, but at least they're happy right up until the end. There now," she said, producing a rag from her pocket and wiping her hands. "I think it'll run just fine. Why don't you try?"

Lucy got back in the car and turned the key, and the engine caught, just like magic.

"I can't believe it!" exclaimed Lucy. "Thanks so much."

"No problem," said Rebecca, stepping back from the car and waving. "You'd best not tarry, as the creek is rising."

Lucy lowered the window. "Thanks again!" she yelled, pulling into the road just as Stoughton's big pickup truck crested the hill. Lucy was relieved to be on her way, suspecting she'd avoided an awkward confrontation, but Rebecca wasn't in a hurry. Lucy could see her in the rearview mirror, standing in the drive, apparently studying the garden. Then her attention was caught by the roaring water of the creek tumbling along beside the road.

CHAPTER NINE

Lucy had never seen little Scorton Creek like this. True, sometimes in spring it filled up with snowmelt and tumbled over its rocky bed in a succession of mini waterfalls, but it always dwindled down to nothing more than a trickle in summer. Fall rains gave it a bit of a boost, but once freezing temperatures arrived, it settled into icy stillness. This torrent of brown, foamy water threatening to overflow its banks was a frightening sight, especially since it was carrying all sorts of debris, and not just tennis balls and fast-food wrappers. Big logs, tangles of branches, mangled garden furniture and even a doghouse went floating by as they approached the bridge.

"Mom, this is scary," said Sara, who was riding shotgun. In the backseat, Zoe was very quiet.

"Everything's going to be okay," said Lucy, who was trying to think of alternate routes so she could avoid the bridge. Problem was, the creek wound its way through the hills around Tinker's Cove, and you had to cross it sooner or later if you wanted to get anywhere, and most of the bridges were older than this one, which had been built about fifteen years ago to replace a dilapidated covered bridge.

"I'm going to check it out," said Lucy, stopping the car and setting the emergency brake but leaving the engine running so she didn't have to worry about starting it again. The wind was blowing hard, and she struggled to force open the car door. When she finally succeeded and stepped out into the storm, the wind immediately blew her hood off and whipped her hair into her eyes. The rain was coming down in buckets; the water streaming down the pavement was ankle-deep. Lucy had never experienced anything like this, and it took all her strength to advance to the bridge embankment. There she held on to the wooden railing and gazed upstream. The filthy brown expanse of roiling water seemed endless; it just kept rolling onward, carrying along everything in its way. It wasn't over the bridge yet, though it was rising, and quite an assortment of junk was collecting against the pilings that supported the bridge. Lucy knew the force of the water must be enormous, but the pilings seemed to be holding up fine. Also in her favor was the fact that the bridge expanse wasn't very wide, maybe thirty feet at the most, and they would be over in seconds.

Back in the car, she announced her decision. "It looks safe to me," she said, releasing the brake. "We're going for it."

"But what if the car dies again when we're on the bridge?" asked Zoe.

"It's running fine," said Lucy, releasing the brake and crossing her fingers. "And we'll be over in no time at all."

Reaching the end of the road, Lucy stopped once more. The rain was pelting the roof and rolling down the windows, and the wipers were swinging back and forth at top speed, giving her pause. "Maybe you girls should get out and run across."

"We'll be over in three seconds," said Sara. "Just go."

Lucy took a deep breath, switched her foot from the brake to the gas pedal, and gently accelerated. The car rolled forward, onto the bridge, and she gave it a little more gas, keeping her eyes fixed on the other side.

Zoe suddenly shrieked, and Lucy turned her head just in time to see an enormous tree in the river, headed straight for them. She floored the gas pedal, and the car jumped forward, reaching safety at the same moment the tree hit the bridge. Behind them they heard a terrible groaning noise, and then a slow tearing sound as the bridge was ripped off its pilings and went sailing off, caught in the leafy branches of the tree.

"That was close," said Sara in a shaky voice.

"You can say that again," said Lucy, struggling to keep the car on the road with hands that shook as they gripped the steering wheel.

Zoe was crying. "I'm scared. I'm so scared."

"Almost home, baby," crooned Lucy. "Almost home."

Minutes later, they were. Lucy parked the car and they all dashed for the porch stairs. Diana and Libby were waiting for them in the kitchen, where Libby had wiggles and wet doggy kisses and Diana had towels.

"I'll put the kettle on for tea," she said, at the very moment the lights went out.

"Thank goodness for a gas stove," said Lucy, precipitating a round of hysterical, nervous laughter. But as she watched her girls laughing so hard they had to clutch their stomach, she sent up a little silent prayer of thanks that everything had turned out all right. If she'd waited a second or two longer before crossing the bridge, they would have been carried downstream in the flood.

After supper, Diana volunteered to wash the dishes. The power was still out, and they couldn't use the dishwasher, so Lucy offered to dry. It seemed an old-fashioned, homey thing to do, especially since they were working by candlelight. Bill had gone into the family room after joking that he was going to watch TV by candlelight; he was making do by reading *TV Guide* so he'd know what he was missing. The girls were there, too, setting up the Monopoly game.

"Did you talk to Peter?" asked Diana, rinsing a plate and setting it in the dish drainer. "I've been worried about him. His place is right on the river."

"I helped him carry things upstairs," said Lucy. "I think his house is going to be flooded."

"Poor man," said Diana. "All this on top of losing Malcolm."

"He didn't seem healthy," said Lucy. "Is he ill?"

"Not that I know of. It's probably grief." Diana was scrubbing a pot.

"He wouldn't tell me much about Malcolm," said Lucy, toweling off a glass. "Except to say the medical examiner is wrong, that Malcolm never would have attempted a dangerous escape trick."

"He knew Malcolm better than anyone," said Diana.

"If he's right, it means Malcolm was murdered."

"I think that too," said Diana, rinsing off the pot. "It's the same old story. People are afraid of witchcraft, and fear makes them do terrible things."

"Don't you want to help the cops find the killer?" demanded Lucy. "It's obvious Malcolm was a member of your coven and Peter still is. What's the point of all this secrecy?"

"It's in the ordains," said Diana.

"Well, if one of my friends was burned alive, I think I would bend the rules a bit to help the police find the killer," exclaimed Lucy, giving the damp towel a snap before folding it and hanging it on the oven door. "Especially if I was getting death threats!"

"I know. You're right," said Diana, slumping into a chair at the kitchen table. "Malcolm was the high priest of our coven."

"Do you think someone in the coven might have killed him?" asked Lucy, slipping into the opposite chair.

"Oh, no! All members of the coven practice perfect love and perfect trust, and besides, we're all one flesh."

"Meaning?"

"We were all initiated sexually by Malcolm."

Lucy's jaw dropped. "What?"

Diana shrugged. "It's not all that unusual. Wicca, unlike most other religions, celebrates sexuality, and sometimes we use it in our rites."

"Oh, my," said Lucy. At the same time, she was congratulating herself on refusing to let Sara attend the Midsummer Sabbat, she remembered that Abby had attended. "Don't tell me that little Abby Stoughton—"

"Don't be ridiculous," said Diana. "She's a novitiate, not an actual member of the coven. It takes years of study before a novitiate is ready to be initiated as a member."

"That is a relief," said Lucy.

"You disapprove?" asked Diana.

Lucy was trying to imagine the congregation of the Presbyterian church she'd attended as a child taking part in Dionysian revelry at midnight. It seemed impossible; all she could think of was the black straw pancake of a hat trimmed with battered velvet violets that her grandmother used to wear every Sunday and the way her bosom used to swell right down to her waist. "Look, as far as I'm concerned, it's your religion and you can do what you want, as long as you don't hurt anybody, and that includes sexual exploitation."

"Of course not," said Diana. "Wicca is life affirming and celebrates the power of nature. Malcolm never, ever took advantage of his position as high priest."

"That may be true," said Lucy thoughtfully, "but if somebody even thought he did, well, that could be a motive for murder."

Diana's face was serious as she returned to the sink and pulled the plug, watching the water drain. "Oh," she finally exclaimed, wringing out the sponge and setting it on the drainboard. "Life would be so much better if everybody was Wiccan!"

But as Lucy folded the dishtowel and hung it on the rack,

she wondered if Diana's faith in the goodness of the coven members was justified.

The next morning, the downpour had subsided to a steady drizzle, although the forecaster they heard on the battery-powered radio warned of more heavy rain, so Lucy and Bill took advantage of the break to get out and check for damage. Their house was untouched, even though there were a number of fallen branches in the yard, some of them quite large.

"Looks like we dodged a bullet this time," said Bill, grinning wryly and whistling for Libby.

"We were lucky," said Lucy as they proceeded down the driveway and up the road to Prudence Path to check on their neighbors.

It was still early and only a few people were out, clearing away storm debris. Toby and Molly's house was unscathed, but a few others weren't so lucky. Shingles had been ripped off Scratch and Willie Westwood's roof, and a tree had fallen on Fred Stanton's garage. Fred was standing in his driveway, studying the situation.

"Much damage?" asked Bill.

"Not that I can see," said Fred. "I'll know more when I get the tree off. The garage is dry inside, so I guess the roof held up okay."

"That's lucky," said Lucy. "They're predicting more rain."

"Hardly seems possible," said Fred.

"You going to try and move that tree today?" asked Bill.

"No. I think I'll leave it for now. I don't want to risk causing more damage."

"That's smart," agreed Bill. "Give me a call if you need a hand."

"I've got my boys," said Fred, referring to his teenage sons Preston and Tommy. "Thanks anyway."

The sky was brightening, and it seemed as if the sun might peek through the clouds as Bill and Lucy walked back to Red Top Road and onto the bridge. Everything was gleaming with wetness, the grass was dotted with droplets of water, the leaves on the trees were bright green against the dark trunks, and puddles in the road were watery mirrors. Libby trotted ahead, stopping only when she reached the end of the pavement. She turned and looked at them with a puzzled expression on her face, as if to ask what happened to the bridge.

Looking at the destruction, Lucy suddenly felt weak in the knees. "We could have been swept away with the bridge," she said, squeezing Bill's hand and watching the muddy water roll by.

"You shouldn't have risked it," said Bill, swallowing hard.

"I know that now," said Lucy, watching Ike Stoughton approaching on the other side, waving his arm. Like everybody these days, he was wearing a rain jacket and rubber boots.

"Hey!" he yelled when he reached the edge of the road. "I'm sure glad to see you! We're cut off over here. No phone, no power, no bridge. Can't go the other way 'cause a tree is down."

"What can we do to help?" yelled Bill. "Do you need anything?"

"No, we've got plenty of food and water, but if you'd call the phone and power for me, I'd really appreciate it."

"Will do," said Bill.

"How's your wife?" yelled Lucy.

"Just fine," he answered, nodding and smiling.

Lucy doubted that Miriam was truly fine; she suspected the woman was seriously ill but had rallied enough to hide her condition from her husband. She also wondered why Stoughton didn't have a cell phone, which had the advantage of working when the electric and phone lines were down. "You should get a cell phone," she yelled.

"Invention of the Devil," he yelled back, grinning, then threw up his hands, indicating the destruction around them: the dangling strip of asphalt that hung over the edge of the riverbank, the barren pilings, the broken branches that lay everywhere. "Makes you wonder if the man upstairs is sending us a message. First the fire and now this. All because of that witch."

Just then, a bolt of lightning flashed, an enormous thunderclap shook the earth under their feet, and the sky opened in a tremendous downpour.

Lucy and Bill turned and dashed for the relative safety of the woods that edged the road. Pausing to catch their breath, Bill noticed Stoughton was still standing in the middle of the road, completely exposed to a possible lightning strike.

"What the hell!" exclaimed Bill, waving at him to get under cover of the trees. Stoughton, however, ignored him, remaining in place and bowing his head in prayer. "He must be nuts," he said, taking Lucy's hand and starting back to the house. "And how crazy is it not to have a cell phone?"

Walking beside her husband, Lucy had figured it out. By refusing to allow cell phones, he was able to limit the ways in which family members could communicate with the outside world. She was willing to bet that phone time was strictly limited in the Stoughton household. There were no long gossipy chats with friends for his wife, no flirtatious conversations for Abby and her brothers, nothing at all that would undermine his authority as head of the house.

CHAPTER TEN

When she left home for work an hour or so later, Lucy couldn't erase the image of Ike Stoughton praying in the midst of the downpour as lightning flashed around him. Was he doing a Moses imitation? Tempting fate? Testing his faith? Showing off? And then there was always the possibility he was simply stupid—she'd certainly written enough obituaries about people who had behaved foolishly. Every spring, it seemed, some ice fisherman misjudged the thickness of the melting ice and plunged through. And then there were the maniacs who had to see the surf when a hurricane was brewing and were caught in a wave and swept away. And she would never forget the guy who lit up a cigarette while filling his lawn mower with gasoline, with predictably horrible results.

But Stoughton didn't seem stupid. He was a talented businessman with a solid reputation and a considerable amount of clout in county politics. Lucy was familiar with his stances on local issues, such as resisting regionalization and opposing the installation of solar panels on the roof of the county courthouse. She always maintained journalistic impartiality even when she disagreed, which she usually did. But now that he had moved his family into the 1799 homestead, she would have to deal with him as a neighbor as well as a newsmaker. She wasn't thrilled at the prospect, especially considering his treatment of his wife and daughter.

Also troubling was his antipathy toward Diana and witchcraft. As she'd gotten to know Diana better, she'd come to like and respect her, even though she had her doubts about witchcraft. She suspected Ike might have been behind the hate mail Diana had received, and she wondered how far he would go. Was it possible that he, perhaps with his sons, had captured and burned Malebranche?

As she followed the familiar route to town, taking note of the storm damage as she drove, she admitted she had no evidence that Ike was violent. But she knew that domestic abuse often escalates, beginning with verbal abuse and controlling behavior and ending in the emergency room. She remembered the words of a nurse she had interviewed for a story. "It crosses all socioeconomic categories," she'd said. "It's not just poor people or a certain ethnic group—it's everybody. I've seen doctor's wives strangled until they passed out, fishermen's girlfriends with broken bones, cops' kids covered with welts. Even a grandma denied her meds because her bank-teller daughter cashed her Social Security checks to play the slots. Anybody can be an abuser, absolutely anybody."

As Lucy parked her car in the driest part of the parking lot that she could find, she suspected that Ike Stoughton was a domestic tyrant who kept his wife and daughter living in fear. It wasn't just the fact that they weren't allowed to see the doctor that caused her suspicion; it was the terrified expression on Miriam's face when Lucy suggested it. But why, she wondered, had Abby reacted so strongly, even dropping a mug of tea? Hadn't the girl been begging her parents to let her see a dermatologist?

"You made it," exclaimed Phyllis when Lucy arrived in a

gust of wind and rain that sent fallen leaves scuttling across the damp wood-plank floor. The lights were on but occasionally flickered.

"I think it's dying down," said Lucy. "The power company's got trucks out. When did the lights come back on?"

"They were working when I got here, about an hour ago," said Phyllis. "But they're still out at my house—at least they were when I left."

"Mine too," said Lucy as there was another flicker. "I wonder if we should risk using the computers."

"Ted said no. The power company warned they might have to cut us off in order to repair the lines farther along."

Lucy nodded, hanging up her jacket. "Did he leave any instructions for me?"

"Said you might as well get out and about, talk to people and get their stories, take some ROPs."

ROPs, as Lucy knew, meant human-interest photos to scatter through the rest of the paper. She sighed, put her jacket back on, and shuffled toward the door in her clunky boots. "If I were a swearing woman, I'd swear," she said. "By golly I would."

Lucy figured she'd start by walking up and down Main Street, taking a few pictures, and hopefully meeting somebody. The problem was that everybody seemed to be staying home. Main Street was deserted; the shops were closed. Nothing was happening except rain. At the hardware store, they had a sign advertising sump pumps and Lucy photographed it. She also took a few snaps of the deserted street; she thought she'd caption it "Plenty of parking." Down at the harbor, she took the obligatory photo of a family of ducks, paddling along in a neat line, and another of a dinghy awash in rainwater and almost submerged. Returning to Main Street, she popped into Jake's Donut Shack, but there was nobody there except Officer Barney Culpepper, buying donuts and coffee to take back to the police station.

"Let the *Pennysaver* pay," she offered, pulling out her

wallet. It seemed like a sound investment in relationship building with a prime news source.

"Aw, I can't do that, Lucy," drawled Barney. His age and weight were increasing in direct proportion to each other, and his crew cut was liberally sprinkled with gray these days. His utility belt hung low on his hips beneath a bulging belly, but his bulldog expression gave him an impressive air of authority.

"Sure you can," said Lucy, plunking down a charge card. It looked like a lot of donuts and coffee; she had no idea how much it would all cost. "It's the least I can do, considering how much you folks do for all of us."

"It's been tough," agreed Barney as Jake took the card and rang up the sale. "I've been working straight through since Saturday. I was only able to snatch a couple of hours of shut-eye in a jail cell." He smiled. "It's been empty since this rain started. I guess it's too damn wet for crime."

"They're just doing it at home," said Lucy, signing the slip. "That reminds me—there's something I wanted to ask you about."

Barney was ready to go, the bag of donuts in one hand and the carry-carton of coffee in the other. "There's no new developments in that burning in the woods," he said. "Not that I know about anyway."

"Uh, thanks, but that wasn't what I wanted to ask you about," she said, holding the door for him. When they were outside, she pulled up her hood and began walking, battling her way against the wind. "It's about a friend of Sara's. I think her father is abusing her and her mother."

"What makes you think that?" asked Barney, striding along, oblivious to the elements in his official foul-weather gear. "Do they have bruises?"

"No. But they sure seem afraid of the father. Even my girls picked up on it."

"We can't do anything unless we have some sort of evidence like a fight in progress or injuries. You know how it is."

"I wondered if there have been any complaints—"

"Now, Lucy, you know I can't tell you anything like that. . . ."

"Just for my own personal peace of mind, that's all. I'm wondering if I should allow my girls to spend time over there." Lucy had known Barney for a long time, ever since they'd been members of the Cub Scout Pack Committee.

"Well, in that case. Who is it?"

"Ike Stoughton. It's a bad situation—the family is marooned since the bridge is out, and the road is blocked by a fallen tree."

He let out a big sigh that shook his jowls. "We can only do so much, Lucy. You know that."

They were almost at the police station and time was running out. "What about Stoughton? Any restraining orders, calls to the house, anything at all?"

Barney shook his head. "Not that I know of, but they just moved into town a coupla weeks ago, right?" He stopped and indicated the police station with a jerk of his head. "You comin' in?"

"No. I'm heading over to the cottage hospital," she said.

"Thanks for the coffee," said Barney, turning up the path that led to the door.

"Enjoy it," said Lucy, consoling herself with the thought that even if she hadn't gotten any leads from him today, she'd made a long-term investment that would pay off down the road. At least she hoped so.

She needed the car to get to the hospital, and then she planned to check on the bridge repairs, after which she could stop at home for lunch. Hot soup seemed like a good idea. She was soaked through and beginning to shiver by the time she got back to the car. She cranked up the heater and switched the radio to a news station just in time for the weather report. It wasn't good; the system that was delivering the wind and rain had stalled over the region. Then the newscaster announced that homeowners intending to file in-

surance claims for water damage were in for a big disappointment unless they had purchased flood insurance, since
their regular homeowner's policies didn't cover flooding.

There was definitely a story there, thought Lucy, thinking
of poor Peter Symonds and his flooded house. With no flood
insurance, he was going to take a big loss, and Lucy was
sure he wasn't the only one. The unusual rain had sent water
into places that had never flooded before, even exceeding
the official computer models.

Arriving at the cottage hospital, she found the parking lot
had become a lake dotted with a few cars and trucks that
looked like scattered islands. She wondered why they hadn't
been moved before the water rose so high, then remembered
that staff members had probably been too busy to notice until
it was too late. She lowered the car window and snapped a
few photos, then drove back along the road until she found a
parking space some distance from the door. With the lot
flooded, new arrivals had sought higher ground, and cars
were parked at odd angles wherever they could fit. When
she stepped out into the downpour, she felt the ground go
squishy under her feet, and as she slogged along on the asphalt, she hoped she wouldn't return to find her car stuck in
mud.

When she arrived at the emergency room, she found it
surprisingly empty. "Where is everybody?" she asked the
woman behind the reception desk.

"It was a madhouse last night, but it's quieted right down
today," she said, looking up from her magazine. "We've had
a few rescue workers in with injuries; that's about it. I can
get you right in."

"Oh, I'm not sick. I'm Lucy Stone, with the *Pennysaver*
newspaper," said Lucy, pulling out her rain-spotted notebook. "Do you mind if I ask a few questions?"

The woman looked skeptical. "What kind of questions?"

"Well, for starters, what kind of injuries did these rescue
workers have?" asked Lucy.

"One guy slipped and fell off a ladder; another jammed his hand in the machinery on a bucket truck, stuff like that."

"Are they still here?" she asked. "Could I talk to them?"

She shook her head. "They were treated and released."

"What about the power?" asked Lucy, noting the rather dim lighting. "Are you on generators?"

"Yeah, we lost power yesterday."

"How long can you run on generators?"

"You know, Lucy, I think you should really talk to Doctor Ryder. He's the one in charge. He's a lot better informed than I am. I just get their names and insurance cards."

"Can you page him for me?"

"Sure. Take a seat."

When Lucy clomped over to the waiting area, it occurred to her that even the cutest polka-dot rain boots can get tiresome when you wear them for three days straight. And whoever made this so-called rain parka, she thought as she draped it over a chair to dry, certainly hadn't designed it for serious rain. A spring shower, maybe, but not the steady, drenching downpour they'd been having, the kind of rain that made you wonder where it could all be coming from.

She'd just finished arranging the parka and had taken a seat when Doc Ryder came striding through the swinging doors that led to the treatment area. "Lucy! I've been wondering when our inquiring reporter would show up."

Doc Ryder had been the town's only doctor when Lucy and Bill first moved to Tinker's Cove, a genuine general practitioner who set broken limbs, delivered babies, stitched up cuts, and diagnosed everything from impetigo to sciatica. As the town grew, he was joined by several others, including specialists and a fancy new family practice and a women's health center, but Lucy had stuck with Doc Ryder and his old-fashioned approach.

"So I'm inevitable, like death and taxes?" she asked.

"Rain's getting you down?" He sighed and took the seat next to her. "You're not the only one."

"So tell me all about it," said Lucy, adopting a fake German accent and propping her pad on her knee. "Have you been depressed lately?"

He chuckled and gave her a quick summary of the situation at the hospital, then slapped his hands on his knees and got up. "Back to the mines," he said. "I'm catching up on my paperwork."

Lucy looked up. "Oh, one more thing before you go, and this is off the record."

"Uh-oh," said Doc Ryder, giving her a wary look through his half-glasses.

"I'm worried about a neighbor. She collapsed yesterday, fainted or something, and it turns out she's been ill for some time, but she won't seek medical care, says prayer is the only medicine her husband allows."

"What are her symptoms?"

"I'm not exactly sure. Listlessness for one, loss of appetite, a general grayish pallor. I suspect weight loss, since her clothes seemed too big for her."

Doc Ryder spread out his hands and shook his head. "Could be anything, from simple food poisoning to stomach cancer. I can't attempt a diagnosis without examining her."

"That's not going to happen," said Lucy. "The husband won't allow it."

"It sounds like it might be an abusive situation, but it's hard to tell," he said with a shrug. "Maybe she also believes prayer is the answer to everything." There was a sudden loud clap of thunder and he grinned. "Hell, maybe they're right. We've had fire and flood—I wouldn't be surprised if plague came next."

"Whoa," laughed Lucy. "I thought you were a man of science."

Doc Ryder scratched his nose. "I am—but I'm the first to admit that science can't explain everything. It wouldn't surprise me if whoever created this beautiful planet for us is angry at the way we've abused it. Maybe all this rain is his—or her—way of expressing disapproval. Or maybe," he added, winking, "maybe that witch who's come to town has cast an evil spell." He paused, scratching his head. "What's that old saw? Something about there being more things in heaven and earth than are dreamed of in our philosophy?"

"It's from *Hamlet,*" said Lucy, who had majored in English. "And if you're going to go all philosophical, it's definitely time for me to bid adieu."

III

EARTH

Always heed this rule you must:
Ashes to ashes, dust to dust,
All creatures alive return to Earth
As death awaits us from our birth.

CHAPTER ELEVEN

"I hate to remind you, but Halloween's going to be here before we know it," said Sue with a knowing nod.

"It's only finally started to feel like summer," protested Lucy.

"I just put my winter clothes in storage," confessed Rachel.

"And I got Ted to put my hammock up yesterday," added Pam.

June's rainy spell had finally ended, only to be followed by an unseasonably chilly July. But now, as August was approaching, the warm weather had finally settled in. The girls were making the most of the fine weather, eating their Thursday morning breakfast on one of the picnic tables Jake had set up behind his restaurant, in the parking lot overlooking the harbor.

"I'm not ready to think about Halloween," confessed Lucy, gazing out over the brilliant blue water dotted with little white boats. "I'm sick of witches."

"One witch anyway." Pam laughed. A seagull, perched on a nearby lamppost, imitated her and let out a few cries.

"I never thought I'd get rid of her, or her blasted cat," said Lucy.

"Well, she's back at her place now, and things have settled down," said Rachel. "I notice she repainted in a new shade, almost gray, just a hint of lilac."

"A very smart move, if you ask me," said Pam.

"Uh, ladies, we're getting off the subject here," said Sue, tapping the table with her perfectly manicured nails. "The Halloween party takes a lot of planning, and the sooner we get started, the better."

The annual Halloween party at the town's community center had been a local tradition for years, sponsored by the women's club, but as the club members aged, it had become a rather sad affair, dwindling down to a halfhearted costume parade and a small treat bag for each child. When Sue, who was part owner of Little Prodigies Child Care, heard complaints about the party, she offered to take it over, sensing an opportunity to promote the center by giving the town's kids a safe, fun Halloween. She also took it for granted that her friends would pitch in and help.

"Lucy, I know I can count on you for publicity. . . ."

"Righto," agreed Lucy.

"Pam, can you rustle up some refreshments, like you did last year?"

"Sure," agreed Pam. "Beastly bug cookies, witch's cauldron punch, and marzipan eyeballs, coming right up."

"And, Rachel, as I remember, you handled the entertainment?"

"Bit of a problem there," said Rachel. "Our magician is no longer available."

They were all quiet for a moment, remembering Malcolm the Magnificent's performance. He had been a big hit with the kids, and he and Peter had stayed long past the agreed time, making balloon animals for each child.

"Was that ever solved?" asked Sue.

"No," said Lucy, shaking her head. Malcolm's grisly

death had been a big front-page story for a while, but when there was no progress on the case, it had gradually receded to the back pages and then disappeared. No one had claimed his body, which was eventually buried at county expense in Potter's Field. Lucy suspected the coven must have held some sort of memorial observance, but it had been kept strictly private.

"Well," said Pam, "I'm sure we can come up with a DJ or something."

"I'm on it," said Rachel. "What's the budget?"

"At the moment, nonexistent," said Sue, laughing. "But I'll be calling the usual suspects—the banks, Rotary, insurance agents, anybody I can think of. I'll keep you posted."

"Good. Are we done with this?" asked Rachel. "Because I heard the oddest thing the other day. . . ."

They all leaned a bit closer.

"You know the giant pumpkin contest?"

They all nodded. For several years now, a number of local gardeners had competed to grow the biggest giant pumpkin, and all the competitors were displayed around town in the weeks before Halloween.

"Well, Rebecca Wardwell came by the other day to visit Miss Tilley, and she said that Ike Stoughton had accused her of hexing his pumpkins."

"Like putting a spell on them?" asked Sue doubtfully.

"Exactly," said Rachel. "Rebecca said she told him to try using raised beds like she does, but he insisted that she's in league with Diana and that they've put the hoodoo on his pumpkins. Apparently, Ike's gourds are rotting on the vine."

"It's all the rain we had—they soak up water like sponges," said Lucy, who had covered the contest for years and had picked up quite a bit of giant pumpkin information. "I seem to remember he came in second last year at the county fair. These growers take it very seriously. I've seen fistfights erupt at the weigh-in."

"You've got to be kidding," said Sue.

"I wish I were," said Lucy. "I hope it doesn't escalate." But privately, she had her doubts. It seemed Ike had chosen Diana, and now Rebecca, as scapegoats to blame for everything that went wrong in his life.

Lucy usually spent Thursday afternoon taking a few hours for herself, getting a haircut or her teeth cleaned or doing her grocery shopping. But today Ted had asked her to do some research for him at the county courthouse, checking old deeds for a story on a disputed piece of land.

She enjoyed the drive over to Gilead, rolling along back roads with the windows down and the radio blasting oldies. She sang along, amazed at the way she recalled the lyrics to so many songs that she thought she'd forgotten. Just how much of her memory was taken up with "American Pie"?

The research at the courthouse was frustrating, however. Some of the deeds were lost in a fire in 1832, while others were written in such archaic language that she couldn't figure out what they meant. She copied down what she could make out of the faded, spidery handwriting, hoping that Ted could make some use of it, and she paid for Xerox copies of the ones that were totally indecipherable.

She had the office to herself, except for the clerks sitting at their desks behind the counter. No wonder, she thought, looking out the window at the cloudless blue sky, the leafy trees, and the green lawn with its Civil War memorial. It was much too nice a day to be inside. There was just one more deed to study, and then she would be free to go; she was planning to stop at an ice-cream stand on the way home and treat herself to a peach cone. She was practically licking her lips at the thought when her attention was drawn by a new arrival. He looked like an architect or a developer, a handsome guy in his thirties wearing chinos and a button-down shirt, carrying a bunch of rolled-up plans. He was obviously a regular, as the clerk greeted him warmly.

"Hi, Kyle," she said. "What are you doing in this musty old place on a day like this?"

Kyle smiled, his teeth very white against his tanned face. "Gotta make hay while the sun shines," he said, passing over a manila folder holding several sheets of paper.

"So what have you got here?" she asked. "Another deed for the Shiloh property?"

"Yup, we're almost there," he said. "Just one last piece and that's in probate. Doesn't look like it will be a problem."

"No missing heirs?"

"Nope, just a nice, cooperative executor, more than happy to wrap the thing up and get the cash donated to some magic museum in Toledo."

The word "magic" caught Lucy's attention.

"Takes all kinds," said the clerk, looking over the documents. "Is your check here?"

"Yup, it's all there," said Kyle. "Take it easy."

"You, too, Kyle," she said, watching as he strode out the door.

"Cute guy," said Lucy, smiling at her.

"Too young for me, and I'm married besides," she said, grinning. "But I can look."

"No crime in that," agreed Lucy. "Who is he?"

"Kyle Compton. Compass Construction. They're putting together a big industrial park over in Shiloh. It's more than a hundred acres. They've been piecing it together for some time, buying up parcels from individuals. There's just one bit left, he says, but the owner died."

"He left the land to a magic museum? Is that what he said?"

"I think the guy was a magician or something."

Bells were ringing in Lucy's head; flashbulbs were popping; alarms were sounding. "Do you know his name?" she asked, trying to maintain a casual tone of voice.

"Not that I recall."

"Would you have a plan for this project?"

The woman shook her head. "This is the Registry of Deeds. All we have are deeds. The towns have the property records."

"Can you give me the book and page?" asked Lucy.

"Sure thing," said the clerk, reading off the numbers.

After she'd written them down, Lucy didn't waste any time. Minutes later, she was in the car, heading for the Shiloh Town Offices.

The clerk in Shiloh wasn't nearly as nice as the woman in the county office—she was sullen and didn't seem to want to get out of her chair. "Yeah?" she asked from behind her desk when Lucy presented herself at the counter beneath the TOWN ASSESSOR sign.

"I'd like to see a site plan," she said, reciting the book and page.

"What for?" demanded the woman.

For a moment, Lucy was nonplussed. "Because it's a public record and I'm entitled to see it," said Lucy.

"Oh, in that case," grumbled the woman, reluctantly rising from her desk and disappearing into a back room. After what seemed an interminable wait, she emerged, pushing the oversized book on a wheeled cart. She leaned heavily on the cart, resting her elbows on the handle as she shoved it across the room. Reaching the counter, she slid the book across to Lucy.

"You better have the right book and page because I really don't want to do that again," said the woman, glaring at Lucy.

Again, Lucy didn't quite know how to respond. The woman was supposed to serve the public, that was her job, but it didn't seem wise to point that out to her. She really didn't seem up to the physical demands of her job, but Lucy couldn't help feeling sorry for her. Maybe she was on chemo or something. "Thanks for your trouble," she said, speaking to the woman's back as she made her painful way back to her desk.

Lucy flipped through the book until she reached the right page, which diagrammed the property between Cisco Road and Aunt Lydia's Way. In all, about ten lots were shown. Most of the owners' names had been neatly crossed out, replaced with "Compass Construction." Only one name did not have a red line drawn through it: Malcolm Malebranche.

Lucy could barely contain her excitement as she asked, "Can you tell me anything about this property?"

"What do you want to know?" growled the woman. "Assessment? Taxes?"

"No, this project. Compass Construction. Do you know anything about it?"

"Check with the Planning Department," said the woman with a huge sigh. "Upstairs."

"Thank you," said Lucy, aiming to kill with kindness.

She took the stairs two at a time. She knew she was on to something here. But when she reached the door beneath the PLANNING DEPARTMENT sign, she found it was closed, locked tight. A tattered paper taped to the door provided the answer: The office was open Monday, Wednesday, and Friday from nine a.m. to two p.m.

Back downstairs, Lucy grabbed one of the town maps from a rack thoughtfully provided by the Shiloh Chamber of Commerce and unfolded it as she walked back to her car. Slipping behind the wheel, she spread the map out on it, scanning the maze of streets until she found Aunt Lydia's Way, not far from the interstate. Obviously a prime location for an industrial park, she thought as she started the car.

Finding the site wasn't difficult, she discovered. All she had to do was follow the signs to the interstate and there it was: a large tract of bare earth bulldozed from the woods, with a lone little house surrounded by a patch of overgrown weeds plunk in the middle. Malcolm Malebranche's house. It had a distinctly forlorn air, like a forgotten wire hanger in an empty closet.

But maybe she was projecting her own emotions on the

house, she thought, turning the car around and heading back to town. A house was just a house, after all. And this house was an obstacle to progress. It seemed obvious that Malebranche had been holding out, either from sheer stubbornness or perhaps hoping to force Compass Construction to raise its offer. It might even, she thought, be a motive for murder.

Back on Main Street, she headed for the office of the *Shiloh Republican.* Like the *Pennysaver,* it was a weekly newspaper, and she had a nodding acquaintance with the editor-publisher-chief-reporter, Howie Unger. He was a big bull of a man given to wearing plaid shirts and jeans, and he had a lush brown beard. He greeted her with a big smile when she walked through the door.

"Hey, Lucy, good to see you. What brings you to Shiloh?"

"A hunch," she said, smiling. "Remember Malcolm Malebranche?"

"Sure," he said, nodding. "Big story. Burned to death in the woods over your way."

"Right. And now I've discovered his house is in the middle of a big Compass Construction project."

He grinned, showing even, white teeth. "And being an investigative reporter, you think these two things might be related?"

"What do you think?" she asked.

He shook his head. "I've known Kyle Compton for years; he's a good guy. And he made every effort to buy Malcolm out. Offered him way more than that place is worth."

"Why wouldn't Malcolm sell?"

"Beats me," said Howie with a shrug. "He was playing a losing game, though. Kyle was going to ask the town to take it by eminent domain."

Lucy was shocked. "Can they do that? For a private project?"

"Yeah. According to the Supreme Court, towns and cities can use eminent domain if a project is viewed as favorable to the general welfare—which means it will increase the tax base."

"I see," said Lucy.

"So even if Kyle Compton was a mean, vicious, greedy, murdering bastard, which I assure you he is not, he had absolutely no reason to wish Malcolm harm." He grinned. "Sorry to spoil your story. Can I treat you to lunch?"

"No, thanks. I'm saving my lunch calories for an ice-cream cone."

He rolled his eyes in mock despair. "Say hi to Ted for me."

"Will do," she said, giving him a little wave. "Bye-bye."

Back on the sidewalk, she considered what Howie had told her as she walked down the street to her car. She was willing to admit that Howie was right about the Supreme Court and eminent domain, which meant that Compass Construction could force Malebranche out of his house, but such a proceeding would not be easy. Compton would have to petition the selectmen, and there would undoubtedly be local opposition; there always was. And even if the selectmen voted to take the unpopular step of acting by eminent domain, Malebranche could appeal to the court, which would entail legal bills for the town and a big delay for Compass Construction. And when it came to construction, time was money, and considering the size of the project, any delay would be extremely costly to Kyle Compton, who had probably financed the land purchases and was facing hefty interest payments. All in all, Lucy decided, Kyle had a jumbo mortgage of a motive.

Reaching her car, she realized she was parked in front of the Shiloh Police Department. Impulsively, she decided to pay a visit to the chief and see what he thought of her theory.

Not much, as it turned out. Chief Strom Kipfer was short and round, and from the way he nodded along as he listened to her argument, Lucy guessed he was a go-along-to-get-along kind of guy. Or maybe not.

"I have to tell you I don't appreciate this at all," he said, nodding away. His apple-round cheeks had grown very red, and he seemed to be restraining his temper with difficulty. Lucy could practically see the steam issuing from his ears. "Kyle Compton is a respected citizen here in Shiloh, and I don't take kindly to strangers coming in here and casting aspersions about a good, upstanding citizen."

Lucy was in Kipfer's office, sitting in the chair he kept for visitors, staring at the photos on the wall behind the chief. Prominent among them were several of the chief shaking hands with Kyle Compton, the sort of picture known in the news business as a "grin and grab," where everybody smiles as a donation check to a worthy cause is prominently handed over. In this case, the worthy cause seemed to be the Shiloh Police Association.

"I see," said Lucy. "I appreciate your time and your frankness."

"Now, I hope you're going to drop this. You're not going to be writing any nasty stories about Kyle Compton, are you?" asked the chief.

"It's my job to follow up leads, wherever they take me," said Lucy, hoping to mollify Kipfer. She gave him a rueful smile. "This one seems to have led nowhere."

"Exactly." He nodded. "Hell of a thing, though, the way that Malebranche was killed." The nods were coming faster. "I'm sure glad it wasn't in my jurisdiction, that's for sure."

"It wasn't pretty," said Lucy, recalling the gruesome discovery in the woods.

"Well, we're fortunate here in Shiloh," he said smugly. "We've got a nice, quiet town with good people, and I aim to keep it that way."

As if Tinker's Cove was a rotten borough filled with criminals, thought Lucy, biting her tongue. "Thanks for your time," she said, rising to go.

"Remember what I said, now," he said, opening the door for her. "And don't go looking for what isn't there."

"I'll remember," said Lucy. But as soon as she was back in her car, she reached for her cell phone and placed a call to Detective Horowitz of the state police. Maybe Chief Kipfer was right; maybe Kyle Compton and everybody else who lived in Shiloh was absolutely innocent of any evil, but she doubted it. The chief had only managed to convince her of one thing: that Kyle Compton was too good to be true.

CHAPTER TWELVE

An automated voice informed Lucy that Detective Horowitz was either away from his desk or on another line,
so she left a message, asking him to call her. While she was
talking, a pickup truck with the COMPASS CONSTRUCTION logo
painted on the door passed her parked car, and noting the
Main Street address, she impulsively decided to pay a visit
on the off chance that Kyle Compton was in his office.

Compass Construction was just a few blocks down Main
Street, at the point where the compact town center gave way
to gas stations, a garden center, and a supermarket, all businesses that needed a lot of space. She pulled up in front of
the neat brick building, with its attractively landscaped bit of
lawn dotted with shrubs, and went inside. A receptionist
greeted her with a big smile, and when she asked for Compton, she immediately relayed the message by phone. Seconds later, Kyle appeared in the hallway, right arm extended,
and grasped her hand in a hearty shake. It was obvious that
Compass Construction did its best to turn every prospect
into a customer. He ushered her down the hall, which was
practically papered with civic awards, and seated her in a
padded captain's chair.

"I'm not a customer," said Lucy, eager to clear up any misconceptions about her visit. "I'm Lucy Stone, and I'm a reporter for the Tinker's Cove *Pennysaver* newspaper."

"Well, what can I do for you?" asked Kyle, smiling affably from his seat behind the desk.

"I'm doing a follow-up story on Malcolm Malebranche, the magician who was burned to death a couple of months ago."

Kyle shook his head. "That was terrible, terrible." He paused, his clear blue eyes meeting hers. "They never solved that case, did they?"

"No," said Lucy. "That's why I'm taking another look at the story. I understand you had some business dealings with Malebranche."

"I tried. I did my best," said Kyle with a rueful shake of his head. "But he resisted all my offers. I wanted to buy his property for a project of ours. I offered him far more than it was worth on the market, but he wouldn't budge."

"That must have been very frustrating," said Lucy.

"You're not kidding," said Kyle, giving her a sideways glance. "You're not suggesting that I had anything to do with his death because of that, are you?"

Lucy gave him her best, most disarming smile. "As a reporter, I can tell you that people have been killed for far less. I know of a woman who killed her neighbor over a chicken."

"A chicken?" asked Kyle.

"It was a prizewinner, and the woman was very fond of it," said Lucy.

"But still," said Kyle, who seemed troubled by the idea. "A chicken seems a poor excuse for murder."

"Frankly, I don't think there's any excuse for murder," said Lucy.

Kyle was quick to reply. "Of course, you're right. There's absolutely no excuse."

"Did you know Malcolm Malebranche, apart from his refusal to sell to you?" asked Lucy, trying to get back on track.

"Yeah, I mean, we live in the same town. I knew who he was. I took my kids to see him perform at the library, things like that. He was an aquaintance—I guess that's the best way to put it. I thought he was kind of unusual, not your average Joe, but I suppose that goes with being a performer."

"Did you dislike him?"

"Are you asking if I wanted to screw him on the deal?" Kyle let out a harsh laugh and looked her straight in the eye. "I've been in this business a long time, and I have a pretty decent reputation of treating people fairly. I've also learned not to take things personally and not to get upset by things I can't control: the weather, stubborn property owners, difficult customers. I focus on what I can do, so I decided to go ahead with the project without Malcolm's land. I have plenty of acreage out there. I figured I'd fence him off, put up some shrubs—nobody'd even know he was there. And there was always the chance that once he saw I was going ahead without him, he'd decide to sell after all."

"I heard you were trying to get the town to take the land by eminent domain," said Lucy.

Kyle grinned, showing very white teeth. "That was plan B," he said.

Lucy was thoughtful. "It seems like you had him cornered. He must have been very frustrated, and when people are angry, they sometimes let it get the better of them. Did he threaten you or try to harm you in any way?"

"He put up some signs on his property accusing me of destroying trees and causing global warming," admitted Kyle. "There was some yelling and shouting at planning board meetings, things like that. It's all in the public record. He made it clear he was going to take this fight as far as he could, even if it meant going to court."

"And how'd you feel about that?"

"Bad, that's how I felt, because I knew he'd lose. I have my ducks in a row, Lucy. That's how I operate. I have every right to build an industrial park on that land, and that's what

I intend to do. I'm following the law down to the teeniest little comma, period." He grinned again, the rueful grin.

"He might have used other methods," said Lucy. "Did
you know he was a witch?"

Kyle's eyebrows shot up and his mouth dropped open.
"You mean he might have cursed me in some way? Put a hex
on me, or a spell?"

"It's possible," insisted Lucy.

"Well, I think that stuff doesn't work unless you're a be-
liever. You know, voodoo only works if you believe it will,
and then the witch doctor points his staff at you and your
heart stops—*boom*—and you drop dead. So, the answer is
no. I didn't know he was a witch, and even if I did, it wouldn't
matter because I don't believe in witchcraft. Or the benefits
of organic food or that coffee is bad for you or that Saddam
Hussein was responsible for nine-eleven!"

"Can I quote you on that?" asked Lucy, laughing. It was impossible not to like the guy. He was smart and good-looking,
and he had a sense of humor. Too bad she was married; too
bad she was too old for him.

"You can write whatever you damn well please, for all I
care," he said, smiling. "Just be sure you spell my name
right."

"You've got a deal," said Lucy, rising from her chair.
"Well, thanks for your time. It's been a pleasure talking to
you."

"Same here," he said, standing and extending his hand.
"And don't forget, I'm here to serve your real estate and
construction needs."

"I'll remember that," said Lucy, taking his hand and once
again finding his grasp firm and warm. The honest grip of a
man who needed no more than a handshake to seal a deal.

That's what she was thinking, anyway, as she left the office and went back to her car, pausing for a moment to ad-
mire the landscaping and to check the identifying tag on one
particularly attractive rosebush. It was called "Knock Out,"

and it was, she thought, a real stunner. Probably expensive, but worth checking out, she decided as she jotted the name down. Then, turning to go, a glint of reflected sunlight caught her eye, and she discovered a witch's ball set among the plants, a reflective globe that was supposed to confuse a witch and thereby offer protection from spells.

Interesting, she thought as she started the engine. Maybe it was purely decorative, or maybe Kyle Compton hadn't been entirely truthful with her. Maybe he'd decided he needed to repel Malcolm Malebranche's evil spells.

What the heck, she decided. She was in the neighborhood, and she had nothing better to do at the moment; she might as well drive back out to Malebranche's place and take a closer look. Oddly enough, "Witchy Woman" was playing on the radio when she arrived at Malcolm's overgrown yard and turned into the rutted driveway. She sat there for a moment, bopping along to the music and surveying the scene.

What on earth made him so attached to this place? she wondered, taking in the sagging roof with cracked and moldy shingles, the ripped screen door that hung askew from its frame, and the drooping porch. Any sane person would have taken the money and ran with it, straight to a bright, clean condominium.

She couldn't find a path amid the tall grass and weeds that reached above her knees, so she walked on through, hoping the many buzzing bees and wasps feeding on the goldenrod wouldn't take offense at the intrusion. She made it safely to the porch and was about to try peering through one of the very dirty windows when she noticed the front door was ajar. Pushing it open, she stepped inside the ramshackle structure and blinked, waiting for her eyes to adjust to the dim light. The scene gradually came into view, and she found herself in a living room, or what used to be a living room. The couch had been ripped open, revealing ugly yellow foam padding. Throw pillows had also been ripped apart, and clumps of white filling were strewn everywhere. Wooden furniture had been broken, and some had been stuffed into the fireplace to burn. The resulting fire had charred the hearth and mantel.

Lucy peeked in the kitchen and found that boxes of staples like cereal and rice had been torn open and the contents thrown around. Empty liquor bottles and beer cans were everywhere, indicating that whoever had vandalized the place had helped themselves to refreshments.

The bedroom was much the same, clothes and bedding thrown everywhere. Malcolm had used another, smaller bedroom to store his magic props, and they, too, had been found and destroyed. His top hat had been trampled flat, bits of glass and wood were everywhere, and a string of colorful scarves fluttered in the breeze from the broken window.

Lucy shook her head at the mess, wondering who would do something like this. There was no painted pentagram, no graffiti, just a lot of broken stuff, as if someone, or more likely some group, had gone on a destructive rampage, fueled by Malcolm's booze. Kids, she decided, partying in an empty house. What a waste, she thought, making her way to the door. It was pathetic that kids did things like this, especially when they could be doing something constructive.

She was almost out the door, shaking her head at all the damage, when something warm and furry brushed against her leg, causing her heart to jump in her chest. Grabbing the doorjamb for support and expecting to see a rat, she instead found a small Siamese cat twining itself around her ankles.

"Well, who are you?" she asked, bending down and picking up the cat. It was as light as a feather and very soft, and it didn't seem to mind being held at all. Lucy could feel its heart beating a mile a minute in its chest and heard it switch on a rumbling purr. "You look hungry to me," she said, and the cat blinked its astonishing sapphire blue eyes. "Let's say we go get something to eat."

The cat seemed agreeable to the idea and allowed Lucy to

carry her out to the car, where it sat sphinx-like on the passenger seat for the short drive to Sue's Summer Shack. Lucy got a small bowl of vanilla for the cat and a double-scoop peach cone for herself. She was sitting in the driver's seat but turned sideways, with her legs outside the car. The cat was on the ground, daintily licking the ice cream. They had the place pretty much to themselves. It was around two, too late for lunch and too early for an afternoon snack, and Lucy was enjoying the simple pleasure of eating an ice-cream cone on a warm, sunny day when her cell phone rang.

It was Detective Horowitz, returning her call. "I hope you haven't found another body," he was saying.

"No, thank goodness," said Lucy. "But I did come across some information about Malcolm Malebranche."

"Shoot," said Horowitz.

"It turns out he had a house in Shiloh that Compass Construction wanted, but he wouldn't sell. It's right smack in the middle of a proposed industrial park."

"Uh-huh," said Horowitz.

"That's it," said Lucy. "That's all I got."

"Thanks for calling," said Horowitz.

"Is that it?" asked Lucy. "Aren't you going to warn me to mind my own business?"

"Well, I would," he said in a resigned tone. "If I thought it would make a difference."

"Oh," said Lucy as the cat seated itself on her foot and started cleaning its whiskers. "Would you like a cat?" she asked. "It's a pretty Siamese, very friendly."

"I'm allergic to cats," said Horowitz.

Lucy looked down at the cat, and it looked right back up, gazing into her eyes. "Well, if you know anybody who wants a cat, give me a call," she said.

"Oh, right," said Horowitz, sounding vague, like something else was demanding his attention. "Gotta go."

When Lucy closed her phone, the cat jumped in her lap and curled itself into a small, purring ball. She sat there, licking her cone, admiring her new little friend and wishing she could keep her.

But back at home, Libby had other ideas. When Lucy walked into the kitchen with the cat in her arms, Libby rose on her hind legs to give her a nosy once-over. Next thing Lucy knew, her arm was scratched and bloody, the cat was hunkered down on top of the refrigerator, and the dog was barking hysterically.

"What's going on?" demanded Sara, rushing into the kitchen.

"I found this stray cat," said Lucy, running cold water over her arm and then wrapping it in a dish towel. The scratches were superficial, but they wouldn't stop bleeding. "Take the dog out for me, will you?"

Sara lunged for Libby's collar but the dog eluded her, running around the kitchen and barking at the cat. She opened the door, but Libby ignored it and kept her focus strictly on the intruding cat.

"It's so pretty," said Sara, reaching up to pet the cat. The cat was in no mood to be friendly, however, and hissed at her.

"Better leave her alone," said Lucy as the cat sailed over her head and ran up the stairs, the dog hot on her tail. They stood for a moment, listening to thumps and bumps, hisses and barks, when the cat sped back downstairs and out the open door followed by the dog.

"Oh, no," said Lucy, standing on the porch and watching as the cat scaled a maple tree, stopping only when she ran out of trunk. Far below, on her hind legs with her forepaws planted on the tree trunk, Libby smiled in triumph, tongue lolling out of her mouth.

"Mom, we've got to call the fire department," said Sara.

"Maybe the cat will come down of its own accord," said Lucy. "It's a nice cat. It seems to like me. I was hoping to keep it."

They both looked at Libby, who was keeping an eye on the cat. "I don't think that's going to work," said Sara.

"Maybe you could take it to Friends of Animals?" suggested Lucy.

"They're still trying to find homes for the spring kittens," said Sara. "It would be better if we could find a home for it—if it ever comes down from that tree." Libby was now sitting, but clearly on sentry duty. No cat was going to get past her.

"Diana likes cats. Maybe she'll take her," said Lucy. But when she called the witch, she declined.

"I couldn't do that to Piewocket," she said. "He's my one and only. It would break his heart."

Nothing Lucy said would get her to change her mind. Not even the fact that it was Malcolm's cat, and Siamese, and apparently very healthy. Resigned, Lucy dragged the protesting dog inside, then diced up some leftover chicken and put it in a dish that she carried outside. She was standing out there beneath the tree, holding a dish of chicken over her head, when Bill came home.

"What in the hell are you doing?" he asked.

"Trying to get the cat down."

"We don't have a cat."

"We do now."

"No, we don't," he said, in a tone that indicated this was his final word on the subject, and marched into the house.

No sooner had the door closed behind him than Lucy felt the cat land lightly on her shoulders. She set the dish on the ground and watched the cat eat; then she picked her up and carried her out to the shed, apologizing for shutting her inside and promising to be back in a minute with more food and a bowl of water. "Don't worry, this is just temporary. I'll find a home for you, I promise."

CHAPTER THIRTEEN

When supper was over, Lucy turned her attention to finding a home for the cat. After working her way through
much of her address book, she got lucky with Rachel.

"I think Miss Tilley would enjoy having a little pet," she
said, referring to the town's oldest resident. Julia Ward
Howe Tilley, Miss Tilley to everyone, was well over ninety,
and Rachel had been her caregiver for years. It started as a
neighborly affair, simply stopping by for a visit and bringing
some nourishing food after the elderly woman had an auto
accident, but it had gradually evolved into a paid home-care
position through the local senior center. Now Rachel arrived
around ten, did the housekeeping and grocery shopping, and
prepared a hot lunch and a cold dinner that she left ready on
a tray before leaving around two.

"I'll bring it over tomorrow," promised Lucy.

"Come for lunch," suggested Rachel. "Miss T loves to
gossip with you."

So at noon, Lucy arrived at Miss Tilley's little Cape Cod
cottage with the cat in a plastic carrier box. Miss Tilley was
in her usual wing chair next to the fireplace, and Lucy set the

box down on the Oriental carpet in front of her and opened the gate. They waited as a sleek brown head emerged, whiskers twitching and sapphire blue eyes surveying the scene. Then with one elegant leap, the Siamese landed in Miss Tilley's lap, where she planted her forelegs on the old woman's chest and raised herself until they were eye to eye. Miss Tilley remained motionless as the cat sniffed at her face, whipping her long brown tail from side to side. Then, apparently satisfied, the cat settled itself like a Sphinx on Miss Tilley's knees.

"My heavens," she said. "That was quite an unusual greeting."

"I guess you passed inspection." Rachel laughed. "The question is, how do you feel about the cat?"

"I think I'm in love," replied Miss Tilley, gently stroking the animal's back with her blue-veined hand. "I've never seen such a beautiful creature."

"What are you going to name her?" asked Lucy.

"Perhaps Cleopatra, but I'm not sure. I need a little time to know her better."

Lucy smiled. "From my brief acquaintance with her, I can tell you that's a perfect choice."

"Cleopatra it is, then," said Miss Tilley. "Now, Lucy, you must bring me up to speed on all the local scandals—the news that's *not* fit to print."

Rachel left the two alone and went in the kitchen to put the finishing touches on lunch while Lucy brought Miss Tilley up to date on her new neighbors and the plans for the Halloween party.

"What about that poor magician?" asked Miss Tilley, just as Rachel announced lunch was ready.

Lucy picked up the sleeping Cleopatra and shifted her to a sunny spot on the sofa, then gave Miss Tilley an arm to hold as she hoisted herself out of the chair. "I don't think there's been any progress," she said as they walked arm in arm to the dining room. "I did learn that a developer over in

Shiloh wanted to buy Malcolm Malebranche's property but
that he was refusing."

"Sounds like a motive to me," said Miss Tilley as Lucy
held her chair for her.

"I thought so, too, until I talked to the developer, who
turned out to be a really nice guy," said Lucy, taking her
usual seat. As always, the table was set beautifully with a
blue and white homespun cloth and matching napkins,
monogrammed family silver, antique flow-blue plates, and a
lusterware pitcher bursting with pink cosmos from the garden.

"They're the ones you have to watch out for," said Miss
Tilley as Rachel brought in the blue and white Canton tureen
filled with deliciously fragrant beef stew.

"You know," said Rachel as she ladled out bowlfuls, "I've
been reading that play *The Crucible,* for an audition. . . ."

"I didn't know the Village Players did such serious stuff,"
said Lucy, passing the basket of rolls. She knew Rachel had
recently appeared in several productions with the local amateur troupe.

"I'm going big-time. It's with a theater group in Portland."

"Rachel's turning into quite an actress," said Miss Tilley,
beaming with pride.

"I probably won't get the part," said Rachel, blushing.
"But I was struck with something in the play. There's this
character, Miles Corey, and he endures the most painful, ag-
onizingly slow death, because he refuses to admit he is a
witch, in which case they would simply hang him and get it
over with. But he stubbornly endures two days of torture because if he admitted to being a witch, his land would be confiscated and his children disinherited."

Lucy stabbed a piece of meat with her fork and chewed
thoughtfully. "I don't think Malebranche's land was the motive. It seems more likely that somebody had a personal motive for killing him."

"Continue," Miss Tilley ordered Lucy, impatient with the delay as Lucy chewed a piece of meat. "It's obvious you know something that you're not telling us," said Miss Tilley, narrowing her blue eyes.

"All I've really got is a hunch," said Lucy.

"We're dying to hear it," said Rachel.

Lucy sighed. "Okay, this is my theory, for what it's worth. You know Malcolm was the high priest of this coven?"

"Diana's coven," added Rachel.

"Right. Well, Diana told me that Malcolm initiated her into the high priesthood by having sex with her, that sex is part of their rites and observances."

"Oh," said Rachel, her eyes wide with shock.

"Hmmm," said Miss Tilley in a tone of disapproval. "That would never happen in the Methodist church."

"And I figure that when you add sex to the equation, you have to deal with a whole lot of emotions and hurt feelings and jealousy. There could be a jilted lover, somebody's jealous boyfriend, even an enraged father. The problem is, Diana won't reveal the names of the members of the coven. And neither will the police."

"Nothing gets people quite as riled up as sex," said Miss Tilley, who was proud of being a maiden lady.

"Speaking of which, I thought for a while that we were going to have a Salem-style witch hunt on our hands," said Rachel, buttering a roll. "Ike Stoughton was really trying to get something going."

"He's been distracted," said Lucy "There was the flood and his sick wife—I think he's got his hands full."

"I was worried too," said Miss Tilley, looking very serious. "I was afraid for Rebecca Wardwell."

Lucy was puzzled. "That's what Rachel told me. That Ike seemed to think Rebecca was a witch, too, and somehow hexed his pumpkins."

"She is a witch," asserted Miss Tilley with a sharp nod.

"She's not one of these silly modern pretend witches with their crystals and candles—she's a *real* witch."

Lucy's and Rachel's eyes met across the table. "A real witch?" asked Lucy.

"She was born a witch. She even has a mark on her back, a witch's mark. She showed it to me once." Miss Tilley speared a piece of carrot. "Her mother was a witch, and her grandmother was a witch too. It runs in the family, like those Mumfords all have red hair and freckles."

"She certainly keeps a low profile," said Rachel. "I would never have guessed."

"Oh, she's not showy like that Diana Ravenscroft," said Miss Tilley, popping the bit of carrot into her mouth.

"Come to think of it," said Lucy, "she does have some pretty amazing abilities."

"Like tickling trout," volunteered Miss Tilley. "I've seen her do it."

"She started my car one day when it stalled," said Lucy. "And when Diana had that awful case of poison ivy, she gave me this bottle of stuff that cured it overnight, absolutely cleared it up."

"She could sell that stuff and make a fortune," observed Rachel.

"Oh, no, she would never sell it," said Miss Tilley, growing serious. "That's why I'm worried about her, you know. She's not practical. She lives in her own world, all those old-fashioned clothes and no telephone. She says she doesn't need one, but how would she get help if she needed it?"

"I don't think you need to worry," said Lucy. "She seems to manage very well."

"Well, I'd feel better if you'd check on her now and then for me," said Miss Tilley, setting her knife and fork together on her plate, signaling she was done eating.

"That's no hardship," said Lucy. "I often stop there to buy eggs and vegetables."

"Well, that's settled, then," said Miss Tilley, turning to Rachel. "What's for dessert?"

"Blueberry pie," said Rachel.

Miss Tilley smacked her lips. "My favorite."

Lucy decided she might as well make good on her promise as she drove back to work, so she detoured out to Rebecca's farmlet by the interstate. A cluster of fast-food restaurants and gas stations had sprouted near the exit ramps, but a large parcel of conservation trust land preserved an extensive old-growth forest. Rebecca's farm was adjacent to this woodland, and visiting there was like taking a trip back in time. When Lucy climbed out of her car, she felt as if she were stepping right into a Currier & Ives print.

Rebecca's little porched cottage was surrounded by flowers, and climbing roses clambered over the wood-shingled roof. A little flock of chickens pecked around in the yard, and goats peered at her curiously over their fence. The goats' pen was next to the barn, which was connected to the house in traditional Maine style by a woodshed, allowing sheltered access during heavy winter snows. Neat rows of vegetables in raised beds filled the area beyond the barn, and Lucy could see Rebecca working out there in her old-fashioned dress and straw sunbonnet, absorbed in her task of picking beans. She looked up, however, just as Lucy was about to call out to her.

"I'm coming," she shouted with a wave.

Lucy watched as she approached with her picking basket over her arm and a tiny owl on her shoulder.

"This is such a busy time," said Rebecca, unlatching the gate. "The beans just keep coming and coming, and there's the Swiss chard and the zucchini and summer squash—it's really all I can do to keep up. And I've got to keep an eye on my pumpkins. I've got high hopes for some of them."

"Are you growing them for the giant pumpkin contest?" asked Lucy, fascinated by the little owl.

Rebecca nodded. "If the weather cooperates, I might have a winner this year."

"Who's your friend?" asked Lucy, watching as the little owl groomed its feathers. "Oops, I didn't mean to make a pun."

"He's Oz, my faithful companion," said Rebecca, indicating the bird on her shoulder. He stared at Lucy with large, unblinking golden eyes.

"I thought owls sleep in the daytime."

"He takes a nap in the morning, but then he's on the job, keeping an eye out for mice."

"So he earns his keep," said Lucy.

"Yes, indeed. He's a working member of this corporation," said Rebecca, getting down to business. "What can I get you today?"

"I've got beans," said Lucy. "But I could use a dozen eggs and some of your amazing yogurt."

"Goats' milk is the best. The fat doesn't separate out," said Rebecca, approving her choice. "I also have herb plants for sale, around on the side—I know you're quite a gardener yourself."

Lucy was definitely interested. She was always looking for new plants to add to her herb garden. "I'll go take a look," she said.

"You do that while I fetch your eggs and yogurt," said Rebecca. "One quart? Two?"

"Just one, and I'll take a quart of raspberries too," said Lucy, planning to serve a healthful dessert.

She wandered along the path that led past the goat pen to the side of the barn. There she found a neat herb garden enclosed by a low boxwood hedge. The plants that Rebecca was offering for sale had been potted up and were arranged on a low bench against the barn wall, but Lucy decided to look over the garden before making her choice.

She was familiar with most of the plants: parsley, lavender, thyme, sage, yarrow, sweet woodruff, and lady's bedstraw that grew between the flagstones in the walkway. Some were new to her, however, especially one rather large handsome plant that bore a slight resemblance to a tomato plant. She remembered seeing it, or something very similar, growing in Ike Stoughton's garden.

"What's this?" she asked as Rebecca approached with her purchases in a recycled supermarket bag. "It's quite impressive."

"Belladonna," said Rebecca, her tongue lingering over the name. "It's one of my favorites. The name means 'beautiful woman.'"

"Do you have any for sale?" asked Lucy.

"No," said Rebecca. "It's a bit tricky to grow; it's not for everyone. But I do have some lovely lady's mantle, if you're interested. It has beautiful bright green flowers that bloom just when the roses do, and you can make gorgeous arrangements. The leaves are shaped like an old-fashioned cape—I have one very much like them myself."

"Is it hard to grow?"

"Not at all. Just give it lots of sun and room to sprawl. That's it there, by the sundial."

"I have just the spot for that," said Lucy, as Oz suddenly rose from Rebecca's shoulder and spread his wings. They were enormous for such a small bird, easily spanning more than a foot. He seemed to float silently over the neat garden, barely moving his wings, until he uttered a sharp cry and dropped straight down between two rows of beans.

"Murder is afoot, I'm afraid," said Rebecca with a rueful smile. "Mr. Mouse won't be coming home tonight. I hope Mrs. Mouse won't miss him too much."

"She has the children to console her," said Lucy.

"Plenty of them." Rebecca laughed. "And probably more on the way."

"Well, I mustn't keep you," said Lucy with a regretful

sigh as she inhaled the lemony, musky garden scent that filled the air. "It's so lovely here. I could stay all day. Is it always this peaceful?"

Rebecca seemed to hesitate for a moment, and Lucy wondered if she was anxious about something, but then she smiled. "I strive to live in harmony with nature—that's why it seems so peaceful."

"So that's the secret. I've got to live in harmony with a husband, four kids, and a boss! So how much do I owe you?"

Rebecca pronounced a shocking sum, but Lucy paid up gladly, telling herself it was important to encourage local growers. And besides, she reminded herself as she carried off her purchases, she'd gotten more than her money's worth, because shopping at the farmlet was a sensual experience. She'd feasted her eyes on beauty, she'd felt the warm sun on her skin, she'd inhaled the heady fragrances of the herbs, and she'd heard the cry of the owl. And now, as she started the car, she was tasting the incomparable flavor of a sun-ripened raspberry.

Back in the office, Lucy found a stack of papers on her desk.

"Ted wants you to go through those letters and decide which ones to print. When you're done with that, I need you to proofread the legals for me."

"Okay," said Lucy with an obvious lack of enthusiasm. Picking the letters wasn't so bad, but reading those complicated and lengthy legal ads was a tiresome chore. However, it did sometimes yield a story, like when a millionaire CEO who owned a luxurious summer home featured in several shelter magazines was included in the town treasurer's annual list of unpaid real estate taxes. That was quite a scoop, but the ads were rarely that interesting, so Lucy started with the letters.

They included the usual complaints about town officials

who wasted the taxpayers' money, thank-yous to the rescue squad paramedics for their "quick response and considerate behavior," and promos for upcoming events such as the Hook Fishermen's "Hookers' Ball" and the "Twice Round the Cove" road race. Lucy decided to focus on the positive this week and set the complaints aside; she was trying to decide which worthy event to include when Phyllis handed her some new letters that had just been delivered.

"Wilf just brought these," she said, in that special voice she used for the mailman.

"How's that going?" asked Lucy, taking the letters. "Is he still bringing you flowers and taking you out to dinner?"

"Yes, he is," said Phyllis, checking her reverse French manicure with white nails tipped with coral. It was the latest thing, according to Phyllis, and all the rage at the nail salon.

"You're a lucky girl," said Lucy. "He's a real gentleman."

"Don't I know it," said Phyllis, gazing out the window and watching as her knight in shining armor—actually blue shorts—proceeded across the street, pushing his little wheeled cart. "He's such a romantic. It's kind of hard not to disillusion him."

"You're afraid of falling off the pedestal?" asked Lucy, attacking the handful of envelopes with her letter opener.

Phyllis grimaced. "I'm not sure our relationship would survive the crash."

"I don't think you need to worry," said Lucy, extracting one of the letters and unfolding it. "You've got a lot going for—" She stopped abruptly as she read the letter. "Here we go again."

"What?" Phyllis was leaning over her shoulder to read the letter, and Lucy could smell her Jean Naté body splash.

"It's Ike Stoughton, going after Diana Ravenscroft again."

"He doesn't mince his words, does he?" said Phyllis. "'Ungodly wickedness, undermining parental authority, corrupting the town's youth . . .'"

"'Must not be allowed to continue,'" quoted Lucy. "He's

calling on the town's God-fearing citizens to take whatever steps are necessary to rid the town of this, and here I quote, 'suppurating sore.'"

"What exactly is a suppurating sore?" asked Phyllis.

"I'm not sure, but it sounds disgusting," said Lucy, unfolding the next letter. "Oh, no!" she exclaimed, reading it. "This is another one, but it's from Cynthia Brock."

"She's a crank, isn't she?"

"Yeah, she usually writes about the school budget." Lucy was opening another letter. "My gosh, this is another one."

"It must be a campaign," suggested Phyllis. "I bet Ike Stoughton's behind it."

"I think you're right," said Lucy, quickly flipping through the remaining letters. "They're all practically identical."

"Are you going to print them?" asked Phyllis.

"Not me," said Lucy, clipping the letters together and putting them on Ted's desk. "This is one for the boss."

Lucy went ahead and compiled a selection of less inflammatory letters for the editorial page and sent it to Ted's queue, figuring he could substitute one or two of the anti-witch letters if he wanted. If it was up to her, she would get the story behind the letters and print that, but it wasn't her call. Glancing at the clock, she realized she had plenty of time left for the legals—too bad.

Fortunately, they were submitted electronically, so all she had to do was read the text and make sure there were no misspellings or omissions. She slogged through several announcements of mortgagees' sales of real estate, always heartbreaking, and notices of a couple of wills presented for probate. She saved the planning board's monthly notice for last, because it was the easiest, merely listing the petitioners scheduled for the next meeting. It was a bit of a shock, however, when she spotted Compass Construction among the petitioners and learned the company was seeking approval for a site plan for a shopping mall adjacent to Rebecca's little farm.

CHAPTER FOURTEEN

Lucy's first reaction was to telephone Rebecca; then she remembered Miss Tilley fretting that her friend didn't have a telephone. So she quickly finished editing the legals, then grabbed her bag and headed back out to the farm. She found Rebecca sitting under the grape arbor, sipping a glass of iced herb tea. Oz, the little owl, was perched on the back of the chair, napping.

"Would you like some?" she asked, indicating a frosty stoneware pitcher. "It's my own blend of rose hips, camomile, and mint, with a dash of strawberry syrup."

"That sounds delicious," said Lucy, easing into a twig chair that was a lot more comfortable than she would have suspected.

"It is," said Rebecca, filling a glass for her. "I was expecting you."

"You were?" asked Lucy, wondering if the witch had ESP or something.

"I got the certified letter from the planning board today, and I knew they'd be printing the legal notice."

"Oh," said Lucy, slightly disappointed. She took a sip of tea and held it on her tongue for a minute, savoring the refreshing flavors before swallowing. "Has Compass Construction offered to buy you out?"

"Oh, yes. A nice young man came by some weeks ago and offered me a shocking sum of money."

"You refused?"

"Of course. I was born in this house. My family has lived here for, well, as long as people have lived in these parts. Mother told me that one of our ancestors married into the Native American tribe that was here when he arrived, so our ties to the land go back further than the European settlers." She shrugged. "There's no way I could sell. The way I see it, it's not really mine to sell."

An unusual sense of calm had come over Lucy, and she sat quietly, thinking about Rebecca's reply. Finally she spoke. "When your time comes, who will the land go to?"

"My daughter, of course."

Lucy was shocked. For some reason, she thought Rebecca was childless, a maiden lady like Miss Tilley. "I didn't know. . . ."

"How could you? She lives over in New Hampshire, with her daughter."

Lucy was relieved. Though it was by no means certain that Compass Construction had anything to do with Malcolm's grisly death, she had been frightened for Rebecca's safety when she saw the ad. But knowing she had an heir changed the situation and seemed to protect her. She looked up, gazing at the forest that surrounded the farmlet. "I thought this was all owned by the conservation land trust," she said.

"Most of it is, to the north and west, but there's about fifty acres to the south that is listed as 'owner unknown.' I guess Compass Construction found the owner after all."

"They tried to buy out Malcolm Malebranche—you know, the man who—"

Rebecca laid her hand over Lucy's. It was warm and much softer than Lucy expected, considering how hard Rebecca worked in the garden. Once again, she felt the same calming sensation flow through her veins. "I know, dear. Now, you mustn't worry about me. Oz and I will be fine."

Hearing his name, the tiny bird opened his eyes, which were as large as quarters, and blinked.

Lucy smiled. "Okay, then," she said, but she knew it wasn't okay. Now, more than ever, she shared Miss Tilley's concern for her friend.

"Now do you want to see my pumpkins?"

"Sure," said Lucy, following Rebecca to a goodly patch of garden filled with sprawling vines in raised beds.

Rebecca pushed some leaves aside, almost as if folding back a blanket to reveal a newborn baby, and pointed to a green globe about the size of a volleyball. "This one is very promising," she said.

Lucy nodded. "How so?"

"It's growing faster than the others, it's nice and round, and I just have a good feeling about it."

"Well, I wish you luck," said Lucy. "I see you're not worried about sabotage, like some of the other growers."

"You mean Ike Stoughton?" Rebecca chuckled. "That man is paranoid." She gave the pumpkin a pat and let the leaves fall back in place, covering it. "Oz and I are concentrating on the real troublemakers: mice and groundhogs."

And with that, Oz soared into the sky and began patrolling the garden.

But as she took the roundabout way home, Lucy worried that Miss Tilley was right to be concerned about her friend's safety and wondered if she could persuade Rebecca to accept one of the cell phones the Council on Aging distributed that were programmed to call 911. But as soon as she arrived home, she received such shocking news that her fears for Rebecca were suddenly insignificant.

"Mom! Mom!" shrieked Sara, erupting from the kitchen door and dashing down the porch steps with Libby at her heels. "It's awful!"

"What is?" asked Lucy, enfolding the girl in her arms. "What's happened?"

"Abby's mother . . . ," she began, then exploded into sobs.

"What happened to Abby's mother?" asked Lucy, wiping tears from her daughter's face with her hand.

"She died," said Zoe, who had followed her older sister outside.

Stunned, Lucy drew Zoe to her, hugging both girls. She'd known that Miriam was ailing, but she hadn't expected this. "Are you sure?" she asked.

"Abby called."

Lucy saw a glimmer of hope and seized on it. After all, teenage girls weren't especially reliable. "What exactly did Abby say?"

"She said the men from the funeral place had come and taken her mother away." Sara sniffled. "She was pretty upset."

"Of course she was," said Lucy, hugging the girls tighter.

"Mom, can we go over there? To be with her?"

Lucy hesitated. She knew the girls were good friends, but she doubted that Ike Stoughton would welcome outsiders at a time like this. "Not today," she said, coming to a decision. "It's too soon and I'm sure her father wants privacy. But tonight we'll make a cake or something and take it over tomorrow."

"Okay," said Sara, pulling away from her mother and sighing. "That's a good idea."

"I wonder what kind we should make?" said Lucy, walking hand in hand with Zoe toward the house.

"I think a pound cake is always nice," said Zoe, sounding like Martha Stewart. "It's so versatile."

That was the wonderful thing about kids, thought Lucy: the way they would surprise you by coming out with something completely unexpected. And then she thought how Miriam would have no more wonderful surprises. She'd never see her children marry; she'd never take a newborn grandchild in her arms. And that's when the tears began to flow.

Lucy was true to her word, and that night the girls mixed up a pound cake while she tidied up the supper dishes. Once again, her little homemaker, Zoe, surprised her by announcing that pound cake was always better after it had aged for a day.

"Where are you getting this stuff?" she asked.

"The cooking channel," explained Zoe. "I've also got some ideas for window treatments, if you're interested."

"HGTV," said Sara, seeing her mother's shocked expression. "We discovered all these shows during that rainy spell when there was nothing else to do."

"And now we're addicted," said Zoe. "You know, Mom, miniblinds are really out. They're the first thing these designers chuck out."

"Leave my miniblinds alone," declared Lucy, tucking a platter in the dishwasher. "They're cheap and functional, and when they get dirty, I just throw them out and get new ones."

"Filling up the landfill," said Zoe in a disapproving tone.

"We should get those energy-efficient lightbulbs too," suggested Sara.

"I guess we could afford those lightbulbs and get new window treatments, too, if you girls give up your new back-to-school clothes," said Lucy, putting an end to that discussion.

The next morning, however, Zoe was right back on the case. "Use aluminum foil to wrap the cake," she advised her mother. "It's recyclable, and plastic film and even wax paper are made from petroleum—that's oil, you know."

"I know," said Lucy, pulling off a length of expensive

foil. "Do you think you could manage to write a note?" she asked.

"On recycled paper?" asked Sara.

"I don't know if it is or not, but I've got a drawer full of note cards and it would be better to use them up, right?"

"I suppose so," grumbled Sara, heading for the secretary that stood in the corner of the living room. "What shall I write?" she asked when she returned with a note card with a drawing of a summer rose on the front.

"Just something simple like 'Thinking of you at this sad time.' And sign it from all of us."

"Okay," she said, bending to the task.

Soon, Lucy and the girls were all in the car, bouncing over the temporary bridge to the Stoughton place. After delivering the cake, Lucy would drop the girls at Friends of Animals day camp where they had summer jobs—Sara's paid and Zoe's volunteer—and Lucy would go on to the *Pennysaver.* She wasn't looking forward to encountering Ike Stoughton, or his sons, and she was hoping that they would be out and only Abby would be home. But it was Mather who came to the door, the older one, who was a spitting image of his father, minus the shoulder-length silver hair.

"We just wanted to say how sorry we are for your loss and to give you this cake that the girls made," said Lucy, holding out the foil-wrapped loaf.

"Uh, thanks," he said, opening the screen door just enough to take the cake.

"Is your sister home?" asked Lucy. "The girls would like to express their condolences—"

"What's going on here?" demanded Ike, suddenly looming behind his son. He was scowling and glaring at them.

"They want to see Abby," said Mather.

"We wanted to say how sorry we are about your wife, and we brought this cake," said Lucy quickly.

"That's very neighborly," said Ike in a gentler tone. "Abby's too upset to see anyone right now."

"Well, give her our love," said Lucy, turning to go. "We're all very sorry for your loss."

Ike suddenly erupted, grabbing her arm. "It didn't have to happen!" he declared. "It was that witch—that evil witch!"

Lucy froze in her tracks. This was exactly the sort of scene she'd been dreading, and she didn't know what to do. She turned and faced him, trying to think of the right thing to say but unsure what exactly that was. When she saw his anguished expression, however, the words came to her. "I think that's the grief talking," she said softly. "Of course you want someone to blame, some explanation—"

"How's this for an explanation?" thundered Ike. "My wife was healthy and happy until that woman came to town. The very day Diana Ravenscroft opened her shop, my poor Miriam started to ail."

"A coincidence," said Lucy. "That's all."

"No! It's no coincidence. Miriam was good, a living saint, and that's why she had to die. Witches can't stand goodness. They have to destroy it."

This was an old theme, thought Lucy, seeing how Ike's son was nodding along. He'd certainly heard this before, and believed it.

Ike's eyes were glittering, and he was spitting out the words. "I believe she's bewitched Abby."

"Oh, no," said Lucy, frightened for the girl. "That's ridiculous. Diana has no special powers. She's a witch the same way some people are Catholics or Protestants. It's a re- ligion, like Hinduism or Buddhism. Just because we don't understand it or believe it doesn't make it evil."

"You're fooling yourself," hissed Ike, looking and sound- ing like a fire-and-brimstone preacher. "I've seen Lucifer in that woman's eyes."

Somewhat unnerved, Lucy saw no option but a dignified retreat. "We have to go," she said, taking the girls by the hands. "Once again, we're very sorry for your loss."

"You never know how grief will take people," she told the girls as they walked down the drive, past the garden that now looked sad and bedraggled. Only the belladonna plants along the fence were thriving.

"Poor Abby," said Sara when they were all back in the car.

"Her father is really scary," said Zoe.

"He's very upset," said Lucy, her heart heavy as she followed the familiar roads. She never would have guessed he was that devoted to his wife, considering the controlling way he treated her, but his enormous grief just went to show that you could never really know how another person felt. She didn't doubt his grief was genuine, but his extreme reaction worried her, especially the way he was blaming Diana. She didn't see how any good could come out of this situation.

When Lucy got to work, she found the funeral director had already faxed over an obituary and a funeral announcement for Miriam Stoughton, which was a big time-saver on this deadline day. She quickly read the obituary, noting that it was extremely brief, noting only Miriam's immediate family, her devotion to her children, and her love of home-making. If she had ever held a job, it wasn't mentioned, and neither were any clubs or organizations. It also omitted the cause of death, so Lucy called the town clerk to find out who issued the death certificate.

"That would be Doc Ryder," said Audrey Lyons.

"And the cause of death?"

"It says heart failure," replied Audrey.

"Well, thanks," said Lucy, ending the call and dialing Doc Ryder's office. She'd caught him at a good time, his receptionist told her; he'd just come in from rounds at the hospital, and his office hours hadn't started yet. Lucy filed the fact away for future reference.

"Well, good morning to you," he said, sounding chipper.

"I'm sorry to bother you," she began.

"No bother," said Doc Ryder. "I was just sitting here, going over lab reports."

"Well, I have a question about Miriam Stoughton's death. According to the death certificate, it was due to heart failure?"

"That's what happens, Lucy. When your heart stops beating, you're dead."

"In other words, you don't really know why she died, right?"

"Exactly."

"In that case, isn't there supposed to be an autopsy?"

He sighed. "The family strongly objected, and it was no secret she had been suffering from some undiagnosed ailment for some time. They apparently have no faith in medicine, and I have to admit I'm not entirely unsympathetic to that point of view. I didn't see any reason to add to their grief."

"I understand. I saw Ike myself this morning, and he's terribly upset. But he's also accusing Diana Ravenscroft of killing his wife by bewitching her."

"Hmmm," said Doc Ryder.

"If there was an autopsy, there'd be no question, would there?"

"Not necessarily," said the doctor. "Lots of autopsies are inconclusive. Maybe she had stomach cancer; that would be nice and neat. But maybe she had a weak immune system, or overdosed on vitamins or herbal remedies. Those things don't show up without expensive lab tests that the town can't afford."

"I suppose you're right," said Lucy, glancing at the clock, which was steadily ticking its way toward the noon deadline. "Thanks for your time."

"No problem," he said, but Lucy disagreed. It seemed to her that the doctor's decision to skip an autopsy was going to cause no end of problems. She reached for the phone to give Diana a heads-up.

"Just wanted to let you know that Miriam Stoughton is dead—"

"Poor little Abby!" Diana exclaimed, interrupting Lucy. "She must be devastated. I must go and console her."

"Not a good idea," said Lucy. "Ike Stoughton is claiming you killed Miriam by bewitching her."

"That's absolutely ridiculous," said Diana. Lucy could hear the shock in her voice.

"Of course it is, but I think you need to be careful."

"This is just absurd," exclaimed Diana. "There's absolutely nothing to fear about Wicca! Do you know that Catholic priest? Father Ed?"

"Sure," said Lucy.

"Well, he called me up last night, quite late, and tried to get me to submit to an exorcism. Can you believe it?"

Lucy knew that Father Ed was a sociable sort who spent most evenings down at the new waterfront pub that had replaced the notorious Bilge. If he'd called late at night, he'd probably had a drink or two and was probably reacting to the scuttlebutt he'd heard from the local fishing crowd.

"You need to take this seriously," warned Lucy. "It sounds to me like people are talking about you and not in a good way. We've also been getting letters here at the paper complaining about you."

"Look, thanks for calling and everything, but I am not going to be intimidated by a bunch of barflies and gossips. Business is up now that summer's finally here and the tourists have arrived, and I'm not about to turn tail and run. It seems to me that the best thing I can do is just carry on, and pretty soon people will get used to having a witch in town—a good witch."

Ted had arrived and Lucy knew she had to get back to work. "Well," she said, ending the call, "don't say you weren't warned."

"I've got a warning for you," said Ted, striding across the office to his desk. "It's a deadline, not a guideline."

"Everything's under control," Lucy assured him, wishing she believed it.

Miriam's funeral was scheduled for eleven o'clock the following Saturday morning. Lucy had an interview scheduled with a woman who was organizing a drive to fill care packages for soldiers in Iraq, so she was running late. The service was well under way when she and the girls arrived, slipping in a pew at the back of the church.

Funerals were always well attended in Tinker's Cove, so even though Miriam had led a secluded life, there was a good showing and most of the pews were full. The choir was singing "The Lord's Prayer," so Lucy took advantage of the musical interlude to consult the order of service. She'd missed Reverend Sykes's sermon, she noticed, but not the eulogy. It was next, and Ike Stoughton was going to deliver it.

Just the thought of this bereaved husband, or any bereaved husband for that matter, or even any family member actually getting up and speaking about such a personal loss, was tremendously moving to Lucy. She knew it was something she could never do, and she wasn't sure she could bear to listen to it, either, so she pulled a handkerchief out of her purse and clutched it in her hand, preparing herself for the tears she was sure would come.

Thus armed, she turned her attention to the choir. Mrs. Wilberforce was in fine voice today, and her wavering soprano clearly dominated as the song came to its crescendo: "For thine is the KINGDOM, and the POWER, and the"— here, Mrs. Wilberforce really let it rip—"GLORY, FOREVER AND EVER." The tones were still reverberating against the clean, white-plastered walls as the final Amen was intoned.

Then Ike Stoughton rose from his seat in the front row

and strode to the lectern set front and center before the altar. Behind him was the church's single stained-glass window, which pictured a white-robed Jesus in a flower-filled garden surrounded by little children and lambs.

"As the reverend so rightly pointed out, a service like this should be a celebration of a life and a thanksgiving for the gift of that life," he began, gripping both sides of the lectern with his hands and gazing at the white coffin reposing in front of him, covered with a spray of pink roses.

"Miriam was truly a gift from God," he said, his voice cracking, causing an eruption of sniffles in the congregation and a fluttering of tissues. "She was better than me, better than all of us put together, and I don't know how I'm going to go on without her."

Now there was a general dabbing of eyes, Lucy's included. She glanced at the girls to see how they were doing, and noticing their brimming eyes, passed along a packet of tissues. Trying not to be too obvious, she glanced around the church, looking for Abby and her brothers. They were sitting together in the front pew, where Abby seemed little more than a wraith herself squeezed between her two beefy brothers.

"Her life wasn't easy," he continued. "My poor wifey suffered terribly, as many of you know. Pain wracked her body. Some days she barely had enough energy to sit up, but she never complained, not once."

Now most women in the congregation were in full flood, and some men were even dabbing their eyes.

"Instead of complaining, my Miriam turned to prayer, praying not for a cure but for the strength to endure her suffering, just as our Lord Jesus suffered on the cross. For Miriam understood there was no cure for what ailed her. There is no medicine that can cure evil, and she knew that her body—the body that had borne our three children—had become a battleground between good and evil."

For the first time, there was a general rustling, a sense that people were becoming uncomfortable.

Stoughton was leaning heavily on the lectern now, his eyes glaring angrily at the mourners transfixed in their pews. "Oh, I know nobody talks about evil much anymore, but believe me, evil walks and breathes and lives among us. It is always with us. Oh, Satan is a crafty one and takes many, many forms. Sometimes a virus, sometimes a fire or a flood, and sometimes the body of a beautiful young woman. But make no mistake," he thundered, raising his hand high above his head with his index finger extended. "Oh, make no mistake—she is here and she will work her evil mischief among us unless we take steps to stop her."

"Amen, amen," chorused a number of people as Ike reclaimed his seat next to Abby. Others clearly looked uncomfortable, relieved that he was done. Lucy sensed that battle lines were being drawn, right here in the white clapboard community church, between those who believed in tolerance and acceptance and those who were looking for a scapegoat. Because it was clear to her exactly who Ike considered to be the evil one, even though no names had been mentioned.

Lucy didn't want to join the procession to the cemetery; she found burials upsetting and tried to avoid them when she could, but the girls were insistent.

"We need to support Abby," said Sara. "It's the only chance we'll get."

"You went to the service," said Lucy.

"I don't think she saw us," said Zoe.

"It really means a lot to me, Mom," said Sara. "She's my friend."

"Okay," said Lucy, adding a warning. "Burials are really depressing."

But when they joined the people clustered around the gravesite, Lucy was surprised to see a black-suited Kyle Compton standing with the family. And when the final words had been said and the casket lowered into the ground, and people were beginning to disperse, she saw Abby slip away from her family to be embraced by Diana. Her absence was noted almost immediately, and it was Kyle Compton who went to retrieve her and bring her back into the family fold, practically shoving her into the waiting black limousine. The town car pulled away, and Diana was left standing alone, a dramatic figure with her abundant breeze-tossed ringlets and the long black dress that clung to her figure, revealing every feminine curve.

And alone she remained, as people scurried past her, eyes averted and offering no greeting as they hurried to their cars.

CHAPTER FIFTEEN

As Lucy went about town in the days following the funeral, she often heard Diana's name mentioned, and not in a good way. "That Diana Ravenscroft has a lot of nerve, showing up at the funeral like that," Mimi Rogers was heard saying into her cell phone as she loaded groceries into her car.

"And what is going on between Diana and that girl Abby? That's what I want to know," wondered Chris Cashman, power-walking down Main Street with a friend.

"I sympathize with Diana, I really do," said Franny Small, picking up a *Wall Street Journal* at the drugstore, "but she seems to be asking for trouble. She'd be smart to lie low for a while."

As far as Lucy could tell, Franny was the only one who seemed to have the least bit of sympathy for Diana. Letters continued to arrive at the newspaper, some calling for an investigation into the witch's practices, others declaring there was no place for her in Tinker's Cove. And if she wouldn't leave of her own accord, wrote several "concerned citizens," she should be forcibly removed.

Lucy found it increasingly difficult to get through each

day. Her thoughts kept turning to Miriam's untimely, shocking death, and she was worried about Abby, now alone with her father and brothers. And she was worried about the way public sentiment had turned against Diana. It was discouraging to see otherwise rational people letting their suspicions run rampant and even succumbing to superstition.

So she was surprised and somewhat heartened when she got home from work on Friday afternoon and found Sara and Zoe elbow deep in a big bowl of dough.

"What on earth are you doing?" she asked.

"We're making bread," said Sara.

"Or trying to," said Zoe, holding up her hands, which were covered with sticky dough.

"I can see that," said Lucy. "But why?"

"For Lammas. It's a traditional Wiccan holiday celebrating the first harvest. Diana gave us the flour and the recipe."

"I thought you were done with that nonsense," said Lucy, sighing. If only they'd been inspired by Martha Stewart instead of Diana. "And you need more flour."

"Are you sure?" asked Sara. "The recipe said six cups, and that's how much she gave us."

"I'm sure," said Lucy. "Bread recipes are approximate. You need to add more flour when it's humid like this."

"How much should we add?" asked Sara.

Lucy peered over her shoulder at the sticky mess in the bowl. "I'd start with half a cup, then add more if you need it. It's supposed to be silky smooth, like a baby's bottom, after you knead it."

Thinking about babies' bottoms made her think of Patrick, and she was reaching for the phone to call Molly, just to check in, when it rang. It wasn't Molly, however; it was Diana.

"Oh, Lucy," she began. "I need to ask a favor."

Lucy found herself agreeing with Mimi Rogers: The woman sure had a lot of nerve. "I have a bone to pick with you," grumbled Lucy. "You know I don't want my girls practicing witchcraft, and here they are baking bread for some holiday or other I never heard of."

"Lammas, or Lughnasa. The first of August. It celebrates the beginning of the harvest." Diana's voice was mechanical, as if she was distracted and was reciting something she'd learned by rote.

The recollection of Diana standing all alone after the funeral popped into Lucy's mind, and she knew she wasn't going to be able to stay mad at her for long. She gave it one last stab. "I don't care what it is. I don't want them dabbling in witchcraft."

"There's no harm in making a loaf of bread," argued Diana. "It's a good housewifely skill. And it's organic wheat flour that was planted under a full moon."

"I give up," said Lucy with a sigh. "Just so long as they're not prancing about the woods by moonlight without a stitch on."

"Not with me, they won't," said Diana. "That's why I called. I'm going away for a while to visit my mother out in Arizona. I was hoping Sara and Zoe could water my plants and feed my cat while I'm gone." She sighed.

Lucy felt a sense of relief; this was definitely a good time for Diana to make herself scarce. "No problem," she said. "How long are you going to be gone?"

"I'm not sure," replied Diana, sounding anxious.

"Has something happened?" asked Lucy.

"Nothing specific. I just don't feel safe." She paused.

"Because of Ike Stoughton?"

"That's part of it, but last night I just had this creepy feeling that I wasn't alone, that somebody was watching me. And I think some things in my apartment have been moved, but I'm not exactly sure. Maybe I'm imagining things."

"I think it's a good time to get away for a bit," said Lucy.

"I'm really torn," confessed Diana. "I don't like to leave the coven, but Lady Sybil has promised to fill in for me."

"That's nice of her," said Lucy.

"I'm not so sure about that," said Diana cryptically. "But I really appreciate the girls taking care of Piewocket and the plants."

"No problem. We'll keep an eye on the place."

"Thanks, I knew I could count on you," she said. "Blessed be."

"Same to you," muttered Lucy, hanging up and turning her attention to the girls, who had just finished kneading the bread, which was now a perfectly rounded ball of dough.

"That's perfect," she said, after giving the dough a poke. "Now you just have to let it rise."

She took half a loaf of the Lammas bread into work on Monday, along with a pot of Rebecca's homemade strawberry jam. She was nowhere to be found when Lucy stopped by the farmlet, but the animals had plenty of food and water, and an array of produce had been left out on a shaded table. The prices were clearly marked, and a box was left for payment on the honor system, so Lucy figured Rebecca had planned for this absence and would return soon. It was the first of August, and Lucy suspected she was off with her family in New Hampshire observing Lammas, a supposition that was supported by the large shock of wheat she'd hung on her door.

Lucy tucked a five and two singles into the slot cut into the top of the cash box and chose one of the little Ball jars of jam; it was twice what she'd pay for a bigger jar at the IGA, but there was something about the color of the jam and the sunshine and the scent of the garden that she found irresistible. Everything at Rebecca's place seemed so alive and vibrant that it was hard to put into words—even for Lucy, who had won prizes for her reporting from the New England Newspaper Association—but she definitely felt it.

So did Phyllis, who never indulged in between-meal snacks since she had lost all that weight. "Just a smidge," she said when Lucy set out the bread and jam by the office coffeepot.

Lucy obligingly cut a slice in half, one for her and one for Phyllis. Ted wanted a big, thick slice, and she cut that for him, too, spreading them all with appropriate amounts of jam: Phyllis got her smidge, Lucy had a healthy dollop, and Ted's was loaded. They all had the same reaction.

"Mmm," said Ted, speaking for them all. "This is amazing."

"I don't know which is better, the bread or the jam," said Phyllis.

"I can't believe my girls made it," said Lucy, wondering if magic was indeed afoot on Lammas.

Thus fortified, they all got down to work. Phyllis tackled the listings, Lucy wrote a summary of the selectmen's meeting, and Ted started his editorial column for the week.

"I'm thinking of calling for tolerance," he said, scratching his chin thoughtfully, "but I don't want to name Stoughton directly. The poor man just lost his wife, after all. But I don't want to dodge the issue either. From the number of letters we've been getting, there's definitely a growing anxiety about witchcraft."

"Diana's leaving town for a while," said Lucy. "This might be a good time to bring it out in the open."

"I'll give it a try," he said, bending to his keyboard.

Soon nothing was heard in the office except the clicking of keys and the tick of the old Regulator clock that hung on the wall. Lucy finished her story, then turned to the legals, noticing that the file was longer than usual. More mortgagee sales of real estate, but none with names she recognized, which was a relief. They seemed to be vacation properties, bought by speculators, and no townsfolk were going to lose their homes this week. She was just about finished when she received a fresh e-mail, from the probate court, and opened it, finding a notice that the will of Miriam Compton Stoughton, late of Tinker's Cove, had been presented to the court.

"Listen to this," she said, reading the relevant parts of the ad aloud.

"Goodness, that was fast," said Phyllis. "The poor woman's barely cold in her grave."

"Ike is a stickler for detail," said Ted.

"I wonder what the 'Compton' means," mused Lucy. "Do you think she's related to Kyle Compton? And did she have an interest in Compass Construction?"

"Well, there's one way to find out," said Ted. "Get over to the probate court and read the will."

Lucy was on it, rising from her chair and grabbing her purse.

"But not today," said Ted. "I need you to proof the back-to-school special supplement."

Lucy couldn't believe it. "Already? Summer's only half over."

"That's how it goes," said Ted. "Like the Christmas decorations coming out around Halloween."

Lucy felt a twinge of guilt, "Halloween! I'm on the committee, and I haven't done a thing," she confessed.

"Well, you better get cracking," observed Ted. "'Cause once school starts, Halloween is just around the corner."

"Point taken," said Lucy, sinking back into her chair. "So when exactly do you want me to check out this will?"

"How about Wednesday afternoon, after deadline? It's kind of a long shot; there's probably nothing in it anyway."

But when Wednesday finally came and Lucy examined the will, she discovered he was wrong. Miriam Compton Stoughton had owned fifty percent of Compass Construction and had left all her shares to her husband, Ike, who was also the executor of her estate.

No wonder Ike was in a hurry to get the will through probate; he stood to become a very wealthy man. Compass Construction was one of the biggest local contracting companies. They undertook large projects like shopping centers and industrial parks worth millions of dollars. Miriam, that meek woman whom Lucy had suspected was abused by her husband, had been a very wealthy woman. The realization stunned Lucy, and she sat for a long while at the table in the probate court office, fingering the thick legal stock the will was printed on.

Did this really change anything? she wondered. Miriam had been wealthy, but Lucy doubted she'd ever exercised her rights as co-owner of the company. It seemed more likely that she had deferred to her husband when it came to business; somehow Lucy couldn't see Miriam opposing him. Money was always a prime motive for murder, but Lucy didn't think it applied here. She believed Ike's sorrow was genuine, but even if it wasn't, he had little to gain by killing his wife since he already controlled everything she did. Or did he?

Compass Construction was a private corporation; the shares were all owned by family members, and Lucy knew from experience that it was very difficult to get information about such companies. Tax records were confidential, and there were no glossy annual reports like the ones big corporations issued. The best way to get inside information was from an employee, preferably a disgruntled former employee. Those folks could be gold mines, but Lucy couldn't think of anyone who fit the bill. Another source could be a competitor, and she realized her neighbor Fred Stanton, who had built the new subdivision on Prudence Path, might fit the bill. She returned the will to the clerk and went outside, reaching for her cell phone as she crossed the parking lot. Seated in her hot car, with the windows rolled down to take advantage of the cooling breeze, she put in a call to Fred.

"I need a little background information," she said after they'd gone through the usual pleasantries. "Strictly off the record."

"Sounds intriguing, like Deep Throat." Fred chuckled.

"Don't I wish," said Lucy. "This is no Watergate. It's

probably nothing at all, but I wondered if you know anything about Compass Construction?"

"Like what?" asked Fred.

"Just basic stuff. Like is it profitable? Are they making
money? Losing money?"

"Probably a little bit—no, make that a lot"—Fred chuckled—"of both. This is a tough business climate. Oil prices
are skyrocketing, building materials, too, at the same time
real estate is tanking."

"But an outfit with capital could make a killing," said
Lucy.

"Sure, there are bargains to be had."

"We run ads for foreclosure auctions all the time," said
Lucy.

"Yeah, I looked into that, but there aren't really any bargains, because the banks don't want to take a loss. Nope, the
best way is the way Compass does it—through adverse possession."

"What's that?" asked Lucy.

"Well, the tax rolls are full of land that's listed as owner
unknown."

Lucy remembered Rebecca using that term, in reference
to land adjacent to her farm. "Right," she said. "There's a
piece out by the interstate."

"It's everywhere in these old towns. People move away,
Uncle Harry dies, nobody can find the heirs, so the land just
sits there. The town's not collecting any real estate tax, sometimes for decades. So there's this procedure. Say a neighbor
starts to kinda expand his boundaries. He puts a vegetable
garden on the land or parks his truck there. If he does this
long enough, and nobody objects, he can take the land. He
just has to pay the back taxes."

"Oh," said Lucy. "That doesn't seem right."

"Nature abhors a vacuum, and so does the tax collector,"

said Fred. "Compass does a lot of that. There's nobody better than Ike Stoughton at sorting out titles."

"So they're acquiring land without paying for it?" asked Lucy, a note of outrage in her voice.

"Well, you could do it too. Anybody can."

"So why don't they?" asked Lucy.

"Because it's a lot of bother. It takes years, and there are costs. The taxes, for one thing. Legal fees. It all adds up."

"But it's worth it for them?"

"Oh, yeah," said Fred.

Lucy was thoughtful as she drove back to Tinker's Cove. It seemed that her original valuation of Compass Construction might be way off base, and it might not be quite as well capitalized as she thought. Sort of like her friend Sue Finch, who dressed in designer clothes and was constantly redecorating her home in the latest style, but she wasn't nearly as wealthy as you might think. Sue was a ferocious bargain hunter who haunted boutiques and off-price stores, buying only when coveted items were discounted, sometimes by eighty or ninety percent, at the end of the season. She was generous with her inside knowledge, often informing Lucy of a terrific sale, but Lucy rarely followed up. She just wasn't interested; it was too much bother to race off to Portland for clothes she'd never wear, even if they were on sale. But bargain hunting sure paid off for Sue, and Lucy suspected it worked for Compass Construction too.

Spotting a roadside picnic area, she impulsively pulled over and called Detective Horowitz, catching him at his desk.

"I was planning to leave a message," she said, stammering with surprise. "You're never in your office."

"I can switch you to voice mail," he offered.

"No, no. This is probably nothing, but I've come across some information. . . ."

"Yes?"

"Well, Compass Construction needed Malcolm Male-branche's land for a big project, and now they've acquired land around Rebecca Wardwell. It's owner unknown, you see, and Miriam Stoughton, who just died, owned part of Compass Construction. It all seems pretty fishy to me."

"You think Miriam Stoughton's death is linked to Male-branche's death?" he asked.

"I think so," said Lucy.

"How exactly?"

"I haven't figured that part out yet."

"I see," said Horowitz. "Would you do me a favor?"

"Sure," said Lucy.

"If you have any more ideas like this, please keep them to yourself, okay?"

"I know I'm on to something," insisted Lucy.

"Don't bet on it," said Horowitz, getting the final word.

IV

WIND

Evil's afoot, wickedness abounds,
All is in turmoil as the earth turns round.
That's when the wind begins to blow;
Close the windows and keep down low.

CHAPTER SIXTEEN

The route back to Tinker's Cove took Lucy past the road leading to Peter Symonds's place, so she decided to pay him a visit, just to see how he'd fared in the flooding. The wind was picking up as she drove past fields and woods, and the tree branches were swaying to and fro. Small branches and leaves were tossed about, almost like a fall day. Except this was summer and the leaves were still fresh and green.

The road followed the river, which wound along on one side and then the other. The water was still higher than usual, tumbling in small cascades over the rocky bed, but it was nothing like the raging torrent she'd seen a few weeks ago. Symonds's house was still standing, which was a relief, but the yard was a muddy mess, with logs and strange objects, obviously detritus from the flood, strewn about

Lucy had to struggle against the wind to open the car door, and she couldn't help laughing as it pushed her this way and that as she made her way to the front door. It was an odd feeling, rather comical, to step in one direction and find oneself going in another. But the wind was warm, almost playful, and Lucy gained Symonds's stoop with little difficulty. There was no doorbell, so she knocked as hard as she could, hoping he could hear her above the howling wind.

There was no answer, even when she yelled, so Lucy decided to walk around back to the kitchen door, which had a curtained window. Her luck was no better there, but she snapped a few photos of the devastated yard so the trip wouldn't be a complete waste. She figured they could run them along with photos she'd taken of the flood, as a sort of then-and-now feature. Then, before leaving the porch, she thought she'd try knocking at the door one more time. She was certain that when she turned around, she saw the dingy curtain twitch, but once again, her knock went unanswered.

Pretty weird, she thought, but the fierce wind blew everything else from her mind as she struggled once again to make her way back to the car. Once inside, she sat for a moment, trying to catch her breath, watching as the trees bent this way and that. It was blowing such a storm that she decided to head straight for home rather than risk going on to the office.

The trip soon became a nerve-wracking struggle against the wind to keep the car on the road, especially in the open stretches that ran past fields of hay and corn. The wooded patches were frightening, too, as the branches whipped around, and Lucy was afraid that a large bough or even an entire tree would fall on the car. She saw a couple of massive branches lying along the edge of the road, and the sweet smell of sap and raw wood was filling the air.

She didn't see any other cars on the road until she passed Packet Landing Road, almost home, where she encountered several vehicles stopped in the road. Braking behind them, she saw the problem—a massive maple tree had fallen across the road, landing on the hood of a black Honda Civic. It had also brought down the wires that ran on poles along the road, making the situation even more dangerous.

"Is anybody hurt?" she asked, reaching for her camera

and running toward the smashed car, carefully avoiding the downed wires.

Two young girls were hugging each other and crying. The drivers of the other cars were trying to comfort them. She recognized Renee La Chance and Sassie Westwood, Sara's friends.

"It was so scary," sobbed Renee. "We were just driving along when it crashed down right on top of us."

"Good thing you weren't going too fast," said one man.

"We called nine-one-one," said another, "but they said it will be a while before they get here. I guess this isn't the only tree that came down."

"What should we do?" asked Sassie, the wind whipping her long blond hair around her head.

"It's much too dangerous to stay out here. I'll give you a ride home," said Lucy.

"Thank you, Mrs. Stone," said Sassie. "Come on, Renee."

"Are you sure I should just leave the car?" asked Renee doubtfully as they struggled against the wind. "In Drivers Ed they said you should never leave the scene of an accident."

"It's not safe, with that power line down. Put a note inside the car and leave the keys—that's all you can do," said Lucy. "It sounds like the rescue squad is overwhelmed, and we don't want to become victims."

Soon a little caravan of vehicles was proceeding down Packet Landing Road, with frequent stops to clear branches out of the road. There were fortunately no more fallen trees, but Lucy, who was bringing up the rear, had a close call when a large pine tree came crashing down behind her. They could feel the road shudder from the impact, and it took all of her self-control not to gun the car and flee, but instead to keep their place in the little procession. She was so busy scanning the sky for falling debris that she didn't realize they had reached the temporary bridge by the Stoughton place until they came upon it. She sent up a little prayer as they crossed the rattling steel structure. Once safely across, Lucy thought of Abby and asked the girls if they'd been in touch with her.

"No," said Sassie. "I called a few times, but they always said she couldn't come to the phone."

"I ran into her brother at the post office, and he said she's been sick," reported Renee.

Lucy was thinking this over when they rounded the bend and her house came into sight, standing straight and tall. But the large oak that shaded the backyard was on its side, its tangled roots exposed.

"That's scary," said Sassie as they passed.

"The house looks okay," said Lucy, more in hope than certitude as she turned onto Prudence Path. She quickly scanned the street, making sure that all the houses were undamaged, especially Toby and Molly's. Reassured that they all seemed to be sound, she parked as close as she could to Renee's front door and watched as the girls dashed for safety, bent double against the wind.

Then she slammed the Subaru into reverse, zoomed out of the driveway, and shifted into drive, speeding as fast as she dared toward home. She parked the car in the clearest part of the driveway, hoping it would be okay, and ran into the house, wondering at the kitchen's unusual darkness; then she realized the fallen tree was blocking the window.

"Mo-o-om," cried Zoe, running into her arms.

"Thank goodness you're home," said Sara in a quavering voice. "You've got to see upstairs. Some of the branches came through the roof."

"Through the roof?" she asked, following the girls up the back stairway.

"Like nails, right through the roof," said Zoe.

"There was a horrible sound, like a big truck roaring down the road, and then this enormous crash," said Sara.

"We were really scared," said Zoe. "Libby went under the kitchen table and we did too."

Upstairs, in Bill's attic office, she saw it was true. Sharp spikes of wood had penetrated the roof, piercing right through shingles and tar paper, sheathing, insulation, and plaster. "Oh, my," she said. "This must be a tornado."

"Weather service says it wasn't a tornado," said Ted the next morning. He'd been up all night, covering the storm and its aftermath. With roads clogged by fallen trees and wires and power out in much of the county, the usual Thursday edition of the paper hadn't been printed yet.

"It's a blessing in disguise," declared Ted. "Now we can run a breaking news story about the storm, as soon as the press starts to roll."

"Any idea when that will be?" asked Lucy. She had borrowed Zoe's bicycle to get into town, frequently dismounting and walking around fallen trees.

"Any minute now, according to our friend Mark McCullough."

Lucy laughed, recognizing the power company's spokesman. "Our customers can rest assured that we are doing our very best to restore electric service as quickly as possible," intoned Lucy, imitating the PR man's lugubrious tone. "In the meantime, we warn everyone to be aware of the danger posed by downed power lines, and in no circumstance should anyone try to move or repair them."

"So how many people are without power?" asked Phyllis. "My lights went out yesterday afternoon and they're not back yet. And wouldn't you know, I've got two turkey breasts in the freezer I bought on sale at the IGA last week."

"I can keep them for you," said Lucy. "I've got power, but I've also got a large tree down. The branches came right through the roof. I think the weather service is wrong."

"The weather service is calling it a significant anomalous event," said Ted, who had all the latest figures at his fingertips. "Over ten thousand homes without power, innumerable trees down, most major roads blocked, emergency room overflowing but no deaths . . ."

"Thank heavens," said Phyllis.

"Property damage in the millions, the old bowling alley collapsed, and the roof ripped off the middle-school gym. . . ."

"Sounds like a tornado to me," said Lucy, looking up as Ike Stoughton strode through the door.

Before she had a chance to greet him, or to ask how Abby was doing, Ike was waving a piece of paper in Ted's face. "Now will you believe me?" he demanded. "This windstorm was stirred up by that witch leaving town on her broomstick."

"I checked with the weather service, and they didn't mention any broomstick sightings on the radar," said Ted, keeping a straight face.

"They're calling it an 'anomalous event,'" sneered Ike. "You know what that means? They don't have a clue. It was that witch—there's no other explanation. I've set it all out here in this letter, and my question is, are you going to print it or not?"

He handed the sheet of paper over to Ted, who unfolded it and read it carefully, peering through his half-glasses. When he finished, he refolded the letter and handed it back. "No."

"Then I want to buy ad space," said Ike, reaching for his wallet. "People need to know the truth."

"We have a policy about ads," said Ted. "No hate language, no slander, libel, defamation of character. No nudity or sexual content—"

"You mean you're censoring the truth?" demanded Ike.

"I practice responsible journalism," said Ted. "At least I try to."

"Well, I've got NEWS for you," said Ike, narrowing his eyes. "Newspaper readership is down, and you know why? Because people don't have to put up with your self-righteous, politically correct, biased reporting anymore. They can get the true news, the real news, on the Internet. I can even crank up my printer and make copies of this letter and distribute them all over town, stick 'em on trees, under windshield wipers, hand them out at the supermarket." He laughed. "You're irrelevant, Ted. You and your pathetic little excuse for a newspaper don't matter anymore. You're obsolete."

"Oh, yeah?" Ted yelled after him. "You're the one who's about three hundred years behind the times!"

But Ike was gone. Ted was yelling at a closed door.

"Don't listen to him," said Phyllis in a soothing tone. "He doesn't know what he's talking about."

"She's right," agreed Lucy. "People love the *Pennysaver.*"

"No, he's right," said Ted glumly. "Sometimes I think I know exactly how the last dinosaurs felt. I'm fighting a losing battle for survival."

Sure enough, as soon as the power was back, Ike's broadsheets began to appear all over town. Lucy saw them stapled to trees and utility poles, flapping in the breeze under car windshield wipers, and blowing about on the sidewalk and parking lots. When she left the IGA, pushing her heavy grocery cart, one of the bag boys offered to help her. When he finished unloading the bags into the back of her station wagon, she noticed one of the flyers poking out of one of the recyclable green cloth bags.

And people were taking the broadsheets seriously. Lucy noticed witching balls sprouting on lawns everywhere, and suddenly everybody seemed to be wearing a chain around their neck with a gold cross. On Monday morning, Phyllis, who had gone to church with Wilf Lundgren, reported the community church was bursting at the seams, standing room only, when just the week before, a handful of people barely filled the first few pews. And it was the same for the Catholics and the Episcopalians, she said, where the parking lots had been packed and cars had lined both sides of Main Street. Ike's campaign was definitely having an effect.

CHAPTER SEVENTEEN

The following Tuesday, with deadline approaching, Ted asked Lucy to retrieve the photo she'd taken of the coven when they were rescued by helicopter from the mountain. "I want to run it with my editorial on tolerance. To show everybody they're just a bunch of regular folks."

"Maybe they'll have faded from the picture," said Phyllis, half seriously. "Vanished into the ether."

"I think that's ghosts," said Lucy, clicking her way through the stored images all the way back to June. "Here they are," she said, enlarging it with a click of her mouse until it filled the entire screen. "Thirteen average Joes and Janes who just happen to be Wiccan."

Ted leaned over her shoulder, studying the faces in the picture. "Just as I thought," he said, stabbing at the monitor with his finger. "You could see these people anywhere—the grocery store, a PTA meeting, lined up at the post office."

"Or prancing around a fire stark naked to celebrate the summer solstice," said Lucy.

"That one's the witchiest," said Phyllis, pointing at Lady Sybil, with her loosely flowing hair and eccentric garments.

"She's supposed to be the leader while Diana's away,"

said Lucy, turning to Ted. "Want me to give her a call, get some quotes to run with the photo?"

"That's not a bad idea, Lucy," said Ted. "Ads are up this week, so I've got some extra space to fill."

Lucy had no trouble getting Sybil Wellington's phone number from directory assistance, and the witch picked up on the first ring. "Spells and Incantations, Lady Sybil at your service."

After identifying herself, Lucy asked Lady Sybil for a brief description of the Wiccan religion.

"How to begin?" she wondered aloud in her rich, mellifluous voice. "It is such a rich faith, with so many diverse influences, which is natural since it is so very old, as old as mankind, and has evolved through the centuries. At root, I suppose, it has to do with man's relationship with nature, with natural forces."

"Could you be more specific?" asked Lucy, typing away.

"Well, we celebrate the changing seasons. Our holidays are tied to the calendar, the sun, the phases of the moon."

"I understand that a lot of our Christmas celebrations are derived from ancient celebrations of the winter solstice," prompted Lucy.

"Oh, yes, absolutely. The mistletoe, a sacred plant to us, the Yule log, bringing light into the home—you're absolutely right about that."

"So why do you think people are so fearful of witches and witchcraft?" asked Lucy.

"People tend to fear what they don't understand," said Lady Sybil. "But really, as much as I'm enjoying our little chat, I'm expecting a client and I really have to go now. All this is in my book, you know. *Modern Witchcraft,* available on my Web site."

"But I'm on deadline," protested Lucy. "I need the information right now."

"Oh, all right," grumbled Lady Sybil. "The thing to remember is that Wicca is a modern evolution of the Old Reli-

gion practiced by our pagan ancestors. In fact, there are remote pockets in the British Isles where the Old Religion is
still practiced to this day. I came upon such a place a few
years ago, and they welcomed me. It was quite remarkable."

"And how is the Old Religion different from today's
Wicca?" asked Lucy.

There was a long silence, but finally Lady Sybil spoke.
"Perhaps the best way to put it is to say that the Old Religion
is more balanced, more holistic in that it accepts the fact that
without death there is no life."

"I remember my mother telling me when I was a child
that the old people had to die so there would be room for the
new babies to grow," said Lucy.

"It's a bit more complicated than that," cautioned Lady
Sybil.

"I know I'm simplifying the concept," admitted Lucy.
"That's how my mother explained death to me when I was
very young. But it's true, nevertheless. The garden dies
every fall, and all that matter and energy is recycled into
new growth in the spring. I understand completely."

"I wonder if you do," mused Lady Sybil. "I'm afraid I
have to go—my client is at the door."

"Well, thanks for your time," said Lucy, hanging up.

She had just finished writing up the interview when she
got a call from Miss Tilley.

"There's entirely too much of this witchcraft nonsense
going on," she said. "Every day there's another bit of trash
blowing about on my lawn."

"It's Ike Stoughton. Since Ted won't print his letters, he's
distributing them himself."

"I don't like it one bit," complained Miss Tilley. "Have
you read the latest one?"

"They're all the same, aren't they?" asked Lucy dismis-
sively.

"No, they're getting increasingly violent. This one has a
drawing of a witch being burned at the stake—it looks to me

to be a copy of a medieval woodblock. It's quite shocking, really."

"He's obsessed. He blames his wife's death, even the cyclone, on witchcraft. He won't listen to reason, so I guess we just have to wait until he gets tired of getting no reaction and gives up."

"I wouldn't say he's not getting any reaction," snapped Miss Tilley. "It seems to me that people are getting all jeezled up and anxious. It worries me. I'm especially worried about Rebecca."

"I've been keeping an eye on her, like you asked," said Lucy. "She's not at all concerned."

"Well she should be!" exclaimed Miss Tilley. "My neighbor spent all morning putting empty bottles on the branches of his Rose of Sharon bush—and he's a science teacher at the high school!"

"Bottles?" asked Lucy.

"To trap witches—don't you know anything?"

"I didn't know that," admitted Lucy. "Maybe we should get a photo."

"Maybe the *Pennysaver* should start covering this and let people know how stupid they're being," snapped Miss Tilley.

"Well, this week Ted is running an editorial—" began Lucy, but Miss Tilley interrupted her.

"Let me talk to that boss of yours. I want to give him a piece of my mind."

But when Lucy reached for the button to transfer the call, Ted was already on his feet and heading for the door. "Coward!" she hissed, covering the receiver. Removing her hand, she told Miss Tilley that he'd been called away from his desk. "Would you like to leave a message on his voice mail?" she asked.

"You bet I do!" snapped Miss Tilley.

It was later than usual when Lucy left the office that afternoon, and she was hurrying to her car when she heard someone calling her name. Stopping in her tracks and turning around, she saw Emily Miller waving and hurrying up the sidewalk, her wrinkled cheeks pink with exertion.

Since Emily was well into her eighties, Lucy didn't want her to overexert herself and trotted down the sidewalk to meet her. "Take your time," she urged. "I won't run away."

"I'm so glad I caught you," panted Emily. "I have big news about the Josiah Hopkins House."

Lucy knew Emily was a stalwart member of the historical society that had restored the town's oldest house as a museum. She also knew the society was chronically short of money and always looking for funding. "A big grant?" she asked.

"No. Unfortunately. But we have some new volunteers, and we're expanding our hours."

"Terrific," said Lucy. "I'll run a short in the paper. What are they?"

"We're now open from eleven to one on Tuesdays, Thursdays, and Saturdays."

"Got it," said Lucy, jotting down the information. "I'll make sure it gets in this week's issue."

"Good." Emily gave a thoughtful nod. "What about these flyers that are everywhere? All anybody seems to talk about is witchcraft."

"Ted's running an editorial, calling for tolerance," said Lucy. "He's hoping it will cool things down."

"I hope it works." Emily leaned closer. "In olden times, people would probably have taken me for a witch, and my sister too. We're old crones, after all."

Lucy smiled at the sweet-faced, white-haired woman who barely came up to her shoulder. "Oh, I don't think so. You're much too nice."

"Lots of nice old ladies got hanged or burned at the stake or drowned," said Emily. "Especially if they happened to have a disagreement with their neighbors."

"Those days are long gone," said Lucy. "Nowadays, people understand that witchcraft is simply a religion. The believers worship nature, that's all. There's nothing sinister about it."

"So you don't believe witches have special powers?"

"No. Do you?" asked Lucy.

"I'm not sure," confessed Emily. "I think it might be like electricity, or the telephone. I don't have the faintest idea how they work, but I know that they do. I think it might be like that with witchcraft. There are forces out there that maybe I don't understand and I'm not even aware of, but some people are sensitive to them. It's like my father, who had a terrific sense of smell. He could smell rain and snow and predict the weather. I never could. I was always amazed when he'd announce snow was coming and a while later the flakes would start to fall."

"Was your father a witch?"

Emily laughed. "My mother used to say he was a devil, but she never called him a witch."

Lucy was still smiling when she said good-bye to Emily and got in the car. The little delay meant she was later than ever, but she decided to take the long way home, anyway, just so she could tell Miss Tilley that she'd checked on Rebecca. She was driving with only half her mind on the road, thinking instead of what would be quick and easy for supper. Spaghetti again? Spanish rice? Soup and sandwiches? She could just imagine Bill's reaction when she informed him it was tuna melts and chowder—again. So when she came around the bend, the last thing she expected to see was a large sign announcing the latest Compass Construction project, the soon-to-be-built Lighthouse Point Mall.

Turning in the drive, she found Rebecca feeding her chickens.

"When did the sign go up?" asked Lucy, after exchanging greetings.

"Yesterday," said Rebecca, scattering a handful of cracked corn on the ground for the birds that were gathering around her. It could have been a scene straight from a story book, thought Lucy, smiling at Rebecca's long, old-fashioned calico dress, her bare feet, and her straw bonnet. And then something caught her eye and she turned her head, seeing the crudely drawn pentagram painted in garish red paint on Rebecca's front door.

"When did that happen?" she asked, horrified.

"Sometime last night," said Rebecca. "I found it this morning."

"Are you all right?" asked Lucy.

"I'm fine," said Rebecca.

"Did you call the police?"

"Why would I do that?"

"It's a crime—and it might mean you're in danger."

Rebecca tossed the last of the feed on the ground and shrugged. "Life is dangerous," she said with a smile. "Now, what can I get you? I've got some nice broilers I just killed." She smacked her lips. "Yummy with a sprinkling of my herbes de Provence."

"Okay," said Lucy, reaching for her wallet. At least the problem of what to have for dinner was solved.

Back in her car, she impulsively decided to stop at the Stoughton homestead. She suspected Ike or his boys had painted the pentagram on Rebecca's door, and she wanted to find out for sure. When Ike opened the door, however, she was so shocked by his changed appearance that she changed her mind about confronting him.

"What brings you here?" he asked. He'd lost weight, his ruddy cheeks had paled, and he looked beyond tired, as if standing was almost too much effort.

"I just wanted to ask if there's anything I can do for you? I know it's a hard time," she said.

"We're doing okay," he said, speaking with effort.

"How's Abby?" asked Lucy.

"As well as can be expected," he said, swallowing hard.

It was clearly not a good time for a social call, and Lucy decided to make it short.

"There's been some vandalism in the neighborhood," she said. "Someone painted a pentagram on Rebecca Wardwell's door."

"Good. It's about time people learned that she's a witch too. Tickling trout. Concocting potions. Hexing people."

"She does seem to have some amazing abilities," said Lucy, defending Rebecca. "But there is not an evil bone in her body."

Ike shook his head. "Why won't you believe what's happening? It's right in front of you, right now, but you refuse to see it. Look around," he said with an abrupt wave of his arm. "It's all gone to hell: the garden, the house, even the goats have gone dry."

Lucy knew it was true. The homestead that was so tidy and promising in June now had a derelict, shabby air. The only thing that seemed to be thriving was the belladonna plant, which was bigger and greener than ever.

Ike continued, squinting at her. "Maybe you're in league with that witch."

It was definitely time to go, thought Lucy. "Not me, and not my girls," she said. "If there's anything we can do to help, please give me a call."

"I can't think of anything," he said, closing the door.

Lucy continued on her way, clattering over the temporary steel bridge and onto Red Top Road, eager to get home and stick the chicken in the oven. Throw in some potatoes and make a salad and she'd have a really nice supper. Maybe she even had a bottle of white wine. A chilled glass of wine would be awfully nice, she was thinking when the house came into view and she flicked on her turn signal. She had to wait for a truck to pass before making the left turn into the driveway; then the road was clear, and she aimed the car for the drive, checking the flag on the mailbox to see if anybody had collected the mail. The flag was down, she saw, and partially covered the angry red pentagram that had been drawn there.

CHAPTER EIGHTEEN

Lucy stood beside the mailbox, staring at the nasty figure of a five-pointed star inside a circle. Was it a joke? Or did it mean something more sinister? Had she—or worse, the girls—been identified as witches? Was it a warning? A threat? Or just a prank? She didn't have a clue, but she sure didn't like it, she decided as she yanked the door down and pulled out the mail. For once, she was relieved to find nothing but a couple of bills. Bills she could handle.

On Thursday, when she met Rachel, Pam, and Sue at Jake's for breakfast, Lucy asked if anybody else had been vandalized. It turned out that she was the only one.

"Maybe it's because Diana was staying with you," suggested Rachel. "I wouldn't worry about it."

"So far they've popped up at Diana's shop, Rebecca Wardwell's place, and my mailbox," said Lucy. "Have you seen them anywhere else?"

Her question was met with blank looks and shakes of the head.

"Now I'm getting worried," said Lucy. "Why would anybody think I'm a witch?"

"Your personality?" suggested Sue, attempting a joke.

Nobody laughed.

"Maybe you should report it to the police," suggested Pam.

"Maybe I will," agreed Lucy.

"Well, speaking of witches," began Pam, just as their food arrived, "we have really got to get serious about the Halloween Party. It's only ten weeks away, and you know how time flies once school starts again."

There was a long silence as they dove into their plates of food.

"I see you're all brimming with excitement and full of ideas," said Pam, biting into a piece of toast.

"Diana offered to tell fortunes," said Sue, sipping the black coffee that was all she ever ordered.

"I don't know if we can count on her," said Lucy, stabbing an egg yolk with her fork so it oozed over the corned-beef hash. "She's left town and I don't think she's coming back until this witch business is settled."

"I can tell fortunes," said Rachel, spooning up her oatmeal. "How hard can it be? I'll dress like a gypsy and make some stuff up in advance. You will do well on your spelling test if you study hard, stuff like that."

"That'll amaze and astound them," said Sue sarcastically, setting down her cup. "To tell the truth, I'm not sure we should go ahead with the party considering the current atmosphere. I've had parents complain about some of the books we have at Little Prodigies, even classics like *Strega Nonna*."

"I love that book," exclaimed Rachel.

Pam set her jaw and slapped her palm on the table. "If they don't want to celebrate Halloween, they don't have to come to the party. It's that simple."

"These days it's never that simple," said Sue with a sigh. "Some people feel they have to impose their beliefs on everybody else."

"So what are we going to do?" demanded Pam. "Are we going ahead with the party or what?"

"I say let's go for it," said Lucy. "I'm not going to let Ike Stoughton—"

"You don't know it was Ike," protested Rachel.

"Maybe he did or didn't paint the pentagrams, but he is responsible for getting everybody all upset about witches," said Pam.

"As I was saying," continued Lucy, "I think we should continue celebrating Halloween just as we always have."

"That's the spirit!" exclaimed Pam, who had been a cheerleader in high school.

"I agree," chimed in Rachel.

"Well, I'm certainly not going to be a spoilsport," said Sue. "So who's going to make the Beastly Bug cookies?"

When Lucy left, she'd not only agreed to make six dozen Beastly Bug cookies, two dozen cupcakes, and a dozen marzipan eyeballs, but she had also promised to ask Peter Symonds if he would make balloon animals, as he had in the past when he worked as Malcolm's assistant in the magic show.

That was the first thing she did when she got to work, after greeting Phyllis and looking over a copy of this week's issue, fresh from the printer.

"Any big mistakes? Angry phone calls?" she asked Phyllis.

"Not so far, but His Nibs hasn't come in yet." She was referring to Ted, who always seemed to find some error that he could berate Lucy and Phyllis about.

Taking advantage of the calm before he arrived, Lucy flipped through her Rolodex until she found Symonds's number. He picked up on the first ring.

"This is Lucy Stone, from the *Pennysaver*," she began.

"I didn't have anything to say to the cops, and I don't have anything to say to you," he snapped.

This was not a promising start. "I'm not—" protested Lucy, but he interrupted her.

"And don't come around here, okay? I saw those pictures you took without my permission."

Lucy had to think a minute before she remembered the before-and-after photos she took of the flood in his back-yard. "I took those pictures from the road. I didn't trespass," she said, defending herself. "And I did knock on your door to let you know, but you weren't home."

"I don't want you coming around my place," he said. "Don't do it again, okay?"

"I don't know that I can promise that," said Lucy. "What if there's a new development in Malcolm's death?"

"Has there been a new development?" he demanded.

"No, not that I know of," admitted Lucy. "But say they find his killer—wouldn't you want to make a comment? He was your friend and partner for quite a few years, wasn't he?" She paused for breath. "But that's not why I called," she began, attempting to turn the conversation back to her original purpose, which was asking him to make balloon animals at the party.

"I'm not talking to you anymore," said Symonds, ending the call.

Stunned, Lucy sat at her desk for a minute or two before she replaced the receiver on the phone. One thing was clear—Symonds was not in a party mood. "That was weird," she finally said.

"What was?" asked Phyllis, crossing the office with a stack of news releases for Lucy.

Lucy shrugged. "Oh, nothing, I guess. Just a disgruntled reader."

"Well don't tell Ted about it, okay?" said Phyllis, setting the stack down on Lucy's desk. "These ought to keep you busy for a while."

"So it would seem," agreed Lucy, but as she typed in the calendar listings for ham-and-bean suppers and yoga classes and nature talks at the bird sanctuary, her mind kept returning to Symonds. What had gotten into him, she wondered, to change his attitude? Had the cops been questioning him? She assumed they'd paid him a visit when Malcolm's body was discovered, but had they made a repeat visit?

When she left work, Lucy headed over to Diana's place to check that everything was okay. The girls had taken the cat to Friends of Animals, finding it easier to care for him there. Piewocket was a big hit with the day campers and seemed to be having the time of his life. Lucy had gotten into the habit of stopping at Diana's every couple of days, making sure the apartment and store were secure and watering the house plants, which had been moved outside onto a shady deck. She didn't have time to tend the vegetable garden, but she had installed a drip hose and picked the tomatoes and squash as they ripened.

As she approached, she braced herself for an unpleasant discovery—at the very least, she expected the pentagram would have reappeared on Diana's door. But there was nothing to mar the fresh coat of paint Diana had put on before she left for Arizona, and the doors and windows were all locked tight.

Lucy climbed the outside stairs that led to the deck and gently hosed down the plants, which were thriving in the fresh air and sunshine. A Christmas cactus would definitely need repotting soon, she decided, and that pothos would have to be cut back before it could return inside. Another tall plant had tipped over, becoming so top heavy that its root system couldn't support it. As she straightened it up, Lucy recognized it as a belladonna plant, similar to the one Rebecca had, and decided to take it home and give it a bigger pot.

"*Belladonna,* beautiful lady, you must have some fine new clothes," said Lucy. She was putting the plant in the back of her station wagon when a Popsicle stick identifying the plant fell out. She happened to glance at it as she replaced it in the pot and noticed it read DEADLY NIGHTSHADE, not belladonna. She immediately pulled out her cell phone, intending to call Rebecca Wardwell, then remembered with annoyance that the witch didn't have a telephone. She would have to drive over there on the way home.

Rebecca was just wrapping up a sale when Lucy arrived, and she waited until the transaction was completed and the customer had left before she asked Rebecca if deadly nightshade and belladonna were the same plant.

"Yes, they are," said Rebecca.

"Why didn't you tell me that before?" demanded Lucy. "Deadly nightshade is poisonous!"

Rebecca shrugged. "I thought you knew. Besides, lots of plants are poisonous. Take philodendron, for example, or mistletoe. And there's plenty worse than those. Like monkshood."

Lucy was looking at Rebecca with new eyes. Instead of the sweet eccentric who dressed in quaint clothes, she was seeing a woman who stubbornly marched to her own drummer and had little thought for others.

"You should have told me when I admired the plant," said Lucy.

"Despite its name, it's very rarely deadly," said Rebecca, folding her hands in front of herself.

But Lucy wasn't listening. She was already heading back to her car, planning to toss the plant on the compost heap as soon as she got home. But first she had to pick up the girls at Friends of Animals.

"Don't touch that plant!" she warned Zoe when she opened the rear door.

"Why not?" asked Zoe as she slid onto the seat and fastened her seat belt.

"It's poisonous! I didn't know and I was going to repot it for Diana."

"What are you going to do with it now?" asked Sara, who was riding shotgun.

"I'm going to throw it out," declared Lucy.

Zoe furrowed her brows, studying the plant on the seat beside her. "Mom, it's a plant. It can't jump up and strangle you or anything."

"Yeah, Mom," said Sara. "Don't you think you're being kind of mean? It is a living thing, after all, part of the circle of life."

"Circle of death is more like it," muttered Lucy. "It's called deadly nightshade."

"Are you sure, Mom?" asked Sara.

"Yes, I'm sure. I even asked Rebecca Wardwell. And why are you questioning me?"

"Oh, no reason," said Sara, who was busy texting on her cell phone. "Oh, phooey," she declared, snapping the phone shut.

"Bad news?" asked Lucy.

"Yeah. Renee and Sassie and I were going to go over to Abby's tonight to try and cheer her up. She's been awfully depressed since her mother died, and they don't have TV, and she isn't allowed to have a cell phone, even. But we figured we could at least visit at her place, so her father could keep an eye on us and see that we're really good kids."

"Sounds like a plan," said Lucy, amazed at how kind and thoughtful kids could be. At the same time, she was uneasy about letting the girls spend time at the Stoughton house.

"Yeah, well, she's sick and we can't go over."

"That's too bad. What's she got? A summer cold?"

"I don't know. Sassie didn't say. She just got a call from Abby's father calling it off."

"I bet she's not even sick," said Zoe, piping up in the backseat.

"Yeah," agreed Sara as Lucy turned into the driveway. "Her father probably figured we'd corrupt her or something."

* * *

But as the last days of summer passed and the first day of school drew closer, Abby didn't get better, and when school finally reopened, Abby was absent. For the first few weeks, Sara kept her up to date on homework and reading assignments, but the school eventually appointed Lydia Volpe, a retired teacher, to tutor her at home.

One day in late September, Lucy ran into Lydia in the supermarket and asked how Abby was doing.

Lydia pursed her lips and shook her head, her dark brown eyes enormous. "She's not improving," she whispered.

"What does the doctor say?"

"The father doesn't believe in medicine, you know. The superintendent is threatening to contact social services, to make him take her to the doctor." She shrugged. "I've never been in a situation like this before. Usually the family is happy to have me, but not these people. They treat me like I'm carrying typhoid or something."

"They lost the mother, you know," said Lucy, looking for an explanation.

"They're going to lose this girl, too, if somebody doesn't intervene," said Lydia. "She's not eating, only drinks this herbal tea." She clucked her tongue. "It's terrible. She's wasting away." Lydia leaned forward, whispering in Lucy's ear, "I think she has anorexia."

"That's awful," said Lucy, truly shocked. "I had no idea."

"God forgive me," said Lydia, casting her enormous eyes heavenward. "I hate to go there. I dread seeing her all skin and bones like this. I have to make myself go. I tell myself that I'm her only hope." She shook her head. "I hope the authorities intervene soon."

"Me too," said Lucy, deeply troubled. As she finished her shopping and loaded the car, she wondered about Ike and how her opinion of him had changed. When he had first walked into the *Pennysaver* office that day in June, she took him for a regular guy and welcomed him as a neighbor.

Then, when she saw him and his family at the cookout, she began to suspect he was a domestic tyrant and that image grew stronger when she learned how Abby and Miriam feared him. She'd discovered his religious bent when the bridge was carried away by the flood and when he began the campaign against witchcraft. More recently, however, she'd begun to feel sorry for him, seeing how he grieved for his wife and began neglecting his property and his appearance. But now that Abby was seriously ill, and he was still refusing to seek medical help for her, she was beginning to suspect that Ike was mentally ill. Taken together, the summer's events seemed to point to a deepening disconnect with reality. She had to agree with Lydia that the sooner the school authorities intervened, the better.

That night, she called Diana at her mother's home in Arizona.

"I was just going to call you!" exclaimed Diana. "I'm coming back. I can't miss Samhain with the coven."

"Samhain?"

"It's our new year, but you know it as Halloween."

"Oh," said Lucy. "I suppose you'll all be riding around on broomsticks."

"Not quite." Diana laughed. "But it is the most important holiday in the Wiccan calendar, and Lady Sybil has called me to help the coven prepare for it. I also promised to help Pam with the kids' party."

"I thought you'd forgotten," said Lucy.

"Nope. I'm on it. I've got all sorts of ideas for games and decorations."

"That's terrific," said Lucy. "I'm glad you're coming home. I don't know if you're aware that Abby Stoughton is seriously ill. . . ."

"No! How long has this been going on?"

"Since before school began. Lydia Volpe's been tutoring her, and she says the situation is very bad, even life-threatening—Abby refuses to eat. They're probably going to take the father to court."

"This is awful!"

"I know. I was hoping you could do something. I know you're very fond of Abby."

"I am! We correspond, you know, through Lydia. She hides the letters in Abby's schoolwork."

"But you didn't know she was sick?"

"Not a word. She never mentioned it."

"What did she write about?" asked Lucy.

"How much she missed the coven, advice on being a solitaire, how much she hates her brothers, things like that."

"Wow," said Lucy, amazed by Abby's behavior. "So when are you coming home?"

"As soon as I can get a flight," promised Diana. "And believe me, nothing is going to keep me from seeing that girl, even if I have to use my six-guns and go in with both barrels blazing!"

As she ended the call, Lucy hoped she'd done the right thing by calling Diana, but she wasn't convinced. Hadn't her mother always said the path to hell was paved with good intentions? Was this one of those times?

CHAPTER NINETEEN

Lucy knew when a story had legs and would run, and Lydia's tip-off about the school system taking Ike Stoughton to court was one of those stories that was full of human interest. Depending on your point of view, it pitted a stern father against a helpless child, or it pitted a taxpaying citizen against a meddlesome government bureaucracy. Did a parent have the right to impose his beliefs on a child, even when it was detrimental to the child's safety and well-being? And how far could society, represented here by the school system, intrude into the privileged sanctity of the home? These were all legitimate questions that would get strong reactions from readers, but Lucy still felt like a muckraker when she called the superintendent's office and asked if the school department was going to take Ike Stoughton to court.

"You know I can't comment on an individual student," said Pete Winslow. "Student records are confidential. Strictly confidential. But I can tell you this," he began, warming to his subject. "We have a strict attendance policy in the Tinker's Cove school system, and we take absences, especially extended absences, very seriously."

Lucy suspected the superintendent wanted to get the word out and was issuing a warning to Ike as well as to any other delinquent families.

"If a student must be absent due to illness for more than a week, we require a doctor's note. If there is no note, the student is considered a truant, and we will prosecute both the student and the responsible—or perhaps I should say irresponsible—parent or guardian."

"So this is simply a matter of truancy? You don't intervene if you suspect abuse?" asked Lucy.

"Frankly, that's the reason for the doctor's note. We want to make sure that a child who cannot come to school is seen by a medical professional. You'd be surprised how many abuse cases are discovered this way."

Actually, Lucy wouldn't be surprised. She'd been a reporter for a long time, and she knew more than she wanted to about domestic abuse. "So is the school department currently pursuing any truancy cases?" she asked.

"Oh, all the time," said Winslow.

"In the courts?" she asked.

"If we have to, we will. There's a process, of course. We start with the guidance counselor. If that doesn't improve matters, we go on to the truant officer, and if he can't make any headway, we refer the case to the district attorney."

"So any case that went to court would be a public record?" asked Lucy.

"Not if the truant is a minor," said Winslow. "Then the file is sealed."

"Oh," said Lucy, disappointed.

"We really try to be sensitive," said Winslow, sounding for the first time like a human being instead of reciting administrative jargon. "We don't want to get people in trouble. All we want, you know, is what's best for the student. A lot of the time we're the only ones looking out for the kid; we're the only ones who can step in and protect the child."

"Have you seen an uptick in abuse?" asked Lucy. "Considering the economy, the high gas and food prices, the foreclosures?"

"These are difficult times for a lot of our families," said Winslow. "Andy French, the business manager, can give you the latest figures on the school lunch program."

Lucy took the hint. "Thanks for your time," she said as an instant message from Phyllis appeared on her computer screen, advising her that there were a large number of legal ads this week.

She opened the file and discovered at least twelve foreclosure notices. Scanning through them, she recognized quite a few names. Some were people whose families had lived in town for generations, and others were newcomers, often immigrants, who'd originally come to Maine as summer workers and stayed on. The very last announcement was a shocker, however: Peter Symonds. No wonder he'd been so angry with her; she'd be angry, too, if she was about to lose her home.

Acting on impulse, she called the police station and asked for her old friend Barney Culpepper.

"Just a follow-up," she began, staring at Symonds's foreclosure notice on her screen. "Has there been any progress in the Malebranche case? You know, the guy who was burned."

"Don't remind me. I think about that poor bastard every day."

"So I guess that means you're not any closer to solving it?"

"You said it."

"It's been a long time. . . ."

"Almost four months."

"I see that his assistant, you know, the guy who made the balloon animals, is losing his house."

"That's not surprising. He lost his job, after all, when Malebranche died." Barney sighed. "I don't suppose there's much call for magician's assistants. It's kind of a specialized thing."

"I suppose not," admitted Lucy. "You must have questioned him, right? He's kind of an oddball."

"That doesn't make him a murderer," chided Barney. "I'm sure he was questioned pretty thoroughly. I never heard him mentioned as a suspect."

Lucy's ears pricked up. "Who was mentioned?" she asked.

"You know I can't tell you that, but off the record, I heard they took a long, hard look at the members of that coven, including your buddy Diana. There was a certain amount of jealousy among the members, and there were some jokes about that Lady Sybil."

Lucy was incredulous. "Was she a suspect?"

Barney was noncommittal. "They all came up clean—and this is strictly off the record, mind you."

"I know. I'm just killing time here, having a nice chat, looking for deep background, as we call it in the news business. Say, do you happen to know who's the truant officer?"

"That would be me."

"I didn't know that," she said.

"Oh, yeah," he replied. "It's not my favorite job. I like the community outreach part of my job a lot better." As community outreach officer, Barney conducted home-safety workshops for senior citizens, organized a bike-safety program for kids every spring, and issued warnings about the danger of fireworks in July and about Christmas tree fires in December. Soon he'd be visiting classes in the elementary school to remind students to wear reflective clothing when they went trick-or-treating and to make sure their parents examined their candy before they ate it.

"I heard a rumor that the school department is taking Ike Stoughton to court because Abby's been out of school for over a month with no doctor's note."

"Lucy, for Pete's sake! I can't talk about that."

"So it's true," said Lucy.

"You didn't hear it from me," said Barney.

"You don't happen to know the court date, do you?"

"What good would that do you? It's a closed hearing."

"If I just happened to be there, in the lobby, I could ask some questions."

"Dinner, at your place?" said Barney, his voice suddenly quite loud.

"What the . . . ?" asked Lucy, puzzled.

"Oh, sorry, we can't make it October fifteenth. Marge's sister is visiting."

Lucy suddenly got it; Barney was afraid somebody was listening to his conversation. "You're a peach!" she said, marking the date in her calendar.

When she left work, Lucy noticed that Halloween decorations were appearing on Main Street. Many of the merchants had filled window boxes and planters with autumn arrangements of chrysanthemums, winter kale, gourds, and pumpkins. The Chamber of Commerce offered a prize every year for the best display of harvest figures, and they were also starting to appear—scarecrow-like figures made from old clothes stuffed with straw—in various and humorous poses. One real estate company had blown up a large photograph of all the agents, then created caricature figures that were arranged in the same poses as the people in the photo. A restaurant had set out a scantily clad female figure in a bikini, lounging in an inviting position on the bench used in summer by tourists waiting for tables, and the Queen Victoria Inn had produced a version of their namesake, complete with voluminous black skirts, shawl, lace cap, and double chin and had seated her in one of the porch rockers.

Feeling somewhat ashamed that the barrel out by the mailbox was still sporting the rather withered impatiens she'd planted last May, Lucy turned in at the IGA, where she'd seen a big crate of pumpkins. She was looking them over, trying to decide whether one big one would be better than several small ones, when she spotted Ike Stoughton coming out with a cart full of grocery bags. It seemed as if pushing the cart took every bit of energy he could muster.

"Howdy, neighbor," she said in a voice she hoped sounded cheerful and friendly.

"Oh, hi," he replied, as if he'd been lost in his thoughts. "How are you?"

"You know how it is," she said conversationally. "School's started, and the girls have cheerleading and field hockey. All of a sudden we're always on the go." She paused. "I heard Abby's been too sick to go to school."

"We're praying for her recovery," he said, glancing toward heaven. "Good is greater than evil," he declared, sounding almost like the Ike of old.

"Well, you've certainly had a difficult time lately," said Lucy. "Perhaps your luck will change. After all, bad things come in threes."

Ike glared at her. "That's Devil talk! I'd be careful if I were you."

"I didn't mean any harm," said Lucy, stunned. "It's just a turn of phrase." She paused, wondering whether or not to say what she was thinking, then decided to go for it. "My girls would love to visit Abby, if she's well enough."

"Maybe sometime," said Ike noncommittally, beginning to push his cart toward the parking lot. "Well, nice seeing you," he said. "Say hi to Bill for me."

"Will do," said Lucy, watching as he made his way across the parking lot, walking like a very old man. His body language told it all, thought Lucy. Ike Stoughton was a troubled man. Or maybe, the thought flitted through her mind unbidden, a man with a guilty conscience.

Back at home, Lucy was unloading the car and trying to arrange the pumpkins in a pleasing way in the whiskey-barrel planter when Sara came running down the driveway, carrying the cordless phone. "It's Diana, Mom," she was yelling. "She's at the airport and wants to know if you can pick her up."

"Right now?" asked Lucy, who was thinking it was time to start cooking dinner.

"Yeah, right now. It won't take long. Can I come too?"

Lucy was struggling with a small pumpkin that didn't want to stay put and was threatening to roll out of the barrel. "Can't she catch a bus?"

Sara had her hand over the mouthpiece. "That's not very nice, Mom," she hissed. "She's a friend. You don't make friends take the bus."

This was a new one to Lucy, but she figured Bill could get something to eat over at Toby and Molly's. Zoe, she knew, would insist on coming along to the airport. "Okay," she said, letting go of the pumpkin, which amazed her by staying in place. Her decision must have appeased the many and various natural forces in the universe. Either that or she was a pumpkin whisperer, able to tame even the most unruly pumpkin.

Lucy's whimsical mood was contagious, and she and the girls were in high spirits as they drove to the airport, fueled by a stop at Mickey D's for burgers, fries, and shakes. The mile markers sped by as they sang along to the Beatles songs on the oldies station, enjoying an unexpected break in their everyday routine. The girls chattered on about school and friends. Lucy listened with one ear, picking up the news that Mrs. Gruber was pregnant, Kyle Saperstein had a crush on Sassie but she told him her horse had to come first, and Tommy Stanton had finally made the varsity football team.

"He's really filled out," reported Sara. "He's looking go-od. I'm hoping he'll ask me to the Halloween Hoedown."

"You could ask him," suggested Lucy.

Zoe didn't approve. "No, she can't, Mom."

"Sure she can—haven't you heard of women's lib? Aren't you a feminist?"

Zoe fell silent, thinking this over as they turned onto the airport road and approached the terminal. Diana was standing outside, along with an enormous roller suitcase, and the girls immediately began shrieking and waving as Lucy braked to a stop and hopped out. They had only a minute, because of security rules, so quick hugs were exchanged, the suitcase was hoisted into the back, Sara hopped out of the front seat, and into the back, Diana took the front seat, and off they went.

"How was your flight?" asked Lucy.

"Don't ask—a nightmare, but that's beside the point. How's Abby?"

"We're not allowed to visit," said Sara.

"Well, we'll see about that," said Diana, drumming her fingers on her lap.

"You better be careful," advised Lucy. "Ike isn't going to welcome any interference, especially from you. He thinks you hexed him. He blames you for all his troubles."

"That's ridiculous," said Diana, fingering a turquoise and silver squash blossom necklace. "But I did pick up a few tricks in Arizona, from a very old, very wise shaman. I plan to stir things up a bit."

"So mote it be," said Lucy.

V

SPIRIT

Our planet spins in Nature's gyre,
Water, Air, Earth and Fire,
Tho mighty be these elements four,
'Tis Spirit rules forevermore.

CHAPTER TWENTY

L ucy couldn't decide whether it was a coincidence or not, but soon after Diana's return, she seemed to notice a new attitude in town. People seemed more cheerful and greeted each other enthusiastically when they happened to meet on the sidewalk, at the hardware store, or at the IGA. Mrs. Mulcahy was telling everyone how the allergies that had been plaguing her all summer had suddenly disappeared, Sally Johanson noticed the rash that had been bothering her husband had magically cleared up, and Molly reported with great relief that little Patrick was now sleeping through the night.

Even the weather was cooperating, as September's warm mugginess gave way to the golden, crisp days of October. One sunny day followed another, and the cloudless blue sky was a luminous backdrop to the changing hues on the mountains, where the tired green foliage was now a blaze of dazzling gold, crimson, and orange.

Festive decorations seemed to appear daily, and the harvest figures that were multiplying like rabbits seemed livelier, almost as if they might rise from the hay bales and old chairs where they were posed and join the fun. Women thronged to Diana's shop, leaving with purple bags clutched tight in their hands and secretive Mona Lisa smiles on their faces. Plans for the party advanced, too, as Rebecca was persuaded to take a turn as a storyteller, and Diana set to work making little black satin protection bags containing herbs for each child.

The one thing that didn't seem to change, however, was a great disappointment to Lucy. Despite Diana's promise to intervene, Abby remained at home, isolated from her friends and completely under the thrall of her father. Ike had even put a stop to Lydia Volpe's tutoring sessions, claiming his daughter was too weak to study. Ike himself seemed to be shrinking, too, and hadn't even made an appearance at the Giant Pumpkin Contest on Columbus Day weekend. Diana was the surprise winner, beating Rebecca's massive 690-pound entry by a mere three pounds. The behemoth had grown largely unattended in her backyard, planted Indian fashion with fish for fertilizer. Now all the giant pumpkin entries were on display in the bandstand on the town common.

The day of Abby's truancy hearing finally rolled around, and when Lucy went to the courthouse, she was shocked at Abby's appearance. The girl was so thin and frail that she had to be pushed into the judge's chambers in a wheelchair, and it was all done so quickly that she wasn't able to question Ike Stoughton, who was accompanied by his dour sons. It was only moments later that an ambulance appeared, and Abby was wheeled out on a gurney and whisked away.

Lucy was considering following the ambulance, which she assumed was going to the state hospital, when Ike exited the courtroom and marched right up to her, trailed by his two boys. This time he had plenty to say.

"This is a travesty!" he exclaimed. "The judge has taken my daughter—MY DAUGHTER—and has committed her to a mental institution. What about the sanctity of the family, the right to privacy? A MAN'S HOME IS HIS CASTLE?

Not anymore, that's for sure, when the state can just come in and take your child away—in violation of your deepest beliefs. WHAT ABOUT RELIGIOUS FREEDOM? What happened to that?"

Behind him, Lucy noticed Pete Winslow, the superintendent of schools, making a hurried exit, clearly only too happy that Ike's attention was elsewhere. But he didn't make the clean getaway he was hoping for; one of the boys noticed him and tapped his father on his arm. Whirling around, he caught sight of Winslow and charged across the lobby to angrily confront him.

"I bet you're real proud of what you've done," he demanded, blocking the doorway. He was gesturing, jabbing at Winslow's chest with an extended forefinger, causing the superintendent to back up to avoid being poked. Winslow was looking every which way for help, but none of the court officers was to be seen, and the handful of people who had been waiting in the lobby were backing away.

"Now, now," he said, trying to placate Ike. "This is for Abby's own good. She needs medical and psycho—"

"Are you saying my daughter is CRAZY? Is that what you think?"

"That isn't the word I would—"

"And I'm neglecting her? You think I don't love her? You think I don't beg her to eat? She's bewitched, I tell you. Bewitched! That witch has cast a spell over my whole family!" Ike's face was red, and he was spraying the superintendent with saliva. Behind him, the two boys seemed only to be waiting for permission from their father to attack Winslow and tear him limb from limb.

Lucy found she was shaking as she tried to write it all down. She was raising her camera to snap a picture when the bailiff finally appeared. She got a good shot of him stepping between the two men, only to receive a jab in the eye from Ike. Then all hell broke loose as he blew a whistle and the other court officials, uniformed bailiffs, and lawyers in suits, all came to his aid. The upshot was that Ike Stoughton was hauled into a courtroom and judged in contempt and confined to the county jail for forty-eight hours without bail. The boys got stiff warnings, even though neither one had thrown a punch.

Lucy followed them when they left the courtroom, pouring on the sympathy in hopes of getting more information and maybe a quote or two.

"I can't believe the judge is sending your father to jail," she began.

"Me neither," said Thomas, who had confusion written all over his face. "What do we do now?"

"Yeah," chimed in Mather. "Dad's in jail and Abby's in the loony bin. And Mom's dead," he added, looking terribly young and sad.

"It's only two days," said Lucy, trying to offer some support. "How long is your sister going to be in the hospital?"

"Two weeks," he replied, shaking his head. "She's not crazy; she's sick, like Mom was."

"They'll do a complete physical, as well as a mental health evaluation," said Lucy.

"And you know what they're going to find, after all their tests and stuff?" demanded Thomas angrily. "Absolutely nothing. Because Dad's right—Abby's been cursed by that witch Diana! She's cursed our whole family!"

"That's not true," said Lucy, but the boys were already walking off, their heads together, as if trying to come up with a course of action.

Lucy reached for her cell phone and called Diana, telling her what had happened and warning her about Stoughton's sons. "They blame you—you need to be careful and watch your back."

"They can't hurt me," said Diana, her voice full of confidence that Lucy felt was entirely unwarranted, "but thanks for the warning."

Lucy ended the call and followed the boys out to the

parking lot, aware that the clock was ticking steadily toward deadline and she had a big story to write. She was starting her car when the boys peeled out of the lot in an oversized pickup truck with the Compass Construction logo on the door.

She wasn't really intending to follow them; it just happened that they were going the same way she was. They were in a hurry, and she was, too, because she had to get back to the office. But when they reached Shiloh and the pickup veered off the main route, Lucy made an impulsive decision to follow it, suspecting she knew where the boys were headed. And sure enough, they followed the familiar route to Compton's big project, out by Malebranche's old place. Except that the magician's house was no longer standing, and a framework of bright new two-by-fours had taken its place.

So the deal had gone through and Malebranche's heir, the magic museum, had sold the property to Compass Construction, just as Fred Stanton had predicted it would. Lucy wasn't surprised, but she felt sad as she made a three-point turn and retraced her route back to the highway and on to Tinker's Cove.

The old Regulator clock on the wall had just struck twelve when Lucy typed the final period and sent the story to Ted. She waited anxiously as he scrolled through it, making a few changes here and there and correcting typos. "Good work," he said when he finished. "This is great reporting." He turned and faced her, narrowing his eyes. "And you just happened to be at the courthouse this morning?"

"I had a tip," she admitted. "But I didn't expect anything like this."

"Again, good work, Lucy. Just goes to show you make your own luck."

"Or unluck," mused Lucy, shutting down her computer. "I hope the Stoughtons understand I was just doing my job."

"If I were you, I'd go see Diana and get one of her repelling spells," advised Phyllis. "I got one and it drove the mice right from my house. And believe me, I tried everything. Traps, bait, a cat, ultrasonic gizmos. None of it worked until I got the spell."

"Somehow I think the Stoughton boys are going to be a lot harder to repel than mice," said Lucy, reaching for her bag and heading for the door. "Especially once their father gets out of jail."

Nevertheless, she decided to pay a visit to Diana, not for a repelling spell but to try and convince her that the Stoughtons really did pose a danger.

"They're going to blame you for everything, you know," said Lucy. "They're convinced you've put a spell on their family. Ike even thinks you cursed his garden and his goats, you know."

"That's just crazy," replied Diana. "The judge only had to take one look at Abby to know that she had to be removed from that house. This committal is exactly what I was hoping would happen," she said, relief in her voice.

"Are you sure you didn't have something to do with this? Did you write to the judge or something?"

"No, not at all." She shook her head, then shrugged. "I did try to visit her, but her father wouldn't let me in the house. Of course, I have been working with incantations and prayers for Abby."

"Did you cast a spell on Ike? I have to say, he wasn't much like himself."

"On the contrary, it sounds like he was very much himself," said Diana. "Strong emotions can shatter that thin veneer of civility men like him hide behind."

Lucy nodded. She'd noticed the same thing many times, when an abuser was challenged. It was the reason cops hated to respond to domestic violence calls—the abuser often turned on them.

"How long will she be in the hospital?" asked Diana.

"The boys said two weeks."

"Oh, good, then she'll be out in time for Samhain."

"Maybe you'd better leave her out of the witch stuff for a while," cautioned Lucy.

Diana raised an eyebrow in shock. "No way," she declared. "That girl needs the craft. The craft will save her."

Lucy was standing at the counter, where a big basket held the protective pouches that Diana was making for the party. She picked one up and fingered it. "What's inside?"

"Some herbs, bay, mulberry and thistle, an acorn—that represents the strength of the sacred oak—a little bit of obsidian. Each child can add a lock of hair or a photo of someone special."

It was odd, but Lucy found she didn't want to return the pouch to the basket. It just felt good in her hand. "Do you mind if I keep this one?" she asked.

"Oh, no, I've got plenty and the girls love making them. Some people wear them on a string round their neck, but I just tuck mine in my bra," said Diana with a saucy smile.

Suddenly Lucy felt silly, and she shoved the pouch into the pocket of her jeans. "Well, thanks," she said. "And remember to be careful."

"You too," said Diana. "Always wear your pouch and it will protect you."

Lucy had hoped the visit to Diana would set her mind at ease, but it only made her worry more. The self-proclaimed witch had returned from her stay in Arizona with increased confidence in her powers, and Lucy wondered what had brought about the change. Diana had mentioned a wise shaman who had taught her some tricks, but Lucy wasn't convinced the shaman's magic was up to the task. Two days in the county lockup weren't likely to improve Ike Stoughton's attitude, and she feared he would come out more determined than ever to get rid of Diana.

When she got home, she tried to settle down with a magazine, taking advantage of the rare opportunity of having some time to herself, but she found herself unable to concentrate on the glossy photos of beautifully decorated homes, the happy smiling people, the well-groomed pets, the impossibly complicated recipes. Hopping to her feet, she grabbed the leash and before she even whistled, Libby was prancing at the door, ready for a walk.

"It's too nice a day to be stuck inside," she said, and Libby agreed, enthusiastically wagging her tail.

The woods were beautiful, almost surreal, as sunlight filtered through the lemon-yellow leaves of the maples. Fallen leaves carpeted the old logging trail that meandered behind their house, a kaleidoscope of vibrant red and yellow that rustled underfoot. Bunches of mushrooms sprouted here and there; Lucy always wished she could tell which ones were safe to eat. Clusters of Indian pipes dotted the ground, too, and enormous tree fungi grew on fallen trees. Lucy remembered how the kids used to collect them and draw pictures on them; if you scraped the flesh with a sharp point, your design would turn brown as the fungus dried. The dried fungi lasted forever, and Lucy bet she could find some of those childish artworks tucked away in the cabinets in the family room if she bothered to look.

She was thinking of the fungi and all the other little projects she'd devised to entertain the kids on rainy summer days: little dolls made from pinecones, leaf collages embellished with macaroni and glitter, Popsicle-stick boxes trimmed with acorns, and always the endless bowls of popcorn and pans of fudge served up to fuel her little artists' flagging inspiration. Those had been crazy years, but she had enjoyed them, and she was thinking about how much fun it would be to introduce Patrick to some of these crafty projects when he was older when her attention was caught by Libby's sharp bark.

Looking up from the path, she shuddered with the realization that she'd come once again to the clearing where Malebranche had died. Here, she noticed, the fiery colors of autumn were subdued, the few leaves that remained on the

The phone itself was so grimy that the buttons on the keypad stuck when she began to dial home. She'd punched in only the first three numbers when she sensed someone behind her. She was turning to see who it was when she was knocked to the floor by a terrific blow to the head. The pain was overwhelming, and she was trying to struggle to her feet when everything went black.

CHAPTER TWENTY-FOUR

Something vile and nauseatingly sweet was in her mouth, and she retched, spitting it out. Her head hurt like hell, and she couldn't see straight—shapes and colors were whirling around her. The trees were dancing against the sky, orange flames were leaping upward, and figures dressed in purple and green and yellow came and went, circling around her. She wanted to lie down but she couldn't move; she was uncomfortably upright. She tried to stretch and found her hands were fastened to her sides. Shaking her head and blinking once or twice, she realized she was tied back-to-back with someone else.

"Wha . . . ?" she managed before slumping forward.

"Lucy! Wake up! It's me, Diana!"

Lucy raised her head; it felt like it was full of lead. "Unh?"

"We've got to get out of here!" hissed Diana, and Lucy felt her wriggling and pulling at the ropes that bound them together. "They're going to sacrifice us."

Lucy was suddenly alert, energized by adrenaline. This was no dream, no nightmare. She was really out in the woods, tied to Diana. She could feel the chilly night air and the dampness on her chest. She smelled bile and wood smoke.

Members of the coven were standing in a circle around them, some with drums, and everyone was chanting. Even Abby was there, pale in the firelight. Lady Sybil was standing at a crude altar, lighting a candle.

> *"Now the tired year comes to its close,*
> *We remember our dying King,*
> *His light is faded and weak,*
> *The birds themselves take wing."*

The group responded together, repeating the phrase "So mote it be" three times. Then Lady Sybil lit another candle.

> *"Well we know this eternal truth*
> *Without death there is no birth.*
> *At Samhain comes the Death Crone*
> *Renewing life upon the earth."*

That bit about the Death Crone didn't sound good, and Lucy felt Diana renew her squirming efforts to loosen the ropes. Her vision was clearer now, and she saw they were in the same clearing where she found Malebranche's burned body. Her gaze turned to the charred tree and she flinched at the sight. Firewood had been piled at its base, and Symonds's red gas can stood alongside.

"C'mon, Lucy," coaxed Diana. "We have to free ourselves NOW."

Lady Sybil now assumed the goddess pose, planting her legs apart and raising her arms to the full moon with the wand in one hand and the athame in the other, as Peter went around the circle, offering a goblet to each member of the coven to sip in turn.

"Who do you think you are? I'm the leader of this coven, a high priestess, and I demand to be released!" declared Diana, her eyes flashing in the firelight as she strained against the rope.

"I am acting for the coven," said Lady Sybil.

"Is this true?" demanded Diana, looking from one member to another and receiving nods. Only Abby seemed to hesitate, looking away and avoiding Diana's gaze before giving her chin a quick jerk.

"We have agreed that we desire a change in leadership," said Symonds, stepping forward.

"All right," said Diana. "I certainly understand. I was away too long. I may have erred. But I demand a trial—"

"We have prepared an indictment," said Symonds, producing a rolled-up sheet of parchment with a flourish. "We believe you and Lord Malebranche have violated the ordains and must be punished."

"That's absurd," scoffed Diana. "And as you well know, the ordains specify that I must be allowed to defend myself."

"Of course," said Lady Sybil, giving Symonds a nod. "Read the first accusation."

Symonds unrolled the parchment and cleared his voice. "The first charge is failing to consult all members before instituting a change in ritual, to wit, the policy of encouraging members to participate in ritual ceremonies skyclad."

"But that was optional," protested Diana.

"It made some members uncomfortable," said Symonds.

"And many of us abhorred the decision to bring sexual practices into the sacred rituals," added Lady Sybil.

"That was Lord Malebranche's idea—"

"For which he was punished."

Lucy could feel a deep shudder run through Diana's body.

"Which brings us to your next offense," said Lady Sybil. "Read it."

Symonds obeyed, reading from the scroll. "You have violated the sacred trust of the coven by sharing secrets about rites, beliefs, and practices with outsiders."

Lady Sybil narrowed her eyes and pointed the athame at

Lucy. "She presented herself to us tonight, a sacrifice sent by the Horned One to complete our atonement."

There was a murmur of assent from the other members of the coven.

"I was only trying to convince the community that they had nothing to fear from us," cried Diana. "And Lucy was helping me. Helping us."

"So you admit your guilt," crowed Lady Sybil.

"No, no. Absolutely not," protested Diana.

Lucy had to speak up for herself. "I only wrote good—" she whispered.

"Silence!" ordered Lady Sybil, turning toward Symonds. "And the final charge?"

"Abandoning the practices that our forefathers established as the very foundation of the craft, to wit, the requirement that blood must be shed and sacrifices presented to the Horned One to perpetuate the cycle of rebirth and renewal. Life brings death and death brings life."

Suddenly Lucy understood it all. She and Diana were to be sacrificed in some ridiculous parody of an ancient fertility ritual. It was crazy, but it seemed as if her life was going to end here in these woods where she'd walked so often, in a nonsensical ritual. She couldn't believe people could be so cruel, and her gaze darted from face to face. No one made eye contact with her. They were all staring at Lady Sybil, as if in a trance.

"That's insane!" shrieked Diana, desperation in her voice. "It's wrong. You're forgetting the first rule: an ye harm none!"

"She's right!" declared a small voice, and Abby Stoughton stepped forward, into the center of the circle. "This is all wrong."

"Quiet, child," snapped Lady Sybil. "You don't know the ways of the craft."

"Oh, yes, I do," retorted Abby. "I'm a powerful witch. I cursed my mother and she died!"

"That's as may be or not," said Lady Sybil, her small

eyes glittering in the firelight. "Seize her!" she ordered Symonds, and he quickly grabbed the girl. She struggled weakly to free herself, but he soon subdued her and bound her hands behind her back.

"Blessed be," declared Lady Sybil as Abby was brought before her and forced to kneel. "Thrice one is three, so may our fortune be."

"You'll never get away with this!" shouted Lucy, looking from one blank face to another. "You'll be caught. You'll all go to jail!"

Lady Sybil raised her staff and looked skyward. "The moon is rising. Now is the time."

The chanting and drumming began anew as Lucy and the two others were dragged, kicking and struggling, to the burned tree trunk where Malebranche had died. There they were held firmly by several brawny members of the coven while Symonds unrolled the fence wire and bound them fast. Other members of the coven began bringing more bundles of wood and piling them at their feet.

It was happening, really happening, but Lucy could hardly believe it when Symonds approached, holding the athame before him. The drumming and chanting were growing louder and more intense. Beside her, she could feel Abby's shoulders trembling and could hear her sobs. On her other side, Diana was standing defiant, muscles tensed. She felt her heart pounding in her chest, and her breaths came quick and shallow. She'd never known terror like this. There was no possible escape; Lucy knew that. There was only one thing to do, and she gave herself up to it entirely, closing her eyes and praying for a miracle with every fiber of her being. Symonds was now in front of Diana. He was raising the knife, about to plunge it into Diana's breast when a dark shadow fell over the moon. The drummers skipped a beat and the chanting faded, and in that moment of pause, something came hurtling silently from the sky, knocking the athame from his hand.

"It's a sign," said someone.

In the distance, they heard the howl of a wolf.

"That's enough for me," said a woman, dropping her drum.

A gentle breeze wafted through the clearing, causing the fire to flare briefly.

"When the West Wind doth blow, witches all best lie low," said another as the members of the coven melted away into the dark woods, leaving Lady Sybil and Symonds standing by the fire.

Lady Sybil fixed her eyes on Symonds, rooting him in place, then stooped down to pick up the knife. "Do it," she hissed, pressing the athame into his hand. "There's time. There's still time."

His hands hung limply, and he refused to take the knife. He stood mutely, his head bowed. Realizing she had lost power over him, Lady Sybil turned and raised the knife over Diana. She was preparing to strike when she was suddenly blinded by a bright light.

Lucy twisted her head, hardly knowing what to expect. An angel, perhaps, or a good witch. Maybe even the Virgin Mary, illuminated in celestial fire. What she didn't expect to see was Ike Stoughton striding into the clearing carrying an enormous flashlight, accompanied by Thomas and Mather.

"Don't move!" he ordered. "The police are coming."

Mather quickly seized the knife from Lady Sybil, who sank to her knees in defeat, muttering curses. Symonds attempted to dart away but was brought down by Thomas, who kept him firmly in place by planting a knee in the middle of his back.

Ike quickly got to work clipping the wires that bound Abby to Lucy and Diana, and suddenly the clearing was bathed once again in moonlight. Lucy heard a soft "whoo," and caught a glimpse of a small owl gliding silently past and disappearing into the trees.

CHAPTER TWENTY-FIVE

"It was thanks to you that we weren't all burned to a crisp," said Lucy, speaking to Rebecca Wardwell. "You sent Oz and he got Ike Stoughton's attention, banging at a window until he came out of the house and heard the drumming and smelled the smoke. He discovered Abby wasn't in her room and came looking for her."

Lucy and Rebecca were seated on Miss Tilley's camelback sofa, sipping smoky cups of Lapsang souchong tea. Diana was there also, seated in a fine antique Windsor chair, on the opposite side of the fireplace from Miss Tilley's Boston rocker. Rachel was passing the cucumber sandwiches.

"I had nothing to do with it," said Rebecca, fingering the large cameo that was fastened to the lace collar of her dress. It was made of plum-colored silk, with leg-o'-mutton sleeves and a full skirt that reached all the way down to the black satin slippers she was wearing, signaling this was truly a special occasion that demanded footwear. "Oz does what he wishes. He follows his own inclinations."

"Well, I wish there was some way I could thank him," said Lucy.

"No need, he is entirely self-sufficient," said Rebecca, biting into a molasses cookie.

"It must have been absolutely terrifying," said Miss Tilley, with a quaver in her voice.

"Oh, it was," said Lucy. "There was nothing we could do except pray for help. I never expected Ike would be the answer to my prayer." She lowered her head. "I really thought he had murdered Malcolm, making it look like he was the victim of a satanic ritual." She turned to Diana. "And you had no idea that the coven killed Malcolm?"

Diana shook her head. "No. He always went to England every summer for a few weeks. Nobody seemed concerned, and since he'd made me high priestess, I thought it was my responsibility to fill in while he was gone. Then when I learned he was dead, I carried on with the practices he taught me. Little did I know the coven were just tolerating me, grooming me to be their next sacrifice. I was never in charge. Lady Sybil was calling the shots, convincing the others to revive some ancient version of the craft."

Rebecca nodded. "There are a lot of different traditions in the craft. They were practicing a much older, much darker druidic religion that involves human sacrifice."

"Like in *The Wicker Man*," said Rachel, refilling their eggshell-thin cups from a fresh pot of tea.

"A most interesting film," said Miss Tilley. "I'd read *The Golden Bough*, of course, but it was quite amazing to see how these wicker giants were really constructed and used."

"What are you talking about?" asked Lucy.

Rachel set down the teapot. "It's a film. They did a remake lately. It's about a cop who goes to a remote British island to investigate a disappearance and discovers the people there are practicing witchcraft. They build a giant figure of a man out of wood and vines, sort of like a cage, and they put sacrificial victims inside and burn the whole thing to ensure an abundant harvest."

Lucy wasn't convinced. "Are you saying my ancestors, your ancestors, did this?"

"Maybe, if they lived in the British Isles. They painted themselves blue, too, and the Romans found them to be fierce opponents in battle," said Miss Tilley. "The women fought alongside the men, bare-breasted."

Lucy bit into a cookie. "Okay, but this was all a very long time ago, right? How come the coven wanted to bring it back?"

Diana tossed her hair back over her shoulder. "I'm not sure they all did. I think Lady Sybil was the instigator, for reasons of her own. She worked on Peter and the others, convincing them that this was the one and only true religion. Peter was easy—he'd built up a lot of resentment against Malcolm while he worked for him all those years. Malcolm didn't pay him enough. He couldn't make his mortgage payments and was losing his house. Malcolm wouldn't teach him the secret of his magic tricks and treated him like a subordinate instead of an equal. Sybil's a smart lady, crazy smart, and she knew just how to play him," said Diana, shrugging. "As for the others, I think they were carried along by the thrill of it all, but they were watchers, not doers."

"What kind of people would take part in something like that?" demanded Rachel.

This was the very question that Lucy was struggling to answer, and she leaned forward, eager to hear what Diana had to say.

"It's easy to think of them as demons, but they're not," she said. "Not at all. Just regular folks looking for a little excitement in their lives. And remember, they all drank that potion that Lady Sybil cooked up. . . ."

Rebecca leaned forward to interrupt. "The police said it was belladonna, which has hallucinogenic qualities."

"And once Abby spoke up, the others began to leave. But even so, they're all being charged as accessories to murder and attempted murder," said Lucy. "There's plenty of evidence, since they left a trail of e-mails, and those things never go away. Some members complained that burning Malcolm took too long and that's why they were going to stab us first." She paused, remembering that dreadful night and how she'd feared she'd never see her family again. "Personally, I hope they all rot in jail for a very long time."

"Not Abby, I hope," said Rachel. "The poor child needs psychological care, but since she confessed to killing her mother . . ."

"Tut-tut," clucked Miss Tilley. "Is it true?"

"Not at all," said Diana. "She did give her tea made from belladonna, but that's not actually lethal. Of course, it probably didn't help, considering the woman was ill to begin with."

"Why ever did she do it?" asked Miss Tilley.

"She was very angry with her mother for not sticking up for her against her father," said Diana. "She wanted to see a dermatologist about her acne, and she wanted a cell phone—she wanted to be like the other girls, and they wouldn't let her. She felt like a prisoner."

"Oh, dear," exclaimed Miss Tilley.

"Exactly," continued Diana. "And then she felt so guilty about it she started drinking the stuff herself and refusing to eat. Rachel's right—Abby does need psychological help. She's struggling with a lot of issues. I hope she gets it."

"Well, looking on the bright side, I think her father is beginning to understand the situation," said Rachel. "He's spoken to Bob about taking her case."

"I know I owe him a huge debt since he saved my life, but I still think he's abusive and controlling," said Lucy.

"He's getting help," said Rachel. "Bob says he's really devastated by his wife's death and totally confused about how to handle a teenage daughter."

"He's not the only one," said Lucy. "Sara's driving me nuts."

"I have some relaxing herbal tea I can give you," said Rebecca.

"I can give you a reading," offered Diana. "Give you an idea what to expect in the future."

"Thanks, but I don't think so," said Lucy. "I'm taking life one day at a time."

"It's the only way," said Miss Tilley. "I find that the older I get, the more exciting life becomes, and I can't wait to see what tomorrow brings."

They sat for a moment; then Diana turned to Lucy. "Remember that first day, when you came to my shop and you said you didn't believe in witchcraft?"

Lucy nodded.

"I wonder," continued Diana, "do you still feel that way?"

Lucy considered, thinking over the past few months. "Everything you said came true, didn't it?"

Diana nodded.

Lucy smiled ruefully. "Let's say I'm open to the possibility."

"So mote it be," said Diana, raising her cup.

"So mote it be," they all said, joining in.

bare trees were drab brown, and the drooping black boughs of the fir trees seemed drawn from a Victorian mourning sampler. The only thing missing was a dull gray slate gravestone, with a skull's head and a mournful text: *As you are now so once was I* or *Prepare to meet thy maker.*

But then she realized no marker was needed—the charred and blackened tree trunk where Malebranche had been bound and burned was monument enough to the terrible deed that had taken place here. She reached out her hand and patted the tree in a gesture of tribute, but snatched her hand back when she felt something sharp prick her finger. Looking closer, she saw that some of the wire that had restrained Malebranche remained on the tree. It was flexible stuff about an eighth of an inch thick, the sort of wire that farmers used to fence in their cows, because it was cheap and easy to string along the fence posts.

Twisting the wire, she found it bent easily, probably stressed by the heat of the fire, and she snapped a piece off. She didn't know why, really, except that she felt it was some sort of tribute. Malebranche shouldn't be forgotten, and this would be a reminder to keep the story alive until his killer—or killers—were found.

She tucked the wire in her pocket and turned to leave when Libby barked again. A small owl suddenly flew over her head, startling her, and perched on the burned tree, where it sat, staring at her with golden eyes.

"Oz?" she asked.

The bird blinked.

"I thought I recognized you," she said playfully. "What are you doing here?"

The bird didn't answer, but suddenly took flight, swooping silently through the trees and inviting her to follow.

CHAPTER TWENTY-ONE

Even as she crashed through the underbrush, raising her arms in front of her face to fend off the branches that snapped in her face, Lucy didn't understand why she felt compelled to follow the little owl. But follow she did, scrambling over fallen logs and weaving her way through the trees and undergrowth that blocked her path and hopping from stone to stone to cross the brook. Libby lagged behind her, following dutifully, although her dragging tail was an indication of her lack of enthusiasm. A nice sedate ramble in the woods was one thing, but she was a lazy Lab, and when the going got tough, she preferred her nice comfy doggy bed in the corner of the kitchen.

When Lucy reached a particularly nasty thicket, Oz was waiting for her, perched on a low branch. Once he'd caught her eye, he took wing, leading her around the tangle of bull brier and brambles until Lucy caught sight of a clearing ahead. Seeing daylight, she stepped up her pace, but Libby seemed to hang back, as if reluctant to leave the cover of the woods. Lucy coaxed her along, keeping up an encouraging babble.

"Come on, girl," she repeated over and over. "Come along."

But when Lucy followed Oz and broke out of the woods into the clearing, she understood Libby's reluctance. She had reached the Stoughton homestead, where Oz sat perched on top of a shed, as if to announce that this was the place they were seeking.

Lucy looked around, taking in the view of the property from the back, instead of the front. She saw the kitchen ell on the back of the house, the clothesline on which a forgotten dish towel hung limply, the barn, a chicken coop with a wire enclosure in which a dozen balding biddies were pecking at the ground, a large herb and vegetable garden gone to weeds, the pumpkin patch filled with withered vines, and a tipsy shed. Once the very picture of rural industry and self sufficiency, it now had a neglected air. It was also much closer to the crime scene than she had realized.

She was trying to decide whether she should return home the way she had come or risk the much easier option of cutting through the Stoughton's property to the road, when Oz suddenly alighted from his perch and flew a short distance to the chicken pen, where he settled on a fence post. The fence, Lucy realized, was made of two kinds of wire; the usual chicken netting was supported by sturdier wire strung along the posts.

She reached in her pocket and felt the protective pouch. Plunging deeper, she found the piece of wire she'd snapped off the tree.

The wire was common; she knew that. You could buy rolls of it at any feed store or hardware store. There was nothing special about it, nothing at all. And as she crossed the yard toward the enclosure, carefully skirting the garden where the shriveled and exhausted tomato vines were still clinging to their rusty wire cages, she expected the fence wire was the same as the blackened piece she held in her hand. Of course it would be. So why did a shudder run through her body when she found it matched exactly?

She looked at the owl for an answer, but he was gone.

Libby gave a sharp bark and she looked up, just in time to see Thomas and Mather arriving in the pickup truck. Before she knew what she was doing, without giving it a thought, she instinctively turned on her heels and ran for the cover of the woods, calling Libby to follow. When she got about twenty feet inside the woods, she ducked behind a big balsam and looked back, and that's when she realized her mistake. Thomas and Mather had spotted her and were running after her.

She should have greeted them, made some excuse about just wanting to check that everything was okay while Ike was in jail. She could have convinced them she was simply being neighborly, but it was too late now. By running away, she'd as good as confessed she'd been up to no good. Snooping around where she had no business being. Her only option was to keep running, hoping that they'd give up the chase.

She took flight, following the path she'd come, or what she thought was the way. Where was that darn owl when she needed him? Nowhere to be seen! She and Libby were on their own. She was running as fast as she could, and Libby was sticking by her side, panting heavily. As was Lucy, who was working up quite a sweat, even as the temperature began to fall and the early sunset approached. It was becoming dim in the woods, and she was increasingly uncertain of which way to go. Her heart began to pound, and she felt panicky as she heard the two boys crashing through the woods behind her, yelling and swearing.

This was crazy; it was stupid. They were her neighbors. Surely she could simply stop and explain, say how they'd startled her and she'd reacted stupidly, but some deep instinct told her to keep running. And as she ran, her muscles burning and her chest feeling tighter and tighter, she wondered if she was replaying the same pursuit that had ended Malebranche's life. Was this what happened to him? Had the Stoughtons chased him through the woods and captured him? Had they caught him and dragged him kicking and screaming to the clearing where they bound him to the tree with wire and burned him alive? Had this all happened before?

Lucy's energy was flagging, and she glanced over her shoulder, finding her pursuers were gaining on her. Their faces red with exertion and anger, they looked just like their father. She had to keep going; she couldn't let them catch her. She snapped her head around and ran straight into a low-hanging branch.

The pain was instantaneous and the impact of the blow made her dizzy. She fell to her knees, clutching her head, and tried to reorient herself, tried to focus around the black spots that were dancing in front of her eyes, tried to stay conscious and get back on her feet but was unable to summon the strength. Behind her, from some distance, Libby was barking. Thomas and Mather were unstoppable, crashing through the undergrowth, leaping over logs with ease, trampling the undergrowth with their size 13 work boots, snapping boughs out of their way with hands the size of baseball mitts.

She placed her hands on the ground and tried to push herself up, but the effort made her so dizzy that she collapsed again, helpless to defend herself. She was losing consciousness. The black spots were growing larger and becoming darker, and her eyes were closing when she heard a huge roar that shook the ground and rattled the trees to their very roots.

Her eyes popped open and she saw an enormous black bear, the biggest she had ever seen, rearing on its hind legs smack between her and the Stoughtons. The two youths stopped in their tracks, awestruck, as the bear batted its paws and bared its teeth, growling ferociously. They knew what to do—they threw up their arms to make themselves look bigger and backed away, aware that running would be a fatal mistake.

Lucy would have done the same if she could, but she was battling to maintain consciousness, fighting like a swimmer against a rip tide that was pulling her farther and farther from shore. She felt herself slipping, yielding to the tug of darkness, then snapping awake, startled at the bright sunlight that was falling all around her. Libby was only a few feet away, nosing at the ground, now vacant, where the bear had roared to life and made its stand.

She had no idea how long she'd been unconscious, but she knew she needed to get out of the woods and back home fast. Concentrating hard and trying to ignore the tremendous pounding in her head, she sat up slowly and looked around. Libby was sitting in front of her, tongue lolling, as if waiting for the word to get moving. Lucy managed to get to her knees, then grabbed a nearby tree trunk and used it to pull herself upright. Once on her feet, she hung on to the tree, waiting for her dizziness to subside. When she finally felt a bit steadier on her feet, she began making her way slowly through the woods in what she hoped was the right direction. Spotting a hefty branch that was caught in some brambles, she yanked it out and began using it as a walking staff and soon found herself on the old logging road.

As she struggled homeward, she tried to make sense of what had happened, hardly believing any of it had actually taken place. Had she really gone into the woods following an owl that for some reason led her to the Stoughton homestead? And when Stoughton's enraged sons pursued her, had she magically been saved by a gigantic black bear that disappeared as quickly as it had appeared? It was insane; it was almost as if she'd been under the influence of a magical spell. Was that what happened? Had Rebecca or Diana or some other witch conjured up the whole thing? And if so, had it really happened, or had it all been a dream?

She was walking along more easily now that she was out of the woods, and she felt her strength returning. The headache was less severe, too, and Libby was trotting ahead of her, following scents that Lucy couldn't smell. Maybe it was the same thing, she thought; maybe she'd encountered a reality she simply wasn't equipped to understand. And maybe, she realized, it didn't matter. Because whether it was her subconscious sending her a message or one of the witches sending a bear to rescue her, she had certainly gotten the idea that Ike Stoughton and his boys were trouble.

There was certainly something seriously amiss in that household; that was obvious from Miriam's death and Abby's sickness. They reminded her of Victorian women who clung to illness as a way of escaping the domination of their husbands and fathers. But even if Ike Stoughton was a tyrant at home, that didn't mean he would actually commit murder.

Although, she admitted to herself, it certainly indicated a moral compass that was somewhat askew. And the more she thought about it, the more likely it seemed, given the fact that he had an interest in Compass Construction. Maybe all his fussing about witchcraft was simply a front; maybe he really had been after Malebranche's property all along. Maybe it was all about the land—he was a surveyor, after all, and everybody knew he was an expert at untangling confused property titles.

Libby was running ahead now, barking to announce their arrival home. Sara and Zoe had just been dropped off and were walking up the driveway, and Libby was prancing around them, wagging her tail. Lucy greeted them in a more sedate manner, with a big smile.

"You look kinda pale, Mom," said Sara. "Are you okay?"

"I took the dog for a walk in the woods and bumped my head on a tree branch—stupid of me."

Sara gave her a funny look, but Zoe was full of concern. "You should put some ice on it," she said.

"I think I will," said Lucy, who was planning to have the girls make supper. "What's the homework situation?"

Assured it was under control, Lucy got the girls started on breading some chicken breasts while she took a couple of pain-killers and slapped a bag of frozen peas on the egg-sized bump that had formed on her noggin. Retreating to the family room, she reclined on the sofa and reached for the phone and called Detective Horowitz yet again.

"What is it this time?" he grumbled.

"I just wondered how closely you questioned Ike Stoughton about the Malebranche murder, that's all."

"I can't tell you that."

"It's just that I happened to discover his homestead is very close to the murder scene."

Horowitz sighed. "We do have topographical maps, you know."

"Hmm," said Lucy. "What about the wire? He uses it on his homestead. Did you send it to the crime lab for a match?"

"No. Wire's wire—of course it would match."

"I know, but I heard somewhere that you can match the cuts—you know, tiny scratches and nicks on a cutter can be matched. . . ."

"Don't tell me you watch *CSI*?"

"Sometimes," she admitted. "But what about it? Did you check for a match?"

"Nope. I had no reason to."

"Are you kidding me? This guy had motive, means, and opportunity. He stands to benefit financially from Male-branche's death. His house is next door to the crime scene and—"

Horowitz interrupted. "Even if the cuts matched, it wouldn't mean anything."

"Why not?"

"Because we don't have a time of death, and we can't es-tablish who had custody of the wire snips at that time. To start with, there are three men on the homestead, and they don't lock the shed."

"Oh," said Lucy, crestfallen. "I didn't think of that."

"Leave this alone," advised Horowitz. "It's evil and nasty, and you don't want to get involved."

"You're absolutely right," said Lucy, knowing that was exactly why she had to find out who had killed Malebranche. If only she could be sure that bear would continue to protect her.

CHAPTER TWENTY-TWO

After sleeping on it, Lucy woke Thursday morning with the conviction that the bear had been sent by Rebecca, who had been alerted to her perilous situation by Oz, the owl. She knew full well that this was utterly ridiculous, that people, even people who considered themselves witches, couldn't create bears out of thin air, and they couldn't talk to owls either. But even though she thought of herself as an extremely rational and practical woman, she could not shake the belief that Rebecca sent the bear, or what appeared to be a bear. She wasn't convinced that a bear had actually been in the woods; it might have been some sort of super-natural force that had taken the form of a bear. That seemed the likeliest explanation, because she assumed that bears were pretty smelly creatures, but this one hadn't left the faintest hint of a stink. And furthermore, it had disappeared awfully quickly, which was also unbearlike behavior. A real bear would have shuffled off on all fours, taking its time, accompanied by a couple of buzzing flies that had been drawn by its rank scent. But this one had simply vanished as soon as Thomas and Mather took tail and ran away.

But even though Lucy was convinced she had figured out the explanation for the bear's sudden appearance, and disappearance, she wasn't about to share it with anyone. Nobody would believe it, for one thing. Bill would be terrified, convinced his wife was losing her mind, and the kids would probably feel the same way. Her friends wouldn't believe it, either, except for Pam, who had great faith in supernatural forces and organic foods. Sue would scoff and tell her she had an overactive imagination, and Rachel would dust off some theory she'd learned in college as a psych major. So even though it was Thursday and she'd be having breakfast with the girls, she had no intention of sharing this particular episode with them.

However, there was one person she most definitely did want to discuss it with, so she took the long way around to town and stopped at Rebecca's to say thank you.

"Oh, no, dear, you needn't thank me," said Rebecca, after Lucy had explained the situation. "I didn't send a bear In fact, I'm not sure I could. I've certainly never tried anything like that."

"But you're a witch," said Lucy, baffled.

"Of course I am, but bears? Not my style."

"But you sent Oz?" persisted Lucy.

Rebecca shook her head. "He's a free spirit, you know. He comes and goes entirely of his own accord."

"I'm so confused," said Lucy. "I really thought I had this figured out."

"You may be right—maybe some other witch sent the bear. But I tend to think it was simply a manifestation of Thomas's and Mather's own wickedness. The bear was an embodiment of their evil intentions, a fine example of the rule of three."

"The rule of three?"

"Oh, yes. 'Ever mind the rule of three—what you manifest comes back to thee.' It's a basic rule of the universe."

"There was more to this than what goes around comes around," said Lucy. "I saw the bear with my own eyes. And the dog was upset too."

"Oh, I don't doubt you for a minute," said Rebecca. "I believe something was there, maybe even a bear. It's possible, you know."

"I don't think so," protested Lucy. "It vanished in a snap, in the blink of an eye."

"Have you considered the possibility the bear might have been your daemon?" asked Rebecca.

Lucy's eyebrows shot up. "Demon? You think I'm possessed by demons?"

"Not demon, *daemon*. Everyone has one. A sort of spirit that protects you. Religious people call it a guardian angel. Pagans believe everyone has an animal protector. Yours may well be a bear."

"If that's true, how come this daemon hasn't made an appearance until now?" asked Lucy.

"Perhaps this was the first time you needed it," said Rebecca, placidly tossing corn on the ground for her chickens. "Or maybe it just decided the time was right. Daemons can be, well, difficult. *Moody* is the best word, I guess. A bit touchy." She raised her head and waggled a bony finger at Lucy. "That's why you must never depend on your daemon—they're flighty creatures and most unreliable."

"Well, thanks for the warning," said Lucy, heading back to her car with the feeling that she was waking up from a rather weird dream. A dream that was so lifelike, she thought it had given her a glimpse of another reality, but now she knew differently. Or did she?

At breakfast with the girls, her mind kept wandering, even though Pam was running through the final preparations for the Halloween celebration.

"We've got a big ad in the *Pennysaver,* and you did a story—thanks, Lucy," she was saying.

Lucy was staring into her coffee cup, wondering why the waxy film on top was in the shape of a bear.

"Lucy? I just thanked you for the story."

"No problem," she answered, staring off into space.

"She's got her mind on something," said Sue, giving her a shake. "Cookies? Cupcakes? How many did you promise to make?"

"Huh?" asked Lucy, coming in for a landing.

"How many cookies and cupcakes are you going to make?" asked Rachel, speaking slowly and clearly, as if to a small child.

"Whatever you said. I've already got two dozen cupcakes with orange frosting and candy corn jack-o'-lantern faces in the freezer, along with two dozen eyeballs. Golly those things are gross. I drew the line at painting little red lines to make them look bloodshot. I just have to do a batch of Beastly Bug cookies."

"Check," said Pam. "Sue, you were going to handle the punch?"

"I've got a cauldron full," replied Sue. "Complete with dry ice for a smoky atmosphere. But believe me, getting that black color was a trick. It doesn't taste too bad, but it could use a touch of vodka."

"No vodka, absolutely not," said Pam, checking her list and turning to Rachel. "I have you down for three dozen cupcakes and assorted wiggly worms."

"You got 'em," said Rachel. "Plus I've put together a terrific gypsy costume, for telling fortunes."

"We've got the Service Club from the high school to help out with decorations, and Diana is taking care of the favors. What have I forgotten?"

"Music?" asked Sue.

"I got this guy who's just starting out as a DJ," reported

Pam. "He's doing it for free, but we have to let him put up a sign."

"Sounds fair enough," said Sue.

"What's fair?" asked Lucy, whose thoughts were still wandering.

"Nothing, honey," said Sue, patting her hand. "You just go back to your comfy little cloud."

"Have any of you seen any bears lately?" she asked out of the blue. "I mean, is there an increase in the population or something?"

The other three all exchanged glances. "Bears, sweetheart?" asked Sue.

"Yeah. I saw one yesterday, and I wondered if they're especially plentiful this year."

The others shook their heads.

"Just checking," said Lucy.

"Okay," said Pam, folding up her list and tucking it away. "Looks like everything is under control—I'll see you all Halloween night. Don't forget your costumes."

Lucy was walking along Main Street, on her way to the newspaper office, when she met Diana coming out of Slack's hardware store.

"I just love this place," exclaimed Diana. "I don't think they've changed a thing since 1950."

"They probably haven't," agreed Lucy. "Did you find what you wanted?"

"Oh, yes," said Diana. "I'm so glad I bumped into you— I want to ask a favor."

"Maybe," said Lucy warily. "What is it?"

"Well, I've been getting calls from a lot of newspapers and TV stations, about Halloween, you know. I guess they think I'm the resident witch or something, and I'm getting a little worried about Samhain."

"Worried? Why?"

"Well, I'm afraid of a repeat of last spring, when they were all camped out around my store and followed me everywhere I went. You see, Samhain is a very special time for Wiccans, and I can't have a bunch of reporters spoiling the ceremony, especially since I'm returning and resuming leadership of the coven."

Lucy saw her point but didn't see how she could help. "So what do you want me to do?"

"Well," said Diana, "I thought that maybe—and this is only if there's a problem—maybe you could kind of lead them on a wild-goose chase while I slip off to meet the coven."

"I don't know," protested Lucy, who wasn't very keen on the idea. "I have to work at the Halloween party."

"This would be after the party, probably around eleven or so."

"Eleven?" Lucy was always in bed by ten, and she didn't relish the idea of impersonating Diana, who wasn't exactly popular with a number of people, most especially Ike and his boys. What if they wanted to do her harm on Halloween night? "That's awfully late for me," she said, taking a step or two away from Diana. "And besides, I'm shorter than you, and I don't have long hair. I don't think I could fool anybody."

Diana wasn't about to let her slip away, reaching out and taking her hand. "Oh, Lucy, I've got a wig you can wear, and it will be dark. And besides, I don't know who else to ask. This observance is the cornerstone of our beliefs, and I can't let the media ruin it with popping flashbulbs and TV footage making a mockery of our most sacred rites. And besides," she added, brightening, "it's all hypothetical. I don't know for certain that they'll even come. But if they do, it would make a great story for your paper, wouldn't it?"

Lucy furrowed her brow. "What do you mean?"

Diana was only too happy to elaborate on her idea. "Oh, something along the lines of '*Newshounds miss big story*,' something like that. '*Paparazzi peeved as Halloween story fizzles.*' I don't know; you're the journalist," she added with a shrug and a big smile. "Hi, Ted."

Dismayed, Lucy realized Ted had come up behind her, and she didn't have a clue how much he'd heard of Diana's harebrained scheme.

Too much, as it turned out. "You know, Lucy," he said, joining them, "that's not a bad idea. I've already gotten calls from a couple of TV stations, putting out feelers, you know. You could do a public service by keeping them away from the coven, and you'd get a terrific story too."

"I could even give you some details about the observance, an exclusive. Isn't that what you call it?" offered Diana, batting her big eyes at Ted.

"That would be terrific," said Ted, picturing a headline. "'*Inside View: The Real Halloween Story.*'"

"I really don't think this is a good idea," protested Lucy. "It's not safe for one thing—what if I have an accident? Or if some crazy like Ike Stoughton tries to do me harm, thinking I'm Diana?"

"You're being ridiculous," said Ted. "Of course I'd expect you would take reasonable precautions for your safety."

"And if you get in a tight spot, all you have to do is reveal yourself. Once they realize you're not me, they'll leave you alone," offered Diana.

Ted was nodding. "It's an assignment, Lucy. Page one. I'm putting it on top of the news budget."

Lucy knew there was no point arguing with Ted once he'd made up his mind. "Oh, well," she said, capitulating. "I guess I've done crazier things." Problem was, she thought as she followed Ted into the office, she couldn't think of anything that rivaled this for sheer stupidity.

"Stop by at the shop," called Diana, giving a little wave. "I've got a disguise all ready for you."

"Okay," she agreed, looking on the bright side. At least

she wouldn't have to come up with a costume for the party. And if things really got out of hand, she reminded herself, she could try summoning her daemon. Just the thought of the bear made her smile.

"And what are you so happy about?" demanded Phyllis, waving the new issue of the *Pennysaver* in her face when she walked into the office. "Ike Stoughton's lawyer has been calling all morning. He's threatening to sue us for libel."

The next forty-five minutes were agony for Lucy as she listened to Ted trying to mollify Stoughton's lawyer. She could hear only Ted's side of the conversation, of course, but even that was excruciating.

"You have no grounds for legal action," he was saying. "The story was accurate, my reporter quoted only members of your client's family who were speaking in public, there was no request for confidentiality, and nobody told her their comments were off the record."

All true enough, thought Lucy, but she knew she had taken advantage of the Stoughton boys' youth and inexperience, as well as Ike's emotional state. If they had known she was going to record their outbursts in the court lobby and print them in the paper, they might have behaved differently. Lucy wasn't completely comfortable with the story. Even though she really thought getting Abby's situation out into the open was the best thing for the girl, she couldn't help feeling guilty about exposing the Stoughton family's tragedy.

"There was absolutely no malicious intent, no desire to defame or expose the Stoughton family to ridicule," said Ted. "This was a public place, and many other people witnessed the scene. We printed a truthful and accurate account of the event, which you can be sure is more than the local gossipmongers will do. We really did the Stoughtons a service by presenting a truthful, unembellished account that demonstrates the highest journalistic ethics."

You had to love Ted, thought Lucy. He was not only defending her, but he was also trying to convince the lawyer that she'd done the family a favor. If only she felt that way.

"Journalistic ethics is not an oxymoron!" exclaimed Ted. "And I look forward to seeing you in court!" he yelled, slamming down the phone.

He sat for a moment, hand on the receiver, before he swiveled around to face Lucy and Phyllis. Ted usually had plenty to say, but this time he limited himself to one word. "Damn," he said.

CHAPTER TWENTY-THREE

The weeks before Halloween passed in a blaze of color as one syrupy golden day followed another, and a steady stream of leaf-peeping tourists passed through town, shopping for antiques, maple syrup, pumpkins, and cider. It was Lucy's favorite time of year: She loved the nip in the morning air, the crunch of leaves beneath her feet, and the comfort of slipping into a favorite sweater. Adding poignancy to her pleasure was the knowledge that these fine October days were fleeting and gray November would arrive like a cold, wet blanket.

For the moment, she was concentrating on what the poet called "this season of mellow fruitfulness." Even Ike Stoughton seemed to have regained a sense of equilibrium. Maybe the brief stay in the county jail brought Ike to his senses, or maybe he was coming to terms with his grief, but he seemed to have ceased his campaign against witchcraft and there was no more talk of a libel suit.

A few days before Halloween the girls reported that Abby had returned to school. "She looks much better, Mom," reported Zoe. Lucy responded with mixed emotions. She was glad the girl had recovered but she really didn't want her daughters getting involved with the Stoughtons again. She expected Sara and Zoe would want to visit and braced for an argument, but the girls never brought it up.

When the big day finally rolled around, she was determined to make the most of it and was in a festive mood as she dressed for the party. She didn't have the first idea about how to wear a wig, so she went for the obvious and plopped it on her head like a hat, tucking the stray bits of her own hair underneath. She was busy poking a particularly stubborn lock out of sight when Bill appeared behind her, wrapping his arms around her waist.

"You look good in long hair," he said, pulling her against him. "Why don't you let your hair grow?"

Lucy looked at her reflection, thinking she was a very poor imitation of Diana. She was shorter and wider, too, which was actually fortunate, because her width took up most of the stretchy skirt's extra length, and the cheap polyester wig with long ringlets that cascaded over her shoulders was way too much hair. She thought it made her look like Chewbacca.

"I'm not tall enough for long hair," she said.

"I think it looks nice," said Bill, his hands straying over her body. "And I like this dress too. It feels silky. How come you always wear pants?"

"I don't always wear pants," said Lucy, reaching a finger under the wig to scratch. The darn thing was itchy, and heavy to boot. And it smelled funny.

"When was the last time you wore a skirt?" asked Bill.

Lucy scratched harder, trying to remember. He did have a point—she almost always wore jeans, because they were comfortable and practical for her busy life. "The Finches Christmas party," she said triumphantly, retrieving the memory. "I wore a red silk blouse and my little black skirt."

"I remember," said Bill, lifting the fake hair off her neck so he could nuzzle it. "You looked sexy. Just like you look sexy now."

"Down, boy," she said, pulling away. "I'm going to be late for the party."

"Be late," he coaxed.

The party was in full swing when Lucy arrived at the community center, where the DJ was playing the "Monster Mash" at top volume. It seemed as if every kid in town was there, most dressed in costumes. Thomas the Tank Engine was popular with the youngest boys, and there were quite a few Spider-Mans and Supermans, and Transformers too. The girls were mostly princesses, though there were also a number of witches in pointy black hats. Lucy herself was wearing a witch's hat, having given up on the itchy wig. The long skirt was a nuisance, however, as she had to be careful not to trip on the hem.

"It's about time you got here," chided Pam when Lucy approached her to ask how she could help. "Is that some new makeup you're wearing?"

Lucy's hand flew to her face, which felt quite warm. "No makeup," said Lucy, smiling to herself.

"Well, you look fabulous," said Pam. "Can you relieve Sue, over at the ball toss? I need her to put out her black punch."

"Sure," said Lucy.

Sue was off in a far corner where a kid-sized basketball hoop topped with the silhouette of a black cat with an arched back had been set up. Each kid got three tries to make a basket, and everybody got a tiny Tootsie Roll prize.

Other games were set up around the perimeter of the room. There were old favorites like bobbing for apples and pin the tail on the donkey, except that today it was pin the nose on the pumpkin. Rachel was ensconced in a pop tent covered with colorful scarves, seated at a small table with a silver garden globe, telling fortunes. Lucy's neighbor Willie, who was married to a vet, had set up a petting corner, bringing along the family cat and her son Chip's pet bunny, as well as some borrowed gerbils and guinea pigs. Rebecca was seated in another corner, in a rocking chair, and a couple of little princesses were sitting at her feet, listening to her read "Pumpkin Moonshines" and other Halloween stories. Most of the kids were running around, dashing from one activity to another, and some were even dancing to the Halloween songs the DJ was playing.

"It's quite the scene," said Lucy, finally reaching the ball toss.

"We got quite a big turnout," said Sue, passing the ball to a very small Dracula. Turning to Lucy, she narrowed her eyes. "Are you using a new moisturizer? What is it? I'm going to have to get me some."

"I think it's the store brand," said Lucy, who always bought the cheapest jar on the drugstore shelf.

Sue's eyebrows shot up in disbelief. "You didn't get that rosy glow from the store brand. What's your secret?"

Lucy wasn't about to tell, not in front of the kids. "Look, Pam needs help with the punch, so I'm supposed to take over here."

Sue was clapping for the little Dracula, who finally got the ball through the hoop on his third try. "Here you go," she said, giving him the candy and taking the ball, which she passed on to Lucy. "Three tries each, make 'em wait in line, and no pushing or shoving."

"I can handle it," said Lucy, passing the ball to a blue and silver princess. A mummy, a pirate, and a tiny Nemo were all waiting their turn, with varying degrees of patience.

"C'mon, Bella," urged the pirate. "You're taking forever."

"Shut up, Jason," snapped the princess, with plenty of attitude. "I can take as long as I want."

"Ten seconds or you lose your turn," said Lucy, starting to count, and the princess heaved the ball, bouncing it off the backboard.

"You killed the cat," crowed Jason, causing the princess to sulk while Lucy chased down the ball. She made the next two tries, however, and Lucy gave her two Tootsie Rolls. She was about to give Jason his turn when the music stopped and the DJ announced the costume parade was about to begin.

There was a flurry of activity as the kids lined up and the judges took their seats; then the music to *The Sorcerer's Apprentice* filled the room, and the kids began marching in a circle. Lucy loved this part best, amused by the kids' expressions. Some were self-conscious in their costumes, while others really enjoyed play-acting and putting on a bit of a show. The Draculas, in particular, liked to show their fanged teeth and wiggle their fingers. The smaller kids really got into their characters, the Thomases huffing and puffing like really useful engines and tiny little Nemo making swimming motions.

Then everyone waited while the winners—there were at least twenty categories, ranging from "Most Original" to "Scariest" and "Funniest"—were announced and prizes awarded. Afterward, everybody lined up for refreshments, which Pam carefully specified were to be eaten sitting on the floor. "There will be absolutely no running," she warned.

"Can we have seconds?" asked Nemo, piping up.

"After everybody has had firsts," said Pam, "and only if there is no running."

The older kids knew the drill, and soon the children were all seated Indian-style on the floor, quietly eating their Beastly Cookies, Wiggly Worms, Eyeballs, and Witches' Brew punch. Lucy took advantage of the quiet to collect the box of favors and stationed herself by the door, ready to present each departing child with a trick-or-treat bag filled with a few pieces of candy, a black or orange flashlight to carry while trick-or-treating, and the protective pouches Diana had donated.

A half hour later and the kids were all gone, all except for little Nemo, and the cleanup was beginning. It looked as if Nemo's folks were running late.

"What's your name?" she asked him.

"Nemo."

"That's your costume," said Lucy. "What's your real name?"

"Nemo."

And people said kids had no imagination nowadays. "So where do you live?" she asked, thinking she probably knew the answer.

She did. "In the aquarium."

Time to try a new tack. "Where does your mom live?"

Nemo chuckled at yet another silly question. "In the aquarium. She's a fish too."

"Okay, Nemo," she said with a sigh. "You stay right here until I get back, okay?"

Nemo nodded and began checking out the contents of his treat bag while Lucy canvassed the volunteers, looking for somebody who knew the child.

"Oh, that's Nemo," said Sue, ripping off a piece of plastic film to cover the leftover cookies.

"So he says," said Lucy.

"No, really. Nemo Anderson. He's a part-timer at the school. His parents are a little sketchy; they're usually late."

"Drugs? Booze?" asked Lucy, who was familiar with the issues faced by many of the town's residents.

"No, I don't think so. They're just free spirits. Throwbacks to the sixties, I guess."

"Can you call them? Tell them the party's over?"

Lucy went back to wait with Nemo, who was now surrounded by a small pile of candy wrappings and discarded herbs. "What's this?" he asked, showing her the little stone Diana had included in the pouch.

"It's a lucky stone. It has a special power, and if you carry it with you all the time, it will keep you safe. At least that's what some people think." Lucy had popped her bag into her bra, as Diana had suggested. She wasn't sure why she did it. Maybe because it was Halloween and it seemed to go with the costume; maybe she subconsciously felt the need for protection on this night when the veil between the living and the dead was said to disappear.

"Cool," said Nemo, popping the stone into the pouch and lifting up his costume to stuff it in his pants pocket.

Lucy could see Sue crossing the room toward them, phone in hand.

"Nemo's mother says her car died, and she wants to know if somebody could bring him home. I would, but I've got to meet Sid at the airport—he's coming back from his annual golf weekend in Hilton Head—and his plane is supposed to be landing right now." She shrugged. "It's probably delayed— they always are these days, but still—"

"I'll do it," said Lucy. "Where does he live?"

"I told you: the aquarium," said Nemo.

Lucy was getting tired of this. "I need better directions than that," she said.

Sue was smiling. "He's actually telling the truth. Remember the old aquarium?" she asked, referring to a defunct tourist trap out on Route 1.

"Yeah," said Lucy, picturing a dilapidated cluster of buildings surrounded by an overgrown parking lot.

"That's where he lives."

"That's almost an hour's drive!" protested Lucy.

"No good deed goes unpunished," said Sue.

Lucy glanced at the little kid, who was busy sucking on a lollipop. "This is how fish eat lollipops," he told her, sucking in his cheeks.

"Okay, Nemo, I'll give you a ride home," she said, taking him by the hand. "Where's your coat?" The coat rack was empty, except for a handful of adult-sized jackets. Her eyes met Sue's, expressing mutual disapproval.

"Fish don't need jackets," declared Nemo.

"There's a blanket in the car," said Lucy, becoming aware as she dashed out to the car to retrieve it that this simple errand was getting a lot more complicated than she'd expected. Then when she tried to drape it around him, Nemo insisted that fish didn't use blankets, not ever, but he changed his mind when they were halfway to the car. The temperature had fallen as night fell. It was just above freezing, and a sharp wind was blowing off the cove. Lucy cranked up the heater when she started the car, rubbing her hands together until she felt the first blasts of warm air flowing from the vents. Little Nemo was seated beside her, wrapped in his blanket and held securely by the seat belt as they drove through town.

The little village had a holiday air, as many people had not only left their porch lights on but had also strung lights shaped like pumpkins or skeletons; others had set up spotlights to illuminate their harvest figures. Candles twinkled inside jack-o'-lanterns; some grinned and others leered or howled, depending on their creators' inclinations. Some people had taped cutouts on their windows: Black cats and witches on broomsticks were favorites. And some folks had even bought crumpled figures of witches that they fastened to a tree trunk as if a witch riding a broomstick had accidentally crashed into it. Lucy loved all the decorations, except for the giant inflatable purple spider that one family always set on their porch roof—that one gave her the creeps, and she tried not to look at it.

She drove carefully and slowly, on the lookout for trick-or-treaters. The kids were everywhere, dashing from house to house, the young ones with parental escorts and the older kids in groups. It was getting late, almost eight o'clock, and she knew things would quiet down pretty soon as the kids went home with their loot. Some parents tried to limit the gorging and confiscated the sweets to dole out later. Lucy and Bill generally let the kids eat as much as they wanted on Halloween night, figuring it was better to get it over with as soon as possible and get back to a healthy diet. Whatever was left went into a bowl on the dining room sideboard for everyone to share; Lucy could never pass it without grabbing a mini chocolate bar, or two, and was glad when nothing was left except a couple of grape lollipops, scorned by everyone. They generally lingered there until it was time to put up the Christmas decorations.

She was thinking about this and hoping Sara and Zoe were having a good time with their friends when the town gradually dwindled down to scattered houses and small strip malls and then to nothing but fields and woods. The old aquarium wasn't in Tinker's Cove but a couple of towns over, beyond Shiloh, and the unlit two-lane road wandered and wound its way over hill and dale and around the mountain. Nemo was a good traveler, however, and Lucy soon sensed he had fallen asleep. The trip seemed endless, but finally she spotted the green neon fish sign that still stood in the old parking lot. Most of the letters were out, however, with only a *Q, U,* and *R* remaining. She tapped the horn, and a figure emerged from one of the buildings and ran to the car just as Nemo woke up. He sat for a minute, rubbing his eyes and blinking under the dome light; then the door was yanked open and a thirtyish woman with a shaved head and numerous piercings stuck her head inside.

"Hi, honey, did you have a good time?"

Nemo blinked and nodded, popping his thumb in his mouth.

"Thank you soooo much," she said as she unfastened the seat belt. "That old car, I keep telling my husband we need a new one but . . ." She shrugged, then scooped up Nemo, blanket and all. "Thanks again," she said, slamming the door shut and running, carrying the child, back toward the lighted building. Lucy got a glimpse of them as they passed an outside light; then they were inside and a moment later the big neon sign flickered out, leaving her in the dark.

At least she said thank you, thought Lucy, shifting into drive and turning back onto the road for the long, lonely trip home. No offer of coffee or a bathroom, not even a glass of water. This was exactly the sort of behavior that really ticked her off. Nemo's mother hadn't shown the least bit of consideration for her. She was one of those who took it for granted that other people, conscientious people like herself, were only too happy to take care of their children. A thank-you was nice, thought Lucy, but a tenner for gas would have been nicer, considering the price at the pump. Much nicer, she thought, checking the gauge and seeing with a shock that the needle was hovering on E. But where on earth was she going to find a gas station out here on this lonely stretch of highway? The nearest was at least twenty miles back, in Gideon.

There was nothing to do but keep driving, hoping that the gas held out until she returned to civilization, but it was nerve-wracking to say the least. She tried to be optimistic, but each flutter of the needle sent her into a panic. And when the engine finally started to sputter, she was just able to glide to the side of the road before it died. She got the emergency flasher going. It ran off the battery, so she knew it wouldn't last very long. She wasn't really expecting her cell phone to work—the area was notorious for poor reception—and it didn't. There was nothing to do but wait and hope that help would arrive.

Lucy hadn't sat there for very long when she remembered she wasn't far at all from Peter Symonds's place, on River Road. He had a big yard; she figured he must have a gas can around for the mower. And she didn't need much gas—even a gallon would be more than enough to get her back to the all-night station she'd passed. Or maybe he'd let her use his phone; she remembered he had a landline. Either was preferable to sitting in the car, especially since she'd promised Diana that she would lead the reporters who were, indeed, camped outside her store on a wild-goose chase. And it was getting late. She'd promised Diana she would be there by ten, and it was already almost nine.

So she turned off the flasher and got out of the car, crossing the road to walk facing traffic, if any should come along. None did, however, and she had the highway to herself all the way to the intersection with River Road. It was a brilliant moonlit evening, with the full moon actually casting shadows of the tree branches on the road. There was enough wind to make the trees moan as they were bent this way and that, and she thought she heard an owl hoot from time to time.

A dark and deserted road, she thought to herself, maybe not the best place to be on Halloween night. But then she caught a glimpse of light shining through the trees and knew she was closer than she thought to Symonds's place. She had just turned up the driveway when the front door opened and two figures came out: Symonds and Lady Sybil. Even in the dark, Lucy knew she would recognize that rotund figure.

"Hi!" she called. "I need some help."

Lady Sybil stationed herself by the front door, waiting for her, while Symonds continued on to his pickup truck. Amazingly enough, he was carrying a gas can.

"Hey, hey," she called, running up to him. "Can I have some of that gas? I've run out. My car's just a little ways down the road."

Symonds set the gas can in the bed of his pickup and turned to face her. "Sorry, but I need it," he told her.

"Can't I just have a little?" asked Lucy, begging. "My car gets really good mileage, and I only need to get to the all-night gas station."

Symonds was looking uncomfortable, but Lucy wasn't about to give up. "You could follow me and I'll fill the can right up for you—I'll fill it to the top, and fill up your truck too."

Lucy was confident this was a deal no sane person would refuse. In fact, if she wasn't so desperate, she'd never make such an extravagant offer that would cost her so much money. But she needed to get back to town to help Diana.

Lady Sybil was sailing down the lawn, her loose ritual garments billowing behind her. "He told you he doesn't have any gasoline to spare," she said, staring at Lucy with those popping frog eyes.

"Okay, I understand," she said, casting her eyes longingly on the red plastic can in the truck bed, resting among the usual clutter of tools and equipment that invariably accumulated back there. "Can I just use your phone to call my husband?" she asked.

"As Lord Peter—I mean, Peter—told you, we're in a bit of a hurry ourselves, so I'm very sorry but—"

"Oh, I understand," said Lucy with a wink. "It's Halloween, or Samhain, and you have, um, commitments. There's no need for you to stay—just let me use the phone and I'll lock up the house. You can trust me. One quick phone call and I'll be out in no time at all."

"Why should I help you?" demanded Peter, but Lady Sybil interrupted him.

"Remember the rule of three," she said in a schoolmarmish voice. "We really can't afford for anything to go wrong tonight."

"Oh, all right," he agreed resentfully. "You'll find the key under the doormat. But make sure you do lock the door."

"I will," said Lucy. "And thank you, thank you, so much."

"No problem," said Symonds grudgingly as he got in the truck. Lucy heard the engine start with a cough when she slipped the key into the lock and turned it.

Entering the ramshackle house, Lucy was almost overcome by the stale scent of dust and mildew. The faded and torn 1930s wallpaper had been stained by the floodwater; the ruined carpet had been removed, revealing scuffed wood planks thickly layered with dirt and leaves carried in from outside on shoes and boots. Lucy hurried down the hall to the kitchen, where she figured the phone would be, and found a dated 1980s wall model hanging beneath a calendar.

Witch's Brew

2 rubber gloves
One 16-ounce envelope unsweetened grape drink mix
One 16-ounce envelope unsweetened orange drink mix
2 cups white sugar
3 quarts cold water
1 liter ginger ale
1 liter cola

Fill the gloves ¾ full with cold water and tie the open end in a knot. Lay one flat in a small baking pan. Arrange the other palm down on a freeze-safe container, allowing the fingers to hang down the side. Freeze overnight.

Combine the drink mixes, sugar, and water in a large punch bowl and stir until completely dissolved. Add the ginger ale and cola.

Briefly run the ice hands under cool water, then cut away the glove. Add the hands to the punch, floating one inside the bowl and placing the other over the side. Serve immediately, as the fingers melt quickly. Makes about 20 servings.

Witch's Cauldron

1 750-ml bottle Midori
63 ounces orange juice
12 ounces vodka
32 ounces club soda

Mix all ingredients in a large bowl with ice. Makes 15–20 servings. (Recipe from Midori.)

Beastly Bugs

For these cookies, use your favorite sugar cookie recipe, cutting the dough into 2-inch rounds and baking. Frost when cool with your favorite butter cream icing, which you have tinted with food coloring. Cut licorice laces into 1-inch pieces and place three pieces on either side of the cookie for legs. Add a gumdrop for the head. You can decorate further with small chocolate chips, candies, or colored sugar.